Wild Like the Wind
Kristen Ashley
Published by Kristen Ashley
Copyright © 2018 by Kristen Ashley

All rights reserved. In accordance with the U.S. Copyright Act of 1976, the scanning, uploading, and electronic sharing of any part of this book without the permission of the publisher is unlawful piracy and theft of the author's intellectual property. Thank you for your support of the author's rights.

This book is a work of fiction. Names, characters, places, and incidents are the product of the author's imagination or are used fictitiously. Any resemblance to actual events, locales, or persons, living or dead, is coincidental.

Interior Design & Formatting by:
Christine Borgford, Type A Formatting
www.typeAformatting.com

Cover Art by:
PixelMischief Design

ISBN 13: 978-1721232611
ISBN 10: 1721232613

Discover other titles by

KRISTEN ASHLEY

THE CHAOS SERIES

Own the Wind
Fire Inside
Ride Steady
Walk Through Fire
A Christmas to Remember
Rough Ride
Wild Like the Wind

DISCOVER ALL OF KRISTEN'S TITLES ON HER WEBSITE AT:
www.kristenashley.net

DEDICATION

For Jizzo . . .
Otherwise known as Jason Bombardier.
Thanks for being a good one and
giving me the perfect inspiration for Black.
But just sayin' . . .
Rosary beads would have been nice.

ACKNOWLEDGEMENTS

Many, many thanks to the fabuloso Jillian Stein for being with me along Hound's journey and helping me to give him Jean as she needed to be. To the point of asking your rabbi all my annoying questions.

You rock . . . and I'm not just saying that because I'm still crushing on Darth.

WILD LIKE THE WIND
A CHAOS NOVEL

KRISTEN ASHLEY

ROCK CHICK
PRESS

PROLOGUE

YOU'LL NEVER BE ALONE

Seventeen years ago . . .

"**D**O YOU HAVE ANYTHING TO say?"

Hound stood in the line with his brothers of the Chaos Motorcycle Club, staring at the man kneeling before them, waiting for him to say something just so they could end this.

There were four drums of fire dancing at the corners of the grouping. Outside of the moon, that fire was the only thing lighting the clearing. It danced on the man in front of them and on the pine trees surrounding him.

There was nothing but nature out there for miles all around.

And no sound but the fire crackling and the men who were talking.

"Go fuck yourself," the man on his knees spat, literally. The words coming out of his mouth included spittle that Hound could see, even by firelight, was tinted with blood.

His face was a mangled mess because he'd been held with his arms behind his back while each brother took a one-two punch, every one of them packed with power, all the power they could muster.

And with their motivation, they'd each been able to pack a lot of power.

Hound was the only one who'd snuck in a third punch, right to the kidneys.

It was the first but not the last time the man had chucked up blood.

His eyes were swelling shut, his mouth dripping blood, the flesh on his cheeks opened up.

His condition meant he was listing. On his knees because he was forced there, keeping his position probably because he didn't have the strength to get up.

This wasn't about the beating he'd taken from his ex-brothers.

It was that he'd taken the slice of each brother's blade carved deep through his back.

This was Tack's idea, and Hound and every brother that stood with him supported it.

It was about obliterating their mark on his back that claimed him brother.

In the rare event a man renounced the Club, he blacked out the Chaos tattoo inked on his back.

If a man played traitor to the brotherhood, by the brothers' hands that tat would be scorched off.

This man in front of them had not renounced the Club.

He had not simply played traitor to it.

He'd betrayed it in a way none of them would have expected.

A way none of them could allow to go unavenged.

He'd stabbed a brother in the back, figuratively.

But that brother was gone all the same, because the man right there on his knees had ordered the hit.

Therefore he'd taken their blades for two reasons.

An eye for Chaos was not for an eye.

It was for your pound of flesh.

Stab Chaos in the back, that's returned.

And then some.

The man kneeling before Hound and all the brothers of the Chaos MC now had a mangled face and a back that was nothing but opened pulp of bloody flesh.

And very soon he would be what he'd made Black.

Gone.

Hound shifted on his feet, impatient, when their new president, Tack, pushed, "That's all you got to say?"

"Suck my dick," the man on his knees replied.

He was known as Crank.

He'd been their president. Their leader. The man who had sworn to honor his brothers. Respect them above all else.

Protect them, even if it meant giving his life to do it.

And for his own greed and pride, not one fucking thing to do with the brotherhood, he'd brought Black low.

Hound's eyes shifted to Tack as he moved closer to Crank.

"You were Chaos, we were you," Tack said quietly.

It took some effort, but Crank hocked up a loogie and spat it at Tack's boots. It didn't hit its mark but it said what he wanted to say.

Hound shifted impatiently again, feeling his jaw tighten.

"You were Black, he was you," Tack continued, speaking low.

Hound felt that in his throat and swallowed hard to wash it away.

"Fuck you," Crank whispered.

"You ordered your own death by ordering his," Tack told him something he had to know, but even if they hadn't made that clear in the proceedings, he knew it before.

What he did could not stand.

Not even out there in the other world, the world not owned and run by Chaos.

But in their world, retribution for what he did was not swift and it had only one end.

"Motherfucker," Crank hissed. "You killed Black, and you fucking know it."

Hound growled, his eyes cutting to Tack to see his jaw go hard, which meant his brother took that in.

All the boys started to get restless.

"Order the fire!" Hound bellowed.

"You've been gagging for the gavel since you were a recruit," Crank bit off to Tack. "It was you that put Black where he is."

"We are not what you made us," Tack replied.

"We're outlaws," Crank shot back.

"We are not what you made us," Tack returned.

Crank swung his torso back and asked sarcastically, "Yeah, right, so I'm gonna walk away from this?"

"No. You. Are. Not," Tack stated deliberately, his face changing from pensive to hostile. "Because we're," he leaned in toward Crank, "*outlaws*. But we're also," he leaned farther forward, "*brothers*." He leaned back and took a step away, ordering, "Get to your feet."

"You take out a man down on his knees, it's as pussy as you're gonna make my Club, so I'll make that statement for you since you'll be taking me out on my knees."

"Face your death on your feet," Tack urged.

"Blow me," Crank clipped.

Tack took a moment to study him.

Then he muttered, "Your call."

After that, he walked back, taking his place in the line.

The men went from restless to wired.

Tack felt it and didn't waste any more time. He couldn't. If someone jumped the gun, this would not be what Tack needed it to be, what the brothers needed it to be.

For Tack, it wasn't about one man taking the right to vengeance from the others.

For Tack, it was about one man shouldering the burden of the end of a human being, even if that being was a man as lowdown dirty, useless and an absolute waste of space as Crank.

They would do it as one.

They would do it as a band of brothers.

That was who Kane "Tack" Allen was.

That was where he was guiding Chaos.

"Brother Crank," Tack called out. "You've been found guilty of a crime against the brotherhood, the worst of its kind, the betrayal of a brother. Your patch has been stripped. You'll rot without the mark of Chaos on your back. Your final sentence is execution. You've had your chance to speak. You've got five seconds to take your feet before you meet your maker."

In the end, unable to do it on his knees, Crank struggled up to his feet.

"Ready!" Tack shouted.

All the men lifted their guns and pointed them at Crank.

But when Hound took aim, his focus was not on Crank.

He was looking at Crank, but everything he had in him was focused on Tack.

So the minute the first sound from the first letter came out when Tack boomed, *"Fire!"* Hound was already squeezing the trigger.

It was a nanosecond before any of his brothers, all who did the same, pulled theirs.

But Hound knew it was his bullet that was the first that penetrated Crank.

And it did this right through his eye.

This made Hound happy.

LATER THAT NIGHT, WHICH WAS the early hours of the morning, Hound was with Tack when they went to the house. He was one of five men with him—Hop, Boz, Dog, Brick, and Hound. They were all, Hound knew, in consideration for being Tack's lieutenants.

For Hound, who was young, this consideration was an extreme honor.

Still.

Hound did not want this.

He had another position in the Club, now more than ever.

And he needed to be free to focus on it.

But he went anyway.

He had to.

For him, there was no other choice.

Tack knocked on the door and she didn't make them wait. She probably hadn't slept in weeks. But she'd know to be waiting for this.

Because she was Chaos.

When she opened it, Hound felt the sight of her hit him like a punch in the throat.

It wasn't about her beauty, which was extreme.

A sheet of black hair that glistened like silk. Lush features that stamped plain her American lineage was either native or seriously exotic. Body, long and lean. Tits, firm and high. Ass, round and sweet. Skin, smooth and tanned.

Hound had rounded the Compound years ago in order to dump a spent keg back there and caught Black fucking his then fiancé, now widow, against the back wall. Before he'd backed away silently, he'd seen that beautiful face in orgasm and he'd never forgotten it.

But it was before that when he'd taken the fall for Keely Black.

So now it was not about her beauty, that punch in the throat.

Now it was about the dead in her eyes, the grief carved in her features in a way each brother knew, Hound especially with the attention he'd given her, she'd not put the effort in to smoothing it out.

She'd met, fallen in love with, married and given two sons to the only man on earth that was good enough for her.

Now he was dead.

And she might be breathing, but she was the same.

"Where are the boys, honey?" Tack murmured.

"Asleep," Keely replied, her unusual, low, smooth voice even on that one word slithering through the air like a ripple of velvet.

She knew the drill and moved out of the way as Tack moved in.

Hop, Boz, Dog, Brick and Hound moved in after her. Each man took time with her, stopping, touching her, pressing lips to her forehead, stubbled cheeks to her smooth one.

Not Hound.

He stopped in front of her and looked down into her dark-brown eyes.

She stared up in his.

I'd take his place if I could, he thought.

But he said nothing.

He just followed his brothers and walked into her living room.

Keely followed him, and after Hound stopped by Brick, Tack spoke.

"It's done."

For a second, Hound didn't know if she heard him.

Then she asked, "It is?"

"It is, darlin'," Tack said gently. "Black has been avenged."

He hadn't, Hound thought. *Not yet. Not fully. But he will be.*

"Now what?" Keely asked, and Hound reckoned he was giving her all of his attention, but at that question he realized he was wrong.

"We—" Tack started.

"I don't care about Chaos," she cut him off.

He felt the men beside him draw in breaths, shuffle their feet uncomfortably, because this wasn't just said about the brotherhood. This was said by Keely, who was an old lady but she was so much a part of Chaos, through Black but also just on her own, she'd loved her place in it so huge, it was also like a punch in the gut.

But Hound narrowed his eyes at her, taking in every inch of her, his lungs on fire, his palms itching, his need to go to her, draw her near, pull her close, absorb her pain, make it all okay so overwhelming, he felt his energy leaking out of him with the effort it took to contain it.

"What I wanna know is, now what? Now what for me? For my boys?" she asked.

"We'll take care of you, Keely. Like Black was still with us, until your last breath, Chaos will have your back. You'll get his cut of everything at the store, the garage. The brothers will—"

"You gonna take out the trash?" she asked.

Yes, Hound thought.

Brick waded in. "If that's what you need, baby."

She looked to Brick. "Okay, so who's gonna make my boys chocolate chip and peanut butter pancakes every Sunday morning?"

I will, Hound thought.

"Keely, darlin'—" Tack began.

"And who's gonna drag Dutch's ass outta bed when he's bein' a pain. He's in kindergarten and he hates school so much, I know I'm gonna have a fight on my hands for the next twelve years until he can see the end of it."

I will, Hound thought.

"We'll be there for your boys," Dog said.

It was like Dog didn't speak.

She kept at them.

"And who's gonna bring me a shit ton of ibuprofen when I get period cramps so bad it makes me sick to my stomach and I can't move?" she pushed. "Who's gonna make up the hot water bottle for me and rub my back until they're gone? Who's gonna do that? Tell me, *who*?"

I will, Hound thought.

No one said anything.

But she still wasn't done.

"And who's gonna fuck me breathless, make me come so hard I think the world is ending? Who's gonna give it to me again and again and again, night after night after *night*, just like I like it? *Exactly* like I like it," she bit out.

I will, Hound thought.

"Keely, honey—" Hop tried gently.

"It's not *done*," she spat, leaning toward Tack, her gorgeous face twisting with an agony no woman should be forced to bear. "It'll never be *done*."

"I used the wrong words, darlin', I'm so sorry," Tack whispered.

"How *done* is he?" she demanded to know.

"Very done," Boz answered firmly.

"Who did it?" she asked Boz.

"We all did," Hop answered.

But her eyes went right to Hound.

And he looked right into them.

She knew.

There was a reason he was called Hound.

It started out as a joke, the guys digging into him about his unusual first name.

But with the hell Crank had thrown them into, it became other things.

Loyalty, one.

Stubbornness, another.

Difficult to rein in, and when he got the scent, impossible to hold back, yet another.

Not giving up and going the extra mile until the job was done, the last.

She was an old lady and she'd been around a long time.

But she was Keely, her heart as open and giving as her mouth was smart. She was Black's and she was Chaos's and she loved it like that. She knew every brother down to his soul. Even if they didn't give her that, she watched, she looked after them in any way she could.

She knew.

Because the first part that made Hound a hound was the most important.

"We've lost Black, but you, Dutch and Jagger haven't lost Chaos," Tack told her, and she turned her attention to him.

Hound felt his entire frame tighten when the change started coming over her features, and he felt his brothers experience the same as the air in the room went flat.

"I can't do it," she said quietly.

"You can," Tack said firmly.

"The boys are lost," she whispered, the agony of a woman who'd lost her man melting into something far more difficult to witness.

The anguish of a mother whose boys lost their father.

"We'll keep them steady," Tack vowed.

"I'm—" she cut herself off and swallowed.

"We got you," Tack said gently. "We'll always have you. We'll always be there."

Keely said nothing, she just stared in Tack's eyes like she was waiting for him to clap his hands, she'd wake up, and the nightmare she was living would be over and she could rest in the knowledge it was all a bad dream.

Tack didn't do this because he couldn't.

So she looked away.

"You want me to get Bev over here?" Boz asked.

Bev was Boz's old lady, and Keely and her were tight.

It took visible effort but she looked at him. "No. If I've gotta go it alone, I gotta learn how to do that."

That was when Hound spoke.

"You'll never be alone."

She turned to him.

"You don't get it," she whispered. "He wasn't the other half of me. He didn't complete me. He wasn't my old man. He wasn't my husband. He wasn't a dick I fell on. He wasn't the father of my sons. He was," her voice suddenly got scratchy, *"my life.* He was my reason to get up every day and *breathe.* He's gone and losing that, losing him, I'll always, *always* be alone."

Hound made no reply because he didn't have one but also because he again felt like he'd been punched in the throat.

"We're gonna look after you," Tack told her, and her gaze went to him. "Please, darlin', he'd want it this way, so will you let us look after you?"

She tossed her head and the sheet of her hair glistened in the light by her couch that was the only lamp lit.

"He'd want it that way, you're right. So . . . yes," she agreed.

"Let me get Bev over here," Boz again suggested.

She looked to him.

Then she nodded.

"Boz, go. Call," Tack ordered then turned to Hop, Dog, Brick and Hound. "Just go. I'll stay until Bev gets here."

Hop, Dog and Brick nodded and moved to Keely.

Hound just moved to the door.

He turned to her and caught her eyes before he walked out.

He had no idea if she read his promise.

But it wouldn't matter.

He was still going to keep it.

HE HAD HER BY HER hair on her knees.

Her girl was standing, pressing herself against the wall, fear stamped in her features, tears running down her cheeks.

"Am I clear?" Hound asked, leaning over her, twisting his hand in her hair.

"Y-you're clear, Hound," she stammered.

"Honest to Christ, if I find I'm not . . ." He didn't finish that.

The flash of terror in her eyes said he didn't need to.

He let her go by yanking her hair and sending her sprawling to her back, her legs bending in an unnatural way not the only reason she let out a cry of pain and surprise.

Without another word, he turned and walked away from the two prostitutes Chaos used to pimp before Tack scraped them clean of that bullshit that none of them, but Chew, who'd renounced the Club before they carried out an execution he did not agree with, wanted to do in the first place.

Hound had no idea how that shit started. He hadn't been Chaos then.

He just knew Tack had plans to end it.

So he'd become Chaos.

They were the two prostitutes that informed Crank that Tack was making maneuvers to take over the Club and clean it up.

The two prostitutes that initiated Crank calling a hit on a brother in order to focus their attention on where he wanted them to be.

"Hop, it wasn't what you think," the one against the wall called out. "We had no choice. We—"

Hop cut her off. "Crank's rotting. Think on that, bitch."

Hound was barely through the door before he heard it slammed.

He looked behind him to see Hop following him.

"If they don't skip town . . ." Hound growled, again not finishing it.

"They'll go," Hop ground out.

Hound didn't say another word.

He turned to face forward and kept moving.

He had things to do.

TACK HAD A HAND TO his chest and was pushing him back.

"This is not who we are anymore, brother," he bit out. "We still got work to do to get ourselves clean, but that part died when Crank hit the ground."

Hound locked his legs and stood solid, staring straight into Tack's eyes.

"It'll get done," Tack told him quietly.

Yeah, Hound thought. *It would.*

Then, quick as a flash, determined, he moved clear of Tack's hand, advanced swiftly to the man tied to the chair, took hold of his hair, wrenched his head back, yanked his knife from his belt and hesitated not an instant before he drew the blade across his throat, going deep.

Blood spewed. The man's eyes got huge. His mouth gurgled.

Hound watched it happen with dispassion.

The man in that chair had carried out the hit on Black.

And now he was going to die like he'd killed Hound's brother. Chaos's man.

Keely's life.

"Fuck yes," High, standing to the side, rumbled.

"The way it should be," Arlo, standing with him, stated.

"Done," Pete, standing behind the man's chair, clipped out.

Hound turned and stopped because Tack was standing right there.

"*Now* that's not who we are anymore, brother," Hound stated.

Then he skirted him and walked out of Chaos's cabin in the foothills.

IT WAS LIKELY SHE HEARD his bike.

Whatever the reason, Hound did not stand too long in the middle of the walk up to her back door before that door opened and she stood in it, her hair perfect, her face exhausted, the shapeless nightshirt she wore drooping on her.

He was covered in blood.

He didn't have to say a word.

She stared at him, not in horror, not in fear.

With sorrow.

And not just for her loss.

For where it took Hound.

"Now it's done," he growled.

He heard her whisper from halfway across the yard.

"Hound," was all she said.

"Heal," was all he said to finish.

Then he turned on his boot and walked away.

One month later...

KEELY SLAMMING THE PHONE INTO its cradle repeatedly set all five men at her kitchen table to alert, and all eyes, including Hound's, went from their poker hands to her.

"Yo," Arlo called, and at the word she stopped with the receiver in the cradle, her hand still on it, and stared angrily at the phone.

"All okay, honey bunch?" Pete asked gently.

She took her hand off the phone and whirled.

"So, my parents weren't all fired up I was dating a guy in a motorcycle gang," she began.

Hound felt his jaw get tight at the word "gang." He knew she was saying that shit because her parents thought that shit. He knew she knew better. They were a Club. An outsider might not see much difference. But there was a mountain of it.

"Therefore, needless to say, they weren't fired up about me marrying him and getting knocked up by him ... twice," she went on. "So it's not like I'm not in the know that they weren't Graham's biggest fans."

At that, Hound fought a flinch.

They didn't call Black "Black" because it was his last name, which it was.

They called him Black because the man was so far from the darkness, it was fucking hilarious that was his last name.

He was goodness.

He was light.

He was brotherhood.

If there was a disagreement between the brothers, Black waded in and had everyone laughing.

If one of the brother's kids walked into the Compound, faster than snot Black would have them up on his shoulders, horsing around.

They all had their place in the Club, and Black's place had been the glue that held them together in shaky times or in times when those shakes were like earthquakes.

But it was also because he was their light. The beacon of the brother they all wanted the Club to be. He was about Chaos. He was about Keely.

He was about his boys. And nothing on this earth mattered beyond that. Not money. Not respect. Not a thing.

He was not Graham.

It was a solid name and Hound had heard Keely calling him that, but usually in a teasing way. The rest of the time, if she wasn't using a sweet nothing, it was always Black.

She'd dropped the Black since he died, and Hound knew it was another way she wanted to drop the brotherhood.

"So now, essentially," she kept going, "they pretty much feel like I made my bed, I made my boys' beds, and we need to lie in them."

Fucking assholes, Hound thought.

"Whatcha need?" Brick asked softly, and her pissed-off eyes went to him.

"I need my parents to give a shit that my husband got his throat slit," she spat.

Hound, nor any brother, could beat back the flinch at that.

She stomped out.

The men around the table all looked at each other.

"They were always motherfuckers," Dog muttered under his breath. "Remember their wedding. They had sticks rammed so far up their asses it's a wonder they didn't come out their mouths."

Hound remembered that too.

"She's better off without them," Arlo put in. "She's got Chaos, she doesn't need their shit."

He knew that was true. Every man at that table knew that was true.

The problem was, Keely didn't know that was true.

He waited until after he won all his brothers' money, they got pissed and it got late so they were all taking off.

He hung back.

She was at the door.

So was he.

He waited again, this time until she impatiently caught his gaze.

She wanted him gone.

"Whether you want us or not, you got a family who wants you. You can't do anything to make that change. Nothing, Keely. We're yours. Forever."

With that, he didn't let her say a word.

Hound gave her what she wanted.

He walked away.

Several months later . . .

HOUND STOOD AT THE END of the walk with his arms crossed on his chest, his leather cut on his shoulders beating back the October chill, and watched as Keely headed back down the walk with Dutch and Jagger.

Dutch had demanded that his Halloween costume be mini-biker, and as much as Keely pushed back, he'd have none of it.

And where Dutch went, Jagger followed.

So they were both in jeans, little-man biker boots, white T-shirts, little leather vests that Bev made for them, with bandanas tied around their foreheads.

Dutch's was red. It was Black's bandana, he wore it all the time. Now Dutch had it all the time.

Hilariously, Jagger's was purple. It was Keely's. She used to wear it all the time too, tied around her neck, wrapped around the top of her skull and tied at the back with her hair flowing out under it. Even wound around her wrist.

Dutch told Jag that real bikers didn't wear purple, but Jag dug in and purple it was.

Keely made it to Hound and stopped.

"You're scaring all the neighbors," she accused.

"Good," he replied.

Dutch laughed.

Jagger pulled his hand from his mom's and caught Hound's.

Then he tugged on it, grunting and demanding, "Let's go! Candy!"

Hound allowed himself to be tugged.

Keely walked next to Dutch.

Hound stood at the end of the walk as they all went up to the next house (Jagger racing to the door, Dutch playing it cool).

He did the same at the next house.

And the next.

And the next.

One year and two months later...

HOUND MOVED BACK UP THE walk, into the kitchen and saw Keely where he left her, at the kitchen table, practically buried under Christmas paper, bows and ribbons.

"Trash is out," he grunted.

She looked to him and nodded.

He looked to the doorway that led to the rest of the house then back to her. "Where's Bev?"

"She has to get ready for her own Christmas," she told him.

He nodded.

He got that seeing as it was Christmas Eve.

"What more you got to do?" he asked.

She was distracted with wrap and boxes and similar shit, and her eyes came to him.

"Jag's mini-Flintstone-use-your-feet motorcycle came unassembled."

"Right," he grunted again. "Where is it?"

"The box is in the basement."

He nodded once, turned on his boot and headed to the door in the basement.

He put the little-kid motorcycle together and hauled it up the steps.

She slapped a bow on it and he put it under the tree.

"You rock, Hound, thanks," she whispered. "Now go home. And Merry Christmas."

He nodded again.

"Later."

Her eyes stayed dead but her gorgeous face got soft. "Later, honey."

Hound walked out her back door.

Four years later...

HOUND DID NOT HURRY THROUGH the halls of the hospital.
 But he didn't take his time.
 He hit the nurse's station and grunted, "Black."
 The nurse behind the station stared up at him with big eyes and such was her bullshit judgment about bikers, she didn't have it in her to speak. She just lifted a hand and pointed down a short corridor at the end of which was a number of curtained bays.
 Hound walked that way.
 When he hit the bays, he looked left and right.
 They were three in to the left.
 He barely moved into the space when Dutch hit him, wrapping his little kid arms around his hips.
 He put a hand to the boy's back.
 The doctor or nurse or whoever was working on Jag in the bed looked up at him.
 "Can I help you?"
 Dutch turned in his hold so Hound's hand was at his chest.
 "He's with us," he said.
 Hound wasn't and never would be.
 And he absolutely was and always would be.
 Hound forced his eyes from a pale Jag with his pinched face and his yellow tee stained with blood to Keely sitting next to him looking even paler and totally freaked.
 Her eyes were glued to Hound.
 "What happened?" he asked.
 "It's my fault," Dutch spoke up, and he looked down at the kid.
 Then Hound turned his gaze to his brother and saw the gaping wound tearing up the inside of his thin, kid forearm that the nurse or doctor or whoever he was, was stitching.

He returned his attention to Dutch.

"How'd you do that?" he asked quietly.

"We were fightin'," Jag put in, his voice usually loud and excited, was weak. "I did wrong."

"It's okay, baby," Keely whispered. "Get you stitched up, it'll all be okay."

"We were just messing around," Dutch muttered.

Hound looked down at him again and his tone was still quiet when he asked, "Tell me how messin' around got your brother that gash, son."

"We were just messin' around then I got mad then Jag got mad then Mom told us to cool it, and she sent me out to the yard and Jag up to his room, but Jag was so mad he went to the back door and slammed his fist on the glass and it went through and he got cut," Dutch answered, looking beaten. He cast his eyes to his feet. "But I shoulda cooled it before it got to that place. So it's me did wrong and I know it."

"What'd you learn from this?" Hound asked.

"Hunh?" Dutch asked back, lifting his head.

"What'd you learn from this?" Hound repeated.

"Uh . . . I . . . dunno," Dutch answered.

Hound looked to Jagger. "What'd you learn from this, Jag?"

"Well, uh . . . not to hit a window with your fist?" Jagger asked back, uncertain his answer was the right one.

Hound beat back his smile and gave them the knowledge.

"What you learned is that life is gonna pull its own punches so you gotta stand strong to fight those. You don't waste your energy fightin' your brother. You *never* fight your brother. Your brother is gonna be in your corner from now until forever. You might get pissed at him. You might have words. But you don't fight. Are you hearing me?"

"Yes, sir," Jag muttered.

Hound shifted his gaze to Dutch.

"Yes, sir," Dutch mumbled.

He looked at Keely and did not allow the look on her face to penetrate.

"The window?" he asked.

"It's messed up," she told him.

He nodded and looked down again to Dutch. "You're goin' with me.

We're fixin' the window." He turned his attention back to Keely. "You got Jag."

She nodded.

He then looked at the doc or nurse or whatever he was. "How many stitches?"

"Probably . . ." he started, still working, "seventeen, maybe a few more."

Hound grinned at Jag. "Boy, when you get bloody, you do it up big. First battle scar."

Jag grinned back.

He felt that particular comment didn't win a soft, grateful look from Keely, but he didn't look at her to get her pissed.

He wrapped his fingers around Dutch's shoulder and said, "Let's roll."

"'Kay, Hound," Dutch muttered.

"Later," he said to Jag, turning to go.

"Later, Hound," Jag replied.

His eyes skipped through Keely. "Later."

"Later."

With that, he and Dutch took off.

When they did, like he always used to do when he was with his Hound but hadn't in a while since he'd reached the age to stop doing it, the situation made him need it, so Dutch found then held Hound's hand.

And seeing as Dutch had reached the age that Hound had lost that from his boy, instead of reminding him it was time for him to think about being the man he was becoming, like he always used to do, Hound let him.

Three years later . . .

USING HIS FIST IN THE collar of his tee, Hound pushed the kid up against the brick wall.

Then he got in his face.

He was the perfect mix of his old man and his momma.

Fourteen and already a heartbreaker.

"Am I gonna have to make another visit?" he asked.

"Piss off, Hound," Dutch Black bit back.

"Scrappin' at school. Skippin' classes. Caught with your hand in the pants of a fifteen-year-old girl. Two months into your freshman year and already suspended twice. This is not Black's boy. This is not Keely's son. This is not *you*. Straighten the fuck out," Hound warned.

"You don't know dick about who I am," Dutch returned.

That was a lie and a ticked one at that, and they both knew it.

But Dutch was gearing up to shut Hound out and Hound could not let that happen. Not when he was fourteen and the measure of the man he was going to be was at stake.

And Dutch was already falling down on that, acting out, doing stupid shit, driving his mother around the bend.

Hound needed to sort this shit out . . . and now.

"Slit the throat of the man who took out your dad," Hound fired back and saw Dutch's eyes get large. "Man who ordered his death took my bullet first, through his right eye. Vengeance is not taken lightly. Vengeance is earned and meted out in the way it's bought. And bottom line, vengeance is carried out in the way the reason it's deserved demands. I didn't blink before I fired that shot. I didn't hesitate before I drew my blade across that throat. And this was because the man who demanded that vengeance was your father. The woman who deserved that vengeance was your mother. And the boys left behind who wouldn't know the straight-up, solid, steadfast, down-to-his-boots good that was your father, needed it. Black *made you*, kid. He raised you or not, not only the goodness of your mother but the man he was means you live, you breathe, you fuckin' *exist* to make them *proud*. Are you hearing me?"

"You . . . you *killed them*?" Dutch asked.

"Fuck yeah, two proudest goddamn moments of my life," Hound answered.

"Whoa," Dutch muttered.

Hound had nothing to say to that.

"Ev-everybody talks about how fuckin' great he was," Dutch said.

"That's because he was fuckin' great," Hound replied, easing up on his fist in the kid's shirt but not getting out of his space.

"I . . . Jagger doesn't even remember him."

"But you do."

Dutch stared up at him.

"You do," Hound repeated. "And you know. You know you lighted his world. You know he was prouder of nothin' than him and his woman makin' you."

Dutch's handsome face got ugly.

"He was so proud, why'd he get dead?"

"Because he wanted to live clean and he wanted to do right by his family. He wanted to slide into bed with the woman he loved and not bring filth into it. He wanted to make pancakes for his boys on Sunday and eat 'em with you, tasting nothin' but goodness in his mouth. Because he was all in to fight for that. Because he was willing to die for it. And it's just life that sucks in ways too mammoth to fully comprehend that he was the man among us who did. Not a brother who's got a patch wouldn't have taken his place. Believe that, Dutch, because it's the straight-up, motherfucking truth. And I would have been first in line. And that would not have been for your mother. That wouldn't have been for you boys. That wouldn't have been for Chaos. That would have been *for Black*."

Dutch was searching for some smartass shit to say to that.

But he couldn't find it.

"Stop fuckin' up and drivin' your mother insane," Hound ordered. "She needs you. You're all she's got."

Dutch had something to say to that.

"I know and that's too fuckin' much. I'm fourteen, man, and Jag's only twelve. We can't be everything to her."

"Your dad would not fall down on that job and he was all she needed. Sayin' that, he would love every goddamn minute of it and woulda killed to have more."

Dutch looked away, a muscle ticking in a cheek that didn't even have fuzz on it yet.

"You got him in you," Hound said quietly. "Be the man he didn't get the chance to fully be."

"How do I do that when he's not here to teach me?" Dutch asked the space at their sides.

"You need a lesson, you find me."

Dutch looked back to him, misery and hope both fighting in his dark eyes.

"If I haven't proved it already, it's you that's not payin' attention. I'm there for you, kid, any way you need me."

"Jag too?" he asked.

"Absolutely," Hound answered.

"Chaos is—"

"Yours," Hound finished for him. "And it's you. You grow up, wanna make that official, every man will welcome you. You just want us at your back, you'll have that until the day each and every one of us stop breathing."

Something washed through his face before his lips quirked. "She was wet and hot down there, man."

Hound let him go but again didn't get out of his space. "You're growin' up too fast. Your looks, you'll get your share of hot, wet pussy. Before he tagged your mother, your old man made an art of gettin' his share. When it comes your time, and by that I mean you hold your shit for another coupla years, first, you see to them. They won't be pantin' for it if you don't give it good. You need pointers on that, talk to me, Hop, Dog, Tack. And second, condoms. No excuses, no exceptions. You can't get your hands on 'em, you call me. I'll make sure you're supplied."

Something else came into Dutch's face.

"People think things about bikers, Hound. I don't even have a learner's permit, no way a bike, and still, my dad, Chaos, kids know things and they say shit. Am I supposed to just take that crap?"

"Fuck no," Hound replied. "But Jesus, son, you don't blow your top on school grounds. Assholes need a lesson, you always do it smart and in a way your momma doesn't feel the pain after you bring it."

Dutch stared at him a beat before he smiled.

"Workout room on Chaos, your ass is there," Hound told him. "I go to a gym, I'll pick you up, take you there too. We'll spar. Make sure you know what you're doin', don't get surprised and can make your point and know when to stop. We got a deal?"

Dutch nodded. He tried not to do it enthusiastically, but he failed.

"I gotta make another visit to you like this one, it won't make me happy," Hound warned.

"But you won't give up on me," Dutch stated.

Hound stared at him.

Dutch's chin moved in a funny way before he made his face hard and he went on, "You won't give up on me. You won't disappear on me. Yeah?"

"You got me, kid," Hound whispered. "Always."

"You won't disappear on me."

"I won't disappear, Dutch."

"Never. You won't go."

Christ.

He'd pull that blade across that motherfucker's throat again right then, no question about it.

"Never, son," he promised.

That thing happened to his chin again before Dutch looked away and drew in a sharp breath through his nose.

"Tomorrow, pick you up at your house, take you to Chaos," Hound said. "Show you around the weights. After school. Wear shorts, tennis shoes, a loose tank. With me?"

Dutch looked back at him and nodded.

Finally, Hound stepped back.

"Need a ride home?" he asked.

Dutch shook his head. "Gotta go get Jag. He gets outta school after me. I walk him home."

Hound nodded.

"Then git, kid. Jag wants to come with you tomorrow, call me and let me know. I'll pick you up in my truck."

Dutch nodded.

Hound moved toward his bike.

"Hound?" Dutch called.

He stopped and turned back.

"I was five," Dutch said.

Hound locked his body.

"But I still miss him," he finished.

"So do I, Dutch," Hound made himself reply.

Dutch took him in.

Then he turned and ran the other way.

Five years later . . .

SHE OPENED THE DOOR, AND like usual, since he was always the one to do it unless he was on assignment, Hound stuck out his hand toward Keely, that hand holding the envelope containing the check Cherry had cut for her.

"Your take this month," he told her.

She took it, her eyes on him. "Thanks, Hound."

He jerked up his chin, and like always said no more and started to move to turn away.

"And thanks for that jumbo box of condoms you supplied Jag with," she continued, making Hound turn around and look at her again. "Gave me one less thing to ream his ass about after I walked in on him drilling the head cheerleader on the couch in the living room."

Christ.

How many times had he told those boys to play it smart when it came to location *and* timing?

"You want me to stop bein' their supplier, you're their mother and I'll stop. Not my place but I'll still say, that ain't smart."

"Please don't stop. I don't need my boys being baby daddy to half the kids in Denver."

That was a good call.

Hound nodded.

He was about to walk away again when she stopped him.

"Dutch wants his name put forward to recruit."

His eyes went again to her, his heart squeezed in a good way, but he said nothing.

"You, Hound, I'm tellin' *you*, don't allow the boys to let that happen."

Now that was *not* a good call.

"You know that shit ain't right," he said low.

"Don't let it happen, Hound."

"He's got Chaos in his blood."

"His father's blood drained out for Chaos."

"Like I said, he's got Chaos in his blood."

She stared hard at him. "I'll never forgive you if you let it happen."

"Black would never forgive you if you did shit to stop it."

He hated it, but after he said that she looked like he'd slapped her.

So he gentled his voice when he said, "That was harsh, but, woman, you still know it was true."

She lifted up the envelope in her hand and said, "You can take off like you always do but thanks for this, Hound. Big, fat check every month bet makes it a lot easier for you boys to live with what *I* lost."

And that was just bullshit.

"If you think for one fuckin' second, Keely, that you were the only one who suffered that blow, it's time to get your head out of your ass, look around you and see how that shit *really* is."

Again, she looked like he'd slapped her but he didn't go gentle because, for fuck's sake, it had been fourteen years.

They knew she'd never get over it.

But she had to find her way past it.

"You're right," Hound carried on. "We've been so damned focused on cushioning the blow for you that in our own ways we all sustained that we haven't seen the kinda care you really need, and that's for someone to tell you that you need to stop wallowing in your bullshit and get it straight, woman. You need to stop shovin' the guilt in our faces that we feel and taste and live every day. And you need to get a fuckin' life."

She didn't look struck by that.

She looked remorseful.

"I shouldn't . . . I shouldn't have . . . not you. Especially not you. You stepped up. They all did. You all stepped up but mostly . . . *you*. I shouldn't have thrown that at you, Hound."

To leave it at that, he nodded and again turned to walk away.

"Thanks for lookin' after my boys, Hound," she called to his back. "With the condoms and with . . . well, everything."

This time, he didn't stop and turn around.

Because he had to. He had to bring her check to her. He had to get his shot at looking at her face. He had to have the mere moments he could get in her space. So he took them. Now especially, with the boys older, with all of them needing him less.

And also because he had to once he got those moments, he got the fuck out of there.

So he just lifted a hand, flicked it out and carried on walking away.

Present day...

"IT GIVES ME NO JOY to say that at least when this asshole takes you out, Hound, you're not leavin' anyone who loves you more than the breath they take behind," Keely shot at him.

He tried to fight it and feared he'd failed at beating back the flinch.

Tack drew her attention to him. "Keely—"

"Do not call me again, Tack," she demanded.

His mouth got tight.

She looked to Hound and everything about her changed. She went from pissed and belligerent to sad and defeated.

Seeing that, it killed.

"Be careful," she whispered to Hound. "Be super fuckin' careful, Hound. Because you might not have a woman who loves you more than her own breath, but you still got folks who love you. So please, God, be careful."

With that, she turned, her hair flying, yanked open the door, stalked out, and slammed it behind her.

He felt Tack's eyes.

He was in control. His face neutral.

But he couldn't stop looking at the door.

"We done here?" Tack asked, and Hound cut his gaze to his brother.

"Yup," he answered, pushing away from the wall.

Tack watched him walk around the other end of the table from where Tack was sitting in the meeting room at the Chaos Compound.

He waited until Hound's hand was on the door before he called his name.

Hound looked back at him.

"You know," he said carefully.

"Know what?" Hound asked.

"You know you don't go there."

Hound drew his brows together. "Brother, you call me when you got somewhere to go no one else can go. What the fuck?"

Tack shook his head but did it with his eyes locked to Hound's.

"You know you don't go there. She's Black's. Dead or alive, she's Black's. She can move on. I hope to fuck someday she does. But she can't move on with Chaos."

At that, Hound got pissed.

Really pissed.

Because he'd been living that hell for so long, it felt like he'd been born to it.

But his voice was quiet when he replied, "You think I don't know that shit?"

"I know you know," Tack returned. "Just remindin' you."

"Don't need a reminder, brother," Hound grated out, so done with it, now more than before after the words Keely lashed out with, he landed it on his brother. "Lived with that for years, bein' in love with a woman I can't have."

Without hesitation, after delivering that, he threw open the door and prowled out. When he slammed it, the door shook.

He knew she had a reason to be mad. Things with the Club were again getting extreme.

So extreme, an enemy had actually kidnapped an old lady. His minions putting hands on her. *Hitting her.*

She was now safe, but that was not on.

Not *fucking* on.

Because they had no choice, even though she'd drifted further and further from the Club as the years passed, Keely was closest to High's kids, so when High's woman, Millie, was taken, Tack called Keely in to get to them and look after them while the boys rolled out.

And since she knew things were again extreme, Keely was pissed.

She had that right. She had reason. More reason than any of them and not just because she lost Black but because, back in the day, her and Millie had been super tight.

When this asshole takes you out, Hound, you're not leavin' anyone who loves you more than the breath they take behind.

He knew she was feeling deep feelings.

But that shit was not right.

It was not right.

It fucking *hurt*.

Over the years Hound did his best and didn't think on it. He lived his life. He had his fun. He covered his Club. He took care of Keely. He looked after the boys.

But fuck him, he'd given himself to a woman who he not only could not have, but who would never have him.

What the fuck was he doing?

He was still tight with her boys. Of all the men, and all the men had kicked in, they were Hound's.

And he'd keep it that way, especially since Dutch was ready to approach Chaos, become a recruit. He was twenty-one, closing in on twenty-two. He'd got his mechanic's license, he'd bought his first bike and he got some experience under his belt. He'd also gotten his other lessons from Hound, as well as all the men.

It was his time.

Jag, at nineteen, was going to follow his father, his brother.

Hound knew Keely wouldn't like it.

But this was not his problem.

If she wouldn't mourn him should he go in the battle that never fucking died to keep the Club clean, so be it.

If she didn't know her boys would be lost again if Hound was not around, fuck her.

They might not love him more than breath.

But he'd stepped up for them, and for her, and he didn't ask for any thanks, didn't want any, it wasn't duty, it was his privilege.

But she was right.

He had people who loved him.

Just not her.
She made that clear.
So it was time to move the fuck *on*.

CHAPTER ONE

COWBOY

HOUND SAT ON HIS COUCH in his wife beater with his hand down the front of his jeans staring at the TV, when the knock came at the door. He moved his gaze to it, his eyes narrowing.

When another knock came, he reached to the gun sitting on the seat beside him.

He pushed himself out of the couch and walked cautiously to the door but not in a direct path.

To the side.

Anyone out there felt like taking a shot through the door, Hound would not take those hits.

His couch would.

And he didn't mind that. His couch was a piece of shit.

He was to the side of the door when he yelled, "What?"

"Hound? It's Keely!"

He stared at the doorknob.

First, how did she know where he lived?

And second, what the fuck was she doing there?

"Hound?" she called.

"The boys okay?" he asked, but he knew at least Jag was. The kid had left just a half an hour ago after bumming fifty bucks from Hound to take his girl out to dinner.

Jagger Black went through money like water. Hound had had so many words about that with him, he should tape that crap and just replay it when he had to do it again.

And he knew he'd have to do it again.

He still gave him the fifty bucks.

But he also gave him shit about it.

"Yes!" she shouted back. "Open up!"

He drew in breath through his nose and moved to tuck his gun under the cushion of his beat-up armchair.

He hadn't seen her in two months. Not since the day Millie had been kidnapped.

He moved to the peephole, looked out and saw her there, staring at the door. Her hair parted down the middle and falling in sheets to either side of her face. Years and grief not having affected the skin on that face even a little. It was smooth from forehead to cheekbones to chin.

She was pushing the Native American gig, something she started doing when she gave up on being a biker babe years ago, and she hadn't let that go. It was something she could do seeing as Dutch and Jag told him they were an eighth Apache since their momma was a quarter. Right then, she pushed it with the hair as well as the three-layer bone choker she had at her throat.

After what she spouted at him at the Chaos Compound, he really didn't want to feel that sheet of hair, those big eyes, those puffy lips and that choker in his dick.

But he did.

He unlocked and opened the door.

She pushed in before he could block her way.

Once in, she did not take in his ratty-ass apartment that he'd lived in for nine years and had not run the vacuum once (mostly because he didn't own a vacuum, but also because he never intended to buy one).

She whirled on him, planted her hands on her slim hips and

announced, "So you're alive."

He felt his mouth get tight and threw the door shut, but that was all he got in before she came at him, both hands up, and shoved him so hard at his chest, his entire torso rocked back.

That was when he felt his whole face get hard.

She didn't hesitate to get up in that face and fuck him, *fuck him*, he felt her tits brush his chest, she was that close.

"You big *jerk*!" she shouted. "You scared the *shit* out of me."

"Stand down, woman," he growled.

"You haven't dropped my check in two months, Hound."

He couldn't stop it.

He blinked at her and did it slow.

"You might miss a month but you never miss *two*," she informed him of something he knew but thought she had not ever noticed.

"As you can see, I'm still standing," he told her.

"I can see that. What I *hear* is that Chaos has got whatever trouble they've got with whoever took Millie and now they're rubbing up against Bounty."

Bounty was another MC in Denver.

They'd never had any problem with Bounty.

Now they did.

"Think you made it clear last time I saw you that you're outta it with Chaos, so not sure how that's your issue," he stated.

"Uh, were you *not* there when the boys voted in Dutch as a recruit a month ago?"

Actually, he was on maneuvers so he had not been.

Though, since he sponsored Dutch, along with every man who'd had his patch when Black died, his official vote wasn't really necessary.

He decided not to answer.

"I thought something had happened to you," she said it like it was an accusation.

He put both arms up at his sides, which he thought pretty much said it all.

It did, but she was clearly not happy about the way he did it and he knew that with the way her face screwed up, all pissed.

"You drop my checks," she declared heatedly.

"Gonna leave that duty to another man," he told her.

"Why?" she rapped out.

"'Cause I got other shit I need to be doin'," he replied, not the entire truth, not a full lie either.

"It's because I was a bitch to you," she said it, straight out.

"You didn't say anything that wasn't true," he returned, and that wasn't a lie at all.

What he left unsaid was that her saying what she'd said sucked dick.

"I was upset," she explained herself.

"That didn't go unnoticed," he shared.

"Don't be an asshole, Hound," she snapped, and his brows went up as his temper caught.

"How's that bein' an asshole?" he asked.

"You're bein' flippant," she told him.

He leaned toward her. "Woman, I don't even know what 'flippant' means."

"Then you need to spend more time reading books and less time doing Chaos's wet work," she shot back.

He leaned away and slowly drew a very long breath into his nose.

She glared at him.

When he had no verbal reaction to her remark, she looked around then back at him.

"For God's sake, Hound, you live in a sty," she declared.

"Got no woman to keep the place nice for, baby," he drawled. "As you pointed out. And men don't mind they live in a sty. It's only women who give a fuck about that shit."

Her eyes got squinty. "Why don't you have a woman?"

He was not discussing this with her.

"That's none of your fuckin' business," he returned.

She threw up an arm in front of her to indicate him. "You're hot."

He did another slow blink.

He was?

"It's a waste," she decreed.

She'd know about waste, all of what was her going without a man for seventeen years.

"You're worried I don't get my wick wet enough, Keely, you can mark that off your list of things you shouldn't stick your nose into in the first place. I get what I need. I just don't keep it."

"Why not?" she asked.

"You obviously won't feel this way, but you don't know me so I'll educate you that for a guy like me, you give it enough time to get time in, snatch becomes a drag and no man needs anything draggin' on him."

"You did not just say that to me," she bit out.

"*Jesus, woman,*" he boomed, looked side to side and back to her. "You're the one stormed in here, gettin' up in my face and my space, puttin' your hands on me, stickin' your nose in shit that's not yours to have. What's your problem?"

"You bring me my checks," she declared.

"Not anymore," he fired back.

"You bring me my checks," she demanded.

He leaned again toward her.

"Not anymore," he snarled.

And then, Jesus, fuck . . .

She was on him.

She was all over him.

Plastered down his front, hands clenched hard in his hair yanking his head down to hers, she had her mouth to his and her tongue in his mouth.

God, nectar.

Fuck, *heaven*.

He ripped his mouth from hers, planted a hand in her chest and shoved her back a lot harder than he'd ever touch any woman (or any woman who had not done Chaos wrong) so she reeled away five paces.

He couldn't apologize.

He needed to draw a line.

For her.

For him.

For her boys.

For Chaos.

"Get your shit together, Keely," he growled.

"Fuck me, Hound," she whispered.

His cock, stirring to attention the minute he heard her voice outside a damned door, got instantly hard.

She was watching him and fuck him, *fuck him*, that needy look on her face . . .

Christ.

It cost him but he replied, "You need it, woman, hook up at a bar or get yourself a vibrator."

"You know how I need it and you know that won't work."

"How did I become your dick to play with?" he asked and did it mean.

She stared him right in the eye and returned, "You know how."

He'd hid it from her.

He'd hid it.

He stared right back at her and knew he hadn't.

"Get the fuck outta my house," he ground out.

She didn't get out of his house.

She also didn't lose eye contact.

Not once, even though he eventually only felt her gaze on him because what she did next, he didn't have it in him not to watch.

She took off her clothes.

Every stitch.

Standing right in front of him.

Then she turned and he watched her round ass and long legs with her sheet of hair swaying down her back walk out of his living room, down his hall where she disappeared at the end in his bedroom.

He drew in a big breath.

Then he drew in another one.

After that, he prowled down the hall and it took everything he had not to stop dead in the doorway, or turn around and walk right out of his house, never to come back, when he saw her curled on her side on top of his dirty sheets, clutching his pillow to her front, her eyes to him walking through the door.

Her hand was between her legs.

He stopped at the foot of the bed and whispered, "Baby, you need to get the fuck out."

Again with her gaze latched to him, she pushed the pillow aside, rolled to all fours, crawled to him, and it was a miracle he didn't come in his jeans when she got close, rose up to her knees and put a hand to his stomach.

"Baby, you need *to do me*," she whispered back, running her hand down his stomach, over his belt, cupping his hard crotch.

Hound clenched his teeth.

He'd told her boys time and again, he did not care if they were drunk. He did not care if they were with a tease. He did not care how far it got.

There was no excuse to lose control.

He believed that. Every word he'd spouted at them, drilling it in. Making it pure, fucking gospel that they never took advantage of a woman.

In that instant, he knew he'd lied.

With a low animal noise he didn't know he had it in him to make, he grasped her at the back of her thighs, yanked forward, making her fall to her back in his bed with her legs open.

And then he dropped to his knees and buried his face in Keely's pussy.

More nectar.

Sheer heaven.

She wrapped her legs around his head, not his shoulders, his head, her calves drawing him deeper and he ate her, beautiful, fuck, *gorgeous*, sucking her clit hard, fucking her with his tongue, licking her glistening black curls until they gleamed.

She didn't groom, not much, enough she could wear a bathing suit.

Other than that, natural, thick, lush, dark, forbidden, Keely.

She panted and she gasped and she bucked under his mouth, and it took way too short of a time to have her wild, writhing, panting, her fingers tight in his hair, her cries piercing the room, coming.

And doing it hard.

He surged up, wiping the back of his hand on his mouth before he grasped her ankles and flipped her to her belly.

She shifted to her side and his hand darted out, spanking one cheek of her round ass.

She stilled except her eyes slid up to him.

"I put you where I want you and I take it like I like it and you give it that way, Keely," he rumbled, and then watched as the slaked look went out of her face and her hungry one replaced it.

"Yes, Hound," she whispered.

He put his hands under her arms, yanked her farther into the bed and followed her there.

Once in, he hauled her ass up so she was on her knees, seeing the mark of his hand standing out red on her cheek.

And again he almost came in his pants.

Instead, he reached long to his nightstand.

"No condom," she breathed. "Just you, baby."

"Condom," he grunted, tugging open the drawer.

"Hound, I've got it covered so just you and me."

He gave her his attention and landed a hand sharp on her other cheek.

She quivered visibly.

Fuck, she was undoing him.

"Stay like that," he ordered, pulling at his belt, undoing his fly, yanking down his jeans, feeling the sweet relief of his dick springing free, watching her the whole time, her cheek in his bed, ass in the air, red from his spankings, the print of his hand marking her . . . both sides.

And he watched her watch him with a need that drew her beautiful features tight as he rolled on the condom.

"Hurry, honey, fuck me," she begged.

He moved around, positioned, grunted, "Spread," and watched her do it, his dick jerking. He then grasped her hip in one hand, his cock in the other. He positioned and then thrust in, watching her pussy take him, her body sway with the force of his drive, and he was buried to the root in Keely.

He closed his eyes at the flawless agony of having her wet tight all around, and he couldn't have stopped it if he'd tried when he mounted her, fucking her rough and fast and deep, curving his body over hers, hand in the bed beside her, face in her neck, buried in her hair, listening up close to her excitement, to what he was doing was giving to her, how much she got off on it, as he dove his other hand between her legs and worked her.

Relentless.

It took everything out of him to hold it back as he pushed her through her second orgasm, her third, then heard her beg for him to stop.

"Too much, baby. Too much, Hound. I'm coming apart," she whispered.

So he pushed her to her fourth and went with her.

It was savage. There wasn't a woman he'd fuck that hard and that rough.

And there was not a woman that had made him come that powerfully, making him feel his cum didn't drain from his balls, but from his goddamned soul.

His face was shoved deep in her neck, his cock buried deep in her pussy, his breath coming fast and uneven, when he came back to Keely on his dirty sheets in his shitty bed in his ratty-ass apartment.

It was all he had left to pull out, fall to his back and lift his hips to hike up his jeans.

He didn't do them up. He didn't even fully tuck his cock inside.

He stared at the ceiling wondering how in *the fuck* he'd let that happen.

He'd fucked another brother's old lady.

He'd fucked Dutch and Jag's momma.

He'd fucked Keely.

Before he could get his shit together to do whatever he had to do to talk that out with her, get her ass out the door and make plans never to see her face again, she rolled into him and did not hesitate even a second to dive her hand inside his jeans and cup his balls like they were hers to claim.

His eyes slid to her.

"That was not smart," he growled.

"Wrong," she returned, giving him a squeeze that made him grunt and honest to fuck, his cock wasn't even soft yet and it started to get hard as a rock. "What it was, Shepherd 'Hound' Ironside is *about fucking time.*"

"Keely—"

Her hand stayed latched to his boys, she lifted up and her other hand yanked up his tank. "Mama's gonna take care of you this time," she whispered, putting her mouth to his chest.

"Keely—" he bit out.

She bit his nipple and threw a leg over him, straddling him and moving her hand to stroke his dick over the spent condom.

Fucking hell, the bitch was in heat.

"Quiet, Hound, got work to do," she muttered against his skin.

"Woman—" he started, but it was another grunt because she was tugging at him hard.

Her head came up and her beautiful eyes in her flushed face were lazy and excited and hungry and goddamn it, he started fucking her hand.

She grinned.

He let out a muted roar, pulled free but only to roll to seat himself at the edge of the bed, dragging her belly down across his lap.

"Spread your goddamn legs when I spank you," he ordered roughly.

She complied immediately.

So that was when Shepherd "Hound" Ironside taught a latent biker mama an important lesson.

And it would be a tough call to say who got off on it more.

♡

HE WAS ON ALL FOURS, neck bent, watching himself fuck her face, watching more how much she got off on it, feeling her nails digging into the crack in his ass, when he couldn't take anymore, pulled out and dragged her up under him.

"I'm on the Pill," she gasped.

"You take me gloved," he bit out, reaching for the fourth time to his nightstand.

"Next time, you better have been tested," she groused.

He wasn't thinking about the next time.

He was tearing a wrapper off a condom.

He got it on and then buried it.

When he was up in her to the hilt, her back arched off the bed, hitting his chest.

He dropped down and pounded her.

"I want top this time," she panted.

"Nope," he declined.

"Baby, no fair, you've had top every time."

"Not the second go," he reminded her through a grunt.

"You let me ride you about ten seconds."

Her little, firm tits bouncing, her head thrown back, her pussy clutching him.

That was all he could take.

He drew up a knee and drilled her.

"Just get fucked and quit your bitchin'," he muttered.

"Hound—"

He locked eyes with her and said, "You keep bitchin', next time you're not takin' me on your back. You're takin me on your belly and I'm comin' up your ass."

He saw she wanted that before he lost her eyes when they closed, she arched her neck and he knew it was time to go in.

He was at her clit for about half a minute before she exploded under him.

He took in that magnificent show and kept fucking her for about two minutes more before he exploded inside her.

HOUND WAS FLAT ON HIS back.

Keely was flat out at an angle on top of him, her tits, ribs and belly to his chest, her cheek in the bed beside him.

When he turned his head, he saw that last part and that her head was turned away.

He stared at the ceiling again wondering if she'd taken a dick since she lost Black.

But when Dutch was eighteen and Jag sixteen and Hound had taken them out for a burger like he did on more than the rare occasion, Jag had been in a shitty mood, Dutch had been quiet, and when he'd coaxed it out of them, they'd shared, "Mom's bangin' some loser."

That had cut him but he hadn't let it show. He'd just had to dig deep to find some glad to give Keely that she was taking care of business and find a way to try to talk her boys around to that way of thinking.

When he took the boys to the firing range a couple months later, though, Jag was all smiles, happy his mother had, "Scraped that loser off."

So as much as it sucked, as gorgeous as she was, as much as she had to give, that her not getting it regular was a goddamn waste, at least she got some.

But he was wondering if getting that four years ago was the last she got.

Because the woman had stamina. He'd found it tough to keep up.

And now he was drained dry.

As he had these thoughts, she whipped her head around, her hair flying and gliding and he looked into her brown eyes.

"I have to go," she muttered.

Oh yeah.

Christ yeah.

She had to go.

"This didn't happen," he said.

Her eyebrows twitched before she asked, "It didn't?"

"Babe," he grunted.

He said no more.

But he didn't have to.

She might have lost her old man seventeen years ago and she'd embraced that choker she wore, but she was an old lady through and through. She knew this would tear the Club apart and put Hound in a serious situation he might not find a way out of.

He just had to hope she had enough feeling for him she wouldn't take it to that place.

Her lips curved up right before she slid up so she was not at an angle, but full out on top of him, her face in his.

He had fucked her repeatedly, ate her the same, spanked her, got blown by her, but in all that, except for the first one she'd laid on him, he'd not kissed her.

His chest heated with her face that close, her mouth that close, that look a look he hadn't seen on her face in years *that close*.

"You're a fantastic fuck, Hound."

"Glad I could be of service," he muttered.

Her smile got bigger.

Then her eyes dropped to his mouth and she murmured, "Mama's feelin' naughty, she knows where to go."

He rolled his eyes back to the ceiling because he was drained dry, and still the bitch could make his cock twitch.

He felt her soft body shaking on his with her quiet laughter.

"Hound," she called.

He looked at her to see she was not laughing anymore.

"This is our secret," she said quietly.

"Obliged," he replied.

Then she blindsided him.

"I need you to bring me my checks, baby," she whispered.

Even as he put his hands to the sides of her waist and dug his fingers in, he returned, "That's not a good idea, Keely."

"I need you, Hound."

He had nothing left, so he dug deep and didn't let it show on his face how much that meant when he said, "You don't need me when you got Chaos."

"You know I need you, Hound. *You*. You know why. You know how it is with us."

He did not.

"Don't pull away from me," she finished.

"Woman—"

Both her hands grabbed his cheeks and she got deeper in his face.

"You're mine and you know it. You're all I have left. Don't take that away from me."

This was about Black.

However she had it fucked up in her head, somehow, this was about Black.

He should set her straight about that, bring her the checks, make sure she knew he was there, he had her back, but do it in a way she knew he wasn't there to tap her ass when she needed an orgasm.

Unfortunately, he wasn't capable of finding the way to do that when she was naked on top of him, also naked in his bed.

"You're rich as fuck, baby, hire a house cleaner," she said when he didn't respond.

"This place is a shithole, Keely, and it's not my dirt that's making it that. You don't hire a cleaner to scrub down an outhouse."

Her head tipped to the side. "It's your home."

"It's a shithole where I crash and watch TV every once in a while."

"Then find someplace nicer. You got the money. A pad where you'd like to hang and keep nice."

He was not moving.

He had a reason to stay and until that reason was no longer, he was staying.

And no matter he spent the last four hours fucking and getting fucked by Keely Black, a dream he'd dreamed for twenty years, she didn't have a right to understand that.

"Babe, you wrung my balls dry. I don't even think I got the energy to lift my head from this pillow. I definitely don't have the energy to spar with you about somethin' stupid like where I crash, which don't mean dick. Give a man a break."

That brought back her smile.

He'd seen zero of those in seventeen years.

And it sucked just how damn good it felt having it back.

"Right, I'll quit busting your balls . . . this time. But when I come back, honey, you best have clean sheets."

His fingers dug in again. "You're not comin' back, Keely."

Her head tipped to the side again. "I'm not?"

"No. It was fuckin' great, but all the same it was still fuckin' stupid."

"I'm focusing on the fucking great part," she told him.

"Keely, do not fuck with me, with this, with where we're at, which I'm takin' from shit you're sayin' means as much to you as it does me. It was great, babe. Fantastic. Fucking spectacular. But it's a one-time thing. I'll bring you your checks. You got me. You'll never lose me. Your boys are so deep in my heart I'd take a bullet for them. But this, what we did, is done. You with me?"

That was when it happened.

That was when Keely kissed him again.

Not deep or long, but it was wet. She touched her tongue to his, giving him a hint of her nectar even as he still had the taste of her pussy on his tongue.

Then she pulled away.

"Okay, Hound," she whispered. "Whatever you say."

He rounded her with his arms, allowed himself to give her a hug with a squeeze, then he rolled her off him and rolled the other way.

He hauled his ass out of bed, muttering, "Get rid of this condom and then I'll get your clothes."

She said nothing.

But by the time he got out of the bathroom, his bed was empty.

He found his jeans, tugged them on and stalked down the hall.

She was pulling her hair out of the back of her top, but was otherwise fully dressed except her shoes and jacket, when he hit his living room.

It was not lost on him that the bone choker had not moved from her neck the whole time they were fucking.

No, and just looking at it right then made him want his face in her neck, her ass in his hands, and his dick buried in her up to the hilt.

She slid her feet into her shoes, swinging her jacket on at the same time, before she tossed a big smile his way.

"See ya later, cowboy," she said as she walked to his door.

He crossed his arms on his chest.

She looked down at his chest and smirked.

"Best tats in the Club," she whispered, her hand on his doorknob. "Walking work of art."

He tensed his jaw so he wouldn't rush her, nab her and chain her to his bed.

Her gaze lifted to his. "Now I know that's more ways than one."

"Stop bein' a pain in my ass," he grunted.

"Pain's in my ass, cowboy," she shot back still smiling, but it went another way and he felt that way drive up his balls. "And I like it like that."

With that excellent parting shot, she disappeared out his door.

Hound growled at it.

Then he went to it, locked it and walked right back down the hall.

He couldn't even look at his bed with its sheets that were fucked up and not from him sleeping in them.

So he turned his back on it and fell to it.

He swiped his face with his hands, and when he was done doing that, he kept them there.

"Fuck me, that was a huge fuckup," he muttered into his palms.

This was true.

It was also the best four hours of his life.

Bar none.

THE NEXT DAY, AFTER TAKING care of his usual morning business, Hound did not strip his bed and wash his sheets.

Oh no.

Fuck no.

He went to the store and spent five hundred dollars on a new set.

CHAPTER TWO

A WOMAN WHO LOVES YOU

THE MORNING AFTER HE BOUGHT his sheets, Hound's alarm clock sounded.
    He did not hit snooze.
    He turned it off, rolled out of bed, went to his bathroom, took a piss, washed his hands, brushed his teeth, splashed water on his face and under his pits then he went back into his bedroom to pull on some jeans, a tee, some socks and his boots.

He headed out, nabbed his keys, unlocked his door, walked through it and down the hall to the door beside his.

He didn't hesitate to insert the key in the three different locks, open them and let himself in.

He also didn't hesitate to walk across the stuffed-full room that was a lot cleaner than his because he *did* pay a house cleaner to come in to that pad once a week, dust, vacuum, mop, clean the bathrooms, change the sheets and take out and bring back the laundry.

Hound didn't hesitate at all on his way to his morning location where he journeyed every day, but he did stop at the door that was cracked open. The door to the bedroom that shared a wall with his living room.

He knocked on the jamb.

"You up?" he called.

He got the usual answer, "Yes, sweetheart."

Hound pushed the door open and further didn't hesitate to stroll right in, his eyes to the woman in the bed.

"Yo," he greeted, smiling at her.

She smiled back.

He stopped at the side of her bed.

"What we doin' this mornin'?" he asked.

"Shower, *motek*. Okay?"

He nodded. Reaching to the side to grab her walker, he positioned it how she needed it then he moved how he needed to move, pulling down the covers and carefully taking hold of the frail, thin body in its granny nightie.

With practice, they went through the motions until she had her slippers on and her hands firm on the walker.

He turned from her and let her shuffle her way toward the bathroom as he walked right to it.

He checked the angle of the showerhead, the seat in the bath, not that they would ever change position since him and her cleaner were the only ones to touch either, but that needed to be like it needed to be so Hound never failed to check it.

He also checked the towels and moved her shit from where it was out of the way to where she'd need to grab it when the time came.

She came in behind him and he helped her get into position. With practice, he was able to look away even as he pulled up her nightie and yanked down her granny panties that she insisted be put on over the adult diaper she wore.

"Good?" he muttered when he had her as she needed to be.

"Thanks, sweetie," she whispered.

Grasping his forearms as hard as she could, which was feeble, he twisted his hands to hold hers as gentle as he could and still do the job that needed to get done. He held her steady while she slowly aimed her ass at the john.

Once she hit it, not looking at her, he walked out, closing the door behind him in a way that it was still open a crack.

He had never made his bed. Even when he'd changed his sheets the day before, he put them on, tossed the comforter on top and that was it.

Every day, he made Jean's.

"Done, Shepherd!" she called.

He threw a pillow to the headboard and walked back to the bathroom.

He left her where she was and turned on the shower so it'd be nice and hot when he got her in there.

And then they danced the dance they'd been dancing every morning for years after he had grabbed a towel and handed it to her.

He never caught a look and by the time he lifted her scrawny body up, she had the towel down her front.

It got totally wet, but he'd bought her a shit ton of them so they could go through three or four, or however many they needed, so she could have her modesty and her shower.

"Shout out, beautiful, yeah?" he told her, still not looking at her and moving to the door.

"Of course," she murmured.

He closed it to its crack and moved in the kitchen.

He made coffee and checked her pill case. Then her pill stash. She was getting low on a few so he wrote that on her grocery list, saw the list was getting long, so he yanked it off and shoved it in his back pocket.

He looked to her easy chair, saw she'd dropped a book to the floor, so he knew she was done with it. This meant he went to the stack he organized for her in the way she wanted it and did the rotation in order that she had a big pile so that she'd always have one to read close at hand, even if she finished one or started three she didn't like the way they were going.

He checked her bottle of Baileys and saw she was good with that but made a mental note to stock her up. He cleared the area, set it up for the day including filling the water pitcher, putting out a glass for that, her squat glass for her Baileys when that time came, and then he went back to her room.

Fresh granny panties. Fresh diaper. Bra. Housecoat.

With timing borne of practice, he'd sorted all that shit right when he heard her call him.

Back to the bathroom, she was sopping wet, sitting on her bath seat, the towel held over her front, blinking up at him. Every morning she took her shower, the most precious thing he'd ever seen.

Except maybe Jagger, years ago, a mini-biker wearing his mom's purple bandana.

Hound set her stuff for the day aside but in reach, turned off the shower, got a fresh towel and they went through the rigmarole that meant she and Hound got her dressed, she powdered, put on her Chanel No. 5, he did up her bra and got her bottom half sorted and then she shuffled out behind him with her walker to her easy chair.

He was in the kitchen starting breakfast.

Two eggs over easy, not a lot of salt, liberal pepper. Two pieces of toast, half burnt and slathered in butter. With that he either opened a tin of some fish that smelled foul or gave her a couple of strips of brined salmon.

He got that shit started and moved to her chair with her coffee and her pills.

She set the comb she was pulling through her wet hair aside as he poured her first glass of water that day, and after she had a sip of coffee and set the cup away, he handed her the pills and glass.

"My sweet boy," she muttered, took them, downed her pills and set the glass on one of the two crowded tables that flanked her chair in order to go back to her coffee.

Hound returned to the kitchen that was, like his, open to the living room.

"Gonna do a shop," he called from there.

"Am I low?" she asked.

"Coupla things." He smiled and knew she could hear it in his voice when he said, "Though, not the Baileys."

"Well, thank goodness for that," she said before he heard the TV go on and a morning program started sounding.

"You down on magazines?" he asked.

"Gotta get my gossip, Shepherd," she answered.

That meant yes.

He let the eggs cook, the toast toast, and dug out the shopping list to add Baileys and gossip rags to it so he didn't forget.

He shoved it back.

"What's on for your day?" she asked.

Do her shopping. Run her errands. Come back and get her lunch. Then continue to attempt to hunt down a maniac, and if that proved futile as it had done for the last months, recon the maniac's minions so Hound could find the weak link, and as he was doing that, try not to ride to Keely's, rush her to her bed and fuck her brains out.

"Gonna work in the shop," he told her.

"That sounds fun."

Except for when he took her to the doctor, the dentist, or the synagogue on Yom Kippur, Passover, Rosh Hashanah and days like that, she didn't leave that apartment.

So anything for Jean sounded fun.

After he flipped the eggs, he took the coffeepot out to her and warmed up her cup.

"Thank you, *motek*," she murmured.

He bent and kissed the top of her wet hair.

Then he went and made up the plate for her breakfast.

He moved the TV tray in front of her before he set it down with napkin and cutlery and returned to the kitchen to get his own coffee.

After he grabbed his mug, he moved back to Jean and sprawled on her couch.

He took a sip and muttered, "Need to call that woman to get her in to do your hair."

She swallowed some egg and replied, "Probably time."

"Want her to do your nails and feet too?" he asked.

"I like that," she told him something he knew.

"I'll sort it then."

While he was taking another sip, suddenly, her gaze came to him.

"I heard a woman shouting in your apartment the other night."

Goddamn fuck.

"Do you have a girl?" she asked.

"Jean—" Hound started, shifting in the couch.

"You need a girl, Shepherd," she whispered. "Why a handsome, sweet boy like you doesn't have one, I really never understood. One that shouts at you about scaring her to death, now that we'll need to talk about."

She wouldn't understand why he was alone because to her he was a sweet boy and to the world he absolutely was not.

But also, she didn't know he'd been in love with a woman he couldn't have since he was eighteen.

The woman who'd been shouting at him.

"She sounded very upset," Jean remarked to her eggs and salmon.

"She's a friend."

Her eyes slid to him. "Friends don't get that upset with friends. Especially not female ones with men."

He knew all about Jean. From the minute he saw her shuffling down the hall nine years ago, juggling grocery bags she was too weak to deal with, telling him plain she had no one to help, it started.

He knew she'd never been married. He knew she lost her fiancé in Korea. He knew she never got over it and lived her life alone. No man. No kids. Friends eventually dropping like flies.

The only help she'd accept was visits from her rabbi and a few members of her community.

And Hound.

How it happened, he couldn't put his finger on. One second, he was helping her get groceries in her pad. The next he was veering his eyes so she could sit on the pisser or take a shower without humiliating herself too much. He figured the progression was natural enough once she trusted him more and more: groceries, cooking for her, setting up her chair, getting her cleaners, helping her get to bed.

And then they were there.

He'd talked to her about getting help in but she wouldn't hear of it. Her pension was shit, she couldn't afford it (she thought), and she refused to let Hound help financially.

Fortunately, part of that progression meant she let him pay her bills and go out and buy her groceries, and he used enough of her cash so that if she looked, which she'd stopped doing, she'd see her accounts dwindling. Just not as much as they would if he didn't pay her rent and utilities, buy her groceries, cover the excess on her medical care and have a deal with her cleaner and hair dresser so that they told her how much they cost was a quarter of what they actually did.

He was a carouser and rough-houser long before he found Chaos, which was why his parents scraped him off. Like Keely's, they were straight-laced, had sticks up their asses and felt living the Christian life was more important than trying to understand their boy, who was simply not straight-laced, hated church and was intense in a way that scared them, but they had no desire to put the work in to understand where that came from.

He'd put himself forward as a recruit for Chaos when he was seventeen.

With Tack's sponsorship, they took him on as recruit when he was eighteen.

And apparently he could hold a grudge, because once he found the family he wanted, he never looked back to the one who didn't want him. And apparently it was no loss to them, because they didn't come looking either.

He had no idea how he took Jean Gruenberg on as family along the way. He didn't know if he'd adopted her or she'd adopted him.

But she was the Jewish grandma to the atheist biker he never in his life expected to have.

And he loved her down to his soul.

"We've never talked about this, but hearing how upset that young woman was, I think the time has come that we should," she told him.

"She's a friend. The widow of a buddy of mine."

Her faded blue eyes grew alarmed, then distressed.

"Oh, Shepherd," she whispered.

"It's been a while, and with some other buds, we been lookin' after her, her kids. 'Cause a' work I've had to skip a few times when I'd do things for her I normally do, and she got tweaked. It's all good now."

That last was a lie, and with anyone Hound spoke to he'd not give a shit he lied.

With Jean, it made his stomach feel sick.

"Perhaps—" she started.

"She's just a friend, darlin'," he cut her off quietly.

"You're not getting any younger. You need to think about settling down. Finding a woman. Making a family," she shared.

"I got a family."

"Your own, *motek*," she added.

He grinned. "I got my own family, Jean bug. I'm good. It's all good."

All of a sudden, those faded blue eyes on him were piercing. "You are the kindest, most gentle soul I've ever had touch mine. If you do not give that to a child, Shepherd, that will be lost to this world and that would be such a crying shame, it'd be hard to reconcile it."

With her words, it shoved right into his head that Keely was forty-three.

Close to past it, but probably not quite yet.

She also had a twenty-one-year-old son, a nineteen-year-old one, and would likely not want to start that shit up again at her age.

Tack and his woman, Tyra, had not thought twice about starting up again after Tyra got in there with Tack, years after he'd rid himself of the bitch who'd been his first wife, Naomi. His girl with Naomi just gave Tack his first grandchild, a boy, and his two youngest with Tyra were barely older than their nephew.

It worked for that family.

The thought of telling Dutch and Jagger he'd knocked their mother up made him want to puke.

The thought that he was even having these thoughts made him want to kick his own ass.

"She was loud then I didn't hear anything for a long time including your door open and close, Shepherd," she said sharply. "Though I did hear it later, very late. It woke me up. Did you go out to a late-night movie? With her?"

This was no one's business.

Except maybe Jean's.

"Took some time to settle her down," he hedged.

"It sure did," she replied, gaze intent on his, lifting her coffee cup to her lips without breaking her regard.

"What happened shouldn't have happened. She's the widow of a dead buddy of mine," he told her.

"I'll tell you what, Shepherd Ironside, in some cultures it's the responsibility of the brother who lives to wed the wife left behind in order to make certain she's cared for."

"That's not our culture," he reminded her, and it definitely wasn't Chaos culture.

"Perhaps it should be. Perhaps there would be very lonely women who struggle, some of them with children, who wouldn't have to struggle so hard, and their children would have a steady man in their lives who provided for them and gave them the understanding their mother was worth taking care of, because that's the truth."

Suddenly, Hound wondered what was behind that emotion.

"Who we talkin' 'bout here, Jean bug?" he asked softly. "We talkin' about Keely or we talkin' about someone else?"

"My Haim didn't have a brother, just a younger sister and she was a spoiled rotten brat."

Hound relaxed and grinned at her.

"I'm old but I'm not stupid and I'll tell you this, I'm sure it wasn't gentlemanly behavior you used to settle her down," she stated.

It was absolutely not that.

She kept at him.

"However, even so, it's the way of the world today and today's brand of gentleman would not have her out the door in the middle of the night. Did she need to get back to her children?"

Dutch had his own place. Most the time Jag crashed with him because he was his brother, not his mother, but also because his pad was closer to where Jag was taking classes to become a mechanic.

So it wasn't just their ages that meant Keely did not need to get back to them.

"Her kids now are grown," he told her.

"So it was you having to take care of me that made you send her on her way," she declared.

"Jean, she left because she wanted to leave. It didn't have anything to do with you."

He felt the coffee he threw back after he gave her that stick in his throat when she said, "You support me and yourself, Shepherd. You seem not to have very many needs, single men often don't unless they have expensive hobbies, which you don't. But it's obvious you have money. Why are you still in these terrible apartments?"

Well, it was now clear she paid closer attention to her accounts than he thought she did.

"Jean—"

"It's because of me," she spoke for him.

It was.

"Jean bug—"

"I'm here because I've lived here for fifty-three years, and it wasn't like this when I moved in and I just don't have it in me to move out. But more, I don't have the money to do it. You're here, in these apartments, in a bad part of town, right where you're sitting now after making me breakfast, because of me. You'll come back to make sure I have lunch. You'll come back and help me get to bed. Boy your age doesn't need a woman mine hanging like an albatross around his neck. You need a woman to love and children to raise, but more, you need a woman who loves *you*. I think it's time we again discuss someone coming in to help, and it's definitely time we discuss how much money you're pouring into looking after me."

"I don't mind," he said quietly.

"Well I do," she retorted firmly.

All right.

He was done.

So done, he found himself maneuvered into sitting on the other side of a discussion they'd quit having two years ago.

"If I don't, how can you?" he asked tersely. "Has it occurred to you that wakin' up knowin' I'd get a dose of you and havin' something important to do in my day, that also bein' lookin' after you as well as stepping up for Keely and her boys, is the only thing feels right about me except my brothers' givin' me their love. But that last, I earned. The rest, those are gifts and you want me to give that up? Move out. Leave you to what, Jean? Some soulless company that offers care and you're just a name on their daily list to tick off and they don't give a shit about you?"

"Language, Shepherd," she murmured.

Hound clamped his mouth shut.

"I despair every other morning when it's time for you to help me shower," she whispered.

"I don't. I don't give a sh . . . oot."

She shook her head. "The beauty you have in you, *motek*, I don't understand why you don't offer that to a woman."

"You don't understand because the only woman I'd let have that is Keely, and her man's been dead for seventeen years and she still loves him like the first day she laid eyes on him."

Christ, why was he giving her this?

Maybe because he needed to say it out loud to remember it.

Her voice was filled with misery when she said, "Shepherd."

"Don't worry, Jean. I've lived with it so long it just is what it is because that's all it can be."

"And this visit of hers the other night?"

"She said somethin' uncool to me and felt bad. She knows I'm hers and she lost one of the three most important things in her life, and the kind of woman she is, that important is *important*. I'm not that but she wasn't feelin' like losing me. So she made sure that won't happen."

"Is this . . . this . . . woman using you?"

He shook his head. "Can't be used when you're gaggin' to be kept on that string."

It was Jean's turn to clamp her mouth shut.

She got over that quick.

"I'm not certain how I feel about this situation."

"She loved him with a love that made even me wonder if there's a God because only something divine could create that kind of beauty."

She leaned toward him over her TV tray, her face earnest. "Please, find that for you."

"It's not out there for a man like me," he educated her.

She sat back. "How can that be?"

For the most part, he was honest with her. That was what he gave his Jean.

But with some things, he held back.

Now, he put it out there.

"Because the man I am in here for you is not the man I am when I walk out that door. And the man I am for Keely and her boys is the man I need to be to replace the one they lost. But the man I am, there's nothing divine about it."

"You're very wrong," she stated irritably.

"I'm all kinds of right," he shot back.

"You can't be different men, Shepherd Ironside. You're the same man who needs to be different for different parts of your life and the different people in it. You cannot tell me and make me believe that a single thing you've done in your life you didn't have your reasons for doing it. So not in this house, Shepherd. Not sitting right across from me. You don't talk yourself down looking right at me. The second man in eighty-nine years who I've given my love to, I didn't give it foolishly. I know the man you are and it might not be divine but it's blessed, because I'm blessed to have you here with me."

Hound looked to her TV, his throat closing.

Jean didn't care she lost his gaze.

She kept at him.

"Now, if this woman cannot see the blessing of you, then you need to find it in you to harden your heart to her and find one who does. She's out there, Shepherd. She's waiting. She's lost and alone and she needs you in her life. So stop messing about and *find her*."

Hound gave her his attention on a scowl.

"If it'll make you be quiet about it, okay. I will," he gave in. "But I'm still lookin' in on you, I'm still lookin' out for you, and I don't want to hear another word about that. And that means with the money."

"I have my own money," she returned.

"You also have mine," he fired back.

"I can pay my own way."

"Good luck with that since you can't pick up your own mail and you don't have your freaking checkbook."

She glared at him.

He pushed it. "So are we square?"

"Fine," she snapped.

"Great," he bit back.

She looked down to her plate.

Hound shoved up from the couch muttering, "You reaming my behind, it's gone cold. I'll nuke it."

"I'm sure it's perfectly all right," Jean replied.

He pulled her plate out from under her fork and looked in her eyes.

"'All right' is not good enough for my Jean."

Tears filled her eyes.

So he didn't have to witness that crap, he took her plate to the kitchen and nuked it.

He brought it back to her hot.

Then he sat in her couch, drank his coffee and watched a morning show where he was pretty sure he would be happy killing every person on it—and none of that would be for good reasons, except no one could pull off that brittle, chirpy fake that early in the morning except them—but he was also pretty sure that wasn't worthy of murder.

Jean ate her breakfast.

Hound did the dishes.

And with her stacks of books and the magazines she had left and her remote right there and her water pitcher fresh and her Baileys close and her box of chocolates closer, he left her on a promise to be back with her groceries and to get her lunch.

THERE WAS SOMETHING HE SHOULD have taken care of a long time ago.

But he never did.

So after his morning with Jean, he returned to her with her groceries and gossip rags and meds, and an appointment with her hair dresser, and getting her to the john then getting her lunch. When he was back on Chaos and he saw Tyra's Mustang at the foot of the steps to the office of Ride—the custom bike and car garage that Chaos owned, ran and worked, and Tyra managed the office—and he saw Tack walk in that door, Hound moved that way.

He opened the door and was thankful to see only Tack and Tyra there, his brother sitting on his woman's desk, his woman sitting in the swivel chair behind it, but she had it rolled close to her man.

They both looked to him when he walked in.

He closed the door.

"Gotta take some of your time," he said.

"You need me to go?" Tyra asked.

"No, Cherry," he answered, using the nickname the brothers gave her that had a lot to do with her hair, but it could be said it was also about her being sweet (Tack called her Red, that was Tack's, and since it was no one used it, not even his older kids that weren't hers). "I mean both of you."

Tack went alert. Tyra kept her gaze pinned to him.

Hound launched in.

"Got a woman, she means somethin' to me."

Tyra's eyes got huge and Tack stared at him, a man who was a master at hiding shit he didn't want seen, he couldn't hide his shock.

Maybe Jean was right.

Maybe it was time to quit banging biker groupies (and definitely Keely) and find a woman to make babies with.

Or something.

Fuck, he was thirty-nine, a biker, and he'd spent seventeen years . . . *pining*.

Jesus.

"She's eighty-nine years old and lives in the apartment next to mine," Hound continued.

They both relaxed.

"She's got me and she's also got no one else but me," he stated.

They both grew alert again.

"If somethin' happens to me, I gotta trust someone will take her on. And I'm askin' you two to do it."

Tyra's lips parted.

Tack straightened from her desk and turned to Hound.

"You look after an eighty-nine-year-old woman?" Tyra asked quietly.

"Groceries, rent, make sure she's topped up with books, her gossip rags, medical bills, personal care, get this chick to come in and do her hair."

"Personal care?" Tyra whispered.

He looked at her. "She trusts me."

With that, her mouth dropped clean open.

Hound looked to Tack. "You're not in, I'll ask Tab and Shy. Tab's a nurse. She'll—"

Tack cut him off. "We got her covered."

Hound nodded.

"Somethin' happens to me, you break it to her gentle," he demanded.

Tack nodded.

"Nothing's gonna happen to you, Hound," Tyra cut in.

And Graham Black was on the way home with pizza for his family when he got jumped in the parking lot and had his throat slit before he could even begin to fight for his life.

"Shit happens, it happens to me, I want to know you got Jean covered," he replied.

Her face got hard.

It was cute.

"Nothing's going to happen to you, Hound," she repeated.

He gave her a look then looked to her man.

"Jean?" Tack asked.

"Gruenberg," Hound answered.

Tack nodded again.

He locked eyes on Tyra when he said, "This is no one's business but mine."

He said this because Tack's woman was gorgeous, she was sweet, she was a fantastic old lady, a loving wife and an amazing mother.

But she also had a big mouth.

"It doesn't leave this room," Tack assured him.

But Hound didn't unlock his gaze from Tyra.

She crossed her heart, held up her fingers and did it smiling.

He'd take that and hope she meant it. Fuck knew the shit he'd have to eat if the boys knew about Jean.

"Right," Hound grunted. "Done," he went on, still grunting. "Later," he finished.

Then he walked right out.

CHAPTER THREE

FLEXIBLE

HOUND'S PHONE BUZZED WITH A text.

He pried his eyes open, saw his alarm said it was nearly two in the morning and he grabbed his cell off the nightstand.

He had a text from Keely.

It said, *Open your door, cowboy.*

He stared at it a second.

Then he lost his mind.

He was out of bed, in his jeans and stalking to the door with his jeans not all the way buttoned before most men could spit.

He'd looked out the peephole and had the door unlocked and pulled open before a woman could say "boo."

"Hey—" she started, giving him a look.

But she got no more out because he wrapped his fingers around her upper arm and yanked her inside.

He slammed the door, locked the three locks then shoved her against the wall beside the door with his hand still on her arm.

"Jesus, Hound, what—?"

He dipped his face right in hers.

"Are you fucking insane?"

"What?" she whispered, staring in his eyes.

"Are you . . . fucking . . . *insane?*" he repeated, slower this time.

"Why are you asking me that?"

"Because it's near-on two, this apartment building is on the brink of bein' a full-blown crack house, it's in a neighborhood that Hell's Angels might find a smidge too scary, and your ass is not in your bed in your sweet crib in your house in your nice neighborhood. Instead, it's at my door."

Her face screwed up. "Why is it safe for you and not for me?"

"Because I got four guns, seven knives, six inches on you, eighty pounds and a fuckin' thousand-pound punch."

"You know the PSI of your punch?" she asked curiously.

"Were you asleep the five thousand times I took your boys to the gym?" he asked back irately.

"No," she mumbled.

He let her go and straightened away, asking, "What are you doin' here, Keely?"

"Well, uh . . ." she started hesitantly, eyeing him up like she wasn't sure how to go on.

"You're here to play with my dick," he bit off.

"How much more mad at me would it make you if I shared that had crossed my mind?" she asked.

"Maybe five, ten hundred *thousand* times more mad, babe," he shot back in answer.

"Hmm . . ." she murmured, still eyeing him.

"I thought we agreed we were done," he reminded her.

"I was kinda hoping you were feeling flexible about that."

Hound looked to the ceiling.

Her soft "Hound" in her low, velvet voice came at him the instant her hand lit on his bare chest.

He grabbed her wrist and she made a surprised noise as he twisted it behind her back, jerked her around, and pushed her chest first into the wall.

He put his mouth to her ear.

"Undo your jeans," he ordered.

Her body trembled against the wall as well as him, and her free hand went to her buckle.

He had no excuse.

Except this was Keely.

And she wanted his dick.

And he was Hound.

He'd give her anything.

When he heard her zip, he let her go and rumbled, "Hands to the wall."

She complied and he yanked her jeans down her thighs, taking her panties with them.

She whimpered.

He pressed his chest to her back, slid a hand around the front and went right in.

Her hips jerked.

"Be quiet, I got an old lady neighbor who sleeps light," he told her.

"'Kay," she breathed, grinding into his fingers.

"I make you come against the wall, make it good but hold some back, baby, because right when that's done, you're ridin' my face 'cause want that wet on my tongue."

"'Kay," she mewed.

Christ.

He pressed his hard cock to her ass.

She moaned and dropped her head back to his shoulder.

After he finished her off, he hunkered down, yanked off her jeans, boots, socks, and then ripped off her sweater and jacket, leaving them and his jeans down the hall before he yanked her into his bed on his five-hundred-dollar sheets and hauled her pussy on his face.

He pulled her down and buried himself in nectar.

Now they were talking.

KEELY ON HER HANDS AND knees, Hound curved over her, an arm around her chest, hand at her tit, other arm straight, hand in the bed by hers, he fucked her fast, tough and hard.

She turned her head, dug her forehead in his neck, and came . . . loud.

Hearing it, he started pounding her inhumanly.

"Can you take that?" he grunted.

"Fuck yes," she said like it was a plea.

"Can you take more?"

"Fuck . . . *yes*," she answered, gasping and panting and slamming back into his ruthless thrusts as if to prove her words right.

He dropped his head, trapping hers against his neck, listening and getting off on hearing the violence of their flesh connecting cracking through the room.

"Hound," she whispered.

"That's whose cock you're taking, baby," he growled.

"*Hound*," she whimpered and then went again, quaking under him, rearing back uncontrollably.

"Yeah, Keely, fuck . . . *yeah*," he ground out then he lifted up, pulled his arm from around her, wrapped his fingers around the back of her neck, and shoved her face into his sheets, his momentum increasing, jacking his cock using her pussy.

"Fuck that pussy, baby," she said in the sheets. "Fuck it and shoot for me."

A noise drove up his throat, thundered out and he let her neck go, clamped onto her hips and rammed her back into him as he fucked her through a staggering orgasm.

It was so huge he couldn't stop himself from collapsing over her, his forehead hitting her between her shoulder blades.

She gave him a few beats before, breathy and hot, she gave him shit.

"Mama wear you out?"

"You okay?" he asked.

"Uh . . . you might be on number one but I'm on number four so . . . yeah," she answered.

He put his hands to the bed on either side of her and found her ear.

"This is not a complaint that your pussy can take that thrashing, baby, but I gotta hear the words and believe them that it can."

She moved her head in a way that it tossed her hair out of her face and

Hound had to lift up to let it. Even so, some of its silk slid across his face.

And fuck, but he liked it.

Then he had her eyes.

And he liked that better.

"You could fuck me harder, I'd take it. You could eat me dry, I'd take it. You could shoot a wad down my throat that was the equivalent of a large milkshake, I'd fuckin' love it. What I don't think I can take, honey, is you saying I can't come back and get more of it."

He slid out, rolled her over, then eased his weight down on her, taking some of it in a forearm.

"We had this discussion," he reminded her.

"Yeah, and I couldn't sleep for two nights needing your dick, so I hightailed my ass to a bad part of town to get it, and you barely pulled me in the door before you had my jeans down my thighs."

He felt his jaw get hard mostly because she did not lie, which reminded him he was weak.

"I need you to ride this out with me, cowboy," she said. "And the way you go at me, I'm thinking you need it too."

"We need to be careful."

"Chaos?"

"You."

"Me?" she asked, sounding confused.

"Keely, you know the shit would be deep I'd be in if the brothers found out about this and straight up, that's a worry. But I haven't put the time in I have lookin' after you to ever make you feel anything but looked after."

"If you don't think I feel looked after coming off of four orgasms in about an hour, you definitely need a better understanding of the concept."

She was being funny and he liked that too.

But now they had to be serious.

"I don't know what you want from me and I'll take that sweet pussy and smack that round ass and take whatever time you wanna give to me but we both have to have a mind to where our heads are at with this, and we pull out, literally and figuratively, the minute it looks like things are gonna get fucked."

"So have fun and don't get in too deep?" she asked.

"So, you wanna give your cowboy a ride, he'll take it, but the minute you get even a hint what we give each other is no longer for you, you clue me in and we go back to where we were before."

"And where was that?"

"I bring your checks. I switch out your thermostats that stop working. Otherwise I live my life and you live yours."

She said nothing to that.

"Sex, babe," he said softly. "Fuckin' great sex. And when it stops bein' just that between two people who dig each other and have history, we cut our losses. Can you do that?"

"You're a magnificent lay, Hound. That could take a while."

"Good to know, Keely. But we both know it's not goin' there so cut a man loose before he gets so tied up, he's strangled."

She got solid under him and he didn't know if it was what he exposed, what he put out there, even if he didn't give it to her straight, or if it was the world "strangled" that was too close to the bone that made her that way.

It would be a relief to find it was the first.

"I'd never hurt you."

She'd been killing him for twenty years.

He didn't enlighten her about that.

"So we're straight," he said.

Her head on his sheets tilted to the side.

"Am I hurting you?" she whispered.

"Come so hard when I'm in you, think my balls are gonna shoot out my dick, but other than that, no," he lied.

She grinned. "That hard?"

"Keely, you're a machine. You're like the bionic fuck master."

She burst out laughing, wrapping her arms and legs around him while she did it.

He watched.

He felt.

Oh yeah.

He'd lied.

Totally fucking killing him.

She stopped laughing but not entirely when she declared, "You got new sheets."

"Apparently, I was flexible about that first time bein' the only time."

She kept laughing softly as she asked, "Tested?"

"That's just now been scratched on my to-do list."

She lifted her head and brushed her mouth against his before dropping it back to the mattress and murmuring, "Good."

He didn't want to ask it, but she'd left him before dawn the last time so he had to ask.

"You need to get home?"

"Jag has discovered Dutch's aversion to grocery shopping and never has any money, which is a mystery since he still has an allowance, now a lot bigger one since he's still in school but mostly on his own, and he's still human so he still has to eat and do whatever boys do, most of which I don't wanna know. So he comes home to fuel up for the day, and he does that shit early."

"Kid's always been an early bird," Hound muttered.

"It's bizarre, and I told them it was for fun we did that DNA test two years ago but mostly it was to make sure he wasn't switched at the hospital."

He would have laughed.

But although part of what she said was funny, part of it was not.

"What DNA test?"

"Those ones you can send off in the mail."

"Someone has you and the boys' DNA on file?"

She stilled again under him.

"Hound—"

"Babe, what the fuck?"

"It's confidential."

"It's not anyone's fuckin' business."

He felt her temper rising even before she stated, "They're not gonna do dick that'll make that a problem. Tack promised me that when he called me to tell me you all had taken on Dutch."

"It's still no one's fuckin' business."

"Hound, you're not outlaw anymore. I gotta believe that because my boy's mixed up in that, and Jag says the minute he finishes school he's gonna jump in."

Hound knew that. The brothers had already agreed to take him on the minute he made his approach.

Still.

"An outlaw never stops thinkin' like an outlaw, even when he's abiding by the law," he informed her.

"Are you abiding by the law?" she asked.

That day?

Sure.

"Yes," he answered.

She seemed to relax under him but still asked, "Should we talk about the problems the Club is having?"

"Nope."

"Is that nope, it's Club business and as such, none of mine, or nope, you're not tellin' Keely that shit because she'll lose her mind?"

Clearly once an outlaw, always an outlaw, and also once an old lady, always an old lady.

"Mostly first, little of the last."

"Fuck," she muttered, and he saw her eyes roll up and stay up.

"You hauled your ass to me at two in the morning to get it tapped, baby," he reminded her gently. "And you did it knowin' the Club's got troubles. We already in the zone where you wanna cut loose?"

Her eyes rolled back instantly.

"Nope."

That was when Hound relaxed.

"We gonna fuck real quick again before you go?" he asked.

"Yup," she answered.

He grinned.

She lifted her head, her fingers sliding into the back of his hair, and she kissed him.

He rolled so she was on top.

She slid the spent condom off his dick and tossed it to the floor beside the bed, which most women would have a problem with doing, most men wouldn't, and Hound didn't.

They fucked real quick.

They did it hard.

Then they got dressed and Hound walked her to her car.

"Next time, you give me a heads up and you stay in your car until you see me," he ordered.

"Whatever you want, cowboy."

With her, it wasn't ever whatever he wanted.

It was taking what he could get.

So he did that right then.

He kissed her.

Then he closed the door on her after she folded in.

And last, he stood on the sidewalk and watched her drive away.

He hit his five-hundred-dollar sheets.

And he woke two hours later to his alarm clock telling him it was time to take care of Jean.

"FUCK," HE GROANED, LOSING THE sight of Keely bouncing on his dick when he was forced to dig his head into the pillows, close his eyes, thrust his hips up into hers and shoot hard.

Before he got over it, he felt her body hit him, her pussy squeeze him and her hair all over his face when she collapsed on top of him.

"You're a lot of work, cowboy," she breathed.

He turned his head and shoved his face through her hair into her neck. "You want it fast, don't swallow a huge load before you decide to ride me."

"So noted."

"That said, if you're markin' preferences, I got no problem with you swallowing a huge load before you bring my boy back to life and bounce on my dick."

He felt her shake with her laughter, wrapped his arms around her so he could feel it better, and she replied, "Preference noted."

He wanted to touch her, smooth his hands over her soft skin, take her in gentle after she'd fucked him hard.

But he didn't do that, and not because he couldn't remember ever doing that with a woman but because they liked each other, they liked fucking each other, but that wasn't who they were to each other.

This was what he thought.

He'd find out immediately that Keely thought otherwise.

He found that out when she lifted up, and with her long, black hair a curtain around either side of her face brushing the skin of his chest, she trailed her fingers across the eagle inked at his collarbone and the top of his chest. The wingspan was spread wide, the tail feathers fanned out, claws outstretched, face fierce, like it was about to attack prey, above it over the top of his collarbone, a thin line of clouds.

She traced her finger down where he had a scroll of intricate fretwork arced across his pecs, and under that was where shit got interesting.

He had the Chaos tat of wind, ride, fire, and free.

To his left abdomen, he had the Chaos scales where one side was high, the scale dripping blood (on Hound that blood was black, all his tats were black, no color, and he was seriously tatted, full torso, back covered in Chaos, two sleeves). There was the word Red on the high side of the scale, meaning Cherry, or precisely meaning Cherry surviving the fact she'd taken a blade numerous times due to shit her girl's now-dead fiancé got all of them up to their necks in.

The other side of the scale, the one that was down, had a reaper drifting up from it, and it was labeled Black.

Chaos's Black.

Keely's Black.

All the men got that tat somewhere on their body to remember what was important: brotherhood, family and keeping both safe.

He held his breath, the ridges of his abs standing out, when Keely put her palm over the reaper, her husband's name, and pushed in hard.

They'd get there, he knew. It would be what would take this away from him, he knew that too.

He just wished it wasn't so soon.

"Keely," he whispered.

Her head, bent so she could stare at her hand, came up.

"The 'Red?'" she asked.

That was the first time she'd seen the tat.

Shit.

"Tyra, Tack's old lady," he answered.

"When she was kidnapped years back and got stuck . . . repeatedly," she guessed.

Hound nodded.

"You got that for her?"

She didn't include Black.

"All the brothers got it."

She studied him a beat before she looked back down, slid her hand off the scales and Hound tensed again, trying to even his breath as she headed to the other side.

There was shit there that was meaningful. A waving American flag. One of his brother, Joker's bike designs, an American bobber Hound wished he'd bought before the customer picked it up because now it was gone forever to some rich fuck who probably had no clue the meaning of something that cool, he just had the money to buy it.

And coming up from his pubic hair, starting close to the root of his dick, a Native American lance with an eagle feather tied to it crossed with a bow, an arrow running parallel to it crossed with a long-handled club that had a rough stone attached at the top with sinew. These ran up his abdomen, through his navel, into his ribs, through the American flag that waved there, and farther up.

Apache weapons.

They weren't the only tribe that used them, but she'd embraced her culture. She was definitely not immune to where Hound had been at when it came to her, she might put it together that he'd inked her in him from dick to where the lance point hit, his heart.

"Keely," he called to take her attention right when she started to trace the arrow through its bow, straight up the middle of his chest.

"I've got no tats," she muttered.

That had not escaped him. It was the only un-old lady thing about her.

"Why?" he asked.

Thankfully, her gaze came to him. "I'd settle on one then change my mind. Settle on another, and change my mind."

"They're not things you can change your mind about," he said.

A ghost of a smile drifted across her lips.

"Your artist is the shit," she said.

"Yup," he agreed.

"You design these or did he?"

"*She* designed them all, except the Chaos tats. Those are inherited or Tack's man did them."

She nodded, her eyes floating down to his chest, already knowing about the ones that were inherited, Black had been buried with his.

"Keely."

"You let a girl ink you?" she asked, and there was something in her face he didn't get.

"She doesn't have to wrestle a tiger before she does it, babe. Then again, a tiger'd probably best me, so it's good she doesn't."

"I mean, she touches you, like . . ." she slid her hand down, into his pubic hair right to the root of his dick, "*here*."

"Not gonna let a dude touch me there," he grunted.

"Did you shave?"

"Had to."

"Did you do it, shave I mean?"

"Yeah."

"All of it?"

His brows drew together. "No. Just where she needed to go."

"Did she see all of it?"

"You mean my dick?"

"Yeah."

"She didn't need all my junk exposed to her to get where I wanted her to go. Now can I ask where this is heading?"

"Have you slept with her?"

It was then his brows snapped together.

"Keely."

"You have," she whispered.

He had. His tattoo artist was a cute pixie badass princess with pink hair, serious as shit piercings that rocked and a magic mouth.

He felt it would be a mistake at this juncture to share that.

"I'll repeat, where you headin' with this?" he pushed.

"I'm bad about sharing."

Ah.

"Took the test today, babe. Not gonna do that, get the results, and if we get the go ahead, come ungloved inside you and put you at risk."

"Okay," she said softly.

But he stared at her because he'd just agreed to be exclusive with, essentially, a fuck buddy.

He slid his hands up her back and into her hair to hold her head with both of them.

"No worries about sharin', Keely. You got my word. But don't lose sight of where this is at and what you're gettin' from me," he warned.

She nodded.

"You gotta get home?" he asked.

"Soon-*ish*," she answered.

"We gonna fuck again?"

She arched one perfect brow. "You have that in you?"

"You do the work, I could rally."

She smiled.

"I blew you, you haven't eaten me," she told him something he very well remembered.

"Happy to oblige, but just sayin', if you're keepin' track, I think you owe me about four."

"I hear that, baby, but mama's mouth is tired."

And he heard that. She gave it her all, did it with gusto and kept going even after he'd blown.

"Guess it's time for me to go down," he muttered.

"It is."

"You wanna swing off?" he asked.

He couldn't imagine why she wouldn't. He still had some hard but he was losing it fast.

She still hesitated.

Then she swung off and he lost her.

The thing that caught at him about that was it was Keely acting like she didn't want to lose him.

He wasn't going to get into that with her.

Instead, he rolled off the bed and headed to the bathroom to flush the condom.

At this rate, the super would be up in his shit for clogging the pipes.

Whatever.

He went back to Keely and took her there with his mouth.

He pushed her there again with his cock and fingers.

Then they dressed and he walked her out to her car where they necked before he stood on the sidewalk and watched her drive away.

CHAPTER FOUR

YOU'RE SO CHAOS

HOUND LIFTED A LEG AND put his boot to the door.

It popped open and he strolled in, seeing bodies scatter.

He didn't have a mind to any of them, but the one he knew belonged to the man who lived in that apartment, an apartment in his building.

The guy tried to take off, attempting to go wide to avoid Hound, but even though Hound was a big man, he could move fast and definitely faster than a junkie.

So he caught the guy at the throat, lifted him off his feet, then slammed him down on his back on his soiled carpet, going down with him to press a knee hard to his chest even as he didn't take his hold off his throat.

He got in his face.

"You gotta do this shit," he lifted his eyes, indicating the dope paraphernalia that was scattered everywhere, "you do it somewhere else. Find a friend who don't have a biker that gives a shit his building is clean. And you need to get supplied, you do that somewhere else too, motherfucker. I see or even hear that kinda scum has walked through the front door again, it won't be the dealer I'm lookin' for. It'll be you. Have I been clear?"

"Yeah, uh . . . yeah. Yeah, man. Totally, yeah," the guy pushed out.

"I am not a man who likes his time wasted. If I find my message has not been delivered, I won't deliver it again. I'll snap your neck," Hound told him.

This last wasn't true but the guy didn't need to know that.

His eyes were glassy but big and filled with fear, his face was red, and he nodded his head even in Hound's hold, because he believed him.

"M-m-message delivered," he stammered. "P-promise."

Hound shoved at his throat as he pushed up, not enough to cause damage, but enough to make the guy splutter and cough, turning to his side.

Hound looked down at him, feeling his lip curl.

Then he saw the carpet he was lying on was the same as his carpet, Hound's not as rank, but it wasn't far from it.

Him and Keely had been at each other now for a week. She had more than a rare occasion to walk on his carpet in her bare feet, especially now that his test came back clean so he went at her ungloved, she liked to clean up in between and he didn't eat his own cum.

She hadn't said dick.

He didn't think about it.

Until then.

Hound walked out of the apartment, out to his truck, swung in and went to Target.

He nabbed a vacuum cleaner, and while he was there, grabbed some Windex, cleaning cloths, paper towels, a mop and some stuff to clean bathrooms.

On his way back to his apartment he called Chill, the recruit they'd taken on with Dutch. A good kid, couple of years older than Dutch. Not tall. Lean and wiry, smart and seemingly dedicated (so far). He didn't know dick about cars and bikes except he liked them, and rode the last, so he didn't work in the garage. Like all recruits, he worked in the auto supply store that was also a part of Ride, but unlike all recruits, he'd stay there after he was patched in.

And Chill was always moving. If he was sitting, his leg was bobbing. If he was talking, his hands talked with him. If he was hanging, his eyes were always darting around the room.

Being totally fucking hyper, of course, they called him Chill.

"Yo, Hound," Chill answered.

"Just downed a junkie at my apartment building because I wasn't a big fan of the element he was attracting to my space."

"Righteous," Chill replied.

Another requirement to be a recruit for Chaos, that being not down with that kind of shit at the same time willing to do something about it.

Chill's mom was a recovering junkie, his dad, out of the picture for years, a non-recovered one.

So Chill was down with that.

"You probably won't think that when I tell you I realized in not cleaning my crib for nine years, it's not a man cave, it's a dump like where a junkie would hang, so you're comin' over and givin' it a scrub down."

"Fuck," Chill muttered.

It wasn't easy being a Chaos recruit, and it wasn't just because you got the shit jobs like stocking shelves, keeping track of inventory and waiting on pain-in-the-ass customers at the store.

It was because you were a grunt, you did what any brother told you to do, you went where they told you they wanted you to be, you didn't question it, you didn't bitch about it and you were on call 24/7 for all that shit.

"Find Dutch, bring his ass with you," Hound ordered.

"Like . . . now?" Chill asked.

"You doin' something for another brother?" Hound asked back.

"No, just workin' the store."

"Someone there that's not Dutch to cover that?"

"Yes."

"Then yes, like now."

"Right, be there in thirty."

"Good," Hound grunted, hung up, drove back to his pad and hauled the shit up to his apartment.

Then he went next door to hang with Jean awhile before he made her lunch.

"SO, TELL ME HOW FLATTERED I should be that you walked me in tonight and the place is spic and span," Keely ordered.

She was naked, astride Hound's lap. He was naked too with his back up against his headboard.

She wasn't holding distant. Her chest was to his, resting on it, but she had her head back so she could look at him.

From their second time until then, Hound got the message loud and clear that they might be fuck buddies, but Keely was not going to let that stop her from being lovey and affectionate.

This meant any time they weren't fucking, she stayed close and touched.

Hound wanted to find some way to warn her off that shit, set that boundary, keep them focused.

But it wasn't just that he wanted it, and where it came to Keely he was weak.

It was that he knew she'd been starved of shit like that for years, and where it came to Keely he wanted her to have everything she needed.

It was the night after Dutch and Chill spent three hours scrubbing down his pad, and not just because she was a woman, but because she had eyes and a nose, she didn't miss it.

"Had to deliver a message to a junkie downstairs this morning, babe," he told her. "Saw his carpet was half a level up from the foul of mine. Men don't mind livin' in a sty, but when it comes clear that junkies don't mind that shit either, he calls the recruits, arms them with Windex and scrubbing bubbles and then goes to have some lunch."

She laughed and it was soft, the sound and the movement of her body against his.

She slid a hand up his chest to his neck, her thumb rubbing down his throat to come rest in the dent in his collarbone.

"What was the message you delivered?" she asked.

"He doesn't do dope in a place where I share a roof with him and he doesn't invite dealers to that place either."

Her head tipped to the side. "He hear your message?"

"He gave indication that he did."

"I bet he did," she murmured, then, louder, "Why do you live here, baby? This place sucks. And you get the same Chaos cut I do so I know you can afford way better."

"Not here enough to bother with movin', Keely," he lied.

"A man like you shouldn't live in a place like this," she returned.

A man like him?

What was the kind of man she thought he was?

He shouldn't let curiosity win.

He shouldn't.

But he did.

"Where would a man like me live?"

"I'd say a kickass loft downtown or something like that, but back in the day before you told the boys it was part of earning their allowance to mow my lawn, I had the best lawn on the block. And the best shrubs. When I added the flowers, it was the awesomest yard for three blocks square."

This was true. He'd put in her sprinkler system. He also did the weed preventer and lawn fertilizer every year so it grew lush and green.

She lived in a graceful, old place in Governor's Park, with big, established trees and thick shrubs. A two-story Victorian that all the brothers would have given Black shit for buying, except for the fact he bought it for Keely about a month after they found out she was carrying Dutch.

She had a decent-sized front yard, for a home in a city. The backyard was bigger.

And before he taught the boys how to take over that shit, he kept it up nice and lush and green so Keely could roll up the drive at the side to her garage and just think it was that. Nice and healthy. Not think anything else, like she had to do dick with it to keep it that way.

"Boys kept that up," he told her something she knew. "They still on that?"

"Dutch has been on his own for a while, but Jag still has to earn his allowance and mama don't take out no trash or mow no fucking lawn."

He grinned at her.

"So, a house," she decreed, sliding her hand back down, curving it over his pec, absently stroking his nipple in a way that was absent for her, but was not at all for him. "A little one. Brick. With a big backyard with a built-in fire pit and grill and the best lawn on the block. Maybe in Englewood."

Hound liked that was the kind of man she thought he was, even though he knew different, and deep down, so did she.

But he'd never thought of getting anything like that for himself. He had his brothers. He had his bike. He had his obsession with Keely. He ate. He drank. He kicked ass. He did his bit for his Club in all the ways he could. He got laid. He partied. He had his apartment, his room at the Compound he rarely hung in unless he got a hankering for a biker groupie and needed a close place to have a hot bang. And he had Jean.

A little brick house with a big backyard and built-in fire pit and grill where his brothers and their women could come and hang, he could slap some brats on the grill and they could get loose around the pit throwing them back, did not sound like it would suck.

Keely walking out back with a bowl full of potato salad she'd made (and hers was the best, he remembered even if he hadn't tasted it in seventeen years) would suck even less.

This thought did not make him do what he should do.

Remind her she should probably think of getting home.

It made him smooth his hands from where they were resting on her hips to the small of her back and then up her spine.

She pressed her chest closer.

"I'll hit Zillow," she said.

"Say what?" he asked.

"I'll hit Zillow. Keep an eye out. Get you a new place."

He blinked at her and it was how he always did it when she surprised him.

Slow.

"Babe—"

"With pot being legal, real estate is insane but I think a badass biker can put the lean on someone tryin' to outbid him. Also thinking you probably got so much dough saved up, you could best even weed-shop owners who got buckets of cash."

"First, baby," he said softly, "I dig that some women don't think men feel shit when they bite, tug and roll a man's nipple, but just to say, that man is me, they'd be wrong."

"Oh," she whispered, stopping her thumb at his nipple and getting such a cute look on her beautiful face, he grinned at her.

"Second, you feel like spending time checking out Denver real estate on the computer, have at it. But I'm not movin'."

"Hound—"

"Babe, I don't like where I'm at but I'm here and I'm not goin' anywhere. Maybe one day I'll settle in. But now my life is outside this place. I got years in me but I'm still wild like the wind. It's not time to tie myself down. I know that time'll come. I'll embrace it when it does and I'll be glad for it. It's just that now is not that time."

"Wild like the wind," she whispered, and now the look on her face made Hound slide one hand farther up so he was cupping her neck and scalp from under her ear.

"Baby?"

"I was once that," she told him.

Yeah she was.

Wild and beautiful and happy and carefree.

"I know you were," he replied.

"Feels like centuries ago."

Where his thumb could reach, he stroked her face. "I know."

She looked deep into his eyes. "I get that back, right here with you."

That hit his gut and it felt far from bad.

He wrapped his other arm around her and pulled her in tight.

"Keely."

Both her hands slid up to his cheeks and she got so close her nose brushed his.

"I'm gonna suck you off right now, cowboy," she whispered. "And you're gonna watch every second of it."

"You want that, baby, I'm not gonna stop you."

She kissed him first, deep and wet and wild, and she held firm when he growled down her throat and tried to roll her to her back so he could take over.

But it was clear it was her time to give him something and she was going to do it.

And Hound was going to let her.

When she broke the kiss, she took her time down his chest. She traced some of his tats with her lips. Nibbled and sucked his nipples until his whole body was clenched, holding him back from shoving her down and forcing his cock in her mouth.

And when she got between his legs, he spread them wide and cocked his knees so he could watch as she went at him, sucking his dick, licking his balls, pulling them one by one in her mouth and drawing deep, digging her lips and tongue and teeth in the junctions of his thighs, jacking his cock with her hand when her mouth wasn't on it.

After a long time of that exquisite torture, he blew down her throat after her hands slid up the insides of his thighs and clenched into his knees, pressing them apart.

But Keely knelt between his legs, her arms out like that, like she was a priestess in a pagan act of veneration to a dick she'd deified, so when he blew, he blew hard, a fist in her hair holding her full of him, shooting a massive wad down her throat that she gulped right back. And after, her head, with her silken hair all around, kept bobbing, milking him dry.

When he came down, he watched her lave him, her arms still out, fingers curled around his knees, her tongue licking him clean from balls up his shaft.

And then she kissed up his stomach, his ribs, his chest, his neck, and he adjusted his legs so she could sit astride him again.

She tucked her face in the side of his neck. Hound rounded her with his arms and didn't even attempt to stop himself from showing her love and affection through his touch. He let his hands roam, taking in her softness, the heat of her skin from ass to hips to back to neck.

"Best head I ever got, baby," he murmured.

"Good," she murmured back.

"Never forget that orgasm. More, never forget watchin' you build it in me."

"Good," she whispered.

He turned his head and kissed her temple.

Still whispering, she said, "No house for you, Hound. You need to be wild like the wind for as long as you wanna be, baby."

He stopped his hands roaming and held her tight.

That could have been for him. That could be Keely telling him she liked that in him, liked it for him, and wanted him to keep it.

It could be her wishing maybe she hadn't hitched her star to Black so young, settled in a big Victorian house in a nice part of the city and started right up giving him babies. Settled in young to something so good it owned all her heart, but finding herself strapped down without release to a life that wasn't what she wanted when her man was no longer in it.

He didn't quiz her about which way what she said went.

He just held her close and smelled her hair that was flowery but herbal and clean and mellow, felt her weight and heat against him, and knew right then, the next time she came to his pad, he should have the conversation with her.

End this.

Because he was in too deep when it began.

And now he was drowning.

At the same time he knew he wouldn't.

It would be her who ended it.

Because no matter how much it took, how deep it dug, how empty it left him, he'd give her what she needed even if it left nothing of him, and after she was gone, he drifted to ash and blew away with the wind.

HOUND SLID UP THE SIDE of her body, cupping her bush, shoving his face in her neck to listen to her heavy breaths even out, waiting until the time was right to stroke her wet lightly with his fingers.

And when that time was right, he did.

"Good?" he murmured, his lips catching against the smooth bone of her choker at her neck.

"I'd say that was the best head I ever got, but every time you go down on me, it gets better. So that was the best head I ever got . . . so far," she answered.

He grinned.

She trailed a hand down his forearm and covered his between her legs.

"Just to say," she whispered, "know there isn't a man who doesn't get when he's got his fingers between his woman's legs, especially after he's just gotten her off, she feels it."

He stopped stroking her but kept his hand there, the rest of his body frozen.

His woman?

He felt her head turn and she asked with her lips against his hair, pressing her fingers into his, "You gonna fuck that pussy, baby? Or just lay claim to it?"

Lay claim to it?

His head came up and he looked down at her to see she was flushed and satisfied but her eyes were still heated, and he knew his bionic sex babe was far from sated.

"Damn," she whispered, her eyes roaming his face then she took her hand from his between her legs and rested it at the side of his head. "You're so fucking hot. I could look at you for hours."

"Kee—"

He got no more out.

She lifted her head from the mattress and kissed him, driving her tongue in his mouth.

Hound liked the feel and taste of that so much, he drove a finger up her cunt and swallowed her gasp, felt her hips move with his finger then allowed her to roll him to his back.

She climbed right on like she could now, and got way off on it, no condom in between.

He let her ride him until it was time to take over and then he *took over*.

He rolled her to her back and rode her like that. Then he got to his knees, pulled her legs up his chest and watched her take his dick like that. Then he pulled out, turned her to her belly, hauled her up to her knees and took her like that.

And in the end, he drove her off her knees to her belly in the bed, and with one hand shoved under her, finger at her clit, taking her there in a wave of orgasms that ended up with her uncontrollably yipping at the same time begging him to stop as well as fuck her harder, he finally shot in deep and clean, nothing in between, jetting his cum into Keely.

He gave her his weight, shoving his hand at her clit deeper so his fingers spread feeling the root of him rooted in her, also pushing his other hand under her, transferring some weight to that forearm as well as curling those fingers around the side of her neck.

"I want you to take my ass."

He had a lot of things to say to her, things they needed to go over after they'd both come down, but that breathy announcement while she was still coming down took him off target.

"Say what?" he asked, lifting his head to look down at her profile.

She twisted her neck to catch his eyes.

"I want you to fuck me up the ass, baby," she whispered.

His hips dug into hers involuntarily.

"Right now?"

She grinned. "You got lube?"

He did not.

Not there.

He did at the Compound.

"Nope."

"Then definitely not right now."

"Keely—"

"I'll bring lube tomorrow night," she offered.

"Babe—"

A strange intensity came over her face and when he saw it, Hound braced.

"I want you up my ass, Hound. I want your cum down my throat, up my cunt and in my ass. I want wild. I want fire. With you, I'm Keely. You take me hard. You ride me rough. I'm not a mom. I'm not the attendance officer at the high school that the kids alternately think is the shit, because I am, or think I'm a pain in their ass because if they miss school, I am.

I'm a woman. All woman. The woman who likes to get fucked however you wanna fuck me."

Keely had never taken her Chaos checks and sat back drinking martinis and watching soap operas all day.

She'd taken her job as the truancy officer at Dutch and Jag's high school during Dutch's sophomore year, this after having a variety of part-time jobs from about a year after Black died to when she got her masters in social work.

She was a mom. She had that job and ones that paid and got her out of the house. She took care of her boys and her home. And she went to school.

Hound had always admired that, considering he eventually had to get his GED before he could get his mechanics license, something he had and kept up but never used since his job for Chaos and Ride was not about holding a socket wrench.

She didn't make a lot but she didn't need to. What Chaos gave her, she could live on easy.

Instead, she fixed up the house like she and Black had plans to do before he died, all reno'ed from basement to roof. She took the boys on kickass vacations every spring break and summer, from places like Disneyland and shit like that when they were young to the Grand Canyon, Yosemite, Aruba, and Alaskan cruises when they got older. When they got their licenses, she got both boys cars (even though she made them get jobs so they could pay for the maintenance and gas) and paid for both boys' schooling. And Dutch and Jag had told him she had accounts for both of them that they'd get when they were twenty-five or when they got married so they could put a down payment on a house.

And these accounts were substantial.

"You said you'd do my ass before, Hound, but are you not into that?" she asked, taking him back to her.

"Babe, you want me to fuck you up the ass, I'll do my best not to shed a tear right now I don't got lube. But just sayin', that's not how we fuck. We fuck tough. No one can take tough up their ass."

"So fuck gentle."

Fucking Keely gentle.

Fuck.

He pulled out, slid his arms from around her and rolled to his back.

Keely, like always—absolutely *always*—immediately got close again, doing this landing her tits to his chest and putting her face in his.

"So am I bringing lube tomorrow night?" she asked.

"You don't need to. I have some at the Compound," he answered.

She shot him a huge smile.

Christ, only woman on the planet that he knew who'd look that happy she was going to take cock up her ass.

Wild. Fire.

Keely.

Yeah.

Christ.

Apparently, he wasn't going to end it tomorrow like he should have ended it that night. But since he didn't, that shit should happen tomorrow.

Apparently, he was bringing lube and coming up her ass.

Hound looked at the ceiling.

"I'll come early, bring some chicken," she stated and his eyes moved back to her. "Say, six?"

He had to get dinner for Jean and help her to bed. She went there early and watched TV until she snoozed.

But not that early.

"Say, eight."

Her eyebrows went up. "Eight? That's late to eat, Hound."

"In case you haven't got it yet, babe, we'll work it off."

She shot him another big smile.

Christ.

He looked back at the ceiling.

She slithered full on him, hiking up her knees so she was straddling him.

More Keely.

She loved to be astride her cowboy, the more body contact she could get, the better, including direct contact of her pussy with him anywhere she could get it.

"Are we done?" she asked.

No.

Hell no.

But they should be.

He looked at her and didn't get into that.

"How did you know where I live?"

She grew visibly confused. "What?"

"How'd you know where I live? Did you ask a brother?"

"You're on Bev's Christmas card list."

So that was the envelope he got from Bev every December.

He reckoned there were at least seven of them in the mountain of mail he never bothered to open on his kitchen counter that Dutch and Chill didn't throw out.

He opened bills.

He tossed junk (or Dutch and Chill had tossed the junk, usually Hound just piled it but that pile had spilled all over the floor about four years ago).

He set aside, evidently, Christmas cards.

"Bev sends bikers Christmas cards?" he asked.

She grinned. "You know Bev's a nut."

He did.

Why Boz got shot of her, Hound didn't get. She could ride a man's ass, and she did. But she'd never done it when Boz, who could be an idiot, didn't deserve it, and this was mostly only when she caught him with his tongue down the throat of some female biker hanger-on or worse, when she caught him with his hand up the skirt of one. Considering that, obviously Boz could be enough of an idiot, even Hound, as his brother who would never normally call that shit, could call it.

But it wasn't often, and even if his transgressions bought it worse, it wasn't that bad.

Mostly she was sweet, really into Boz and a nut.

He couldn't think on any of that.

He had to think about something else.

"So Bev knows you came here?"

"I told Bev I was a bitch to you and you weren't givin' me a shot to say I'm sorry, so I asked if she knew where you lived and she told me. So the answer to your question is, yes. She knew I came here. But no, she doesn't know I'm still coming here."

Hound relaxed.

"She's still totally in love with Boz," she announced.

He focused on her, not sure he wanted to get into this with her for a slew of reasons.

"I'd interfere with that if I still wasn't so ticked at Boz for not reconciling with her after she broke it off with him for being an asshole," she went on.

"Babe, you know you don't get involved in that kind of shit," he warned.

And he was right.

Except for the fact that Tyra Allen had now been head old lady for nearly a decade and she stuck her nose in anything she wanted. To the point it sometimes caused friction with Tack, the most recent being when she got in there when High and Millie were getting back together.

Tack had not been happy.

The part that sucked was that the end result could not be argued. It wasn't the end result that sucked. It was the fact it didn't would give Cherry excuse to do it again.

He didn't share this with Keely because they should absolutely not do this. Her being a part of the Club the way she was and always would be, him being a brother of the Club, if she was his old lady, post-fuck conversation would be just like this.

But she would never be his old lady so this was a boundary they definitely should not cross.

"You know what drove him to not taking her back?" she asked.

"I know you know I'm never gonna share that shit with you. I also know you know it's not your business. I further know you know that you don't stick your nose in that shit or it might get bit off. And last, straight up, babe, as cute and hot and beautiful as you are, you know all this enough to know we're never goin' there no matter how cute and hot and beautiful you get to try and get it. Yeah?"

She scrunched her nose, which witnessing it was so cute it made Hound wonder if what he'd just said was true.

"You're so Chaos, it's kinda annoying," she snapped.

"Well . . . yeah," he replied.

She rolled her eyes.

"Are we done fucking tonight or what?" he asked.

Her eyes went up to his alarm clock and he tilted his head on his mattress to do the same.

It was nearly one in the morning.

She usually texted him around nine or ten that she was downstairs and he went down and brought her up.

She also usually left around now.

"I best get going," she muttered.

Hound hugged her. He kissed her. He rolled them both off the bed.

She cleaned up in his now clean bathroom.

They got dressed.

And they necked by her car before she got in it and drove away.

Hound did not do what he normally did, go up to his crib, take off his clothes and collapse in his bed, falling asleep smelling Keely.

He went to the bathroom and flipped the light on.

It was cool how much better he could see himself with a mirror that wasn't covered with water spots, toothpaste splashes and grime.

And that made him mark cleaning his pad as part of Chill and Dutch's recruit duties, and Jag would get in on that shit when he was prospect, but maybe even before if he came and begged money off Hound again.

He pulled off his tee and stared at himself in the mirror.

He had a mess of dirty blond hair that fell in his eyes, so sometimes he jacked it back with a band at the back of his head, and hit his shoulders.

He shaved maybe every two weeks, not having the time or inclination to maintain a mustache or goatee or the patience with it itching at first to grow a beard (that itch heralding a shave), so the dark stubble on his cheeks and jaw and down his throat was thick, but not long.

His eyes were blue. Just blue, nothing interesting about the color or shape.

His brow was heavy. He had lines in his face that maybe made him look older than he was. But seeing as he wasn't in his twenties anymore, and even when he was he didn't care, it didn't matter.

He worked on his body, he was tall, so he could see a chick thinking he was fit.

And his tats were fucking awesome.

He got his share of pussy, and he didn't have to work hard for it but he always thought that was because biker groupies were easy.

Hop was in a rock band before he joined the brotherhood and he told stories of pussy on the road, but Hound could see how Hop got in there repeatedly even if he couldn't sing and play guitar. The man was just good-looking.

Tack too.

Rush (Tack's son, who got the best of his dad and the only good she had to give of the bitch of his mom, her light-blue eyes), Shy, Joker and Snapper could all be in magazines. Biker magazines, but those boys had looks.

He could see women not thinking High was hard to look at either.

Dog, who was now in Grand Junction with Brick, Arlo, Bat and Tug setting up their new store there, was the same. And Brick had that teddy bear thing going on that not only made women fall at his feet, it made them think they could treat him like shit and he'd eat it (and he did, until he was done doing that).

Pete was an old guy, not past it but he'd rode hard, lived hard, played hard, fought hard and that was not lost on anyone who looked at him.

Boz, Roscoe, Tug, Bat, Arlo and Speck, they all had biker cool but they had to rely on that. Though Hound didn't think they thought on it too much. They just caroused and hit the snatch that opened for them, which for Chaos was always abundant.

He'd never thought on it either. But if someone made him do it, seeing as this was the first time ever he'd taken himself in in a mirror when he wasn't doing it to examine a wound or shave, he would have thought that was it. He was a biker. He was Chaos. He knew how to use his dick. So snatch opened.

Definitely he'd heard he was hot, handsome, good-looking, but he thought that was just bullshit to make him hit something, that something being the pussy of a biker groupie.

Keely calling him "so fucking hot" made him stare hard.

He didn't see it.

Then again, he had no interest in dick, except his own, and these days he didn't have to jack it himself, far from it. Any time away from Keely was recuperation time, so he wouldn't.

And it didn't matter.

She did see it.

That mattered.

Definitely too much, seeing as he was standing in his bathroom looking at his damned self in the mirror.

He stopped doing that, flipped the light switch and tugged off his boots, socks and jeans.

Then he hit the hay to get five hours of sleep before he had to go see to Jean.

CHAPTER FIVE

BROOKIES

HOUND LAY ON THE COVERS in bed next to Jean, his back up her headboard, legs stretched out, stocking feet crossed at the ankles, watching her TV with her under the covers, slouched into him, her head on his shoulder.

Keely would be there in half an hour.

But he would be with Jean if she wanted him for that half an hour.

"I know she's coming to see you."

Hound looked from the TV to the top of Jean's wispy, white-haired head.

"Darlin'," he murmured.

She lifted her head from his shoulder, twisted her neck and looked up at him.

"You know, sweetheart, after I lost Haim, I couldn't find it in me to look anywhere else. But that doesn't mean I didn't think in the back of my head, 'maybe tomorrow,' or 'maybe next week,' or 'I'll just give it to the end of the year and then I'll open my heart again.' Well, days turned into weeks and weeks turned into months and months turned into years, and now I'm here with you. I'm lucky because you're all I need, and that's because you're the kind of man whose heart is generous so I have all I need. And I'm glad I'll have you in the end. But I still spend a lot of time looking back wondering what if and feeling regret."

"I hate that for you, Jean bug," he replied, and he did.

He hated worse her saying the words, "in the end."

And if Keely ever did that, looked back and asked what if, he'd hate that for her too.

"You lost your heart to this woman years ago, does she know that?" Jean asked.

"I don't know if she knows how deep it goes, but I know she knows I'm hers."

"Take backsies."

His brows drew together. "Say again."

"You're hers, take yourself back. Take backsies."

He grinned at her and shared, "Not sure it works that way."

That was when she said, "Bill Withers."

Hound took her in hoping like fuck she wasn't losing it. Her body was letting her down. Her heart was weak, the doctors worried about it (and Hound worried about it more). Her lungs weren't great either. Her strength was in the shitter, seemed she slowed down more and more every time he came to her. But her brain was as sharp now as it had been the day he met her nine years ago.

"Jean, darlin', think you need to explain," he prompted.

"You young people, I know, can get hold of music real easy these days. So get one of your gadgets and listen to the song 'Use Me.' And I think . . . I think," she bit her lip before she finished, her voice getting quiet, "I think you might like it like that, and okay if you do. But don't let her use you up."

Hound felt the warmth hit his gut that she cared about him so much to worry about him that much and knew it was in the small smile he gave her.

"Don't worry about me, Jean bug," he whispered.

"Impossible, Shepherd. But I'll try."

He leaned in and kissed her forehead.

When he pulled back, she turned to face the TV and dropped her head to his shoulder again.

He dropped his head to hers when she did.

They watched some TV.

She was snoozing when he left her.

And he wasn't in his pad for five minutes before he got the text from Keely that she was downstairs in her car with chicken.

"TODAY HAS JUST BEEN *INSANE*," Keely declared, walking to the bar of his kitchen, dumping some fancy-ass grocery bags that Hound reckoned rich women who gave a shit about global warming took to LeLane's gourmet store when they bought groceries, but they still kicked ass because they were Keely's.

She shrugged off her suede jacket, unwound the long scarf from her throat, sent them and her purse flying toward his beat-up armchair, and suddenly Hound felt a need he'd never felt in his life.

To go furniture shopping.

She started digging in the bags, stating, "I've got this kid, who's just a little *shit*. Now, I volunteered at King's Shelter for three years, did an internship there when I was in school, had two boys of my own and it isn't like I started my job a month ago, so I know kids can be shits. But most of them are just finding their way or have some reason that's making them be total pains in *everyone's* ass or seriously, hormones make you do whacky things. But this kid . . . no. His parents are rich. They're still together. They spoil his punk ass rotten but neither of them are pushovers. They're always at school events. All over coming in to chat with me when he skips. They care. And he's still a punk ass. Skips school at least once a week. I've had so many meetings with his parents this year, I'm about to put them in my will."

Hound wanted to laugh.

He didn't laugh.

Because she was unearthing shit from those bags that was not grocery-store-bought chicken.

It was Tupperware and stuff folded up in foil.

"Babe, what's that shit?" he asked.

She turned to him with one hand holding what looked like a glass container filled with brownies.

"What?"

"What did you bring to eat?"

"Keely's Buttermilk Goodness Chicken Tenders, my potato salad, homemade biscuits, I brought butter, honey and apple butter because I'm guessing you have none of that, but I'm hoping you have water and a pot because I need to blanch the green beans. And we're having my brookies for dessert."

"Brookies?"

"Brownies with cookie dough cooked in them."

Her potato salad was enough.

The rest . . .

"You said you'd bring chicken," he reminded her.

"Well, I should have said I'm bringing my Keely's Buttermilk Goodness Chicken Tenders but it's a mouthful and bottom line, it's still chicken."

"In other words, babe, you cooked."

"Uh . . . yeah," she drew all that out, staring at him like she thought it best to check his temperature.

At this juncture, Hound was seeing the error of his ways.

She wanted his cock up her ass, he should have brought the lube from the Compound, refused the chicken and given her his cum whatever way she wanted to take it.

What he should not have done was opened himself up to Keely's Buttermilk Goodness Chicken Tenders (something he'd say out loud only if a gun was pointed to his head), the return of her potato salad, the goodness of whatever the fuck brookies were—but with what was in them they couldn't be anything but great—and her bitching about her work, which he wanted to hear so bad he might need to do something he would never in his life admit he needed to do.

Find a shrink.

"Pan, Hound," she ordered, back to organizing food. "Water, on the stove. The rest is still hot. It won't take long to deal with the green beans and then we can eat."

He needed to draw this line. They didn't have this. They fucked. They might cuddle and chat between fucks, but that's what they had.

Not this.

Hound drew no line.

He went and filled a pot with water, and not only did he do that shit, he got out two plates and some cutlery.

"So, I think I need to read my employment contract, but my guess is, they don't spell it out in the contract that you can't slap a kid upside the head . . . *repeatedly* . . . for being a punk ass. Still, I think they'd frown on that. Now I'm at a loss, because I honestly just want to write him off and let the principal suspend him and let his parents take him in hand and not let him waste more of my time, but that will fuck with my perfect average of keeping kids in school or at least getting them back there and making them stay, which I've worked my ass off to do for six and a half years."

Hound had the water going under the pan and was facing her over the bar.

"You have a perfect record of keeping kids in school?" he asked, surprised.

"It's not my job not to let them smoke pot, meth, crack or inject heroin on school grounds. Or not to stick each other during fights. Or make them stop fucking each other in the bathrooms or fingering each other at assemblies. It's my job to bring them back so they can do all that on school property."

Hound stared at her a beat then threw his head back and busted out laughing.

When he righted his head, she was smiling at him in a way he was way too amused to let penetrate.

"Baby, not sure you take your job serious enough," he told her.

"I have enough to handle with what I've got and that's more serious than is cool. There are a lot of parents who do not give a fuck about their kids, Hound, not even a little bit. They care about their cars or their designer shoes and handbags. So many of them are Jeremy. So many, it isn't even funny."

"Jeremy?" he asked.

"Pearl Jam. 'Jeremy,'" she answered. "Kids are not something Mom can wear. So they don't give a fuck. They go shopping. The kids come home to an empty house but their bed is covered in shopping bags. They've got great clothes, the latest phone, hot wheels, and no love. But by the time they get to high school, Jeremy is not gonna be talking in class. That hurt is gonna have burned so down deep, no social worker attendance officer is gonna be able to heal it."

"Baby," he whispered.

She was needlessly arranging food on his counter she wasn't going to open until the beans were ready and studying herself doing it.

This should have been a clue.

Hound was tuned to her, very tuned, and still, he did not field that clue.

And he'd wish he did.

"My boys thought it was a pain in the ass that we sat down to dinner every night. Every night. This was even before I heard this stuff from the kids, learned about it in school. I just know the way my folks were and the way . . . the way," she lifted her eyes to him, "Graham came from money, but not the good kind, the up-its-own-ass kind. He didn't fit and they treated him like shit."

"I know," he said when she stopped speaking, watching her closely now that she'd brought Black right out there, right there, between them.

"So we talked about it, him and me. And unless Club shit got in the way, we were going to have family dinner every night. Even if we got McDonald's. We'd sit down and look in each other's eyes and talk and ask about our days and let them know we gave a shit. I let them know I gave a shit. You know that. You've sat down to dinner with us."

He nodded.

He had.

Not often.

But he had.

"It's really that easy," she continued. "I swear to God. I gave my boys a lot. Chaos gave my boys a lot. But I swear, the most important thing I gave them was my time every day during dinner."

"You're probably right, baby," he agreed.

"And you."

Hound's chest caved in on itself.

This was such an extreme sensation he had to push out his, "What?"

"The only other thing I gave them that was important was not cutting them off from Chaos, which meant not cutting them off from you."

Christ.

Christ.

"Keely—"

She shook her head, lifted her hand palm out his way and interrupted him.

"It's about time I said it and it requires no response. I know you did it for me, for them, for Graham, and you didn't even think about it. It's in your blood. It's in all you all's blood. But yours especially. I know, Hound. It's just what you do. But I'll never forget you standing in my backyard covered in blood, and what that meant you did for me, for us, for Black. I know with every lawn you mowed and every time you took the boys for burgers and every time I'd see you close to one of them, your head bent to them, and I knew you were delivering a man lesson I'd have no hope to give, but they soaked up like a sponge, how important what you gave them was. They love you down deep to their souls, and I'm grateful to you down deep to mine and it's about time I said it."

He just stood there staring at her over his countertop that had not, in nine years, ever had that amount of food on it and not ever had food that good on it, and he knew that shit before he'd even tasted it, and he said not a damned thing.

Not only because what she said meant so much he couldn't speak.

Because what she said meant so much, there were no words to say.

"This is not about that," she said low, her voice rippling over him like a soft touch. "What we got right now. What we have in your bed. Why I come to you every night. That's about you and me. Please never ever, please, *please,* baby, never ever mistake what this is between you and me. And it's not about that."

He had no idea what it was so he couldn't mistake it.

But she didn't want him to think it was gratitude, so he could give her that.

"I won't mistake it, Keely."

"Now, the look on your face makes me want to suck your cock but I'm hungry since you made me wait forever to eat, so we're gonna do that first and then we'll get down to the good stuff."

"I have a feeling, your potato salad, babe, the good stuff starts earlier."

She smiled, it was smaller than usual and a little unsure, a little uneasy, and he worried after that, but she still did it.

"I remember you liked that," she said. "But you'll fall in love with my chicken."

Hound had no doubt.

He had no fucking doubt at all.

And he'd find he was right.

HOUND MADE IT SO SHE could take him.

With him ass to his calves, her straddling with her back to his chest, sitting on his cock, her hole primed with his fingers and lube and so much foreplay, they had to have broken a record, his dick slathered in lube too, she took him up her own ass, doing it slow.

It was agony.

She was hot and tight up there.

So hot.

Unbelievably tight.

He was working her tit with the fingers of one hand, her clit with the other and having not a small amount of trouble not taking over.

"God, this is . . . it's . . ." she breathed then inched down on him farther. *"Nice."*

He shoved his face in her neck and tried to think of things that didn't include wrapping his arm around her hips to hold her steady and driving his cock up her ass.

"You okay?" she asked.

He was not.

"Totally," he answered.

She took more of him.

He growled into her neck.

"Okay?" she asked.

"Baby, it's you gotta be okay," he told her.

She slid down farther, pushing out a breathy, "I'm okay."

"Then it's okay," he grunted.

"Can I . . . are you good with . . . more?" she asked.

He wanted to shout it.

Instead he gritted it through his teeth.

"Yeah."

She slid down farther, feeling it, taking more and then he felt her ass hit his thighs.

And he was in.

"Fuck," he groaned.

"Good?" she asked.

"Babe, my cock is buried in hot tight. I don't wanna hurry you but—"

"Fuck it," she whispered.

"What?"

"Take it, baby."

"Keely—"

She twisted her neck, he lifted up and she looked him in the eye.

"Fuck my ass, Hound."

He went in, taking her mouth, clamped on her tit, kept at her clit and moved, bouncing her up, gliding out, pulling her down.

He went slow. He went gentle. He loved every fucking stroke. She got off on it too. He kissed her through it all.

And when she came, she sank her teeth in his lip so hard, he tasted blood.

Then when he came, he ground his cock up her ass so deep and shot so huge, he was worried he'd never quit coming.

When he did, her forehead was in his throat so he rested his jaw on the side of her head.

"Fuck, that was fucking *awesome*," she said into his skin.

He smiled into her hair.

"Are you . . . ready to, uh . . . lose me?" she asked.

Never, he thought.

"I'm ready when you are, baby."

She slid up, another agony, doing it slow, and he lost the heat of her but not for long.

She turned and climbed into his lap, legs open and rounding him, grasped his hair on either side and made out with him with his cum sliding out of her ass, getting all over his thighs.

When she was done, she kept her hands tight in his hair, her face so close all he could see was her eyes, and the look in them made the blood in his veins freeze.

"I broke the seal earlier, you know how, and I'll break it again, right now, real quick. But you deserve it and it's important so you're going to get it but I was virgin back there, Shepherd. So that's all yours. No one else has had that. It's just yours."

She was talking about bringing out Black.

And his brother never had that.

She gave it just to Hound.

When the blood started flowing through his veins, it did it racing, fiery hot and so fast it roared in his ears so he had no control over his actions. In fact, he wouldn't even be aware of them until later. But in that moment, he surged up, carrying her wrapped around his hips to the bathroom. He dropped her ass to his basin, turned on the taps, wiped her clean, him clean, then carried her back.

He turned her and tossed her on his bed on her belly, shoved her deeper in using her hips, then pulled them up.

He entered the bed twisting to his back, slithering up. He then yanked her pussy down on his face and ate her.

He also fucked her again, her face and her cunt.

He was barely down from coming and she was still in the middle of it when he rolled her and smacked her ass, hard, twice.

Her body jerked, her head came up, and her pussy still wrapped around his dick clenched tight.

"Was I bad?" she asked.

"Don't land shit on me like that without warning, woman."

She grinned. "I take it you dug that news."

He cracked her ass twice more and her eyes shot wide then got lazy when he was done.

"He liked it," she muttered like she wasn't talking to him.

He pulled her hair back in two hands but only roped the long length around one, holding it to the back of her head and curling the fingers of his other hand around the side of her neck.

"You'll get this one warning, Keely, just this one, baby. You need to be a lot more careful, yeah?"

He knew she knew exactly what he was saying when something stole over her face, a look of surprise chased with a feminine satisfaction so profound, no way unless she worked him up to it again his cock could get hard, but witnessing that look, he wondered if that was true.

It was then Hound knew he wasn't in too deep.

He was totally fucked.

And for some reason he wasn't sure about but it pleased him the same as it made him uneasy, he knew she was glad about that.

"I hear you," she said.

"You sure?" he asked.

She brushed her mouth against his. "I'm sure, Hound."

"We done for tonight?" he asked, because he never thought he'd think it, but he needed a break.

"Fuck no. Cold chicken is *awesome* chicken."

Her chicken couldn't be bad unless it was coated in a layer of shit.

"And we haven't eaten the brookies," she finished.

"You're gettin' that shit," he replied, unwinding his fist from her hair. "I'm recuperating."

She gave him a sassy smile that was almost as much as a turn on as the other one.

"I can do that," she said, beginning to slide him out.

His arm around her waist grew tight.

"And bring me a beer."

"Beer and brookies?"

"Beer goes with everything."

"Only in Hound's world."

He let his eyeballs dart side to side before he said, "Where you think you are, woman?"

That got him a beam.

Yep.
Totally.
Fucked.
She slid off.
Then she cleaned up.
Then she brought cold chicken, brookies and beer.
They ate it in his bed.
And before she left, they fucked again.
It was magnificent.
And he wasn't just talking about the brookies.

THE NEXT AFTERNOON, HOUND LAY on his back in his bed at the Compound where he'd connected to the Wi-Fi and downloaded a song to his phone.

He already had "Jeremy."

Earphones in his ears, he listened to it four times, wondering how Keely, who got so much so soon and lost it so ugly, could go to school every day and deal with that kind of shit.

He then listened to "Use Me" four times.

And he had proof that Jean had not lost any of her mental faculties.

Even so, not knowing Keely, she hadn't hit it right.

But listening to the words, he still took her point.

He was a man drowning and he knew that shit.

He also knew he didn't care.

Jean worried.

His brothers would be seriously pissed at him. They shared women, but no old ladies, not ever.

Though back in the day, Chew had fucked one of Crank's ex's, that "ex" being legally untied after being legally tied, and Crank had lost his mind even though she was no longer his to claim.

The circumstances weren't the same, but Chew had felt the displeasure of the rest of the brothers and Hound knew it bit deep. So deep Hound sometimes wondered if no one taking Chew's back on that was one of the reasons he'd renounced the Club.

But this wasn't that.

This was Keely.

And for his brothers, it would only be about Black.

He had shit to do with Club business, the mess they were in with Bounty, and there was Benito Valenzuela, who had been fucking with them for years and was not exactly behind the kidnap of Millie but he'd sent men out to freak her shit, they just took it too far (and got dead because of it, apparently Valenzuela wasn't hip on his soldiers fucking up) but he was still responsible.

But Hound had spent months trying to get a lock on Valenzuela, who had disappeared (though his operation was still running smoothly, so they knew he wasn't gone), or trying to find a way in to find him and use his unique way to stop him, or put the screws to one of his higher ups to unravel his organization from the inside out.

He just kept coming up empty.

He should be concentrating on that. All the old ladies had constant vigilance from brothers because the men were so tweaked about what happened to Millie, High and Tack most of all. High for obvious reasons. Tack because Cherry had been taken by an enemy years ago and nearly died of the stab wounds he'd inflicted. Tack didn't mind making it clear those flashbacks were unwelcome and he wanted this business they'd been fucking around with for years done so they could all rest easy.

Hound needed to focus on something other than drowning in Keely.

On that thought, his phone went with a text.

It was from Keely.

Eight. I'm bringing Irish stew. The American kind without lamb but with big hunks of beef. Don't tell the Irish and don't have dinner because it sticks to your ribs. See ya later, cowboy.

Over stew he should tell her he was in too deep and it was time for him to deliver checks and look after her boys as they did their time as recruits and then beyond.

He knew he should do that just as he knew he wouldn't.

And as the days went by with Keely in his bed during the nights, he had less and less in him to give a fuck.

They love you down deep to their souls and I'm grateful to you down deep to mine and it's about time I said it.

Yup.

As the days went by, he had less and less in him to give a fuck.

"NO, SERIOUS," HOUND TOLD KEELY through her shouts of laughter.

"S-s-stop," she said, putting her spoon in her bowl of stew and waving a hand at him.

They were on his shit couch like only Keely would sit to eat a bowl of stew and dumplings.

That was, Hound was in it normal, feet up on the scratched and chipped coffee table.

She was in it sideways, legs over his lap, ass to his hip, twisted a little so she was lightly leaning into him.

In other words, as close as they could get while eating stew.

"Bev didn't tell me that," she said when she finished laughing. "Only Hop would kidnap his woman in order to make her marry him."

"She was pregnant with Nash. He wanted his ring on her finger when she pushed him out. After that shit went down with her fiancé getting her drilled with a few holes, she wasn't hip on a big wedding, but she had it twisted in her head she wanted *no* wedding. Hop found a way around that and they got married in jeans in Vegas by a fake Liberace."

She cracked up again at his last and he found himself relieved that him mentioning Hop's wife, Lanie, got drilled with holes did not make her troubled at all.

She finished laughing, scooped up more of her kickass stew, but before she shoved it in her mouth, she said, "I hear she's gorgeous. Lanie, that is."

"She is. But I prefer Apache pussy."

Her gaze shot to his, it got soft, his dick started to get hard, and she chewed, swallowed, leaned in and touched her mouth to his.

She barely pulled back before she purred, "I know you do, baby."

He shook his head. She pulled away and he went after more stew.

"I hear Tabby had a boy," she said quietly.

"Landon Kane," he told her. "Named after Shy's brother and obviously, Tack. He's cute as shit. They call him Playboy because that kid is two months old and he's already a total flirt. In other words, got a lot of his daddy in him."

"Her old man, uh, Shy, is a flirt?" she asked.

"Was," he answered. "Not anymore."

She grinned, happy for Tabby having that.

"Too bad I never got the chance to see Tack flirt," she remarked. "I can say straight up, when Bev told me he scraped Naomi off, we went out, bought a bottle of champagne and toasted that shit."

Hound grinned at her but said, "Tack doesn't flirt. He gets a bitch drunk, gives her so many orgasms she doesn't know her ass from a hole in the ground, then he puts her in her car and she's lost sight of him before she turns the ignition. Even did that to Cherry. But she proved she had staying power."

"Cherry?"

"Tyra."

"His new old lady."

"They been hitched, I don't know, seven, eight years, so not that new, babe."

She nodded. "New to me."

"Yeah," he muttered.

"She sweet to him?" she whispered.

That meant a lot to her, that Tyra did Tack right.

And that meant a lot to Hound that Keely felt that way.

He looked her in the eye. "He loves her and doesn't hide it. Loves her fierce, Keely. And she deserves that."

"Good," she replied.

It didn't need to be said, they were talking Chaos.

So another line he should have drawn Keely had erased.

And Hound again couldn't find it in him to give a fuck about it.

In fact, now they were into it and she was interested and laughing, he loved that she wanted to know about her family again.

Better, with Dutch in and Jagger going to follow him, that legacy was secure and she needed to be a part of it again, even if it was in little ways.

Bottom line, with her boys in, she had to stop drifting away.

"Dutch is doin' good, baby. He's committed, and the brothers all loved him before but he's earning respect. They aren't making it easy. Maybe to make sure Chill knows Dutch isn't getting it easy because of his legacy, they're a little harder on him. But he sucks it up. I knew he had it in him, but he's even impressing me."

He knew that was a risk, bringing that up, Dutch, his legacy, but she gave him no indication she had any issue with it.

"It isn't like he hasn't been in Chaos training since birth, babe," she replied.

"True," he muttered, going after more stew and hiding his relief she seemed cool he brought it up.

"Jagger heard about having to clean your place, he told me he's rethinking recruiting," she shared.

Hound chuckled, knowing even that wouldn't hold Jag back. "Jag's a lazy fuck unless it comes to charming some girl. He's lucky Playboy has been taken or that'd be his Club name."

"He's pretty desperate to work with the brother called Joker. He says his builds are *sick*."

Hound quit chewing his stew, swallowed and said, "Joker is a genius and it's been noticed. Did you see that magazine spread?"

She nodded. "Bev showed me. That chopper you all were pictured around was freaking inspired. And his designs . . . I don't know anything about that and it made me want one. Street safe but hotrod cool."

He grinned at her. "Joker'd set you up. Not sure he'd paint any car pink though."

She assumed an expression of fake ticked.

"*Pink?*" she asked with disgust.

"Okay, purple."

She lifted her chin and her spoon filled with stew, "Purple is cool. Case in point, Prince, may he rest in peace," she declared and shoved stew in her mouth.

"I'll get Joke on that. Girlie car with purple cool."

She rolled her eyes.

Hound memorized that.

And the feel of her legs over his thighs.

And the taste of her stew.

And the warmth in his gut that he had this shot to play at this, Keely his on his couch talking Chaos shit like she belonged to him. Like she was his old lady.

Maybe he'd been wrong.

Maybe he shouldn't have fucked up his own head with those boundaries.

Maybe he should take what he was getting, having wanted it so bad for so long, and relish it while he had it.

"Want your beer, babe?" she asked.

"Yeah, Keekee," he muttered, not thinking about it, giving her a name that was his, he'd heard no one call her, so it was theirs, and also focusing on his stew so he didn't see the look on her face when he said it.

But he did feel her reach for his beer on the coffee table and was chewing when he took it from her and decided this was it.

For as long as it lasted, even if it was play, make believe in his head for a man who was far from a boy, he'd take it and get off on it.

It'd end soon enough.

But even after it did, he'd always have it.

And he knew all too well, that was a whole lot better than not having it at all.

CHAPTER SIX

YOU DESERVE BETTER

"**D**ID YOU GET MY TEXTS today?"

Hound was ass to his couch.

Keely was in his kitchen cooking.

It had been near on three weeks since she gave him a version of her virginity then the next night her version of Irish stew. In that three weeks she'd cooked dinner for him every night, at first bringing it over like the chicken and the stew, and then he was lugging up her fancy-ass grocery bags because she cooked it in his shit kitchen.

Since he didn't allow her to show until after eight, this meant they ate late.

But Keely was a great cook and Hound usually ate fast food, so he was good with waiting.

Keely wasn't, she bitched about it all the time.

But she had him, all of him, no boundaries, and since he still gave that to Jean, she had to wait her turn.

"Babe," was all he said about the fifty texts she'd sent him that day.

This was because they were pictures of furniture. Couches. Armchairs.

Recliners. Dressers. Beds. Barstools.

In other words, his thought was they didn't need a reply.

Or a discussion.

His furniture was such crap he didn't even remember where he got it. He just remembered he'd got none of it new.

But it had been established he lived in a shithole, so as much as he hated having Keely with him where she had to use it, it worked.

"Babe?" she queried.

"I'm not buying furniture," he told the TV.

"Why not?" she asked the side of his head.

He looked to her at his stove. "Because anyone sees that shit delivered, the first time I took off, it'd be in this crib for about five minutes before someone lifted it."

"You have three locks, Shep, and you're you. Do you honestly think anyone is gonna break in here, *ever*?"

She got his Keekee, he'd earned her Shep.

His girlfriend in high school had called him Shep and that was the only person in his life he'd allowed to call him that shit.

Except Keely.

He didn't tell her about his high school girlfriend though.

And he had to admit, that part of town, as rundown as his building was, it was a constant effort to kick tenants' asses in line, but he never tired of giving it that effort, not because he gave a shit but because Jean lived there.

So he had a reputation and Keely was probably right.

He didn't tell her that either.

"Not real hip on droppin' a load on new furniture and finding out."

"So get rental insurance," she returned, looking back to the taco meat she was stirring on the stove, his apartment filled with that aroma, and he had to admit something else. That goodness in the air, a woman as beautiful as her cooking in his kitchen, his furniture didn't fit the scene.

And it had rattled around in his head for the last couple of years that he needed to get quit of his mattresses. They sucked. He'd just never done anything about them.

"Keely, first, I don't pay bullshit scam artists like insurance agents money to fuck me up the ass and second, even if they're bullshit scam artists, not a one of 'em would ever give me a policy for a place in this 'hood. And if they did, it'd cost through the nose."

"You don't have insurance?" she asked.

"On my truck and bike, yeah. Otherwise, no."

"I can see this," she said to the taco meat.

He grinned at her profile then looked back to the TV.

"You deserve better."

That comment bought her his eyes again.

"I dig why you live in this place and don't want to bother moving, babe," she went on. "But I hate that you come home to a pit. You deserve better."

Christ, he loved her.

It would never have entered his mind in the years since he'd taken that fall that she could get more of that from him.

But having her like he did now, she totally did.

"What were your favorites, baby?" he asked quietly.

She didn't hesitate to answer. "That black leather sectional. The barstools that the base is made out of a crankshaft. And that leather studded headboard."

He remembered all those pictures.

Vaguely.

And from what he remembered, if she outfitted his crib like that, it was going to look like the Harley-Davidson furniture god puked all over the place.

But if she liked it, he didn't give a shit.

"I give you the cash, you go get it. Let me know when it's gonna be delivered. I'll get Dutch and Chill over here and we'll cart this shit to the dump."

Her eyes were big. "Really?"

"Yup."

"All of it?"

"Whatever you want, but make sure you get new mattresses too, Keekee. Mine suck. And think on that headboard, 'cause if I remember what you're talkin' about, I can't tie you to it."

Her face screwed up with fake irritation. "Don't make me hot when I'm making tacos."

"You know I'll fuck you tough after you feed me so don't bitch I make you wet before you do."

She turned the stove down and came to look at him from over the bar. "You need end tables too."

"Whatever," he muttered, turning back to the TV.

"And new nightstands and a dresser and new lamps, like, everywhere."

"I got stacks of cash in the safe in my room at the Compound. Tell me how much you need. I'll have it here tomorrow night and give it to you."

"I have carte blanche?"

He again looked to her. "You think I'll like it, I'll probably like it. More likely I won't notice it unless it's uncomfortable, goofy, girlie or preppy. I reckon you know to avoid any a' that shit so, yeah. You got carte blanche."

"I'm taking tomorrow off and going shopping," she declared.

He grinned, turning his head back to the TV, repeating, "Whatever."

"You wanna come with me?"

That slashed through him like a blade through his heart.

Slowly, he looked again to her.

"Babe," he said quietly.

"Is that . . ." She weirdly had to take a moment to get her shit together. "Is that a 'babe' no way in hell I'm going shopping or a 'babe' you don't want to be seen out in public with me? Because I'm pretty sure no Chaos brother is gonna be at furniture stores."

"Their old ladies might."

"So it's you don't wanna be seen out in public with me."

Why was she asking this shit?

If it was up to him, he'd be out in public with her, she'd be on the back of his bike, he'd fuck her in his bed at the Compound, she'd be deep in his life every way he could get her.

But it wasn't up to him. It wasn't something she could give him the way he was guessing she knew he wanted it, so it wasn't something he could have and she knew that shit, so why the fuck was she going there and dragging him with her?

He turned in the couch to face her, trying not to get pissed. "Keekee—"

"It's not like we don't know each other, Shep."

This was true.

"If on the extreme off chance we run into someone remotely associated with Chaos," she continued, "we can say you needed new mattresses or whatever and since you don't give a shit about that, asked me to help out or just were there to hand off the cash. But since it's not gonna happen, who gives a shit?"

"Honest as fuck, babe, it's mostly because I don't wanna go furniture shopping so you getting wound up about this is pointless."

She looked to the wall.

He needed to guide them out of this, for both of them.

"Is the food ready?" he asked.

She looked back to him.

"Yeah," she snapped.

"Are you gonna be pissed while we eat it even though I'm gonna hand over thousands of dollars in cash to you tomorrow that you can spend decorating my ratty-ass apartment for me?"

She tried to hold on to the pissed but couldn't do it.

Still, she verbally stuck to it, but without the sting, and bit out a, "Yeah."

He got up and moved toward the kitchen, "Then tonight's a spanking night, baby. You got a sting in your ass and my cock up your cunt, no way you can stay pissed."

"I told you, Hound, don't turn me on when you're not imminently gonna do something about it, and I'll add, don't turn me on when I'm mad at you."

He caught her at the waist and dragged her up against him, clamping his other arm around her, and taking her mouth in a wet kiss.

He lifted his head and stared in her eyes.

"Still pissed?" he asked.

"No," she answered.

"Good. But you're still getting a spanking," he told her.

At that, she smiled.

WITH HIS BODY HIDDEN, HOUND leaned against the corner of the building and watched Camilla Turnbull come out of another building down and across the street.

She was covered in Valenzuela soldiers, four right on her, one at the car they were escorting her to, one down the street keeping an eye on things, and then there was the driver.

Camilla Turnbull was Valenzuela's snatch.

She also ran his girls and her name was listed as executive producer on all his porn video credits.

Her man had disappeared but Hound was finding she was everywhere.

He was also getting a funny feeling about that. About two of Valenzuela's boys fucking up and taking Millie, one of them clocking her, then both of them getting dead. The hits his soldiers took, Millie had witnessed. But by the time the cops got to anyone to ask for statements, a man not the man who did it came forward to confess to the killings and no witness had seen Valenzuela anywhere near the scene.

Not to mention Turnbull gave him an alibi.

But that colossal fuckup happened, Valenzuela was now gone, she'd stepped up and this surprised Hound.

She had her place in Valenzuela's operation and that place had always been firm. Valenzuela made it very clear how he felt about gash. He fucked it and he used it to keep his girls in line and his production facilities cranking out bad sex tapes.

Now she was coming out of Valenzuela's swank apartment complex with a shit ton of bodyguards looking like she not only owned a pad there but the entire building and every one on the block.

Topping that, the woman was young. Hound didn't know how young but he'd put money she wasn't even out of her twenties.

Too young to be doing all she was doing—not that anyone should ever be doing anything she was doing—and way too young to be heading an operation the size of Valenzuela's.

It could be Valenzuela was laying low knowing Chaos would lose their shit after Millie was taken. He was hoping in that time they'd cool off (they would not) and he was concerned they'd seek retribution using his woman to do it (they would not do that either, or Chaos wouldn't, Hound would consider it), so he put extra men on her in the meantime.

But he would not ever put her in charge. And although Valenzuela seriously compartmentalized his operations and was never the direct line of communication to any of his people, Turnbull was proving she felt like being more hands-on with things, and the impression she was giving Hound, because he was watching, was that she was running the show.

So yeah, Hound had a funny feeling about this, not only because that didn't sit right but because she had been such a minor player, he didn't know dick about her.

She got in the car with one of Valenzuela's goons holding the door open for her. Hound turned from the edge of the building he was leaning against and walked the other direction, down the block where he'd parked his truck around the corner.

He did this pulling out his phone and making a call.

"Hound," Knight Sebring answered.

Knight Sebring owned the hottest nightclub in Denver.

He also had a side business he took very seriously, which meant he was in the know about a lot of things.

Those things being pretty much everything happening underground in Denver.

"Sebring," Hound replied. "Got some time?"

"Yeah," Sebring said.

"You know Camilla Turnbull?" Hound asked.

"No," Sebring answered. "Of her, yes. Know her to her face, no. But recently we've been getting acquainted."

That was interesting but it didn't make Hound feel any better.

He started with the first part. "What do you know of her?"

"She's a cunt. She's got a wicked backhand and I don't mean tennis. If a girl is producing, whatever way she uses her, and that girl wants to cut ties, she doesn't let her go and has nasty ways of keeping her girls under her thumb. And I wouldn't mind Denver saw the back of her in a permanent way."

"That's it?" Hound pressed.

"Outside of me havin' a couple of phone calls with her recently to share how I feel about how she runs her girls and her pretty much tellin' me she doesn't give a shit, yeah."

Hound stared at his truck as he turned the next corner and walked to it, not liking this.

Not many people would mess with Knight Sebring. If he told you he wasn't feeling good about what you were doing, the way he rolled, there weren't a lot of people who wouldn't ask for a written list of what he'd like changed in order of priority so they could tick it off as they went down the line.

"So Valenzuela thinks he's untouchable and that's rubbed off on his snatch," Hound muttered.

"That was my take," Sebring replied.

"And where are you with that?"

"Getting impatient for Chaos to make a move so I don't jack your play," Sebring told him.

Hound opened the door to his truck, swinging in, sharing, "Valenzuela's been proving slippery since his soldiers took an old lady."

"I know. Heard he's on vacation."

"He must need a lot of rest because it's been a long one and just to say, you got snatch, you take it on vacation with you. You don't leave it behind to look after your shit."

Sebring didn't hide his surprise when he asked, "Turnbull is looking after Valenzuela's operations?"

"Can't say for sure but she's no longer in the director's chair on the porn set and instead out on the street givin' a lot of facetime to his lieutenants. That started slow, but as time wears on she's out more and more doin' it."

"Takeover?" Sebring asked, still sounding surprised.

"I don't know," Hound replied, scanning the street, sidewalk and his mirrors. "Been putting time and effort in to getting someone to share, but they're bein' stingy with the information."

"Yeah." Now Sebring sounded amused. "Heard about that bad fall one of his soldiers took down the stairs. How long was he in the hospital? Three weeks?"

"Freaky how he didn't hit a landing and stop, just kept rollin' down flight after flight."

He heard Sebring chuckle before he asked, "And that brought nothing?"

"Nope."

"You know I'm in on this with you boys and I've heard dick, Hound. But just to say, I mentioned being impatient and I'd take that to Tack. I'm good to sit down for a meet. But the way she's runnin' her stable has to stop. I was done months ago. So now you could say I'm really done."

"Word, man. I'll share with Tack and he'll be in touch."

"Cool. That all you need from me?"

"For now. Thanks and later."

"Later, Hound."

They disconnected, Hound shoved his phone in his back pocket and looked at the street.

It had now been three months since Millie had been taken.

And no Valenzuela.

But a lot of Camilla Turnbull.

Maybe he'd been asking the people he'd been asking the wrong questions.

Maybe he needed to start asking about Camilla Turnbull.

"SO? WHAT DO YOU THINK?"

Hound was naked on his back in his bed and Keely was naked on all fours over him, a hand on each side, a knee on each side, bouncing on his new mattress that was delivered that day.

It had been three days since they'd had the conversation about furniture.

And now his place was gutted, all his shit he and the recruits had taken to the dump, because it was Friday and the rest of the deliveries were going to start coming tomorrow.

The mattresses were boss.

Keely bouncing on all fours naked over him was fucking *inspirational*.

"It works," he said through a smile.

"It *works*? It's da freakin' bomb diggity *bomb bomb*."

He started laughing, wrapped his arms around her and pulled her down to him.

She didn't fight it and settled in.

"You're a nut," he muttered when he got her close, still smiling.

She grinned at him then stated, "Speaking of nuts, you need to kick Boz in them."

He lifted his brows. "What did Boz do?"

"It's what he's not doing," she informed him. "If he doesn't get his head out of his ass about winning Bev back, she's going to settle for this new man she's seeing and that would be *bad*."

"Babe—" he started, giving her a squeeze with his arms.

"I know, I know, I know," she cut him off, waving a hand between their faces. "The brotherhood vow of not sticking your nose in. But seriously, this guy she's seeing . . ."

She made a face.

It was a funny face but he didn't like it.

"This guy fuckin' with her?" he asked, his tone having a bite.

Keely got serious and melted into him.

"No, baby," she said quietly. "It's not like he's hitting her or stepping out on her or anything. I haven't met him yet and she doesn't really say a lot about him but I still know he's not the guy for her."

"How do you know that?"

"Well, we don't have all night so I'll run down the highlights. He's got a small dick."

Hound gave her his slow blink.

"Say again?"

"Thumbeleen-*oh*," she stated.

Hound's body started shaking.

"Now, I wouldn't know because I've been lucky in life and have never seen a small dick, but I would guess if you aren't exactly endowed you'd make up for that by acquiring other skills."

His word was shaking too when he asked, "No?"

She shook her head. "Bumbeleen-*oh*."

The bed started shaking with Hound's silent laughter.

"He's like, well, she says he sells insurance so my guess is he's probably kinda a wimp too," she continued. "I mean, nothing wrong with that if that's your gig, but it isn't Bev's. She's seen some good ones since Boz, but it has to be the right mixture, the perfect balance, and they've always got too much of the bad parts."

Now he was confused. "What're you talking about?"

"The bad boy," she told him. "The alpha. The biker. She goes for a hint of goof because Boz had that and it was cute, if you're into that kind of thing, which I'm not, but she is so it worked for them. But, you know, the badass, half a step up from caveman has to be tempered."

Since she was lying on top of him, meaning spending time with him, so he was catching her drift and he didn't know whether to start laughing again or start getting ticked.

"Half a step up from caveman?" he asked.

"Shep, honey, you drink beer with brookies."

"That makes me half a step up from caveman?"

"And your pans are made of tin and the last time they were used was by hobos displaced in Oklahoma during the dust bowl crisis."

That settled it.

He started laughing again.

"And it can't be lost on you that you have a dominant personality," she went on.

No, that wasn't lost on him.

"For a woman who is not a pushover, this could go bad if things aren't balanced the other way," she declared.

"And what's the other way?"

"If her man isn't protective, like you. And thoughtful, like you. And sweet, like you. And funny, like you. And especially if he doesn't have a gorgeous cock and knows how to use it, like you do."

Hound now wasn't finding anything amusing.

He was finding it something a lot better.

"You think I'm all that shit?"

"Babe, the first bite you take of food I make you, every time you give me a look that tells me how much you like it that immediately makes it worth the effort of buying the food and cooking it for you."

"Just to say, not to take anything away from the food you cook for me, which I like and appreciate you make that effort, but before you started doin' that, Keekee, all I ate was fast food so pretty much anything would be better."

"I'm sure, but that doesn't matter. What matters is that you don't act like you expect me to serve up good food as your due because you have a penis. Like you said, you appreciate it and you make that known. That's the difference. Now I can continue to blow sunshine up your ass but that would not be me talking you into having a word with Boz about getting his head out of *his* ass."

"Keely, it sucks Bev is gonna settle for this guy but it isn't my business, or yours, and since they split years ago, it isn't Boz's."

"And from what you know about their split, he doesn't care Bev moves on?"

He couldn't say that.

What he said was, "From what I know about the brotherhood, I don't get involved."

"Hound—"

He gave her a firm squeeze to cut her off.

"No, babe, it's not gonna happen."

She gave him a stubborn look.

He kept his mouth shut and took it.

Her look vanished and a concerned one took its place.

That was harder to withstand.

"I want her to be happy," she said.

"This guy doesn't make her happy?"

"He pays attention to her, and if they settle in, he'll help her pay the bills. That's what this guy does for her."

He liked Bev. That sucked for her. She deserved more.

It still wasn't his problem.

Or Keely's.

He didn't have to say that again.

Keely got it.

"Right," Keely muttered. "We'll quit talking about this because it's making me sad."

He rolled her and gave her some of his weight, getting all of her attention.

"Just talk to her," he advised. "Tell her she should hold out for what she wants."

"She isn't twenty-two anymore, honey."

"No. But she is a good woman and she shouldn't give up."

She slid a hand up his back, did it light and did it sweet.

"You sure you won't talk to him?"

He shook his head, liking the touch but not giving in to it.

"You know how it goes, Keekee."

Her eyes drifted away from him and something moved over her face that disturbed him more than the subject of their current conversation merited, even as tight as she was with Beverly and as obvious as it was this was bothering her, as she answered, "I know how it is."

"Babe," he called.

She came back to him and it didn't make him feel better that it looked like she wiped her expression clean, like she'd lost track of it, knew what she'd exposed and was hiding it from him.

"Wanna tell me what's in your head?" he asked.

"Just that this is one of the bad parts that you have to balance with the good."

He could get that.

"Sorry, Keekee," he whispered.

"It is what it is, baby," she whispered back.

It was definitely that.

He touched his mouth to hers and left it there when he asked, "You want more?"

"Do you seriously have to ask that question?"

He grinned against her mouth and when he went in again, it wasn't a touch.

◆

"WHAT D'YOU THINK?" HOUND ASKED Jean.

She'd taken a rare shuffle down the hall because all of Keely's furniture had shown up, Jean had heard the commotion over the last six days, and she was curious.

So since his place wasn't a sty anymore (not that she hadn't been over before, just that she was Jean, he didn't subject her to that when she had a fussy pad full of stuff, but it was way better than his), he showed her.

Keely had even come over on Saturday morning before anything was delivered and steam cleaned the carpets. Some of the stains didn't come up, but it still looked a load better.

"Was what you had before not good enough for her?"

Jean's question made him look down at her, leaning on her walker inside his closed door.

"She didn't like me living in a pit," he told her. "She said I deserve better."

Jean studied his face for a beat before she replied, "You do. Was her telling you this what caused you to allow her to spend a great deal of *your own money* on you?"

It wasn't simply that Hound was keeping the two best parts of his life all to himself, not letting them meet each other because he knew it would end with Keely eventually, but also because Jean wasn't her biggest fan and the fact it would end eventually was part of why she wasn't.

Among other reasons.

"I had other motivation, Jean bug," he shared. "I'm spendin' more time here, and yeah, that's with her, but it *was* a pit."

She threw a bony hand out toward the room that didn't actually look like a Harley-Davidson god puked all over it. The crankshaft barstools were cool but Keely left it at that for anything unusual, and all the rest of it was just masculine and comfortable.

"Is this her style?"

Keely's house was not black leather and chrome.

It was bold and in your face. If he was forced to describe it, it was like junked-up-cool, biker gypsy rock 'n' roll.

"No."

"So she doesn't just come here, hiding with you. You've been to her home," Jean stated, but it was a question.

"Yeah," he answered.

"That said, you're still hiding."

"Jean—"

"You know I don't understand this, Shepherd. You seem to be taking this in your stride but it makes no sense to me. She's here every night. If she feels you deserve a better place to live and puts the work into making that happen, because I know it was her that cleaned this carpet, I heard it, then why is this what it is?"

"It just is."

"It makes no sense."

"You don't live in our world."

"I know if I was a young woman who caught your eye and owned your heart, I would not hide that in an ugly apartment that can be made nicer with decent furniture but it's still no better. I'd shout it to the world."

"That isn't in the cards."

"Because of you or because of her?" she demanded.

Because of her, he thought.

"Because of my brothers," he said.

"And they matter this much to you that you can't have the woman you love, who I'm hoping from the time she spends with you and the effort she takes to make your life better, cares about you too?" she pushed.

"Yeah."

"And you think this makes sense?" she asked.

"I think it is the only way it can be and we're both takin' what we can get, how we can get it, until shit happens where we can't have it anymore."

"Would you give up your brothers for her?"

"That's like asking me to cut off my own arm."

She studied him again before she nodded. "I see. And this Keely understands this so she allows you to hide her away in this ugly apartment taking what she can get."

He'd deal with whatever the brothers decided to dish out if it meant in the end he'd have them and he'd have Keely.

But she had the man she gave it all to, and he was dead. And although she had more to give, she couldn't give it all making it worth it to butt up against the brothers to have her. She knew that so she was taking what she could get and giving it all the same.

He didn't explain this to Jean.

He said, "The man she loved, my brother who died, there'll be no one else like that for her."

"Of course not," she returned. "She loved him. She married him. She gave him children. But does that mean she can't find another to love, if not the same, a different way that's just as beautiful?"

Hound stared at her.

She didn't wait for his answer.

She declared, "It's clear she can't. She may care enough to clean your carpeting, Shepherd, and she may think you deserve better, and I would very much agree." She leaned his way slightly, just enough not to take her off balance. "You deserve *better*," she stated.

"She's a good woman," he told her firm.

"I'm sure. But evidence suggests you still could do better."

He felt his mouth get tight and forced through it, "Maybe we shouldn't talk about this."

She examined his mouth and murmured, "Maybe we shouldn't." She looked back to the room and finished it, "I like it very much. Whatever one can say about what's happening, she had a mind to you when she furnished your apartment. It's very much you. And it is definitely better than what you had and it looks very fine." Her eyes came back to him. "What you deserve."

He nodded, more than ready to do a snail's walk with her back to her place and still pissed because he didn't often want to leave Jean. Need to leave her because he had shit to do, yeah. But she was the calm in his life that was always a storm.

His preference, it was the life he chose.

It still was good to have a place that was calm.

"Don't be angry with me for worrying about you, *motek*," she said softly.

He wasn't angry at her for that.

He was angry that she pointed out shit he was trying not to think about.

"I can sustain bein' pissed at you for about ten seconds," he replied.

Her brows went up. "Have you been upset with me before?"

"When you had that cough that lasted two weeks and refused to go to the doctor and they found out it was pneumonia."

"Oh, of course," she muttered.

"And when you got up in my face that you could still make your bed, then you took that fall and hit your head on the nightstand and I found you on the floor three hours later, out of it, and had to take you to the hospital."

"I forgot about that," she mumbled.

"And that time you got ticked at me for goin' outta my way to borrow my brother's car 'cause it's easier for you to get in and out of than my truck when I had to take you to synagogue."

Her eyes got intent on him. "You can stop now."

He grinned.

Her eyes wandered beyond him.

"She didn't buy you a new television," she remarked.

He looked to his boxy TV that he vaguely remembered picking up outside a dumpster then calling in a marker from a TV repair guy he knew who was a biker to fix it.

"That's my gig. Pickin' one up tonight with a mount. I'm thinkin' sixty inch."

She shuffled with her walker toward his new couch. "Well, now it's lunchtime, not tonight, so I say we eat some of the leftover food she makes you and enjoy your new furniture by giving your TV one last go. There's a *Law and Order* marathon running on TNT."

As far as he could tell from being in her pad as often as he was, there was always a *Law and Order* marathon running.

"Her name is Keely, darlin'," he said quiet.

She kept shuffling toward the couch, didn't look back, and replied, "I know."

He felt his mouth twitch.

Then he watched until she made it to his couch and he kept watching as she shuffled around, aimed her ass to it and made it *on* the couch.

Then he went to the kitchen to nuke some of Keely's leftover food.

He wasn't going to give Keely the chance to win Jean over.

But he had a feeling her food would help the cause.

In the end, he didn't know if he was wrong or if he was right.

He did know the huge-ass portion of spaghetti with homemade garlic bread he made her . . .

She cleaned her plate.

CHAPTER SEVEN

PAWNS

HOUND'S ALARM WENT, AND HE opened his eyes seeing and feeling a naked Keely draped on top of him.
Fuck.
They were nearly two months into their gig and she hadn't spent the night once.
But last night she wanted him up her ass, and he was feeling creative. They'd been settling in these past weeks with less sex (but it wasn't less good, it was always spectacular) and more cuddling and pillow talk, so last night they went bionic.
He remembered his last orgasm.
He didn't remember passing out.
He was lucky it wasn't a weekend. He was having trouble getting Keely to go home on the weekends now. She didn't have to get to work and Jagger didn't have to get to school so he didn't show for breakfast, which meant she had no reason to go and didn't want to.
But now she had reason to go, get home, get ready for work, but mostly, get gone from Hound's crib so he could see to Jean.

He was pissed about this for a variety of reasons.

The most important was he'd passed out so he wasn't conscious to enjoy the first time Keely spent the entire night with him.

Equally important was that they had a situation where he had to get her to haul ass at all.

Out there in the world, they were nothing to each other but members of an alternate-style family.

In his apartment, they were biker and old lady.

And as Hound had feared, having it all and not having it was getting under his skin like a tick, digging in and sucking out his soul.

Hound reached to the alarm clock.

Keely moved.

"Shit, it's six?" she asked his alarm clock.

"You gotta haul ass, baby."

"Shit!" she snapped. "It's six!"

She kicked off the covers that were only over her legs and rolled over him, taking her feet by the side of the bed.

Slower, Hound followed her.

She took off for the bathroom.

He reached for his drawers.

He had them on and was pulling on his jeans when she raced in and started to yank on clothes.

"Jag's home before you get there, what are you gonna tell him?" Hound asked curiously.

"Seeing as I'm gonna have to go to work unshowered and with fuck hair, this is not my biggest concern right now," she replied. "But this is also not like the time he got his nose where it wasn't supposed to be and I found him brandishing my vibrator, telling me it was a light saber. He's not six anymore. If he hasn't figured out mama's gotta get laid every once in a while, it's time he learned."

Dutch was the oldest and except for his brush with fuckery when he was fourteen, from the minute he could, he'd stepped up for his mom and his brother.

Jagger, the baby, wasn't exactly spoiled but he also hadn't quite cottoned on to the fact his mother didn't exist to make his life golden.

Case in point, the last time Jag figured out his momma was getting laid and not liking it.

Another case in point, showing at her place for her to make him breakfast before school every morning when he was nineteen and essentially living somewhere else.

"We need to be more careful, Keekee," he said, reaching for his tee and straightening to tug it on.

"You need to be less awesome with your dick, Shep," she shot back.

He pulled his shirt down his stomach and grinned at her.

She cut a fake pissed-off look at him and clasped her bra at her front before she twisted it around the back.

She put the rest of her clothes on.

He put his socks and boots on.

She grabbed her jacket and purse from the living room and he walked her down to her car.

They didn't have time to make out so he gave her a quick kiss, closed the door after she folded in and then went to the sidewalk.

But he was late for Jean and Jean would worry, so instead of watching her drive away like he always did, he started right up the walk to the building, and through that, he played that cool.

However, when he was about to hit the building he started jogging.

Inside the building, he took the steps three at a time.

He let himself in Jean's apartment, and right when he was about to make it to her bedroom door, she called, "Everything okay, Shepherd?"

He pushed in. "Everything's cool."

They did their thing. She'd had a shower the day before and she didn't like to make him do it every day so it was about toilet, teeth brushing, making her bed and getting her dressed before breakfast.

They were finishing that when there came a pounding at the door.

Not a knock.

Pounding.

He twisted his neck and narrowed his eyes that way, feeling his mouth turn down as Jean murmured, "What on earth?"

"Stay here. I'll find out," he growled.

He left her leaning on her walker by her bed and stalked into the other room.

The entire time he did that, the pounding didn't stop.

When he looked through the peephole and saw what he saw, his vision exploded in sparks of fury.

He unlocked the door, yanked it open and moved immediately to press back a visibly enraged Keely.

But hearing the locks go, she was ready for him, hands at his chest shoving hard.

She pushed in, pushing him in with her, shouting, "Who you got in here, Hound? Who's your side piece means I come to you after you do her and you get me gone so you can go back? Who, Hound? Who is this bitch?"

"That would be me."

Hound was pulling in oxygen so he didn't black out with rage, and this effort was not helped when both he and Keely turned to see Jean in her slippers and housecoat shuffling with her walker down the hall from her bedroom.

"Holy shit," Keely whispered.

"As Shepherd knows, I don't allow foul language in my home so if you'd refrain, I'd appreciate it," Jean declared.

Keely said nothing.

Hound continued to expend effort so he wouldn't do or say anything he'd regret, and this took so much, he couldn't take any to speak.

Jean stopped at the mouth of the hall. "You're Keely, I presume?"

"Yeah," Keely answered.

"I'm Jean Gruenberg. As you can see, I'm Shepherd's neighbor. We're friends. Close friends."

"Uh, Shep and I are, um . . . close friends too," Keely shared.

"I know."

"He didn't tell me about you," Keely told Jean.

"I'm realizing that."

It was then Keely looked at Hound, and he might still be pissed as fuck at her but the look on her face said she was no longer that with him.

The look on her face was something else entirely.

And that look sliced clean through his gut.

"You didn't tell me about Jean," she whispered.

Shit.

"Keel—"

He said no more as her head jerked Jean's way and she stammered, "I'm s-sorry. So so so so *sorry*. That was rude. Incredibly rude. I'm so very sorry."

"Your apology is accepted, dear," Jean said carefully, watching Keely closely.

Hound put his hand on her arm but she pulled that arm away, slouching to the side and looking up at him. "I, well, obviously, I should go. I'm sorry."

"Babe—" he tried again.

"I have to get to work and you have to—"

He moved toward her but she backed quickly to the door, still talking.

"I have to get to work," she repeated. Hand on the handle, she looked again to Jean. "Terrible way to do it but it's, well . . . nice to meet you. Have a lovely day."

With that, she opened the door and flew out.

Hound was pissed again.

Because he was stuck, half his head with one woman, half his head wanting to run after another.

"*Motek*," Jean called and his gaze swung to her. "If you don't chase after her, I fear that would be a very bad mistake."

That was all he needed.

"I'll be back," he told her, and then he threw open the door and sprinted down the hall.

Keely was folding in her car again when he hit her driver's side door.

She kept folding in but he put a hand to the top of the door to keep it open.

She didn't even try to close it.

She just stared at her steering wheel.

"You need to go up and take care of Jean, Hound."

"Look at me, Keely."

Her eyes came right to his. "I get it."

"Not sure you do."

"I get it. I've got what you'll let me have."

She had what *he* would let her have?

"Like I said," he growled, "not sure you get it."

"I think maybe we should have a break for tonight. It's been intense."

Oh no she did *not*.

He leaned into the car and got in her face. "Oh no. Fuck no, Keely. You don't get to do that shit. Your ass is here tonight at eight o'clock and if it isn't, I'll find it and drag it here."

"Hound—"

"*Eight*," he ground out, pulled back and slammed her door.

He walked around her hood, jogged up the walk, in the door and up the steps.

He walked right into Jean's apartment and found her in her armchair.

She looked surprised.

And worried.

"You're back a lot sooner than I thought you'd be," she remarked cautiously.

"She needs time to get her head straight," he stated, walking to the kitchen to start breakfast.

"Can I ask why you haven't told her about me?"

"Because you're none of her business."

"Now can I ask why that is?"

He walked back to the side of her chair and looked down at her.

When he'd locked eyes with her, he gave it to her.

"Because you're mine. And you're important. Outside my brothers, and her, you're the best thing I got. She's keepin' something important from me. I don't give a fuck if it's immature and mean, I'm keepin' something important from her. You."

"I'll let that F-word slide seeing as you're this upset," she murmured. "And, of course, that was sweet, even if I'm thinking you understand right about now it was quite foolhardy."

"She doesn't get you," Hound bit out.

"And I love you, my handsome boy," she whispered. "But has it occurred to you that keeping her from me is keeping me from her?"

"Say what?"

"Although it says little about her upbringing that she'd pound on the door and force her way in like that, considering she thought you were seeing another woman, I must admit that it's understandable. After she realized that she was in error, she was very considerate."

"Maybe we shouldn't get into a blow by blow," he suggested.

"And maybe, sweetheart, you need to start paying closer attention, because after she was considerate it became clear she was very hurt."

"She forces herself into a part of my life that's my decision whether or not it's hers to have, she doesn't get to feel hurt."

"You can't tell anyone, especially a woman, how they can feel."

"Tonight when she comes over, since the lid is off about you, Jean, you can come over and watch me."

"I fear this would be a mistake, Shepherd."

"This is another part of the world I live in and *she* lives in that you don't that you don't get," he shared. "But she does."

Her eyes got intent. "I hope that you never, *ever* don't put in the effort to find it in your heart somewhere, even if it's the tiniest place, to try to understand what those you love are feeling. I hope that deeply, Shepherd. Very, very deeply."

He was done.

"You want breakfast?" he asked.

She studied him a beat before she nodded.

Hound prowled to her kitchen.

Jean didn't let up on him.

"She's very beautiful."

"Yeah, she is," he told the inside of her refrigerator.

"You were right those weeks ago, she knows you're hers."

"Yeah, she does," Hound agreed, putting the carton of eggs on the counter.

"What I fear you're not understanding, *motek*, is she's yours too."

She wasn't.

She would never be.

He had her cunt and her cooking and her smiles and her time.

But if he had her, she'd be on the back of his bike faster than he could say her name.

She was not his.
She was Black's.
And she always would be.

※

AROUND LUNCHTIME, HOUND WENT EARLY back to Jean's because that morning he'd fed her and cleaned up after but he was in a mood he didn't want to hang around.

So he didn't.

But now he was calmer.

Not about what Keely pulled.

About understanding where Jean was because she knew one biker her whole life, him. And right now her whole life was mostly her apartment, so she'd never get it. But she loved him, and he had to have more patience with her and not take the shit going down with Keely out on her.

He knocked on her door like he usually did to give her the heads up he was outside, then he let himself in.

She was in her chair, her chin to her neck, motionless.

The air rushed out of his lungs and it felt like someone sucker punched him in his gut, so he had to press out his, "Jean?"

She didn't move.

She might nap and he might wake her when he opened the door.

But he woke her when he opened the door.

Cautiously, he moved toward her feeling his skin start itching all over.

"Jean!" he called sharply.

She gave a jerk and her head came up.

Hound was so relieved he fell back on a foot as he swallowed the feeling that shot up his throat.

She blinked at the TV before she turned to look at him. "Shepherd, sweetie. You're early."

He walked to her, bent in and kissed her forehead.

He lifted away and said, "Was ticked earlier. Took off. Didn't get my time with Jean bug."

"Making up for it," she said on a smile.

"Don't get my daily dose of *Law and Order*, might quit breathing."

Her smile got bigger.

He surveyed her area and asked, "Need anything?"

"Since you're here, can we go to the bathroom?"

"You got it," he muttered.

They did that.

They watched *Law and Order* with some *Judge Judy* mixed in just for shits and giggles, and he made her lunch.

Hound stayed longer than he normally did.

He needed to be out on the streets.

He needed to be doing the job he did for his Club so they could breathe easy.

But he stayed with Jean.

Benito Valenzuela and Camilla Turnbull unfortunately weren't going anywhere.

That scare earlier with her asleep in her chair . . .

He needed to take his time with Jean.

THAT NIGHT, IT DIDN'T START good.

This was because at eight oh three, there was a knock on the door, not a text on his phone telling Hound that she was there and he needed to come down and get her.

He went to it and saw Keely outside through the peephole.

So he opened the door fast and with such force, it was a wonder it didn't come off the hinges.

"What'd I say about—?" he started to bite out.

But she scuttled in and said, "Please, let me start."

He was about to slam the door.

But since he left Jean snoozing, she'd hear it and it would wake her up, he closed it quiet, flipped the locks, turned to Keely, crossed his arms on his chest and then didn't move.

"It was wrong. It was . . . was wrong," she began.

"You bet your ass it was," he agreed angrily.

"Please, Hound, please let me get out what I need to say."

He clamped his mouth shut.

"I know that . . . I know that . . ." She cleared her throat. "I know that the man you are, that was out of line. Unacceptable. I know that. I know that with what . . . uh, we have, that was also out of line."

When he opened his mouth to speak, she hurried on.

"But you always watch me drive away. Always. This morning, it was morning. Not when I usually leave. And it was just weird that you, I mean, a biker doesn't keep a schedule. Chaos boys don't do that kind of thing especially. They do what they do. They are where they are. So you never . . ." She stopped and started again. "After eight every night, like a schedule. It was strange. And then you didn't . . . well, you don't mind me going. You've never asked me to spend the night. It's okay that I go and a lot of the time it's you that reminds me it's time I go, and I just . . . got it in my head . . ."

She shook that head, took a deep breath and then kept going.

"We agreed that there was no one else and I got it in my head you were not honoring that and I acted on it and invaded your privacy with Jean and I'm sorry, Hound. I'm really sorry. It was out of line, I was rude in Jean's home, and just . . . please, honey, I'm really, *really* sorry."

"You think I'd ever do that shit to you?"

"No," she said softly.

"This morning you thought I was doin' that shit to you," he reminded her.

"I was wrong this morning," she replied. "I just was . . . you watch me drive away, Hound. And what we have, it's intense, and you don't mind me leaving in the middle of the night?" She shook her head. "I just got twisted up. I didn't know you were looking after your elderly neighbor. How could I know that?"

He had to give her that.

But he also had to underline that point.

"I would never do that to you, Keely."

"I know," she whispered.

He stared in her eyes.

She now knew.

So he let that go.

"How'd you know I was in that apartment? Did you sneak up after me?" he asked.

"No." She shook her head. "You didn't watch me drive away so I didn't pull out. I watched you go into the building. You started running like you were in a hurry. I did think about it, Hound. I really did. Then I . . . well, came to the wrong conclusion, turned the car off, came back in and went to your door. I was going to have it out with you here but you have a deep voice. It carries, and I heard you through the walls. I couldn't hear what you said but I also heard Jean, just barely, but I knew it was a woman and I . . . well, I guess I flew off the handle."

"You did that," he agreed.

They stared at each other.

She had on her killer suede jacket with a big scarf draped around her throat that had fringe and was the pattern of a blanket. She also had in long earrings made of beads, a tee on under her jacket and scarf and he could see she had a tangle of long necklaces over that. A kickass belt in the loops of faded jeans that were frayed in different places across both thighs. And she was wearing on her feet what she wore a lot, her beat-up cowboy boots that were light brown and had a lot of stitching on them, some of it in ivory.

Her hair was in sheets down either side of her face, tangled with her scarf, her earrings and feathery over the suede.

He'd had her every night but one for two months and he'd known her for twenty years, and he'd never gotten used to her brand of beauty.

He could tell she was what she said she was. Sorry. It was written in her face, the line of her body.

She was also all he ever wanted and everything he could never have, standing in his dumpy apartment among thousands of dollars of kickass furniture that he bought but she picked.

He gentled his voice when he asked, "Do we need to end this, Keely?"

"No!" she cried, making a move like she was going to burst from her space and launch herself into his before she stopped herself.

Hound's body locked solid as she lifted both hands and pressed them down in front of her once, dropping her eyes to the floor for a beat before she lifted them to him again.

"No," she said quieter, calmer. "I . . . that won't happen again, Hound. I swear."

He loved her initial reaction. He shouldn't, it troubled him, but he still did.

But the fuck of it was it was looking like it was going to have to be him that looked after the both of them.

Like always.

"Seems to me we're both gettin' in over our heads, babe," he pointed out.

"What we have is good."

"What we have is good cooking, good company and good sex and we can't let it get beyond that."

He felt his chin go into his neck as he watched the flinch hit her face at his words.

A flinch that hit him like a stone in his gut.

A big one.

"Babe?" he called.

"You're more than that to me," she whispered.

He liked that.

But he already knew it and it didn't change shit.

Because it would never be enough.

"You're more than that to me too," he returned. "But that still doesn't mean that isn't all we got."

"I want more."

"Keely, I'm asking you to look out for you, but I'm asking you to look out for me too."

That got him her look like he'd slapped her face.

That he did not get.

So he growled, "What's on your mind?"

"Do you *want* this to be over?" she asked back.

"Fuck no."

"Then why does it sound like you're ending it?"

"Because I'm looking out for you," he explained shortly, and the short part of it was that he didn't feel it needed explaining.

"And how is it looking out for me when I don't want it to end?" she rapped out.

"I look after Jean. I mean I look after her . . . totally. I help her hit the pisser. I help her shower. I cook for her. I get her groceries in for her. I pay her rent and for the cleaner that comes once a week, even though her house doesn't need it but she needs the company. The trust she's got in me built up over nine years of knowin' her and that's where we're at."

"The real reason you won't move," she murmured.

He nodded at her once and kept talking.

"And the only ones who know I got Jean are you, because of this morning, and Tyra and Tack, but I only told them recently. Though I should have told them before just to make sure someone knew she needed looking after."

She nodded at that when he stopped.

So he started again.

"What I'm sayin' is, you're right. I got a life that I go where I go and no one's the wiser that I come home a lot to look after Jean. What they're gonna be the wiser about is the fact that I don't go back to the Compound at night to throw a few back or I don't hit the pool tables or a biker groupie when they're hangin' around. I haven't been around much for two months, not because a' Jean. Because a' you. Now, Dutch or Jag put that together with their mom gone at night, every night, what do you think is gonna happen?"

"They don't come around at night."

"Ever?"

She didn't answer that.

He knew those boys.

They visited their momma.

And he knew now that she'd been putting them off.

"They come here and see me too, Keely," he told her. "It's luck of the draw Jag hasn't needed money for somethin' since he pissed away whatever he's got, but sayin' that, we've connected the last two months just because. It just happened during the day when I was able to meet up with him and not tell him to haul his ass here."

"So you can keep putting him off," she replied.

"They're gonna figure it out."

"Dutch is so caught up in Chaos, and Jagger is so caught up in charming as much skirt as he can find, they're not gonna figure anything out."

"You sure about that?"

She again didn't answer.

She wasn't sure about that.

"How you think your boys are gonna take it that ole Hound is hittin' their momma?" he demanded to know.

"Right now I don't care," she whispered.

"Well I do," he bit out.

She suddenly threw her hands out to her sides and tossed her hair.

"Can't I have a *little* happy?" she asked, then lifted a hand and gave him a thumb and forefinger an inch apart. "Just a *little* happy, Hound. Just some time to be me, nothing but me, and do that with you, the only one who *gets* me. The only one who doesn't handle me with care. The only one who doesn't look at me with sorrow in their eyes that Black died and I pissed my life away after he did. The only one who sees," she slapped her hand on her chest, *"me. Keely.* A woman who likes to cook for her man and laugh and get fucked hard and get his soft touch after. Can't I have just a little *more* of that, Hound? Just a little."

"You can have that, baby."

The words were out before he could stop them.

And Christ, the second they were, bright filled her eyes with her tears.

"Fuck, Keekee, get over here," he muttered.

She flew into his arms.

They closed around her.

"I'm n-not gonna cry," she told his chest, burrowing into it.

"Good, 'cause I hate bitches that cry," he replied.

She threw her head back, her hair flying over his arms and aimed a screwed-up face at him, those tears still in her eyes.

"Don't be a dick, Shep."

He grinned at her. "You like my dick, babe."

"Now don't be *more* of a dick, Shep."

"You walked up here without texting me, which I'll let go this time 'cause we've had enough drama today."

She rolled eyes that were clearing.

He kept going.

"Does that mean I gotta go down to your car to lug up the groceries?"

She shook her head. "I didn't buy groceries. I didn't know the state of play between us. But if I won, I figured we'd get something delivered if we could talk someplace into sending a delivery person to your 'hood."

His brows went up. "If you won?"

"If I won."

"So this is a game," he noted, pretty sure how he felt about that, and it wasn't all that good.

"Life's a game, Hound. People don't play it. We're pawns. It plays us. And every day you don't know how it's gonna play you. You could wake up a winner, or you could wake up a loser." She pressed into him, tightening her arms around him. "But when you're wild like the wind like we are, you roll with it. Today, I woke up a loser. But I'm gonna end the night a winner."

He couldn't argue with that.

So he didn't.

"I want to spend the night on the weekends," she declared.

Now she was pushing it.

"Keely—"

She gave him a squeeze and a shake. "If you need to go over and be with Jean, and you don't want me a part of that, I'll hang and watch TV while you do. Or snooze, because, baby, you wear me out. But what sucks about this is that it's been made clear that this might not be the end, but there will be one. So I want all I can get while I've got it."

It's been made clear?

"It's always been clear," he stated.

She looked him in the eye and it took her a beat to say, "Yeah."

He didn't get that, but he had Keely in his arms and they had an understanding.

Hound wasn't sure it was the right one, but it was an understanding.

They both knew where this was at.

And she wanted more of him.

He wasn't sure it was the right thing to do to give it to her.

But he still was going to do it.
Because they weren't done.
Not yet.
And he wanted more of her.
Since she was offering . . .
It was dumb as fuck.
But he was going to take it.

CHAPTER EIGHT

PROPER BIKER GRANDMA

KEELY WAS GOING DOWN ON him, body slightly to the side, legs straddling his cocked thigh, rubbing her wet pussy along its length, and Hound had had enough.

He pulled out, took hold of her and heard her breath catch as he flung her on her back, gripped her behind her knees and yanked them high and wide, pulling her hips clean off the bed.

He looked her in the eyes as he grasped hold of his dick and led it home.

He had the head in when he returned that hand to the back of her knee and drove inside.

He caught the first moment of her head jerking back right when his did as he felt her slick wet close tight around him.

He bent his neck to watch her face and alternately watch his cock plunge inside her again and again and again.

"Clit and tit," he bit off.

She immediately moved hands as she was told.

And Hound fucked his Keekee, watching her fingering herself and twisting and pulling at her nipple.

It took it out of him but he held back until she went.

Then he ground as deep inside as he could get and let go.

HIS ALARM CLOCK SOUNDED AND he opened his eyes to feel Keely draped on him again.

This time, it wasn't chest to chest.

This time her chest was over his hips, his morning hard pressing into her tits, head in the bed, the covers tangled around their legs, her round ass, the sway of her back and arc of her neck all he could see.

He ran one hand over that ass and reached the other out to the alarm clock as she shifted, lifting her head, twisting.

The alarm went silent. He felt her eyes on him and looked to her.

It was a few days after their big blowout. Since then, the sex had gone from bionic to stratospheric. With the reminder shoved right up in both of their faces that their time was limited, they obviously were both committed to sucking everything out of it they could get.

Last night was Friday. She'd brought a bag and enough groceries that they didn't have to leave the house for a month.

He didn't say dick.

"Gotta take care of Jean, baby."

She shifted on him, slithering up, putting her face in his, hers was soft and sleepy, something he'd never seen on her. The only time she'd woken up in his bed, she'd had to rush out of it.

He could get used to that look.

Just like he'd gotten used to all she gave him.

Yup.

Burrowing in and sucking out his soul.

And he was the goddamned motherfucker letting it happen.

She touched her mouth to his, whispered, "I'll be here," brushed her mouth along the side of his neck then slid off him, reaching to yank the covers up her naked body.

Hound got up to sitting and let himself watch as she settled back in, stretching just an arm behind her to tag his pillow and pull it over her so she could hug and curl into it on her side.

She looked good in his bed.

Then again, she'd look good in any bed because she looked good any time.

He rolled the other way, did his morning gig and moved his ass to Jean's.

It was not a shower day so he had her taken care of, in her chair and was in the kitchen when she remarked, "I didn't hear Keely leave last night."

"She didn't," Hound grunted to the skillet he put on the burner.

"She didn't?"

"Nope."

"She's still over there?"

He grinned at the carton of eggs he pulled out the fridge. "Think we went over the fact you know about these modern-times, man-woman gigs, Jean bug."

"I do know," she stated tartly. "What's she doing?"

"Snoozin'."

"Does she not eat breakfast?" Jean asked.

Hound turned to her. "Say again?"

"Shepherd, I'd like to get to know your girl. We could do that over sandwiches and *Jeopardy!* but I get tired in the afternoons. I'm bright-eyed now. So before you crack those eggs, get home and ask her if she'd like to join us," she ended all this on an order.

He was considering the "tired in the afternoons" mention, something he suspected due to her naps, but not something she'd ever spoken about.

He was not liking what his consideration was bringing up when she prompted, "Well? Or, even though the cat's out of the bag, are you still keeping me all to yourself, leaving your girl right next door when you make excellent eggs."

With the back of her chair to the kitchen, she was peering around her seat at him.

"Jean—" he started.

"Please go get Keely, Shepherd," she requested quietly.

Shit.

Fuck.

"Right," he muttered, stalked to the door, out of it, down the hall to his place.

He went in, moved down the hall and saw that Keely was what he said she was. Snoozing. In fact, she was dead to the world curled around his pillow.

He sat on the bed and put a hand to her hip.

Her body did a soft jump, her eyes opened and she turned her head on the pillow.

"Hey," she mumbled. "Everything okay?"

"Jean wants to know if you'd like to have breakfast with her."

She stared at him, sleep receding, then it was him that jumped and it wasn't light, when the covers and his pillow hit his side with a slap.

She scrambled out of the bed the other way and said, "I'll . . . I . . . a shower might take too long. I just need to, uh . . . brush my teeth and drag a comb through my hair and . . ."

She trailed off and turned at the door of the bathroom to look at him.

Hound had tugged the covers off him but other than that was unmoving from his spot on the bed, watching her.

"Do you . . . are you gonna wait or do you want me to just go over and knock on the door?"

Fuck, she *really* wanted to have breakfast with Jean.

"She gets why you did what you did, babe," he told her.

"I . . . well, I hope so, but, um . . . I need to get dressed."

Then she disappeared in the bathroom.

Hound dropped his keys on his (new) nightstand at the base of his (new) lamp then went to the bathroom door.

She was brushing her teeth so vigorously, her bare ass shook while she did it.

His cock started to respond so he looked into her eyes in the mirror.

"Keys on the nightstand, Keekee. Lock this place up when you come over. Knock first but you can come in after that."

She nodded, still brushing.

He grinned at her.

She lifted a hand, gathered the sheet of her hair behind her neck, and bent over the basin.

That jutted her sweet ass his way.

Christ.

He walked back to Jean.

Her eyes were on him the instant he walked back through her door.

She looked hesitant but excited.

"Is she coming?" she asked.

"She's brushing her teeth."

Jean beamed.

Fuck.

Hound moved to get back to business in the kitchen, announcing, "She's nervous."

"I'll settle her down," Jean told Saturday morning TV that she'd now turned down.

Hound had nothing to say to that and nothing to say at all because this was not something he expected to happen, or expected he'd want to happen, some part of him thought it shouldn't happen, and another part thought it should.

Faster than he figured she would, even in the tizzy he'd left her in (or maybe because of the tizzy he left her in), there came a knock on the door.

Hound turned from the toaster to the door to see it open slowly, not far, and only Keely's head coming in.

She glanced at Hound before she found Jean.

"I . . . is it okay if I come in?"

"Of course, dear," Jean replied.

She pushed the door open, came in, closed the door, but stopped there, and it sucked she was cute in her anxiety and not because she was anxious. Because it sucked Hound found it cute.

"Let's put this to bed, shall we?" Jean said immediately to Keely. "We didn't meet under great circumstances but you apologized, and it says nothing about the person who receives a sincere apology if they don't accept it, set what happened aside and simply carry on. I accepted it. I set what happened aside. And now we're carrying on. So, Keely, tell Hound how you like your eggs. And do you like lox?"

Keely stood there and stared at her.

"Also, please sit down," Jean invited.

Slowly, Keely moved to the couch and sat her ass down where Hound usually sat.

"Shep can make eggs?" Keely asked.

"Very good ones," Jean replied.

"I do all the cooking for us," Keely told her.

Hound watched Jean lean over the arm of her chair toward Keely and say conspiratorially, but loudly, "He makes sandwiches and soups for lunch, which are rather nice. But I cannot say his dinners are as good as his eggs."

"I heard that," he grunted, and decided to just let this be.

Jean wanted it.

Keely wanted it.

Right now they were his two girls.

So who was he to say dick about it?

He returned his attention to the toaster.

"Please do not take that as me being ungrateful, *motek*," she said to his back.

"Whatever," he muttered.

"Shep loves my cooking. So do my boys. When I cook for him, I can make more for you so he can bring it over for dinner."

"I must admit, I had some of your leftover spaghetti a few weeks back and it was on the tip of my tongue to ask Shepherd if he would share more of what you had left over."

"I'll totally make more," Keely said, and Hound heard the smile her voice.

"That's very sweet," Jean replied, and Hound heard the smile in hers.

"Can I ask, what does *motek* mean?" That was Keely.

"It means 'darling' in Hebrew," Jean explained.

"You're Jewish?" Keely asked.

"The mezuzah usually gives it away," Jean said on an amused cluck.

"I hadn't noticed it when I walked in." Hound looked to Keely to see her twisted to look at the door. She twisted back. "Wow. It's beautiful."

"From Jerusalem. A friend of mine brought it back for me, oh, I don't know, maybe thirty years ago. Outside of Shepherd, it's my most prized possession."

He felt Keely's surprise at that, and then he heard her hilarity when she burst out laughing.

He looked from the frying eggs to the ceiling rethinking his decision this was okay.

"Bikers aren't usually owned, Ms. Gruenberg," Keely stated through her continuing fit of laughter.

"I slipped it past him when he wasn't looking," Jean told her.

Keely busted out laughing again.

Hound shook his head, his mouth quirking at the skillet.

Then he called out, "Babe, best give me your egg order or you're getting over easy like Jean."

"Over medium, honey," Keely replied.

Jesus, how in the fuck did he find his ass in a kitchen taking egg orders from a woman?

But there he was, doing that.

"I'm not sure I've ever tried lox," Keely told Jean.

"Then today is your lucky day. And just to say, please, Keely, call me Jean," Jean replied then louder, "Shepherd, sweetheart, make sure to add some lox to Keely's plate."

He turned to the living room. "You women want me to put on an apron while I'm servin' you?"

"No, babe," Keely said. "Your outfit is just fine."

That was when Jean busted out laughing.

KEELY WAS NAKED ON TOP of him, tracing the eagle tat across his collarbone, her attention on it.

"You're cute with her."

She meant Jean.

And she'd know.

She'd gone over for breakfast.

And lunch.

And she'd ordered Hound to go escort Jean to his own damned

apartment so she could make the woman dinner.

Through this time, Hound had watched Keely falling in love (it happened during *Jeopardy!* when they both shouted *"The Fonz!"* at the same time for some TV question, and then Keely reached out and Jean actually gave the woman a high five).

Jean took that dive not long later (about a second after she put a bite of Keely's fried beef cutlet smothered in mashed potatoes and gravy in her mouth).

"Shut it," he replied.

"It's absolutely *adorable* you call her 'Jean bug,'" she told his tattoo.

He gave her waist a warning squeeze.

Her gaze came up to him and she had a sassy smirk on her face.

"She's like your proper biker grandma. It's hilarious that you don't cuss in front of her."

He lifted his brows. "Didn't I say shut it?"

The smirk remained but quickly faded away and the look that replaced it, Hound had learned to brace.

"It's incredibly beautiful the way you are with her. The way you take care of her. How much you guys love each other."

"Keekee," he murmured, lifting a hand to her cheek.

She turned her head and kissed his palm before she righted it and tipped it to the side, resting her cheek in his hand.

"I'm not surprised," she whispered. "You seem to have all the time in the world for everybody else, Hound. Live in a crappy apartment with old furniture and worn-out pots and pans and making Jean eggs, giving her guff, handing over money to Jag . . . which you should not do, his allowance is plenty . . . putting Dutch forward for Chaos and looking out for him, and just being all you are to your brothers in the Club."

"Not gonna let my boy look bad in front of a date," he murmured. "And just to say, babe, every man in Chaos backed Dutch."

"Yours was the one that mattered the most."

He slid his hand to the back of her neck, gripped it and used it and his arm around her waist to pull her up his body, repeating, "Baby, *shut it.*"

"You're the—"

She cut herself off.

He didn't want to know what she was going to say. What he did know was that whatever it was wasn't healthy to his peace of mind.

He asked anyway.

"I'm the what?"

She shook her head, let her lips curl up a little and murmured, "You're just a really, *really* good man, Hound."

So she'd shut up, he lifted his head to kiss her.

She let him, got into it when he pushed it further, then he broke the kiss and used his hand on her neck to settle her face tucked in his throat.

"I'm worried about her."

That was in the room and it came in his voice.

Fuck, now shit was just running right out of his mouth.

He needed to get a tighter grip, seriously, or that would get him into trouble.

Big.

She pushed on his hold to lift up and look down at him again.

"About Jean?"

He said it, and she was now in it with him with Jean, so he knew she wouldn't let it go.

"She fell asleep on my couch tonight, Keekee," he said.

Keely looked confused. "She's not young. I thought that was normal. Is it . . . unusual?"

"She goes to sleep early. Sleeps light. Wakes up a lot. She's up before I get there every morning and alert enough I figure she's been up awhile. But lately, she's been nappin' a lot more. She doesn't take that shuffle down the hall often, but she's never been as slow as she was tonight or as obviously worn out after."

"How old is she?"

"Eighty-nine. Ninety is comin' up in April."

And it was end of February.

"She's not young, Shep. She's gonna slow down."

"This fast?" he asked.

"It's been fast?" she asked back.

"Lately it seems like it."

"Can she get out and about? Go to the doctor?"

"She fusses because I don't have a year to help her get down the stairs so I carry her, but yeah. I take her to synagogue. I take her to get her eyes checked. I take her for her checkups."

"When's her next checkup?"

"Around her birthday."

"Maybe it's best to go out of schedule and get her in sooner," Keely suggested.

He was going to do that. Jean wouldn't like it but it was going to happen.

"Need to borrow Boz's car," he muttered.

"Why?"

He focused on her. "She has trouble gettin' up in my truck and she's old but she's got her pride. I help her out of bed. On the john. Into the shower. Just think the stairs and lifting her ass into my truck are those last straws that bug her that she can't handle."

"Use my car."

She had a little, sporty, black Nissan Juke.

No way in fuck Keely shouldn't have bought American.

But it had zip and it suited her.

"I'll go with you," she carried on then immediately put her middle three fingertips over his lips. "And before you say anything, there is no way in hell anyone having anything to do with Chaos is gonna see us escorting an old lady to a doctor's appointment, and if they do, we have an excuse. You needed my car and my help. And for you, I can distract Jean from getting grouchy while you look after her even more. For Jean," she shot him a sunny, smug smile, "she digs me. She'll be glad I'm around. So it's a win-win."

There was nothing she said that was wrong.

He wrapped his fingers around her wrist and tugged it down.

"What about work?" he asked.

"I'll tell them I need a few hours of leave so I can take my granny to the doctor."

"They gonna believe that?"

She gave a shrug.

That was part of the biker mama that never left her. She did what she did and if The Man gave her shit about it, especially if it was important, they could go fuck themselves.

She'd find a way to get time off.

"I'll make the appointment and let you know," he decided.

Another sunny smile, this one not smug. "Cool."

He rested her hand on his shoulder but didn't release her wrist. She shifted it, dipped a thumb into the dent in his collarbone and started to stroke.

"Why doesn't she get around very much?" she asked.

"Because she's old," he pointed out the obvious.

"Could that be contributing to this? I know she uses a walker and she's not all that fast, but maybe a few more trips down to your place a week. Some outings. Just liven things up a little bit, give her some exercise."

"Babe, she's near ninety with a ticker that isn't doin' her a lot of good and lungs that aren't firing on all cylinders. This makes her weak and slow, so she's not supposed to tax either."

"Oh," she muttered.

He grinned at her and asked, "We done talkin' about Jean? 'Cause I need at least a whole half hour of talking about somethin' else before I can fuck you again."

Back came the sassy smirk. "She is *so* your proper biker grandma."

"Shut it," he warned.

"Shepherd 'Hound' Ironside, badass brother of the Chaos MC, adored by his Chaos family, feared by everyone else for the lunatic he absolutely is if you do his brotherhood wrong, owned by an old Jewish lady."

He rolled her, hitched a leg, digging his junk into hers, and growled, "Babe, I said *shut it*."

"You're a lot of things, Hound, right now seriously hot, but also totally adorable," she teased.

"Had your warning," he muttered.

She opened her mouth to say something.

But he kissed her.

And when he had her like he liked her, he moved down and ate her.

He worked them up to it, but eventually he drove her into his bed fucking her face and then her cunt.

She passed out, leaking him all over his thigh, which she was straddling, face shoved into his neck, hair all over his chest, shoulder and arm.

Hound took a moment to feel her dead weight right there.

Then he passed out with her.

─────

THE NEXT NIGHT, KEELY DID not make Jean walk down to his crib.

She made Hound haul the groceries she needed down to Jean's.

And it was Hound sitting in the couch where he normally sat while Keely moved around Jean's kitchen like she'd done it a million times, preparing their meal, doing this jabbering.

Keely could jabber and Jean could too, so as they got in their competition of who could jabber the most, Hound sat there with his eyes on reruns of *Mike and Molly* wondering if either woman knew he was there.

"So, Hound says your birthday is in April. And it's a milestone. I'm totally making you a birthday cake. What's your favorite?" Keely announced.

At that, Hound's neck muscles grew tight but he still had to power through that to turn his head from the TV to look at her bustling in Jean's kitchen.

She thought they'd still be together in April?

Christ, he fucking hoped so.

At the same time, for the torture to be over of waiting for it to end, he hoped that they would not.

"Oh, I don't do much for my birthdays, dear. You have as many of them as I do, they're not as special."

Keely shot him a glare and he'd understand why when she asked Jean, "Shep doesn't do up your birthdays?"

"I didn't say that," Jean told her, eyes to the TV. "He gets me a store-bought cake with my name on it and everything. And he brings me a huge feast from that kosher deli off Virginia. Matzah soup and chicken schnitzel for dinner. And he always brings flowers when he comes for lunch."

Hound looked from Jean to Keely right in time to catch her mouthing silently, "You are so fucking adorable."

He squinted his eyes at her.

She shot him an amused smile and got back to work.

"Okay, so do you want a store-bought cake this year too?" Keely asked.

"Do you bake as well as you cook?" Jean asked back.

"I have two boys with sweet tooths, so if I didn't when they were born, I learned."

"Chocolate cake with vanilla buttercream icing," Jean ordered.

"I'll be all over that," Keely replied.

Hound looked to Jean.

She was grinning.

There it was.

It had been the right decision to let these two get together.

Maybe not for Hound.

But for Jean.

"Now, just to say," Keely launched in again. "I have some leave that I have to take at work the next couple of weeks and Hound says you prefer to go places in cars. So that he can use mine, he says you also have a birthday checkup but we'll set that up early so he can have mine and I can take some leave and come with. We'll go to that deli in person for lunch. Sound like a date?"

Hound kept studying Jean, wondering if that had been a deft maneuver on Keely's part or if she'd fucked it.

Slowly Jean turned her head and caught Hound's eyes. From her place in the kitchen, if she was looking, Keely wouldn't be able to see Jean holding Hound's gaze.

Her face was wrinkled. She had old-lady skin that was thin and papery.

But that didn't mean she didn't have an expressive face.

And right then, it was soft.

"Sounds like the perfect date," Jean answered Keely, gaze on Hound.

It wasn't a deft maneuver. Jean knew exactly what Keely was up to.

But still, she hadn't fucked it.

Yeah.

This had been the right decision. Keely had horned right in but in truth stepped right up, because Hound wouldn't have found it that easy to trick Jean out of her house for an early visit to the doctor.

Keely was probably lying about the leave she had to take. If she had that leave, she'd have mentioned it.

She just did what she had to do to get done what had to get done.

He wanted to get up, go to the kitchen and stick his tongue down Keely's throat.

He just watched Jean turn back to the TV and did it himself as Keely cried out an enthusiastic, "Awesome!"

Jesus, he was going to fuck her so hard tonight she'd think she'd never stop coming.

He adjusted in his seat so his cock wouldn't get stiff at that thought and lifted his feet up to Jean's coffee table.

"Boots, Shepherd," Jean said.

He growled but used his toes to flip off his boots.

He heard Keely's soft laughter.

"You frickin' women are gonna be the death of me," he muttered.

"From at least one of us, you can only hope," Jean muttered back.

Hound went still and he felt the stillness of Keely in the kitchen, but not in a bad way.

In a way he was trying to figure out if his Jean bug just used sexual innuendo.

From her own version of a sassy smile he could see from her profile she did.

It was then, he howled with laughter.

Jean turned her head and smiled baldly at him as he did.

And in the kitchen, Keely dissolved in giggles.

It was then Hound realized life was good.

So yeah, it was a life that was good for now.

But he would take it.

CHAPTER NINE

SEED OF THE BROTHERHOOD

THE NEXT AFTERNOON, HOUND WAS sitting at the bar in the Compound, Boz at his right side, Hop and Tack behind the bar, Shy and Joker both on his left, Joker sitting next to him, Shy standing, leaning into the bar.

Shy was exuding bad vibes.

Then again, their conversation wasn't exactly cheery.

"She hangin' in there?" Boz asked Tack, and Hound had his gaze on the beer sitting on the bar in front of him, but his attention was on Shy.

He was sure he was not the only one doing this.

"Snap's seeing to her. She's healing up. And Snap is also seein' to the other kinda healin' she's gotta do," Tack murmured.

Hound lifted his gaze to Tack without lifting his head and saw Tack was locked on Shy, his son-in-law, the father of Tack's grandbaby, and his Chaos brother.

"She's gonna be okay, Shy," he went on. "She's strong and she's handling it great."

"Shit went south," Shy returned shortly.

"This is old ground," Hop said carefully. "It happened. It's done.

We've already talked about it and we've already dealt with it."

"It's worth goin' over since it didn't just go south, it got totally fucked up," Shy fired back.

"It did. And that was out of our control," Tack returned. "You asked me, I'd never guess Bounty had that in them."

"No, you're wrong," Shy bit out. "It was *in* our control when we used her to make our play against Bounty, against Valenzuela. And part of that control was us not doin' that. That being somethin' I'll remind you I was not happy about then. Now we got a beef with Bounty, which I don't fuckin' blame them for the reason they first got that beef, and we got a woman who got beat to shit on *our* watch."

Hound felt the hairs on the back of his neck raise.

This was true.

She was Bounty, but she had Chaos protection.

It had been Speck that fell down on that job.

And it had been Speck that felt the displeasure of his brothers. A displeasure that was extreme.

They didn't really have to do dick, though. Speck felt like shit and when Snapper had backed him against a wall, squeezing the breath out of him with his hand at his throat, it might have taken three brothers to pull him off.

But Speck had not done one thing in his own defense.

It was like he wanted Snap to take him out.

Nope, they didn't have to do dick.

"That's been taken care of," Tack said low.

"Yeah, which got us a bigger beef with Bounty," Shy shot back.

"You don't think we should have gone in and dealt with those assholes?" Joker asked in disbelief. "Take a hand to a Chaos woman, you get taught a lesson. And she mighta been takin' Bounty dick, but she made that deal to back our play, and when she did, she became Chaos."

"For fuck's sake, no," Shy replied. "Agreed, the lesson needed to be taught. The problem is, it was *us* who led it to that shit."

"Maybe Hound didn't have to slice that Bounty's face. What's his name? Throttle? Blood for blood but no one sliced Rosalie. And he played the massive dick card, but now he's goin' all out to atone," Boz muttered.

Hound did not agree with Boz's assessment.

Hound was also surprised with Boz's assessment. It wasn't like him.

Throttle had been Rosalie's boyfriend. And Throttle had not only handed her ass to his club to kick the shit out of when he found she was informing to Chaos about Bounty's security operations for Valenzuela's drug transports, he'd been the first to land his blows.

Rosalie had just wanted her man out of that. She was in love with him. Thought he was a good man, just one messed up in bad shit. He wouldn't listen to her so she went another route.

It wasn't Hound's call to make if it was the right route, or the wrong one.

It ended up bad for her, except Tack was right. They beat her down huge, but she was recovering. And now she knew her man had that in him, he wasn't the man she thought he was, and she could move on.

And seemingly doing that with Snapper, which was good since he was into the bitch, and big.

Problematic to all these problems, Rosalie was Shy's ex. She never got that deep in with him, but they had time together, he'd liked her, she'd fallen for him. But for Shy, it had been Tabby, Tack's daughter. And it had been Tab for him for years. So that didn't end real good for Rosalie and she found another biker in another club.

But Shy had been inside her and Hound could get that. Any biker babe that hung around who he'd dipped his wick in had put her ass on the line for good, for Chaos, and got it whipped, he'd go gonzo and it wouldn't be beat-downs and sliced faces.

Bodies would pile up.

"You'd let me in on that shit, I'd have carved his face right off," Shy clipped.

Hound's lips curled up at his beer.

He'd always liked that kid.

Tack had made the call to keep Shy out of it.

In the end, not surprising to the woman she was—a biker princess grown up—it was actually harder to keep Tabby out it.

The woman, new mother or not, lost her motherfucking *mind*.

It was cute.

But she had nothing to worry about.

Hound took her blood for her.

"Blood for blood. Women in the hospital," Shy bit out. "I'm beginning to wonder if Rush isn't right and this shit isn't worth the massive mindfuck, time suck and pain in the ass it is."

He had no more to say and all the men knew it when he prowled out.

However, Hound knew they all had heavy thoughts.

Rush, Tack's son, was not a big fan of their beef with Bounty (to say the least) or their maneuvers to push back Valenzuela.

He wanted it all turned over to the cops and to be done with it.

But Chaos had for years claimed turf around Ride, the store, garage and their Compound, which was all housed on the same lot. Once Tack guided them free and clean of the shit Crank had mired them under, they made it clear no drugs or whores anywhere on what they considered "Chaos"—a five square mile area around their property.

The brothers back then who put their asses on the line to get clean felt that turf was their due.

So they'd taken it.

Then came Benito Valenzuela.

Valenzuela pushed, Chaos pushed back. Valenzuela pushed more, Chaos pushed back. This went on for-fucking-ever. Shit went down where Tack felt they had to make a move, the brothers voted, it passed (not unanimously), and to make a statement, they pushed back—harder—and claimed ten miles around Ride.

Rush was not happy but Rush did not have a lot of support for his idea of retreating just to Chaos—meaning their store, garage and the Compound—getting out of the vigilante street-cleaning business, leaving that to the cops, and just looking out for what was legally theirs.

With the shit going down, Millie kidnapped, working with the cops to dismantle Valenzuela, Rosalie getting her ass in a sling, constant surveillance of their women so they could be sure they were safe, and more area to patrol, Rush was finding new interest in his ideas.

This had included Snapper.

It now seemed it included Shy.

"Okay, nobody open me up for this, but I'm just gonna say . . ." Boz started, and Hound's head stayed down but his eyes slid to Boz, not liking how this was beginning. "We're informin' on another club to the cops. Tack, brother, that shit is not us. Half that fuckin' MC was locked up in that takedown. It's not the MC way to get in bed with cops, hand deliver biker brethren to them. We shoulda found another way."

"And what way would that be, Boz?" Tack asked, his voice stone cold.

It was a good question for Boz. He was a soldier. He wasn't a general. He wasn't a strategist.

Without Tack saying it, it was said.

If you don't have any ideas, shut the fuck up.

"I don't know, I'm not a mastermind, Tack," Boz threw back, not stone cold, pissed as shit. "Since you are, how 'bout *you* come up with a scheme to get us outta this fuckin' mess, because seriously, brother, it's gettin' tired."

"Boz," Hound murmured, and felt Boz's attention land heavy on him.

"And you. You're supposed to get this in hand, man. What the fuck you been doin' for the last fuckin' four months? Only time I seen you pitch in, including on guard duty to the old ladies, is when you could get your jollies kickin' Bounty ass."

Slowly, Hound straightened from slouched at the bar and turned in his seat toward Boz.

"Dial it down, Boz," he heard Hop warn, quiet and irate.

"Fuck that," Boz returned. "We're all steppin' up and this guy hasn't even taken patrol in fuckin' months." He said this jerking a thumb at Hound.

"He's on his own mission," Tack said.

"Well, he's failin'," Boz fired back.

Hound felt his neck start burning.

"Check yourself, brother," Joker warned Boz, also quiet, also irate.

"It's not only me who's noticin'," Boz bit back.

"You and the boys henpeckin' over me, Boz?" Hound asked with casual curiosity.

"Fuck you," Boz spat.

"Has it occurred to you I might have shit happenin' in my life where I don't got time to be suckin' your cock?" Hound asked.

Boz's face went hard, his torso swung back, then his face turned nasty. "Hell no, Hound. Known you decades, man. You're about pussy and blood. The deeper the shit Chaos is in, the happier you are 'cause you'll have asses to kick and then bitches to fuck as you ride the adrenaline high."

"Am I lookin' in a mirror?" Hound returned, because his brother just described his own damned self.

"Not from where I'm sittin' 'cause I don't have a *mission*," Boz said that snide. "But least I'm on patrol and takin' old ladies' backs when it's my turn."

"You sayin' I'm draggin' this Valenzuela shit out after High's woman was taken, hit in the face, watched two men die, and Rosalie got the shit kicked out of her?" Hound returned.

"I'm sayin' you're not a man who's gonna be happy sittin' in a rockin' chair in front of the Compound when this shit is done," Boz replied.

"No. I'll drink tequila and fuck broads and raise hell and sleep real fuckin' cozy, brother, smile on my face the dog that's Valenzuela is put down, whatever way that is, and he's not sellin' pussy on my patch. Sellin' junk that fucks people up on my patch. Doin' anything to smear his oily, nasty shit *on my patch*. I stood side by side with you, brother, when it went down years back. But it was *me* who got bloody to avenge this Club, avenge my brother, keep us on the path to bein' clean. So if you're feelin' a little impatient things aren't movin' fast enough, get your thumb outta your own goddamn ass and step the fuck *up*."

"That's a point you should take, Boz, but I'm gonna get in here between you two and say this shit doesn't fuckin' help," Tack growled. "We fight ourselves, we're not gonna have the focus to fight the real fight. So quit this shit and get over it."

"Sebring's done and he's said that to you, Tack," Boz reminded him of Knight's repeated warnings over the last month. "He's over this shit. Let him deal with it. You don't do that, I know you're tight with those cops and Hawk, but this is a brothers' problem and the brothers best get to handlin' it."

"Why are you standin' there tellin' me shit I already know?" Tack asked. "If I could snap my fingers and have this done, I would. Since that's not an option, find some patience, brother. Or take a break, get on your bike and ride. But don't bring this shit on Chaos. You or any of the brothers have a problem with how things are handled, you bring it to the table. You don't spill that shit all over the bar where nothing can get decided. And if you got any bright ideas, I promise, Boz, I'm all fuckin' ears."

While he was talking, the door opened and Hound was looking at Tack.

But Hop had looked to the door.

Then vibes came off Hop that made Hound look to the door.

And he had to put it all in to stop his own vibes from choking all the oxygen out of the air.

This was because Keely had strolled in.

What in *the* fuck?

"Keely," Hop muttered.

"Jesus, never met her. Fuck, she's amazing," Joker said under his breath.

Tack turned to Keely as did Boz.

Hound kept his seat and stared at her strolling in.

She *was* amazing.

Jeans, scarf, suede jacket, boots, a bunch of jewelry that was kickass Native American or just kickass, hair shining, gorgeous face alert, she could have walked right out of a magazine.

Unfortunately, since the timing was shit, she'd walked right into the Compound.

"I come at a bad time?" she asked, rounding the curve to the bar.

"Never a bad time for you, darlin'," Tack answered. "Everything okay?"

"No," she told him, her attention moving direct to Boz.

Hound's neck started burning again.

Oh no, she was *not*.

"What's going on?" Hop asked, an edge to his voice, thinking she was dealing with some shit she wanted Chaos to handle, not having any clue Keely didn't actually have a problem.

She was there to throw down with Boz.

Guess an entire weekend of Jean and Hound's dick didn't shore her up to be in a good mood for anything that came her way. It was Monday, she'd reset his alarm clock and left him in his bed at five that morning.

And now she looked like she wanted to kill someone.

Namely Boz.

"She said yes," Keely told Boz.

Fucking hell.

"Who said yes, sweetheart?" Boz, like all of the men, careful and attentive to Black's widow.

"Beverly," she stated, tossing her hair. "She said yes this weekend when her guy asked her to marry him."

Christ.

This was the worst possible time for her to be doing this.

Boz, wound up, got jacked up. Hound could feel it pounding off him.

"So, you want me to make sure she sends you an invite?" she asked fake sweet, tilting her head to the side.

It was on the tip of his tongue to intervene.

But who he was and who she was right there, in the Compound, on Chaos, he could not fucking intervene.

Someone had earned a goddamned spanking, that he knew.

"Keely, babe—" Boz started pacifyingly.

Standing a few feet in front of Boz, she put her hands on her hips. "You down with that, Boz? You good she's gonna marry a wimpy guy with a little dick who doesn't make her happy, just makes her not alone? You okay with that?"

Shit.

Joker made a low noise at "little dick," but other than that wisely remained quiet.

"We were done a long time ago, honey," Boz murmured.

"So you *are* good with that," she declared. "You're okay she's still totally in love with you. Has been waiting years for you to pull your head out of your goddamned ass and—"

Boz was getting even more jacked up, all the men felt it, but Hound acted to do something about it.

He scraped his stool back, got off, rounded Boz and stalked to her.

Grabbing her upper arm, she snapped, "Hound!" but he whirled her around, dropped her arm, caught her hand and dragged her out.

He pulled her right to her car, jerked her until she was back to her door, got in her space, and bent his neck to get in her face.

"Are you *insane*?" he asked.

"Well, *you* wouldn't do anything about it and she called me at school today to give me the happy news and then immediately burst into tears. And they weren't tears of joy, Hound. So what do you expect me to do?"

"I expect you to go to her house, get her loaded and talk her outta marrying a guy who's not for her. Not waltz into the Compound and get up in a brother's shit."

"Someone has to do it."

"And that someone can only be you because you're Black's widow and you're the *only* bitch breathing any brother would put up with that shit."

She snapped her mouth shut and her eyes flashed.

"You know it," he growled. "You know every brother would walk a mile with bare feet on broken glass for you. You haven't used it but the situation obviously never came up. Now, it's come up and your ass is here, stickin' your nose in shit that," he got closer, "*I fuckin' told you* to keep your nose out of."

"*You're* their dog on a leash, Hound, not me," she threw in his face.

He leaned back.

Her expression instantly untwisted, going from pissed to repentant.

"Fuck, that was outta line," she whispered.

"Damn straight," he agreed. "Now go see to your girl and we're off for tonight."

He started to move away but she grabbed his wrist, murmuring, "Shep."

He yanked it free and hissed, "Don't fuckin' touch me. Not on Chaos. I'm Hound on Chaos. The dick you play with belongs to Shep. Don't forget that, Keely."

She looked like he hit her but he didn't give a shit.

He walked away.

Right into the Compound.

"You set her straight, brother?" Boz called as he stalked toward the door at the back that led to the brothers' rooms.

Right.

Apparently they were all good when Hound was dealing with Boz's problems.

Hound kept moving, turning only his head to Boz, having all the men's eyes, but feeling only Tack's stare.

"She's right. Bev loves you," Hound said. "You never stopped lovin' Bev. She's lonely and tired of goin' it alone. Get your head outta your ass and do somethin' about that, Boz. Or it's gonna be too late. If it isn't that shit already."

He stopped at the door, turned to the room and lowered his final blow on his bud.

"And if you ever fuckin' say shit like you said to me earlier again, *brother*, we'll have problems. We got enough problems. Shit nearly tore this Club apart when we weren't all in, takin' each other's backs. I'm doin' my fuckin' best for this Club at the same time dealin' with my own problems. The fact you doubt that cuts deep. Think on that, Boz. We're all impatient with this shit. You cut a brother because you can't sort that in your head, you need a reality check. And I'm all up for givin' it to you."

He said that.

Then he disappeared through the door.

BY THE TIME HOUND PROWLED out, all the brothers were gone.

Except Tack was still behind the bar.

"You off?" Tack called.

"Got shit to do," Hound told him, still on the move.

"Hound," Tack said.

Hound rocked to a halt and took the conversation he didn't want to have in hand.

"You got anything more on Turnbull?"

"Only Sebring's desire to see her put outta commission turning more and more rabid," Tack answered. "You?"

"Got dick," Hound answered. "And Valenzuela hasn't resurfaced."

"You've told me that, brother," Tack replied quietly.

"Far's I can tell, she's closed ranks," Hound declared.

"You've told me that too," Tack said.

Hound told him something else he knew. "And she's pulled off Chaos."

She had.

For the last week, maybe two, no Valenzuela whores or dealers had been found on their patch.

All clear.

All clean.

All Chaos.

"I'm uneasy about that," Tack shared.

"You're not alone," Hound replied. "I can't get near one of her boys. They don't roam alone or in groups of two anymore. She's the wiser to me. They roam in packs. I try to dig into one, they'll rip me to shreds."

More likely fill him with bullets. They were clinical motherfuckers. They had a problem, they shot at it, had good aim, and then walked away. It wasn't about brotherhood or family. It was about getting the job done. He fucked up one or he fucked up fifty of their soldiers, it was all the same to them.

"Then you need to pull back," Tack told him.

"And where's that get us?"

Tack didn't look happy and the hard line of his jaw said just how less happy he was to say, "Waiting and watching, brother."

"Unleash Sebring," Hound advised.

Tack nodded. "I'm thinking, Turnbull is leaving Chaos turf, that's our only choice. I'll bring it to the table."

Hound nodded back and started moving again.

He didn't get far before he was stopped by Tack calling his name.

"Keely good?" Tack asked.

That didn't make his neck burn.

It set it on fire.

"She's pissed as shit at Boz."

"He's made the wrong plays with Bev for years," Tack muttered.

He could say that again.

"I know how you feel about—" Tack started.

"No you don't," Hound bit out.

He'd told Tack he loved Keely.

But now that didn't even come close to explaining where he was with her, even after that scene they'd just had.

"You were holding her hand, Hound," Tack said carefully.

"I was dragging her ass out so she didn't stick her foot deeper than it already was, walkin' in with us the way we were and landin' that shit on Boz."

Tack nodded again. "You wanna talk about what shit you're dealin' with?"

He didn't.

At least not all of it.

"Jean's slowin' down," he said.

"What?"

"Jean. Lady I look after—"

"I remember," Tack cut him off.

"She's slowin' down. And fast."

"Fuck," Tack murmured.

"That's about it," Hound replied.

"You need anything? Tyra'd be happy to pitch in. And you know Tabby could help."

He said both with pride because he had two girls like that. But that pride rang deeper with Tabby since she was a nurse and there wasn't a father who wouldn't be proud his daughter did that.

"I'm gettin' her a doctor's appointment. I'll let you know."

And Tack nodded again. "Hang tough, brother."

He had no choice.

He lifted his chin to Tack.

Then he walked out.

HIS PHONE RANG AT EIGHT o'clock sharp, about half an hour after Hound left Jean because she was already asleep.

Not a good sign.

It was Keely.

His mouth tightened but he answered the phone with, "We'll talk later."

"I'm in the bathroom at Bev's. She's practically catatonic on tequila. And I can't let it go any longer without saying I'm sorry for what I said."

She sounded like she was in the bathroom and also whispering.

And fuck him running, it was goddamned cute.

"We'll talk later," he repeated.

"I lashed out because I'm mad about Bev, and this shit fucked with the glow of a great weekend. We lash out the worst at the people we care about because we think they'll forgive us. But it isn't cool."

He said nothing.

But she was right.

She could cut him to shreds and he'd stay standing as long as he could and then accept her apology even while he continued to bleed.

"Saying that," she continued, "we disagree about how that should be handled with Boz. I get that he's your brother. But what you aren't getting is that she's my sister. You'd bleed for them. Do you think I wouldn't do the same for Bev? She's the best friend I've got. She's the only aunt my sons have who's worth dick. She's like blood. Proved better than blood. She's always been there for me. I've always been there for her. That's the way it is, Hound. You'd not think twice about wading in for one of your brothers. Turn the tables, honey. I'm sitting on the other side."

It fucked him that she had a point.

He didn't tell her that.

He again didn't speak.

"Hound?"

"You pour that woman in bed, you come over and text before you come up, Keely," he growled.

"Okay, baby," she whispered, sounding pleased with herself.

She won again but she was smart enough not to crow.

"And I told Boz to get his head out of his ass about Bev," he told her.

She was still whispering when she replied, "You what?"

"We were having a heavy conversation before you showed. You couldn't have worse timing than if you'd waltzed in five minutes before the sun exploded. So I'm not sure either of us got in there. You give me a heads up next time, I might be able to tell you that shit."

"Right," she murmured, and how he knew she was crowing now, he had no clue.

He just did.

So he said, "You're sleepin' with a red ass, baby. Serious as shit. I'm resetting the alarm to five. So pour Bev into bed soon. You're gettin' a workout before you pass out, Keekee. So you best get over here so I can dole out that shit and we can both get some sleep."

"I'll be there soon's I can, cowboy."

Now the woman was purring.

"Go take care of Beverly," he ordered.

"On it. See you later, baby."

"Later, babe."

He hung up.

Then he opened his fridge.

He made his decision and nuked some of Keely's leftovers for dinner.

❤

THE BEGINNING OF THE END started that night.

He'd spanked her, fuck yeah, he had. Like the naughty brat she'd been, her jeans pulled down her ass, he'd given it to her.

Then he'd shoved his hand between her thighs held tight together with her jeans, found her sopping wet and made her come on his lap.

After that, he'd given her a workout, giving himself the same while he did.

Her ass was pink but her mood was still victorious, and after he pounded her fourth orgasm out of her (his second), he'd rolled to his back with her on top and let her give him all of her weight.

It took her a while to recover, but she did and she did it doing her pagan priestess act, lavishing every line and curve of his tats with the tip of her tongue, like it was her that put them there, her they belonged to and she was worshipping at the altar of her own creation.

Her hands were on him too.

But Hound just lay there, one arm thrown to his side, the fingers of his other hand wound in her hair, cupping the back of her head, and he felt what she was doing to him. What she was giving to him. Taking it, memorizing it, hoping like fuck it filled him up for the time when he'd have nothing like this and no hope to find it.

And then her tongue slipped over the reaper.

After it did, it traced the word "Black."

His eyes opened and he stared at the ceiling, feeling her touch on him now burn like acid.

She could worship him, fuck yeah, he'd let her do it for hours.

But she sure as fuck couldn't worship her old man using him.

Except for the fact that she did, she was doing it right then, and she had been for months.

That was what this was.

He let her move to the "Red" and trace that and the scale before he took his fingers out of her hair and put both of his hands under her arms.

He hauled her up his body then slid her off to his side, turning her so her back was to his chest.

"Shep—"

He wasn't Shep.

He hadn't been Shep since his girl called him that in high school.

He was Hound.

Chaos's dog on a leash.

And he was fucking proud of it.

"Quiet," he ordered.

He reached behind him to switch off the light. Then he pressed into her to reach to the light on her side and he switched that off.

Finally, he yanked the covers over them and tucked her in the curve of his body.

"Are we done?" she asked quietly.

They were done before they started.

How she could not know they were totally done now, he couldn't fucking guess.

What he did know was that this was about Black. This was about using Hound to get her wild on. This was about going back to the glory days and getting fucked so hard she was breathless, made to come so hard she thought the world was ending.

It didn't matter who it was, as long as it was Chaos, as long as she had that link to her old man, as long as the cum that jetted up inside her was the seed of the brotherhood.

It was just that Hound, for years, had been giving her the opening.

And she finally needed it enough, she'd walked right through.

"Shep—"

"Go to sleep," he grunted.

"I was—"

He squeezed her belly, pressed his body hard into her and growled, "Keely, go to fucking sleep."

Her frame was strung tight, and it felt like she forced it to relax before she replied, "Okay. We'll talk in the morning."

They wouldn't.

They'd talk tomorrow night, somewhere private, quiet, not there, not at the house that Black bought her, not anywhere a brother could see, not anywhere an old lady might catch them, not anywhere anyone in the biker world might witness the end of something that hadn't begun.

She linked her fingers in his at her belly and held on tight.

He let her, not because he liked the feel, just because he couldn't deal with the shit.

He waited until she fell asleep.

It took a long time.

But finally her body loosened, as did her grip.

Only then did he slide his fingers from hers.

But he didn't let her go.

He had one more night.

A few more hours.

A few more hours of make believe.

He was going to fucking take it.

Then it would be over.

CHAPTER TEN

DEFEAT

HOUND WAS AWAKE BEFORE THE alarm sounded.

Keely started in his arms and lifted her head.

"Fuck," she muttered.

He slid his arm from around her waist, muttering back, "You best git."

It was dark but he still saw the shadow of her head turn his way.

"Shep, baby—"

"You got work, I gotta get some more shuteye before I see to Jean then I got shit to do for the Club."

And he fucking did.

It was time to knock some teeth down some throats and do it hoping he was bulletproof.

"I think something happened last night," she said softly.

She thought?

"Keely, you need to get moving," he reminded her.

"You told me we'd talk in the morning," she reminded him. "It's morning."

"And we're talkin' but we don't got a lot of time because, like I said, you got work and I got shit to do."

"Hound—"

"Woman, shake a fuckin' leg. We'll talk tonight."

She studied him through the dark before she asked, "You sure?"

"Sure I'm sure."

And he was sure.

They were absolutely going to talk that night.

More studying but he didn't take it. He rolled the other way and turned on his light.

Then it was him that got out of bed, murmuring, "Before you go in there, I'm gonna hit the pisser."

He did that and she came in wearing her underwear while he was washing his hands.

Her eyes were steady but searching on him in his mirror.

He didn't touch her as he walked out.

He didn't know what to do then.

Get in bed, which meant watching her put on clothes and get ready to leave his place, her not knowing it was for the last time, him feeling a hole in his soul because he did.

Or get in bed and turn his back to her like a sulking kid.

Uncomfortable and feeling like a fucking moron in his own goddamned house.

He should have kicked her ass out the night before.

In the end, Hound did neither.

He yanked up his jeans commando and strolled down the hall to his kitchen.

He didn't have a coffeemaker, something Keely gave him shit for, told him last weekend that was her next addition, but he didn't need one. If he wanted coffee, he went over to visit Jean.

So he had no reason to be in his kitchen either.

He still stayed there, leaning into a hand on the counter of the bar that faced his living room and scowling at the furniture she picked for him, wondering if it'd fit through his windows so he could just shove it out.

She walked into the room, and he stopped scowling at his furniture to turn a blank face to her.

Keely didn't miss it.

But she powered through it.

"You want me to come earlier? I can make dinner for Jean before we talk," she offered, like nothing had happened.

Like she hadn't touched her tongue to her husband's name on his fucking body with Hound's cum up her cunt.

"That might be good," he lied. "I'll ask Jean and text you."

She seemed to relax at that.

"Okay," she said quiet, then came to him, put her hand on his stomach and tipped her head back.

He went through the motions, putting his lips to hers, even setting his hand on her waist.

When he lifted away, she looked confused and worried again.

"Are you gonna walk me to my car?" she asked.

Fuck.

He was so deep in his own head, he forgot.

"Right, yeah. Be back," he grunted, walked around her, down the hall, tore on a tee, jammed his feet into his boots and then walked back.

He nabbed his keys off the kitchen counter and he was the first out.

She followed him.

He went down the stairs first too.

She followed him again.

At her car, so he didn't have to tell more lies, eat more shit, he took her mouth in a kiss that was a fuckuva good-bye.

She just had no idea that was what it was.

But it worked. Her pretty eyes were hazy, her face soft, her body plastered to his when he finished it.

"Get home, babe. I'll see you tonight," he murmured.

"Okay, honey."

She rolled up on her toes to give him one last lip touch.

Her good-bye.

And she didn't know that either.

Then he waited until she folded in her car, closed her door for her and he was sure to stand on the sidewalk and watch her drive away.

When he went up to his place, he didn't find his knife and slash the furniture to shit like he wanted to do. He didn't yank the lamps out of their sockets and smash them against the walls like he wanted to do. He didn't drag the stools and end tables out into the hall and send them crashing down the stairs like he wanted to do.

All that shit would have woken up Jean.

Instead, he got his phone, got his ear buds, walked to his bed, laid on his back and listened to "Use Me."

Withers could write and sing a song.

But the motherfucker was fucked up if he thought that shit was all right.

THE END OF THE END started thirty-eight minutes later.

It happened after he'd brushed his teeth. Taken off his shirt and splashed water on his face and in his pits. Toweled off, put his shirt back on and went over to Jean's.

It happened after he let himself in.

It happened after he walked down the hall.

It happened after he knocked on her door and called, "Jean bug?"

That was when it happened.

Because she didn't answer.

He pushed open the door and saw her lying on her side, her back to him, in her bed.

"Jean," he called.

She didn't answer.

She also didn't move.

Dread and fear filled him. Dread that felt like a hand closing around his throat. Fear that built to terror that felt like a set of claws had sunk into his gut and was tearing up, splitting him open on a trajectory to his heart as he put one boot in front of the other on the way to her bed.

He had a moment when he made it to the side and he saw the covers up, her head on the pillow, her soft, wispy white hair framing her face, her eyes closed. A moment he thought she was just still asleep, like when he'd walked in on her napping in front of the TV.

"Jean," he whispered, bending to her, reaching to her, his fingers out and searching.

They closed around her ice-cold hand.

He stared at his big hand around her little one, his knuckles scarred from fights, the veins standing out at the back, his calluses catching at her soft skin.

He didn't need to look for her pulse.

He did it anyway.

But he got what he thought he'd get.

Nothing.

He moved his hand back to hold hers.

And then Shepherd "Hound" Ironside stood beside the bed of the old Jewish lady who owned his heart and he held her hand.

"I hope," his voice came rough, raspy, tortured, "you knew even a little how much I fucking loved you."

She lay there . . . sleeping.

Hound let her go.

He could only manage one step back before he fell right to his ass beside Jean's bed.

He stared at her beautiful, peaceful face right there before his.

Then he cocked his knees, drew his wrists up to rest on them.

And he dropped his head in defeat.

CHAPTER ELEVEN

RIDE FREE

Keely

Just over two months earlier . . .

I SAT IN MY CAR at the cemetery, staring at Bev's text on my phone.

It was an address.

Hound didn't live in a very good part of town.

I dropped the phone to my lap and looked out the windshield not seeing anything.

I'd seen it all before.

I'd been there a lot.

But Hound wasn't bringing my checks anymore.

So today's visit was going to be different.

I drew in breath and closed my eyes.

Things flashed in that dark.

Memories.

The first time I saw Black, over a barrel of fire, the most beautiful man I'd ever seen.

The time he had me against the wall, his cock buried deep, his fingers digging into the webbing of mine, cutting the ring he'd just put on me into my flesh, pressing it against the wall, promising me, "We're gonna ride wild and burn bright, baby. We're gonna tear this life *up*."

The look on my husband's face when I told him I was having his baby.

The look on his face when I told him I was giving him another one.

The look on his face on the slab in the morgue when, Tack at my side, Hop, Dog, Brick and Hound at my back, I identified him.

Hound at my back.

I opened my eyes but the visions didn't stop coming.

Hound walking up the stairs from my basement carrying Jagger's little mini-bike on Christmas Eve.

Hound sitting on my front steps with Dutch, not touching him except the side of his leg was pressed to Dutch's and his shoulder was dipped, his neck bent, his head turned to Dutch, his lips moving, after Dutch's first girlfriend dumped him.

Hound on his back under my kitchen sink with a wrench after those assholes installed my kitchen and didn't put the pipes in right.

The look Hound gave me when I told him no woman loved him.

I'd been pissed.

But I had a bad habit of lashing out when I got pissed, always did, and it didn't get better after Graham died.

The worst part of me doing that was that most the shit out of my mouth, I didn't mean. I just meant it to hurt, like me hurting someone could take away the pain in me.

Would I ever learn?

Hound was not bringing my checks anymore.

I had to learn.

The cemetery came in focus, like a sharp, savage blow, telling me to get with the fucking program.

Yeah.

I had a lot of lessons to learn.

I got out of my car. Walked to his grave. It was a wonder there was any snow or turf under my heels I'd walked that path so often.

It was cold. The December chill biting through my jacket.

I should have worn the sheepskin but I really didn't feel the cold.

The only thing on my mind was what I had to say, how much I needed to say it, and how hard it was going to be.

I sat on my ass in the snow and I didn't feel that either. It'd get wet through when it melted about two seconds after I sat in my car, but I didn't care.

I stared at the black marble gravestone with the Chaos insignia etched at the top.

In a fit of rage at life, but mostly at his family, sticking it particularly to his sister, an uppity bitch who'd detested before but did that more when she thought she had a say about the gravestone of a brother she hadn't seen in years, I didn't allow his full name to be put on the stone.

So under the insignia, it just read "Black" and gave the dates he'd been put on this earth and then left it.

Under that, it said, "Ride free, baby."

That last was mine.

"I know you're so totally pissed at me," I whispered.

We're gonna ride wild and burn bright, baby. We're gonna tear this life up.

"I can feel it through the dirt," I said. "Just how pissed at me you are."

Burn bright, baby.

"I just loved you so much."

We're gonna tear this life up.

"I couldn't find it in me to burn bright without you. You were gone, I was so empty. I gave everything I had to our boys and it felt like there was nothing left."

We're . . . gonna . . . tear this life up.

"I gotta burn bright, honey," I said softly. "I gotta start tearing this life up."

The black stone just stood there.

It might be there forever.

It might fall through the sky when the earth fell out of it.

"I love him."

It was choked, my admission, choked with the betrayal I had to get over so I could get the fuck on with it.

"I love him and he loves me. I know that last. He doesn't know the first. Not yet. I didn't mean for it to happen. Not with Hound. Not with a brother. Not with Chaos. But you've seen," I leaned toward the stone, *"you've seen*. He's been everything. Everything I needed. Everything you would have been to our boys. He's been *everything*, baby. Every-*fucking*-thing. And I fell in love with him. I tried to blank my heart. I tried to hold it back. But when I hurt him, I knew. When I said that shit to him, I knew. When I found out the Club was in the thick of it again and all I could think was that Hound would be the deepest in that shit, *I knew*."

Ride wild.

I pushed up to my knees, leaning forward, reaching out a hand, putting it to the base of the cold marble.

"You love him like I do. If you were breathing, you'd never want this. You'd break the brotherhood to claim me. But you left me, Black. A brother stepped up. And shit happens. You're not breathing. I gave you years and then I gave you more and I can't do this anymore. He's given so much, baby. He's been there through it all. He sent the man who took you from me straight to hell, maybe earning his ticket there when he did it. He did that for you. You need to do this for him. You need to let him have me. And you need to forgive us both."

I sat back, wet ass to heels and stared at cold stone.

"We'll work it out in the afterlife, honey," I whispered. "Somehow, we'll make it work. And we'll all burn bright, tear it up and ride free. I know we will. You wanna know how I know?"

There wasn't a sound.

Not even a rustling.

"Because that's how much you both love me."

My man lay still in the earth, his beacon of black marble gleaming dull in a gray sky.

"You know I'll come back. Maybe not every week like you're used to, but I'll be back. And I'll see how he feels about it, but if he's up for it, I'll bring your brother." I tipped my head to the side. "And don't get pissed. You know you wanna see him. You dig down deep, you know where you stand with this. You know, it was you wearing the other boots, Hound would want this for you. You know I told you your future before it happened, then what he'd hand over to me, to *us*, you'd give this to me. So now you gotta get your shit together, baby. You gotta take my back like your brother's been doing. And you gotta shine your badass biker light down on us because this is not gonna be easy."

It didn't happen right then. Shit like that doesn't. It isn't like the movies.

It happened later.

After I sat with him for longer.

After I reminded him that I loved him more than my own breath.

After I told him his sons were pains in my ass but they were the best boys on the planet, and I filled him in on their lives, telling him stuff he totally already knew.

After I got back into my car.

After I drove away wondering if I should pull over because the vision before me was wavy since I was staring at it through tears.

It was when the Denver sun broke through the clouds that I knew I had the permission I needed to finally again burn bright, tear life up, be wild . . .

And ride free.

CHAPTER TWELVE

ENFORCER

Keely

Present day...

I STOOD OUTSIDE HOUND'S DOOR and checked my phone again.
Three texts from me.
On my way.
Downstairs, honey.
I'm here. Everything okay?
None of them answered.
I'd gone up, even knowing he'd be pissed at me, and knocked on his door.
No sound inside. No sense of movement.
I went to Jean's door, knocked and got the same thing.
This did not give me a good feeling because his bike was outside and so was his truck, and at this time he might not be at his place, but he would be at Jean's.
I thought about texting Boz, finding out if for some scary-ass reason Hound needed his car for Jean, and because I was at work didn't bother me.
Or because whatever had happened with him last night, shit was not

good between us.

I wasn't an idiot. I knew he was reacting to me being at Black's name on his body.

But he didn't give me a chance to finish what I was doing.

He then didn't give me a chance to explain.

And he got so freaky cold and remote, I panicked, froze, didn't push it.

But he didn't lose his mind, kick me out of his bed, shout at me.

He held me tucked close. He let me lace my fingers in his.

He might have been distant and weird that morning but he'd kissed me at my car and watched me drive away like normal.

So I told myself it would be okay. I told myself maybe he understood what I was doing with his tats. I told myself maybe he was getting there too. Where I'd been guiding him. Where I needed him to be to take on the brotherhood so I could have him, he could have me, we could have Chaos and it would all be what it should be.

He was pushing back. I knew he felt he was betraying Black. I knew he felt that digging down deep. I knew it was on his mind his brothers would lose theirs if they knew what was happening, what we both wanted, how far it'd gone and how fast, and how, in the end, it needed to be.

Hound and Keely.

That was what needed to be.

The end of Black and Keely was years ago.

It wasn't just me who had to learn that, and once I did and where I intended to go, I knew I had a long row to hoe ahead of me.

So before that, we needed to be solid. We needed to be a unit. We needed to be a team.

And that was what I set about doing.

He wasn't making it easy. But I'd been ready for that and I intended to do whatever I had to do to see it through.

Unlike Hound, I was not worried about my boys. Dutch, I knew, remembered his daddy and missed him even if he'd lost him young.

Still, the only father he truly ever had was Hound. He felt that. He'd understand. And if I had to guess, my guess would be that he'd not only not be shocked Hound and I got together, he'd be super fucking happy.

Jagger was, sadly (all my fault, but I didn't feel too badly about it), a momma's boy. He was still a badass-in-the-making, what with Graham's blood and Hound's and Chaos's upbringing.

But he loved Hound as the *only* father he ever knew.

He might have issues with it at first, but he'd come around.

It was Chaos that would be the toughest nut to crack.

They owed me and they'd paid in the ways they thought meant something.

But this was the way I wanted.

This was the something that meant everything to me.

And not only for that they were going to give it to me.

But for Hound who'd given his very soul to that Club.

That was the most important reason they were going to give this to me.

Because they were going to give it to him.

Before I tried Boz and maybe opened the lid on something, making Boz curious as to why I'd ask or why Hound had borrowed his car, first I tried the doorknob.

I didn't expect it would open. Now that he had the stuff I'd picked for him, Hound locked his door even when he came down to get me in my car.

But the minimal pressure I put on the door expecting it not to open, opened it.

I stared at it, cold invading my veins.

He'd never leave his door open, not if he wasn't in there.

And if he was in there, he'd answer when I knocked.

If he was in there, he'd have come down and gotten me.

As terrible thoughts rushed through my brain, I didn't think.

I pushed open the door and walked into the dark room.

I saw him immediately, on his sectional, facing the door, feet up on the coffee table I'd picked out for him, sitting casually in the dark.

Was he sitting?

Or was he something else?

I had to go with sitting.

So why was he sitting silent, alone in the dark and not even calling out when I knocked on his door?

"Hound?" I called carefully, a frog in my throat.

"Right," his deep voice sounded, cracking through the room like a thunderclap. "Our talk."

I stood still in his open door.

"You played with my dick," he stated, matter of fact, like he was reading out instructions for something. "You got your orgasms. You rode that wild wind, Keely. You did that last real good every time you did that on me. Gratitude for that. Now we're done."

Oh God.

He totally, *totally* did not read what I'd been doing with his tat.

"Shep—"

"Call me that again, I'll rip your throat out," he growled.

I went solid as the marble of my dead husband's gravestone.

"Now turn that ass around and get the fuck outta my space," he ordered. "And if that's not clear, Keely, that means now and don't come back. You want your checks, use another brother. You're done usin' me."

Oh yeah.

Fuck yeah.

He *totally did not read* what I'd been doing with his tat.

"Using you?" I forced out past a closed throat.

"To get your biker bang," he explained.

"That's not what it was," I said quickly.

"Bullshit," he clipped out, and before I could say more, the shadow of him leaned slightly forward and he kept biting. "Now I'll say it only once more. Get the fuck out."

"Hound—"

He took his feet, fast as a blink, and I put a boot back in preparation to flee when he roared, *"Get the fuck out!"*

It hit me then, panic coursing through my system, barbed, tearing away at the insides of me.

It was past six.

But it wasn't past eight.

"Why aren't you over at Jean's?" I asked.

"Get out," he growled, his tone, as impossible as it was to believe, deteriorating.

That panic started scoring away huge chunks of me.

"Why aren't you over at Jean's?" I repeated.

"There's no winning this, bitch. You played your hand. You earned your loot. The pot's dry. Time to cut and run."

"I—"

"Woman, I do not have the patience for this."

He might not.

But I couldn't give up.

Not now.

Especially not now.

Why wasn't he over at Jean's?

"I think there's a lot we need to talk about," I told him.

"Time when you can talk me into dick so you can play with mine is done, Keely."

"Really, Hound, honest to God, there are things to say. Starting with why you aren't over at Jean's."

That was when he came at me.

And the manner in which he did, the feel roiling off him and thundering into me, I wanted to do what he said.

Cut and run.

But this was Hound.

He was mine.

And I'd spent two months proving I was his.

If he took a goddamned *breath* and paid attention, he'd know that, calm the fuck down and *listen to me*.

So I stood my ground.

It was a mistake.

I knew that when I took his hand in my chest, a hand that slammed me so hard against the wall, my skull cracked against it.

And then I took his fist in the back of my hair and had to expend energy I did not have not to cry out in pain when he used it to jerk my head back.

Finally I saw some of his features come into focus with the weak light from the hall filtering in the door as he put his face in mine.

It was then I knew.

It was then my heart tore apart.

He didn't even have to tell me.

But he did.

"Jean died in her sleep last night," he spat.

No.

"Now, just in case you haven't wrapped that stupid, *fucking*," he pulled again at my hair and I failed at beating back a wince, but he was so deep in his grief and his fury, he didn't notice it or he didn't care, "head of yours around this, it wasn't Black's cock you were sucking. It wasn't Black's cock you were fucking. It wasn't Black's cock you begged to have thrust up your ass. It was *mine*. And I'm *done*. And when a man like me says he's done bein' used by some washed-up, washed-out, tired, old, biker groupie pussy, bitch, he . . . is . . . *done*."

With that, agony tore through my scalp as he jerked me by my hair to the side but he didn't put me out of his house.

He left me in it, stalking out his door, leaving it open, disappearing into the hallway.

I stood there a long time.

Long enough to hear his bike roaring away.

I DROVE INTO MY GARAGE, feeling like a functioning open wound.

That must have been why something that had been like a razor's edge slicing through me for weeks, months, years, but as shit like that had a way of being, it had become part of the scenery, for the first time since that visit when I told my husband I was moving on, I saw his bike under its cover.

I switched off the ignition and sat in my car, my head turned, staring at it.

The boys both had vehicles, with Dutch now also having a bike. They also both parked in the drive in a line behind the door that led to their father's bike. They fought and bitched at each other about who pulled in first because neither wanted to be fenced in when they were ready to take off, and I'd laid down the law that neither of them fenced me in.

So like their father.

And so like their non-biological father.

I got out of my car, went right to Black's bike and ripped the cover off, tossing it aside.

He had a shit-hot bike.

And my man on that bike . . .

God.

Not once, in all the time together, did I not get wet the instant I saw him astride that bike.

I told him that happened to me about two weeks after we started seeing each other.

About five minutes after that, we were fucking on that bike.

It was our first time on his bike, but not our last.

I would not tell the boys that.

That fucking hideous night, he'd taken his truck to get pizza, for obvious reasons.

So it had been my man who'd backed that bike right there.

I'd put the cover on.

But other than that, that bike had never been touched.

Never been moved.

It was where Black had put it.

And now that shit had to end.

I left the cover off, walked out the back door to the garage, walked the walk that led along the back of the house and moved up the stairs to the back door to my house.

I tried not to remember the day years ago I stuck my head out that door during a huge snowstorm, when Hound was standing out on that walk at the place between detached garage and house, and he was staring at the thin line of space between both.

I failed at not remembering this and froze, staring at my hand on the handle of the storm door.

"Hound! It's half a blizzard out here! The bad half!" I'd shouted. "What in hell are you doing?"

He'd been wearing his Chaos cut, like always. The black leather jacket beat up with use, the Chaos insignia patch stitched to the back, small rectangular patches stitched where a breast pocket would be, one said Hound, the one under it said Enforcer.

Hound's cut still said Enforcer. But back then Tack had the patch that said President (and still did), Dog's said VP, Brick's said Sgt at Arms, under which was another one that said Road Captain. Hop's jacket had Tail-Gunner.

There was a secretary and treasurer who at that time of the snowstorm I no longer knew (and still didn't, though I knew Hop was now VP and Tack's son-in-law, Shy, was Sergeant at Arms). The rest had Member or Prospect (even though Chaos verbally called them "recruits" because the founders not only were all ex-military and that felt natural, they also felt like bucking even MC traditions—they didn't name their club "Chaos" for nothing).

I just knew after Tack took over and cleaned up the Club, Big Petey had been given the patch that said, Chaplain.

"Behind this wall is your laundry room!" he'd shouted back.

I knew that. He knew that. I just hadn't known why he was shouting it through a snowstorm.

"Yeah!" I'd yelled.

"Need to attach your garage!" he'd yelled back. "Gonna get the boys here to see to that."

In the end, he'd never done it, mostly because I'd pitched one holy hell of a fit at the thought of a bunch of bikers pounding a hole in my wall to attach my garage.

To see that didn't happen, I'd talked to Dog, who was one of the more level-headed ones (though not when it came to me, but still, he was more level-headed generally) and convinced him I was going to see to that as part of all the work I was doing, dedicated to giving my boys the home Graham and I had promised each other we'd make for them.

I never did it.

But right then, I remembered Hound standing outside in the snow, staring at that space, and I knew then (but buried it) like I knew now he didn't like me to walk through snow.

That could have been when the tears came.

It wasn't.

I had shit to do.

And that shit was opening my door, walking in and unraveling my scarf from around my neck. Tossing it and my purse and my jacket on my kitchen table. Running up my stairs.

And, after I turned on the light by the bed, going straight to my closet.

In the early days, as a form of self-torture, I'd hung it on a hook at the back of my closet door so every time I opened it, he'd be right there, the smell of leather, the hint of my man waving at me.

Eventually I'd torn our bedroom apart to usurp another room, "To give you the bedroom of your dreams, baby," Black had said. "To build a bedroom and big closet and kickass bathroom for the biker queen you are."

Before the workers had started tearing down walls, I'd folded it carefully, put it in a flat plastic crate, and tucked it away safely.

Now, I found that crate in the big-ass closet I'd had to give myself, took it out, moved to my bed with it and set it down.

I crawled in, pulled the box deeper into bed with me, and sat there, cross-legged, staring at it.

It took a second but finally I flipped the lid on it.

I'd put it in, not like a brother would do, back—and Chaos insignia—up.

I'd put it in like an old lady would do.

Front, the patch that said Black, the one under it that said Secretary, and the one under that that said Road Captain up.

Graham's cut.

It took a second before I could reach out and touch the tips of my fingers on the Black.

And just like always, just like it always would be, even if I'd been able to win Hound, the tingle of love and memories, and laughter and loss coursed over my fingers, up my arm, across my chest and straight to my heart.

They'd cleaned it.

Or Tack had given it to Boz so Bev could do it.

Probably paid a mint, cleaning that leather.

And I'd hated them for it. All of them, even Bev.

I'd railed and screamed and even went at Tack with nails bared (not surprisingly it had been Hound that had pulled me back) when they took his cut and had it cleaned.

But it was covered in his blood.

I wanted that blood and the scent of him. Even if one of his goddamned hairs was there, I wanted it.

They'd cleaned it, taking all that from me.

A Chaos brother's cut was buried with him.

I refused to allow that.

And Chaos allowed me to refuse.

Now I knew why.

They probably knew it before.

Because a time would come that I'd be giving it to one of my boys, and when I did it'd need to be as it was, not have the life blood of their father crusted into the leather and threads of the patches that meant everything to him.

Absolutely everything.

And that time was now.

I gathered up my husband's cut, put the lid on the box, nabbed it and walked down to the kitchen.

I shoved the stuff I'd thrown there aside, put the cut on the table, spreading it out carefully, then walked the box out to the trash and dumped it.

Only when I was back inside, locked up tight, did I go back to my room, turn out the light, lie in bed and stare at my dark ceiling.

Jean Gruenberg had died last night.

And Hound was done with me.

The first wave came like a hiccup.

The second made me sound like I was strangling.

So I turned to my side when the sobs overwhelmed me.

THE BACK DOOR OPENED THE next morning when I was at the stove.

"Hey, Ma," Jagger called.

I didn't look at him.

He'd see me in a second. He'd see my face and know I'd had no sleep. Know I'd been crying. Know pain was at the surface.

With what I had planned, he'd mistake the reason why. Or not exactly. It was just that what he'd think was only part of the reason.

But that was okay. It was how it needed to be. He'd never know and I'd never tell him. Hound certainly wouldn't.

It was done.

Over.

Now I knew why he didn't push through the feelings of betrayal and concern of what his brothers would do to start things, really *start things*, to begin to build a future with me.

Now I knew he thought I was so sad, so pathetic, so selfish I came to get my rocks off, using him.

Using him.

So yeah.

It was done.

Over.

I could forgive him anything.

Even the way he put his hands on me, the ugly words he'd hurled at me, knowing he'd lost Jean, knowing how you could lash out at the people who mattered when you were wounded, knowing all that, I could forgive.

But him using Black against me, thinking I'd put Black between us, thinking I'd *ever* do what he thought I'd done to him, to Hound, hell, to *anybody*, but especially not him, I would not.

Not ever.

The start and end of Keely Black and Shepherd Ironside moved just a few feet down a hall but was otherwise entirely contained to a shitty apartment in a bad part of town.

Where it should be.

Right then, in my kitchen, I had to pull it together to do what I was doing.

I knew when Jag saw it. I felt it in the air.

"Ma?" he called.

I turned.

He took one look at my face and his blanched.

"You're gonna become Chaos, yeah?" I asked.

His eyes were darting from his father's cut to me, back and forth.

God.

I'd wondered the answer for years if God loved me or hated me, giving so much of their father to my boys.

They didn't look exactly like him.

But they both had his voice. Identical. Sometimes, I didn't know which was which or would even think in my wildest moments it was Graham who was calling from beyond the grave when one of them phoned me.

They also both had his mannerisms, his walk, his long legs, his superior ass (I could think that, even as their mother), his broad shoulders.

They both had his hair, dark and wavy. Not mine, dark and sleek.

And they both got his jaw, strong and square.

Jag had the wide of my eyes, both in setting in his face and in the actual feature.

Dutch's eyes were set deeper in his head, hooded by his brow, like his father's.

I had brown to my skin, which Dutch got.

Graham had had olive in his skin, which Jag got.

Dutch got his father's nose, strong and narrow and perfectly proportioned.

Jag got my nose, the masculine variety, straight along the bridge, slightly upturned at the end, flaring out at the nostrils.

They were beautiful boys that had turned into good-looking kids who had grown into knockout men.

Dutch was watchful, responsible, sober and quiet.

Jag was fun-loving, teasing, reckless and loud.

Graham had miraculously been able to be all of that.

And because he was, I was free just to be like Jag.

Until I was not.

They loved and looked after their mother more than they should, especially at their ages. Even Jagger, who did it by making an excuse to come eat breakfast with me nearly every morning when he could hit a fast food joint and get some egg and sausage Croissan'wich.

I'd been, of late, encouraging them to live their lives and not spend so much time worrying about me.

It had been a lie to give me the time to be with Hound.

That lie was now done but I wasn't going to go back.

They had to live their lives.

Burn bright.

Tear it up.

"Everything okay, Ma?" Jag asked carefully.

"Are you going to join your father's Club?" I asked the same question in a different way.

His eyes flicked to the cut and longing hit his handsome features for a moment.

But even at just a moment, I felt that carve through my belly, rending pain like it was the first time, not one of innumerable, it sliced through me that my baby boy had never really known his father.

He looked back into my eyes.

"Yeah," he told me.

"When you were born, both of you, he was at my side. When you came out and they cut the cord, he didn't let them hand you to me. He didn't even let them put a blanket around you. He tore off his shirt and held you, flesh against flesh, at his chest. That was the first vision I had of either of you. Held against your father's flesh, gunked up and bawling, tight and safe in his arms."

I watched my boy swallow.

I did the same.

Then I kept at him.

"One of you gets his cut," I announced. "One of you gets his bike. You decide between you who gets which. You know this but I'll tell you, they aren't equal. The patch means everything. Whoever gets that can't wear it until they've earned it. But I'll tell you something you don't know. That bike was an extension of him. It was a symbol of the man he was. It was a symbol of the life he lived. He might have had women before me but he never put one single female ass on the back of that bike until he met me. He told me that. His brothers confirmed it. And I believe it down to my soul. So that bike is also a symbol of him and me. He loved it. He was proud of it. So what I'm saying is, neither of you will get the raw end of the deal. Now call your brother and make your decisions. But before either of you get either part of your dad, you come to me and tell me who's getting what. I want to say good-bye to both before I let them go."

His face got sweet.

Sweet and tender.

My baby boy.

"You don't have to let them go, Ma."

"Yes, I do," I replied quickly, before I decided something that was very wrong, that he was right. "Your father would want you to have them. So you're going to have them."

Jag nodded, not taking his gaze from me.

"Who would he give which?"

If he'd lived, he'd give Dutch his cut, Jag his bike.

If he'd known he would die when he did, he'd give Dutch his bike, because Dutch got more of him, and he'd give Jag is cut, because he did not.

But he wasn't there.

So they were going to make that decision.

"I'm not saying. You boys are deciding. And that's all I'm gonna say about it. Now sit down, I gotta get to work so I need to feed you."

"'Kay, Ma," he said gently, letting it go immediately because he knew I needed that, but still watching me.

I turned back to the stove.

What was Hound doing right then without Jean to take care of?

I felt the tears well in my eyes at the same time I felt like getting in my car and going to Hound's and kicking the shit out of him, even if I had to do it verbally.

Two months, he kept her from me.

I got a weekend.

And now she was gone.

That was an entirely selfish thought.

But to get through breakfast with my son on the second day that had dawned without Jean Gruenberg existing on this earth and with the second man I'd loved in my life lost to me, I was clinging to it.

With everything I had.

I GOT THE NEWS FROM Bev.

She'd gotten it from Tyra, who had no idea it had happened and who Bev had told me had her work cut out getting Tack to rip it out of Hound.

But Tack got it.

So the next morning, I walked up to the gravesite wearing a simple black dress, my black wool overcoat, as modest as I could get black boots (mine had spike heels and were crazy-sexy, but I didn't have time to shop), my hair pulled back in a ponytail at my nape, minimal makeup, no jewelry.

I'd looked up how Jean would want to be laid to rest on a website and dressed accordingly.

And that was how I approached the semi-sparse mourners surrounding an unfinished wood casket that might have alarmed me if I hadn't read that website.

Hound had done her right.

Hound was giving her the Jewish burial she would have wanted.

I wondered if they talked about it but I doubted they did.

He wouldn't be able to think of the end of her.

Until he had no choice.

I also wondered what would become of her mezuzah that she cherished so much.

And I hoped Hound asked her rabbi if it was okay to move it to Hound's lintel.

Because that's where she'd want it.

It wasn't shocking to me that the few sitting in the scant seats did not seem to have much reaction to what made the congregation for Jean Gruenberg the "semi" part of semi-sparse.

This being the wall of bikers wearing Chaos cuts that were standing at Hound's (who was standing at the head of the casket) back.

Those others knew Hound was hers.

The only people standing close to him, right at his back, were my boys.

They both looked to me as I approached. Jag gave me a small sad smile. Dutch watched me closely.

I gave them both my own small sad smile then turned my attention to Hound.

He only glanced at me when I arrived.

I drank him in.

"If it wasn't you, it'd be him," I'd teased Black long ago after the first time I'd seen Hound, then a recruit.

"Shut your mouth," Black had said back, amusement laced in his rich voice, not having a problem with what came out of my mouth, knowing he had me.

"He's a looker," I'd said.

"He's a dawg," Black had said.

"So were you," I reminded him.

He'd clamped a hand on my ass, open to him to do that since I was lying on him on a couch in the Compound. "Until you."

This was very true.

I tried not to be smug but it was hard.

Black had grinned up at me.

"He's still something," I'd muttered, turning my head again, looking over Hound's tall, brawny length, disheveled dark-blond hair and his intense stare with those unusual lapis blue eyes that were aimed at the pool table.

"Woman," Black called, and I looked down at him. "He's a good guy. Before we voted him in, coulda stuck a knife in his vein and seen his blood ran Chaos." His hand at my ass squeezed and it was his gorgeous face that had turned smug. "He's also smart like his brother. So don't worry. He'll get himself a hella good old lady."

Black had been wrong.

But I'd tried.

I tore my gaze from the haggard but hard face Hound wore and moved to stand with Chaos. I came to a stop next to one of the brothers, who came after Black, who was standing at the end of the line whose name I wasn't sure about, but I thought it was Roscoe.

Boz reached across him and pulled me in until I was standing between him and High, who I was happy to see had his arm around Millie's shoulders.

Back in the day, she and I had been tight.

Then I, like everyone else, had felt the betrayal when she'd got shot of High.

Now, through Bev, my Chaos grapevine, I knew why she'd done that, and it was the right reason even if it was unbelievably heartbreaking.

I gave her a trembling smile.

For a second, she looked relieved.

Then she returned it.

Boz took my hand.

I tried really hard not to start crying.

Fortunately, I succeeded.

I saw Dog, Brick and Arlo there, and that surprised me. Bev had told me they'd moved to the western slope to expand business operations.

But it shouldn't surprise me.

Hound had lost family.

And they were Hound's family.

They probably rode all night to get here for this.

Bev was there too, far away from Boz. Arlo's arm was slung around her shoulders.

She gave me a look.

I pressed my lips together, sucking them in.

Hers were trembling before she did the same but they curled up a bit, a grimace of a smile.

Bev and I both looked at the casket as someone started talking.

We stood as family for Hound.

But I stood also for Jean.

And I kept standing as they laid her to rest.

After it was over, everyone moved to Hound.

Except me.

I knew some would question it, but those ties were cut.

I definitely came there for him.

But that was the last he was getting from me.

It took a lot to do it.

But Jean would have wanted it that way.

Now it was over.

So after I went to my boys (as close as I was going to get to Hound) and kissed both their cheeks, I walked away.

I felt eyes following me, and when I got in my car, I looked back and knew which ones.

They were not Hound's.

They were Dutch's, which didn't surprise me. He always had an eye on his momma.

They were also Tack's.

And they were his beautiful, redheaded wife's. Tyra.

I lifted my chin to them standing there, Tack's arm around his old lady, her body twisted, front to his side, both her arms around his middle.

Tack's first wife had been a cunt. I'd hated her.

But Tack got his name because he was sharp as a tack. He'd not make the same mistake twice.

From the look of them, I knew that still ran true.

Then I looked to the space where Jean's casket was before they put it in the ground.

"Good-bye, sweet lady," I whispered to my window. "Thanks for taking care of him for so long."

With that, I started my car and drove away.

CHAPTER THIRTEEN

FUCK YOU

Keely

I DIDN'T SEE IT COMING.

It was unlike my boys to play it like that.

But after it was done, I'd realize why.

It started in my kitchen. It was the Sunday afternoon after Jean had died and Hound and I had ended.

I was baking cookies because I was dedicated to the act of dulling the pain of all that had happened through sugar instead of tequila because my life might be over (again), but my life wasn't *over*. My boys didn't need some alcoholic momma swishing in and making a fool of herself during their wedding ceremonies (whenever that happened—for Dutch I hoped it was at least ten years so he'd have some fun for once—for Jag I hoped some woman settled him down in about five).

They came in the back door together.

It was their home and I'd not given them any indication, since they'd both essentially moved out of it and were living together, that they couldn't come and go as they pleased.

But it was me (not Hound or the boys of Chaos, definitely not) that had ingrained politeness in them. So they had the sense this was their home (because it was) but it was mostly now only mine, so they didn't spring themselves on me and texted or phoned to say they were coming by.

This was usually a heads up prior to me making a meal that I should make more to feed them.

But I knew their game. They were checking on their momma, making sure she wasn't lonely, giving her some company.

It was just, if they were going to do that, they were going to get themselves some of her cooking.

For a second I thought that maybe my biological connection with them sent them vibes that I was making cookies, and both my boys loved my cookies, and that had sent them on a trajectory straight to my kitchen, like a homing beacon.

But with one look at the serious on their faces, I knew this was not it.

"What's up, boys?" I asked.

"Hey, Ma," Jagger said.

"Ma," Dutch said.

My eldest came to me first. Putting a hand to my waist, he also bent down and put his lips to my cheek.

I was tall. Black was tall. It was impossible that my boys would not be tall.

So they were both *tall*.

Dutch was taller, taller even than his daddy. He was six-two.

Jag was his father's height, six foot.

Dutch was wearing his prospect cut. It didn't have his name on it or the Chaos insignia patch on the back. Just Prospect at his chest with the arced word Chaos in their Wild West font on the back. His faded jeans hung on him like a girl's wet dream. His black thermal needed to be dumped since it'd been washed so often, it was no longer black. But still, it fit his wide chest like someone had tailored it to match his proportions like armor.

Dutch had always had serious girlfriends. He didn't take a girl out unless he was interested enough that, if she didn't blow it on the first date, he knew he wanted to take her out again.

It was only his first that had broken his heart. Whatever Hound had told him, he'd avoided that in the future with his next two girlfriends and he'd been the heartbreaker.

But he'd done it as sweet as he could.

It still had cut him up.

I'd liked both of his last girlfriends (not that first one, she was beautiful, knew it, so was up her own ass). But for whatever reason Dutch decided they weren't the one, he put an end to it.

I was glad. He was way too young to get serious with a girl. He'd chosen the course of Chaos, but he still had time to put in to find the man he was going to be.

The weird thing was I sensed he knew this. I sensed he wouldn't settle down until he could give the woman he chose the man he intended to be.

That didn't mean he didn't want company along the way.

Jagger was wearing a long-sleeve, gray tee that would, if animate due to its close proximity to his skin, have had to have been in love with him. His jeans were probably selected because they attracted attention to the parts of his lower body that would set a female to drooling. He wore this stuff like his brother, with a casual confidence that was *so* their father. But there was a hint of cocky to Jag.

He knew he was hot.

Dutch probably knew it too. He was just quieter in that knowledge.

They both had great bodies that came partially from genetics, partially from them learning from Hound they should put time into honing them. They still were members of Hound's gym and they both still hung out with the Chaos boys at their workout equipment at the Compound, Dutch now more since he was on Chaos all the time.

So Dutch was bulking up, even in that department larger than his father.

But he was not larger than Hound.

Jag came to me second, doing the same thing and staying close as he sucked in breath through his nose, gave me a jaunty smile and said, "Cookies."

"Yup," I replied, smiling back at him.

"We gotta talk," Dutch put in.

I watched the smile fade from Jagger's face as he stepped away and glanced sideways at his brother.

This was when I mentally prepared for whatever was coming next.

My thoughts were, they were going to tell me their decision about their father's cut and bike.

What was strange about this was I'd told them to make a decision, so I didn't understand why they both were acting so cautiously.

"Jagger called Hound," Dutch announced.

Oh shit.

I hadn't prepared enough.

I shored up my defenses so I would do nothing but hold my boys' eyes and nod.

"He asked Hound to put his name forward officially to recruit," Dutch went on.

Okay.

This was all right.

I was expecting this, though not for a while.

I thought it was too early. I'd like Jag to wait until his brother was a full member. Until after he'd finished school, which would be at the end of May. And then even later.

He wasn't even legal to drink.

Of course, his birthday was next month (he still wouldn't be legal to drink), his brother's birthday came two days after Jag graduated.

Still.

I looked to Jag. "Might be hard to recruit and go to school, Jagger."

"Hound knows that and the brothers know it too. Hound told me it might take longer that way to earn my patch. But they'll give me space to get my degree and I'll still be on the road to the patch," Jagger replied.

He'd thought it through. Discussed it with Hound.

I should have realized with how close my boys were with Hound that I couldn't exactly erase him from my life. He would steer clear. I would steer clear. We'd have the bond of Chaos and have to deal, especially when the boys patched in and I was again sucked deeper into Chaos in the way that would pull me in, which wouldn't be that bad. It wasn't like I was an old lady and expected to show at events or sit on the back of a bike during a ride.

So it was then I realized I'd never be fully quit of Hound, and not because of history old and new, and memories old and new.

But because of my boys who he'd never let go and I wouldn't want him to, but even if for some insane reason I did, they'd never let him go either.

"If you have it worked out, it's your decision, your life, but like your brother, you have my support," I told Jag.

This brought to mind that, years ago, when Dutch first started talking to me about it seriously, I hadn't wanted him to put himself forward to join Chaos.

Hound, of course, had set me straight about that.

In thinking about it the past few days (and months but the last few days especially), I'd realized that was when I'd started to fall in love with him at the same time realizing (finally) he was already gone for me.

He hadn't treated me like porcelain.

He'd laid it out like I was the biker bitch, old lady I damned well was. Like I could take it. Like I had to do what he'd told me to do. Get my head out of my ass and restart my life because I'd let my grief get out of hand.

It hadn't felt good at the time, but in the end, I appreciated it.

I'd also gone out and got myself a short-term man.

It wasn't like I hadn't gotten laid since Graham died. It had taken years but I found one-night stands to deal with the basic needs. It was rare and I went far afield to sort that shit for myself.

But I hadn't found someone that I went back to even twice, much less was with for a few months.

That man didn't last. He wasn't Black. He wasn't even a biker.

But mostly, even though I didn't realize it at the time, he wasn't Hound.

In the end, after Hound had laid it out for me and I'd thought on it and realized he spoke true, I gave Dutch my support for his decision to give his life and loyalty to the brotherhood.

It was what he wanted.

It would make his father ecstatic.

And it was what Hound wanted.

Now, I'd do the same for Jag.

"Thanks, Ma," Jagger replied.

"The Club has shit goin' on so they're sittin' the table tonight and they're gonna vote on a lot of it, including Jag. We all know that's gonna swing Jag's way so he's gonna be a recruit soon," Dutch said. "But he doesn't have a bike and to be a recruit, he's gonna need one."

My gaze slid between my boys and I saw Dutch's face was noncommittal.

I also saw Jag's jaw get slightly hard.

Uh-oh.

They both wanted Graham's cut.

"Jag told me about Dad's cut and his bike and we been talkin'," Dutch continued.

Yeah.

They both wanted their father's cut.

"All right," I said when he didn't go on.

"We can't decide."

Shit.

I didn't want to be in the middle of this. It was already hard enough to give up what I was giving up, even if I knew in my heart it was already theirs. I couldn't make the decision of who got what.

"It really has to be you boys that decide," I told Dutch.

"We can't," Dutch said firmly. "So we asked Hound to come over and help us make the decision."

What?

Shit.

No.

Fuck!

No!

"He's gonna be here in a few," Jagger put in.

Shit!

No!

I hid all this from my sons. I had no choice.

And I wondered what Hound was thinking.

He had to know the meet wouldn't be here if I wasn't here. If they wanted to talk just to him, they'd meet at the Compound or at Hound's or at Dutch's.

A swift wave of hope washed through me that maybe, since some time had passed since Jean died, he'd seen the error of his ways with how he'd touched me, what he'd said to me, and he was using this as his in.

I rode that wave and let it crash me to the shore, because the way he was, what he thought, I found it very doubtful he'd reflect on that and come to the correct conclusions.

But also, what he thought, there was no going back.

In all this madness, it did not give me any warm fuzzies to note how both my boys, particularly Dutch, were watching me so closely.

It could just be they got how tough it was for me to let go of the final two, most important pieces of their father.

It could be something else I didn't want to contemplate.

They knew me, even Jagger was watchful of me, tuned to me. And they both were tight with Hound. I knew they'd spent time with him that week. Jag had mentioned being mildly pissed that Hound hadn't shared Jean with him and Dutch, but he wasn't letting the fullness of that through because it would interfere with the support he was giving Hound now that he'd lost her.

It sucked I was glad Hound had that from my sons.

I was still glad he had that from my sons.

"While we're waiting," I said nonchalantly, "do either of you want cookies?"

Jag slid another sideways glance at his brother that continued not to give me warm fuzzies.

Never had I offered either of them cookies when they hadn't pounced. They actually never even waited for me to offer. They took their bodies seriously. They still ate the shit out of my cookies.

"Yeah," Dutch murmured, finally moving forward.

"Cool, Ma. Thanks," Jagger said, like always, if Dutch gave the approval (or not) in a certain situation, Jagger followed his brother's lead.

They ate cookies.

I took the last tray out of the oven, turned it off, and was in the act of scraping the cookies off and onto a wire cooling rack when the back door opened and Hound strode through.

He didn't even knock.

That was new.

Actually, the back door was new.

He usually came to the front.

And knocked.

One look at his handsome, blank face told me what he was thinking in accepting the meet with my boys with me in attendance.

He was a badass biker who lived life wild, took it by the throat, and shoved aside anything he didn't want in it.

I'd been shoved aside.

He was over me.

"We gonna do this shit in the kitchen?" he asked.

Not even a greeting for my boys.

I stared at that handsome, blank face.

It had been studiously blank for years, trying to hide what his actions screamed, how deep he felt for me.

That was different now.

It was just all gone.

Two months of watching him smile, laugh, climax, tease me, get pissed at me, it was all swept away, shoved aside, and he was moving on.

No, he'd moved on.

Standing in my own damned kitchen after he'd slammed me against the wall, caused me physical pain using my own fucking hair. Hair he'd slid his fingers through. Hair he'd wound around his fist. Hair he'd tangled his hand in while I went down on him. While doing that, he'd said the vile things he'd said to me.

And it was him that had moved on.

Fuck him.

"Let's move this to the living room," I said, and then I put down the tray, took off the oven glove and started them doing just that.

My house looked like the women who owned that Junk Gypsy business had come in, taken over and gone a little insane.

It was all, every inch wild and bold, bright colors, clashing prints (except the boys' rooms, which I'd let them decorate, the extent of this being motorcycle, souped-up cars and mostly-nude women posters as well as dirty clothes on the floor).

I even had a round copper tub in the middle of my bathroom that was tarnished green on the outside, had a checkerboard of mismatched-colored square tile floors, a piece of distressed furniture made into a basin, red walls with stuff all over them, including a huge mirror with a wide, stamped-tin frame.

It was totally over the top.

I loved it.

Black would have loved to hate it.

And I loved that too.

Hound, I had no idea. He existed in his surroundings, filling them up with his badass biker vibe, but they didn't matter to him in the slightest.

The last two months I'd wondered (often) if we'd both fit in my tub.

Now, I'd never know.

My living room we walked into had a red-orange velvet sofa and matching armchair, both nearly taken over with huge teal velour pillows mixed with ones covered in burnt-orange patterns with thick, little tufts of fringe around the sides. The wood floor was topped with a huge rug patterned in reds, golds, bricks, teals and browns that might cause a headache if all the other prints weren't clashing with it, adjusting the eye to sheer design insanity. Gold-based lamps with shades that had a complicated print in hues of brick red sat on the two end tables.

This fed into the dining room that had a long, tall dining room table with bright red stools around it, ten of them, like I had huge dinner parties where I played happy hostess to all my friends.

Which I did not.

Mostly because, over the years, Bev had become my only true friend.

But maybe I would.

Maybe I'd ask some of those straight-laced, middle-of-the-road, hadn't-tossed-back-a-shot-of-tequila-since-high school people I worked with over for a biker bitch meal that'd knock their socks off.

I'd tell them to Uber their asses to my house.

Then I'd get them drunk out of their brains and show them how to live.

How to burn bright.

How to *tear life up*.

When I took my position opposite my gold-rimmed glass coffee table and faced off with Hound, I fought tossing my hair, because if he wasn't going to give me anything, I sure as shit wasn't going to give *him* anything.

Hound stood behind my couch, my dining room table behind him.

Both the boys stood to the side, opposite the armchair.

"Right, Hound, told you Jagger and me gotta make an important decision about some seriously important shit and we can't," Dutch started it, not earning Hound's regard.

He hadn't looked at me since he walked into my kitchen.

He'd been about blanking me out and the boys.

So Dutch already had Hound's regard.

"What I didn't say was that Ma's ready to let go of Dad's cut and his bike, and me and Jag gotta pick which one is gonna get which," Dutch carried on.

At that, Hound's gaze sliced to me.

I didn't move. Didn't even lift my chin.

I just took it for a beat before I looked back at my boys.

"We can't pick which gets which, we both want both, but most of all, we both want Dad's cut," Dutch shared. "And Ma won't say which one of us Dad would have wanted to have what."

"If your father was here, he'd give you his cut, Dutch," Hound's deep voice sounded immediately. "And he'd give Jag his bike."

I was not surprised Hound came to the same conclusion I did. I was also not surprised that Dutch took this without reaction but Jag took it trying to hide being pissed, which meant disappointed.

"If he knew he'd end when he did, though," Hound kept going, "he'd have made it clear to your mother that you should get the bike, Dutch, and Jag would get his cut 'cause he'd feel it, he didn't have more time with his youngest boy. And he'd know you'd become the kind of man who'd get that."

Okay, now that was just uncanny.

And now I was noticing Dutch was having trouble holding back his reaction and Jag looked relieved.

"It was up to me," Hound continued, and my gaze shot to him because he'd never said dick about what he felt if it was up to him.

He did, always, what he felt Black would do with the boys.

He'd never given his own opinion.

"Way you manned up early to look after your ma and your brother, you'd get Black's cut and Jag," Hound's attention moved to Jagger, "you'd get his bike. It might suck, son, and it might not seem fair. But you think hard on it, you'll understand that circumstances gave your brother two more years of your daddy but not at a time when he could get what he needed outta that. At a time when the time would come when he'd need to step up in a way a boy wouldn't have to if he had his father. And you didn't have to do that. You got to be you. So in one way, your brother earned that cut. In another, it's an expression of gratitude for the brother he was to you that you'd give it to him. Sayin' all that, Black had a shit-hot bike. So you aren't exactly getting a bad deal."

God, *God*.

I hated it that I so totally loved him and he was standing right there in my own goddamned living room demonstrating one of the reasons why when he was such a huge, motherfucking *dick*.

It occurred to me I was glaring at him so I stopped doing that, fortunately just in time to feel my youngest boy's eyes come to me.

"Ma?"

I looked to Jagger. "I'm not in this," I said, and when his expression grew impatient, I carried on, saying, "But Hound speaks sense."

Disappointment slid to devastation and my stomach clutched before Jag did what the blood in Jag's veins guided him to do. What the direction Hound had been giving him most of his life guided him to.

He turned to Dutch and said, "You take Dad's cut, man. I'll take his bike."

Dutch gave him a beat before he asked, "You sure?"

"No," Jagger answered immediately. "But Hound's right. You earned it."

Something came over my eldest son's face that settled low in my gut in a beautiful way, and I knew from the vibe Jagger was now giving off that he saw it and felt the same thing when Dutch murmured, "Thanks, Jag."

"You become a brother and ride my ass as a recruit more than the other brothers, I earn my own patch, I'll kick your ass," Jag returned. But I knew from the tone of his voice he felt the extent of his brother's gratitude, it meant a great deal to him, and he knew this was the way it should be.

Still, he was going to give him shit.

And there it was.

Brothers being brothers.

Dutch just grinned at him.

And again there it was.

Proof, if my oldest wanted to be a player, panties would be dropping all over Denver.

I looked to the ceiling.

"We done here?" Hound asked.

I looked to him and again had to fight back my glare.

"Uh . . ." Jag started.

"Just—" Dutch began.

"We're done here," Hound decreed and honed in on Jagger. "Men are meeting in a coupla hours. Be at the Compound. We'll call you in after we vote." And with but a glance cut sharply through the boys, though not me, he ended it, saying, "Later."

Then he strolled across the living room toward my front door.

He'd fence me in with his bike, and probably did, since he had no problem parking it right behind my side of the garage, and I'd never said anything to him about that.

It wasn't the time to say anything about that, because I had a feeling this would be the last time he'd ever be in my house.

No.

It was the time to say something else.

"Eat cookies," I ordered my sons. "I'll be back."

And with that, I marched out behind Hound.

I knew he had to know I was following him after I opened and closed (okay, slammed) the front door he'd already been through.

He still didn't even hesitate as he walked through the early March Denver sunshine to his bike, not even turning to look at me.

Yep.

Parked fencing me in.

I waited until he'd swung a meaty thigh over his bike (Lord, I loved that man's thighs—focus, Keely!) but I got in there before he made it roar.

"A coupla minutes, you can find that in you, Hound," I called.

He was facing front, and at my call only turned his head to the side.

But he didn't turn on his bike toward me.

When I made it to him, I found it fortuitous that I could look down at him.

His long torso was proportioned well with his long legs so I didn't get to look *too* far down on him.

But at least I could look down at him.

"First, the preliminaries, and no matter the colossal motherfucking dick you've proved yourself to be, it has to be said, I'm very sorry about Jean," I declared to start.

The blank left his face, and I felt him rocket right to fury, not at me bringing up Jean, at me calling him a colossal dick, but I did not give that first shit.

"Second," I kept going before he could even open his mouth, "it's clear you misinterpreted what I was doing when I was at your scales tat. If you even have a *smidge* of respect left for me, you'll allow me to explain that I was trying, like I had been for two fucking months, to guide you to a place where you'd get past feeling you were being disloyal to your brother, where you'd get to the point you were willing to face what the brotherhood might land on you if they knew we'd become what we'd become, and you'd fight to make it to the other side with me."

"Do not try to feed me this shit, woman," he rumbled.

That pissed me off (more).

But I ignored him and kept talking like he had not.

"In all we had, and there was a lot, one of the things I felt was beautiful, not the most beautiful, other stuff we had was far more beautiful, but I still thought it was beautiful, and that was that we both had him. We both loved him. He loved both of us. I'm sure you'll twist this, and hey, it might be twisted. But I don't give a shit. I loved that. I loved that you got what he was to me. I loved that wasn't something I'd ever have to explain or hide. I loved that you loved him so much you had him inked into your body. I loved that he wasn't between us, he was a part of us. *Both of us.* I loved that I got to have something new and beautiful with you at the same time I got to share him with you. And last, I loved you had that reaper and would understand how important it was to be smart and stay safe so you wouldn't be torn away from the people who love you."

I also ignored how his expression had now changed.

The fury was gone.

Shock had replaced it.

"Then you put him between us," I went on. "Dragged his spirit right there not like the shield you'd been using, but like a weapon. That I *didn't* love, Hound. That was fucked up. And how you put your hands on me made it worse."

His face started to soften and warm and he turned his torso my way so he was sitting on his bike still, but fully facing me.

"Keely—"

I talked over him.

I had to.

He'd had his chance.

He wasn't getting in there again.

"For two months you didn't pay one single bit of attention to one single *fucking* thing I did. Not one, Hound. Not that first one. If you did, you'd know I knew *precisely* whose cock I was sucking. Whose cock I was fucking. Whose cock I," I leaned toward him, "*invited* up my ass because it was damned important to give that to you. To make sure *you* knew you had something of me he never got. To make sure *you* knew I was inviting you inside me *every way I could take you.* You missed that, Hound. You missed it, but you had enough hold on it to twist it into something ugly and foul and shove it in my face while you had your fist in my hair and you made us done. So just to confirm, I got your message and we're done. *So fucking done.*"

"Baby—" he tried to get in.

I did not let him.

"Now, you gave my boys that," I flung my arm behind me, "and as ever, I appreciate it. What I would appreciate from this point on is if they need something like that and you're gonna be in my space, you give me a heads up. I don't wanna see you. I don't wanna breathe your air. But you mean the world to my boys so I'm not gonna get that. So again, if you have any respect left for me, give me warning I gotta endure your presence. Yeah?"

"Keekee—" he whispered, his expression now haggard, like he wore it at Jean's graveside.

God.

Christ.

"Fuck you," I whispered back. "I'll never forgive you for what you thought of me, what you did to us. Fuck you for not being the man I thought you were. Fuck you for not being the man I needed you to be."

That did not get me haggard.

That got me *wrecked*.

"Kee—"

He cut himself off because I had to end it there before his reaction started working on me.

So I turned and trooped up to the house, fighting real hard not to do it running.

I slammed the door behind me and stomped right to the stairs, starting up them, yelling, "Enjoy the cookies. After that big decision got made, Momma needs a bubble bath."

And hearing Hound's bike roar outside, I realized I really, *really* did.

Motherfucking *dick*!

"Ma," Dutch growled in a way I turned halfway up to look down to see him at the foot, staring up, Jagger coming to stand by his side. "You sort your shit with Hound?"

I stared back at him, my heart tripping over itself, fast, furious and full of fear.

In the time my sons had been spending with him after Jean, had Hound shared?

"What shit?" I asked.

"You two bein' broken up," Jag said.

Oh *fuck*.

He'd shared.

"What did Hound tell you?" I snapped.

"Nothin'," Dutch said. "Hound cleaning up his place, clearing out old furniture to get new and your car at his pad told us. Jag went up once, didn't see your car, just wanted to see Hound's new shit, and heard you in his apartment, laughing with him. When he left, that's when he saw your car."

Shit.

Shit, shit, *shit*.

"You know about Jean. You were at the funeral. You didn't even walk up to him, say that first word. What the fuck's up with you dumping him right when he lost that old lady?" Dutch asked.

Oh my God.

My boys were taking Hound's side.

Before I could answer, Jagger threw his own question in. "And did you know her? Like, before. When she was alive?"

"Shortly," I pushed out.

That visibly did not make either of my sons happy.

"I get you kept shit under wraps with Hound, though you coulda told us and not snuck around like a goddamned teenager," Dutch clipped. "But it woulda been nice to have met a woman that meant what that old lady did to Hound."

Um, excuse me?

It wasn't *me* who kept Jean from my boys.

"And speakin' a' that," Jagger butted in again before I could make a peep, "you're our mother and he's been our stepdad without sleepin' with our mom for, oh . . . I don't know, fuckin' *ever*," he bit out his last. "Maybe call a family meal with Hound where he should have been for about the last decade, at our table, and say, 'Okay, boys, your momma and your Hound have finally got their heads outta their asses and we're doin' this. Now pass the mashed potatoes.'"

That was kinda funny.

I was not laughing.

"This isn't any of either of your business," I told them truthfully.

"And that's full of shit," Dutch shot back. "Because you're ours and he's ours and we've been a fuckin' family since Dad died, and we got a shot at makin' that real and somehow it got dicked up and that's impossible because he loves you like Tack loves Cherry, like Hop loves Lanie, and you know what that kinda thing means. Now we arrange this so you two will be forced to get your heads outta your asses, *again*, and you're having a bubble bath and Hound's . . . whatever the fuck he's doin'."

So they'd arranged this.

They obviously needed help making the decision and knew only Hound could offer that guidance. But they didn't need me.

They just made it so Hound and I could have the confrontation we'd just had.

Regrettably, they thought it would go another way.

It didn't. And they were my sons but I didn't owe them an explanation.

I also didn't need them piling this on me.

"Again, this isn't your business," I declared, and when both opened their mouths to speak, I kept at them. "It isn't. Hound and I are done and how that happened is not yours to have. I know you love him. I know you love me. I get what you're saying. What you need to get is, a breakup is a breakup for a reason, there's always pain involved, sometimes more, sometimes less. This time, it's more. A lot more. So think on that and back," I lost it a little, leaning down toward them before I finished, "*off.*"

They looked stubborn.

They also looked contrite.

God, I so *knew* neither of them would have a problem with Hound and me.

It didn't matter.

It was over.

The contrite won out.

"You ever need to talk," Dutch said quietly.

"I love you, boy, but I'm your mother. I'm not talking to you about my love life," I replied, trying to do it gentle, but for God's sake.

I needed a bubble bath!

"We just don't get it. He's been so into you for so long, we thought, when you finally noticed that you'd . . ." Jagger trailed off.

Oh I did.

"Can we stop talking about this?" I asked.

"Yeah, Ma," Dutch answered quickly.

"But—" Jag started.

Dutch kicked the side of Jag's boot with the side of his.

Jag shut up.

"Ziplocs. Take as many cookies as you want," I told them. "And lock up when you leave."

"Right, Ma," Dutch said.

"Right," Jag muttered.

I looked over my two handsome sons.

"Love you boys," I said, and that came out gentle.

"Love you too," Dutch said.

"Yeah, Ma, love you too," Jag muttered.

I let my gaze rest on them for another second.

Then I dashed up the steps to run my bubble bath.

It wasn't until I was in it that it hit me that Jagger was getting Black's bike, Dutch getting his father's cut.

Just like Graham would want.

Hound had wrangled that.

On that thought, the first tear fell.

Damn it.

So after that thought, I slapped my face in the water in front of me and kept it there until I had to pull it out to breathe.

CHAPTER FOURTEEN

I LOST COUNT

Keely

THAT NIGHT, I STARED AT the dark outside the window in my kitchen, eating a cookie, my phone to my ear.

The boys had left me six cookies.

I should probably have been grateful they'd left me that.

It was coming on to late. I'd had my bath and gone gung ho. I gave my legs a clean, close shave since I hadn't shaved once since the day of Jean's funeral seeing as I was no longer fucking Hound, so I felt I didn't need to see to that little chore.

I also gave myself a facial because I would never, *ever* attempt to catch another man's attention, but that didn't mean I wasn't going to have the best skin I could until the day I died.

And I'd done the hot oil pack on my hair that made it gleam even more than it naturally gleamed (God loved me and I knew this because he gave me Black for the time I had him, he gave me my beautiful boys, and he gave me long legs, a great ass, a metabolism most women would kill for and fabulously shining hair).

I was now in undies and my red robe that hit me several inches above my knees, had three-quarter sleeves that were wide and feminine, almost bell but not quite, and was made of this soft cotton-knit material that was supposed to keep you warm or cool, whatever way you needed it.

And it did.

I was also on the phone with Bev.

"So it's probably official," I told her through my cookie munching. "I expect a phone call any minute telling me Jagger is a Chaos recruit. Or one from Dutch since the boys will get Jag smashed out of his brain to the point he'll puke his guts out for the next week."

"Happy for you, Keely," Beverly replied softly.

Her tone brought me up straight.

She and Boz never had kids.

This was because Boz had repeatedly cheated on her while they were dating. Though, as far as I knew, he never did that shit while they were married.

Except once.

The reason she left him.

And after she did and tried to reconcile, he never took her back.

I did know Boz was one of those bikers who was of the mind that priorities in life came in a certain order: Club, brotherhood, freedom, bike, country, and if he wasn't an atheist, God. If he had enough of him left over on a certain day to give a shit, last came his woman.

In other words, he thought he could do exactly what he wanted and anyone in his life had to put up with that.

Bev had been all in for that, mostly. She loved him. She was not a nag. She got the life. In fact, she *loved* the life. She loved the Club. She was about freedom, country, God, having a good time, being among people where she could be herself, and she dug Boz on his bike.

What she wasn't a big fan of was Boz sleeping with women who were not her.

She put up with it before she had his ring (this might have started her problem, though I wondered if he'd have ended things with her if she'd tried to put a stop to it before she'd accepted his ring).

She put her foot down when she got it.

This caused their first marital fight. One of many. That seemingly (to a woman) natural but important request when she gave him the freedom to be everything else he needed, she didn't get why he couldn't give her. But he railed against it, mostly with fighting with her, sometimes with getting caught necking or groping women, not her.

Though, until the end, as far as I knew, he'd never taken it all the way, that made no never mind to me. I was not of that mentality. Necking was a form of cheating, groping, definitely.

Fortunately, Black had agreed with me.

It was me for him and him for me, totally.

That didn't help, Bev having to watch Black and me (while Black was alive). And how totally devoted High was to Millie. And the fact that it seemed Tack could barely stand the sight of his first wife, Naomi, but he'd never strayed.

The other brothers, back then, felt the same way Boz did, which solidified Boz's position (to Boz).

Through Bev, I'd heard that had turned somewhat around with everything Tack had turned around in the Club.

Now Tack, Hop, Dog, and the new brothers, Joker and Shy, not to mention now Millie was back, so High as well, were all devoted to their old ladies like High had been with Millie way back in the day.

Like Black was with me.

In other words, during their marriage, more fights surfaced when Beverly refused to give Boz a baby if he refused to give her his fidelity.

In the end, he'd refused.

And in the end, I thought she was upset that she'd held out, and even now apart didn't have a part of him like I had so much of Black through my sons, but just simply the fact she didn't have her own family.

She loved my boys. Unlike my own sister, and Graham's (a long, ugly story), she was a great auntie to them and always had been.

She also still loved the Club, keeping her finger on the pulse and having earned the respect of the brothers who she could, in her way.

She was definitely happy for me, for Jag, that he'd taken up his father's legacy.

I knew by her voice it still stung she had no son to take on that legacy.

"You need to break up with that guy," I announced suddenly.

"Keely—" she began.

"You totally need to break up with that guy," I repeated.

"Boz is never getting back with me," she replied.

"So?" I asked. "He lost out. Hold out for what you want."

"There aren't many of them out there."

"Who cares? Hold out for one."

"You know, I still live mostly paycheck to paycheck."

The abrupt sharpness of her tone had my back coming up again.

"Beverly—"

"He's an insurance salesman. A good one. He makes good money. His clients love him. He's very likable on the whole, actually. He could sell the London Bridge back to the people who bought the wrong one, even pointing out it was the wrong one, that's how good of a salesman he is. And he thinks he scored with me."

"He did," I shared, because Boz might be a little goofy, but Bev was like a biker babe cheerleader, all exuberance and sweetness and liveliness and affability, totally "Go Team!" with the bright-eyed, girl-next-door looks that matched.

"I'm just so fucking tired of it all," she stated.

And the way she stated that sounded like she wasn't tired, she was exhausted.

"Tired of what?" I asked quietly.

"Everything. Paying the bills. Dealing with the roof leaking. Buying all the groceries. Putting them away. Having to unload the dishwasher. Even me being the only one putting dishes in the damned thing."

"The boys would deal with your roof," I offered, knowing it was lame.

But they would.

"You know," she began in a tone that made me, already vigilant in our conversation, start to brace, "you and me, we gave everything to that Club. They didn't ask for it. It was *us* who gave them everything. And it's been a long time that I've been wondering if we haven't wasted the best years of our lives in loyalty to a bunch of men who, for your part, gave back out of guilt, and for my part, didn't even want it."

"Bev," I whispered.

She was still my friend because unlike everyone else, early on, she'd pulled off the kid gloves with me.

But I'd never heard her say anything like that.

"So I'm gonna marry an insurance salesmen who wouldn't know his way to a woman's clit if he had a fifty-page instruction booklet, but he loves me. He'd never cheat on me. He's over the moon I said yes. He came over Friday night with this basket his secretary made, filled with bridal magazines, and champagne and pretty flutes and a box of chocolates, and Post-it notes, saying we were going to spend the evening going through the magazines and he wanted me to stick a note on anything I loved."

Wow.

That was sweet.

She kept going.

"So I have to spend some time introducing him to my clit. And I never felt with him the way I felt when I made Boz laugh. Whatever. He's one thing Boz is not. Chaos is not. Good for me."

"I—" I started to say something but I heard my front door open.

I turned that way.

The boys usually came in the back. It wasn't unheard of for them to come in the front.

But they usually came in the back.

Maybe Dutch was there to tell me in person they'd taken his brother on as recruit (Jag would be celebrating, though tomorrow, even as sick as a dog as he'd be, he'd be cleaning up the mess of the celebration afterward, starting at oh-dark-hundred, no matter what that mess might be).

Though it was a given Chaos would take him on, so I couldn't imagine why one of the boys didn't just text me.

"Can you just be happy for me and try to help me find the way to happy?" Bev asked.

I couldn't answer.

Not immediately.

Hound stood in the double-wide doorway to my kitchen.

Chaos cut. White thermal. Faded jeans that did things to his substantial package any woman, even one not into bikers, would give her favorite pair of shoes, her most beloved handbag and anything else that was requested for a shot at. Hair unkempt and wild from his ride, falling over his forehead and into those beautiful blue eyes that were wary and locked on me.

In other words, hot.

In other words, if he wasn't such a motherfucking dick, and I wasn't on the phone with Bev, I'd take about a second to think about it.

Then I'd pounce.

It was then I cursed the day I'd had double-paned windows put in to replace the old ones. With the rest of the built-to-last house, back in the kitchen, I never heard a bike approach. I never heard anything.

Damn it.

And he had a key.

A lot of the guys had keys.

Definitely Hound.

Damn it!

I stared (okay, glared) in his guarded eyes and fought throwing my half-eaten cookie at him.

"Keely?" Bev called.

"I can do that," I told her.

The relief reached through the phone at me. "Thanks, babe."

"I think one of the boys is trying to get through to tell me about tonight's meet," I said.

It wasn't a lie.

Hound was one of the boys.

"Okay, text me even though you don't really need to text me. Text me anyway," she requested.

"You got it. We'll talk more about your wedding later. Especially the bachelorette party."

Hound's head tipped to the side and his eyes went to my phone at my ear.

The gratitude was practically dripping from her repeat of, "Thanks, babe."

"I'll text later and we'll plan some facetime," I replied.

"You got it. Later, Keely."

"Later, babe."

I took my phone from my ear and made sure the call was disconnected before I caught Hound's gaze again and opened my mouth to blast him.

He got there before me.

"You said what you had to say earlier, baby," he said gently, his deep voice wrapped around the words like a snuggly blanket. "I couldn't get into that with you with the boys here and the meeting coming up. The meeting's done. Jag's in. So now I'm here so we can talk this shit out."

"You said all that needed to be said, Hound," I pointed out. "The only thing left right now for you to do is leave your key and get out of my house."

"Keely—"

"Get out of my house."

"Baby—"

Right.

Enough!

I threw the cookie at him, it bounced off his shoulder, fell to the floor, and I shrieked, *"Get out of my house!"*

He stared at me a beat (and I'll note, did this and did not get out of my house) then his eyes dropped to the cookie on the floor.

Okay, the cookie was a loser move and I shouldn't have let him see me lose my cool like that, especially on a loser move that huge, but he wasn't *getting out of my house*.

He looked back to me.

"You threw a cookie at me," he stated.

Were his lips quirking?

Oh no, they were *not*.

But they were.

They were quirking!

"Do you find something funny?" I asked dangerously, slowly reaching out to put my phone on the counter so I didn't throw that at him too.

"You threw a cookie at me." His eyes glanced down at it and back at me before he amended, "Half a cookie."

"This is not funny, Hound."

He wiped his face clean of amusement.

"Jean had died," he said quietly.

"That's no excuse."

He flinched.

Christ.

Hound *flinched*.

Still with the quiet. "My head was messed up."

"You didn't fail to communicate that to me," I shared sarcastically.

"You're right, I missed the signs."

That admission had me clamming right up.

"Been playin' it in my head since I took off earlier," he told me. "Got no idea what votes I cast at the meeting tonight and they were important. I don't give a fuck. All I could think about was you. What you said. What you'd been doin'. All I'd missed. And gettin' my ass back here to work this out."

That felt good.

But it wasn't enough.

"It's too late," I shared.

"Babe—"

"I'd forgive anything from you, Hound. *Anything*," I stressed. "Not because you stood on my back walk with the blood of Black's murderer all over you. Not because all you gave my boys. But because all you are *to me*. That, what you said, what you thought I'd done, I can't forgive."

"You came apart when he died," he reminded me.

"Of course I did," I snapped. "I loved him. He was my husband. He was the father of my sons. And he'd had his throat slit. So of course I did, Hound. But that was seventeen, almost eighteen fucking years ago."

"You put yourself back together two months ago, Keely, and don't try to tell me that wasn't when it happened. That was when it happened. You gave him that amount of grief, suddenly you're at my crib, strippin' buck naked, comin' on to me, what the fuck did you think I'd think?"

"Not that I was out for my biker bang," I hissed.

His mood started deteriorating, and I could tell it not only by his vibe but by his voice.

"No indication, nothin' before that and suddenly you're naked in my living room, Keekee."

"You know me better than that."

"Didn't hear dick about you givin' up Black's cut and his bike until after I blew my stack with you. So what's that, babe? You held on even when you were with me so let's get to the real of this. You weren't ready to let go until you realized how far we'd gone and thought it was lost."

He wanted to get to the real of this?

Well, we'd do just that.

"If his bones could talk, Hound, they'd tell you about the visit I took to them right before I showed at your apartment that first time and shared with him right at his gravestone that he was going to have to suck it up and let you have me because I wanted you, and he had to let me be free."

That was when Hound clamped his mouth shut.

"So yeah, that last scene at your place . . ." I nodded. "Yeah. It was time to totally let go. But that was more about my boys being twenty-one and nineteen, almost twenty-two and twenty, and finally getting what was their due from their father. I can't say it didn't have to do with that shit that went down with you. What I can say is it would have come earlier, except I was spending so much time trying to get through to you, I didn't have time to do that. When we were done, I took that time. And now it's done. All of it."

"We're not done," he growled.

"You made the call, Hound. I just answered it."

"I found her."

"Yeah you did," I purred, leaning back suggestively, then leaned forward and bit, "And you lost her."

"I'm not talkin' about you, Keely. I found Jean dead."

I shut up.

"Would only ever be me and I thanked fuck she had me or who knows how long she'd be lyin' dead in her bed before someone found her," he shared.

Okay.

Shit.

God.

He'd found her.

I hadn't thought of that but of course he did.

God.

"Hound—"

"My head was messed up with you and I know for a goddamned, fuckin' *fact* if I hadn't lost Jean and it hadn't been me that found her, spent the day with paramedics, at the hospital, callin' her rabbi, sortin' shit out 'cause Jews try to get their own put in the ground as soon as they can, I woulda listened. I was in no mood to listen. And you might not think that's an excuse, babe. But I loved her, and I held her cold dead hand and I knew she'd died right beyond a damned wall from where I was, died all alone, so you'd be wrong."

I would.

He was right.

I was wrong.

It was an excuse.

"Now," he kept at me, "you say you can't forgive I put him between us, *you* didn't put the shit out there you needed to put out there even *knowin'* I had that shit messin' with my head. And don't pretend you don't know what I'm talkin' about. You gave it to me earlier standin' by me on my bike. You didn't tell me your goals with comin' to me and you knew I'd put him right there between us. And you touched your mouth to him on my body and you knew then I lost it about that and you still didn't say dick. So I blew my stack and I fucked up huge. But you played a game with massive stakes not lettin' me in on what would be the ultimate prize and life kicked me right in the balls in the middle of shit takin' us to where we'd hammer it all out, and I fucked up. I did it huge. You laid it out. And I'm here. So, where we goin' now, Keely? You gonna hold on and cut me out and die alone one day? Or are we gonna find our way past this and figure out what's next with the boys, with the brothers, and fight our way to the other side?"

There was a lot about that I could argue.

But in that second, I wondered what was the point.

Because I wanted to fight my way to the other side with Hound.

I had no idea what I should say to communicate that, I just needed to say something.

It came out, "Hound—"

But that was all that got out.

He lifted up a hand, palm my way.

"Before you say dick, first, I'm fuckin' Shep to you and second, even when I was still pissed at you, convinced you'd played me for my cock, I couldn't sleep remembering the way I put my hands on you. So I'm standing here giving you my vow that will never happen again. Never, Keely. Whatever comes of this, we work it out, whatever comes our way, you never have to fear that from me again. Not ever. If you give me nothing from makin' that ride from the Compound to here to have this out, I gotta beg you to give me that."

I gotta beg you to give me that.

"I knew that was about Jean," I whispered.

He stared at me half a beat before he closed his eyes and turned his head away.

Oh yeah.

Even ticked at me, thinking what he thought of me, that's what had him sleepless.

He could have done worse, a big guy like him, absolutely.

But what he'd done to me, I wondered, even though I'd forgiven him, if that was something he could forgive in himself.

"I already forgave you for that," I told him.

He opened his eyes and looked at me.

Hope.

Oh my God.

His eyes, Hound's eyes, that crazy-cool, bright lapis blue, were shining with hope.

He really, totally fucked up.

But he really, totally loved me.

"The boys know about us," I shared. "You having the recruits clean it then clear it out and you got new stuff, Jag came around to check it out. Saw my car at your place. I think both of them did. My guess, repeatedly. Jag even came up and heard us in your apartment together."

The hope fled and aggravation took its place.

"Fuckin' you?" he asked.

"Laughing," I answered.

He blew out a breath.

I almost giggled.

Instead, I shared, "They're mad at me because they thought I broke up with you right when you lost Jean."

That sent his brows up. "No shit?"

"I'd appreciate you disabusing them of the notion that their mother is the cold-hearted bitch who dumped 'their' Hound, and that's what Dutch called you, 'ours,' right when a woman he cared about died."

"I'll get on that later," he replied.

"They like us together. They, well . . . want us together."

Hound said nothing to that.

But the hope came back.

He was hot. I loved looking at him. I'd always loved looking at him. Even when I had Black.

But he'd never been more beautiful to me.

"So, it's kinda just the brothers we have to win around," I kept babbling.

"Babe?" he asked.

"What?" I asked back.

"How can you make just a robe look so fucking gorgeous?"

And man, he thought I was hot too because this robe was nothing.

I shrugged. "Maybe because I have nothing on but panties underneath."

Again the hope fled but this time something that made my nipples tingle took its place.

"Am I fucking you on the kitchen table?" he asked.

My pussy saturated with wet and my legs turned to jelly.

By a miracle, I remained standing.

"Yes, please," I whispered.

And suddenly there I was, back to the kitchen table, panties down my legs, feeling Hound's hand work between them, then feeling his cock drive into me.

Okay, maybe I let him get off easy.

But I suspected I was now going to get off a whole lot easier, so it was worth it.

We could hammer out the details later.

Now, I was all in for my man to hammer *me*.

My back arched into him and I lifted both my hands to fist them in the back of his hair.

He thrust into me, bent over me, eyes locked to mine.

"Do you know how many times I thought about fuckin' you on this table?" he asked on a grunt.

"How many?" I asked (or kinda panted) back.

"I lost count," he answered.

"Hmm," I mumbled, wrapping my legs around his hips.

He started going harder, his face growing darker, his arm curling around the top of my head to drive me down into his thrusts.

Nice.

"Kiss me, Shep," I begged.

"No," he declined.

"No?" I asked.

"Gonna watch you get fucked on your kitchen table and gonna watch you come for me right here. I'll kiss you after."

My whole body shuddered.

I was in for that plan.

His lips twitched.

"That's my Keekee," he muttered. "She likes it like that."

"Just ride it, cowboy," I breathed, and God, a week without him, it just took his cock and him pounding into my clit to tumble right over. I got there like a shot, dug my heels into his ass and whispered, "Shep."

"Go," he grunted.

I went. I did it loud. I did it hard. I did it long. It was fabulous. And in the middle of it, I felt Hound topple over with me.

Lord, I loved listening to him come. The rolling, snarling, low groan he always gave me made my pussy ripple automatically in response.

When I was done and started to resurface, I realized he wasn't gliding.

He was in, all the way, buried deep and still watching me.

Yeah.

Hound was in.

All the way.

Buried deep.

"Baby," I said softly.

That was when he kissed me.

I let go of his hair with my fists but held the back of his head in both my hands and kissed him back.

I thought he'd make it last a long time. I mean, it was a makeup kiss after all.

He didn't.

And when he spoke again, I was glad he didn't.

"I'm so fuckin' sorry I laid that shit on you, baby. You said we land the heavy on people we care about the most because we think they'll forgive us but it isn't cool. And that wasn't cool. But fuck, I was feelin' so much I could not see past it, and then you opened that door and it boiled over and I came at you like I did and—"

"Hound, Shep, baby," I cooed, running my hands over his hair, letting them come to rest at the sides of his head. "I get it."

"I loved him."

I went still.

Hound was inside me on the kitchen table in the house Black had bought me where I raised his boys . . . with Hound.

"I would not forgive him for this," he whispered.

"Are you going to make me happy?" I asked.

"I'm gonna fuckin' try," he answered.

"Then yes you would."

He stared in my eyes before he shoved his face in my neck.

Okay, suffice it to say, I'd underestimated the battle Hound would wage within himself taking what belonged to a brother, even one that was no longer breathing to claim it, we both knew in a way I was still his and a part of me always would be even as I was free to be another's.

I knew it'd be rough.

I still underestimated it.

"Jean didn't get it," he said in my neck.

"Sorry?"

He lifted his head. "Jean didn't get it. She had another perspective. She lost her man before she could ever really have him, and then let her life slip away not letting herself have anything. She didn't get why two living, breathing people who cared for each other would not grab hold." He ran his hand to the side of my face and his thumb across my cheek. "I'm beginning to see her perspective."

I understood a little something about allowing the extremes of grief to lead you to letting your life slip away.

I hated that for Jean.

But it made me feel wonderful I'd put a stop to it and went all out to find some happy.

I just wished we could tell Jean we were both going to go for some happy.

Sadly, we couldn't.

I had a feeling she knew anyway.

I gave him a shaky smile. "Good."

"The boys are really okay with it?"

I nodded, I should have done it emphatically since "okay" did not cover it. But I'd let Hound experience that for himself.

"The brothers won't be."

I pressed my lips together and nodded again.

"Keely?"

"Right here, baby," I whispered.

"Let's not fuck this up."

The smile that earned was not shaky.

"Deal," I agreed.

"And baby?" he called.

"I'm here, Shep," I reminded him.

"No more cookie throwing. I've had your cookies and that one hittin' the deck, even half of one . . ." he gave me a rakish grin that made even badass Hound look downright adorable—wicked, but adorable, "cryin' shame."

I narrowed my eyes. "Don't make me pissed when I'm post-orgasmic."

"That was lame," he decreed.

"You'd rather I came at you with my nails?" I asked.

"That would have meant I'd have to subdue you, which would no doubt turn into angry sex, which would turn into makeup sex and I woulda learned a lot quicker all you had on under that robe was panties."

"Women don't normally put bras on after they have a bubble bath."

That surprised him. "You take bubble baths?"

"Is that shocking?"

"You're a biker babe."

"There's one operative word to that, 'babe,' and many of us like bubble baths."

"Just to say, it had not escaped me you're a babe," he remarked.

"Don't try to sweet talk me after you've annoyed me."

"How many cookies are left?" he asked.

"If you make the five second rule the fifteen minute rule, five and a half, but time is swiftly running out on that half."

His body started shaking on mine.

It was glorious.

"Dutch and Jag cleaned you out," he noted.

"They haven't stopped producing chocolate chips, Shep."

He grinned. "My babe's got a smart ass."

His babe.

Hound's babe.

Was that finally me?

I wasn't going to ask for confirmation.

If I did, this bubble might burst and I'd be back where I was and that didn't stand contemplating.

Instead, I declared, "So we've come to the understanding that if I'm pissed, I should pounce so we can have angry sex and your woman has a smart ass. Now, are you going to keep me pinned to the kitchen table all night?"

"Maybe."

"My bed is a lot more comfortable."

Something drifted across his face.

"He's never been there with me," I told him quietly. "The bed isn't the same. The room isn't even the same. No one has been there with me."

"We got shit we gotta get past," he muttered.

Boy, did we.

I nodded but shared, "I'm not feeling taking this slow."

He looked deep in my eyes and rumbled, "Agreed."

"So I need to text Bev about Jag and then we need to break the seal on my bed, and tomorrow, if Jag shows for breakfast, we'll make it official. At least with the boys."

"He won't. Boys got plans for him. He'll also miss a day of school, Keekee."

Shit.

Okay.

He was nineteen, almost twenty, and I'd cut the apron strings (kind of).

This was his choice.

He'd make it up.

"Right. So, family dinner as soon as we can plan. Make it official for both boys at the same time," I said.

He considered this for about three seconds.

Then he nodded that he again agreed.

I scored my thumbnail lightly through the thick stubble on his cheek and reminded him, "I want this. You want this. We'll make this happen. We just gotta be more out there and look after each other along the way."

"Yeah," he muttered.

"Let me up, baby. I need to text Bev."

"She goin' through with the wedding?" he asked.

"Yeah," I answered.

"Fuck," he replied.

With that he slid out and pulled me to my feet.

He yanked his jeans up but didn't do them up.

He bent and tagged my panties from the floor, and as I was lifting my hand to take them, my breath stuck in my throat when he dropped to a knee in front of me.

He held them out.

I stood unmoving.

He tipped his head back. "Step in, Keekee."

Shepherd "Hound" Ironside, kneeling at my feet.

He'd been there figuratively for years.

Now he was right there, for me.

I put a hand on his shoulder and stepped into my panties.

He slid them up gently, coming up with them, settling them on my hips and then smoothing my robe over them.

He put his lips to mine. "Text Bev. Got beer?"

"Yeah, honey."

He pressed those lips to mine.

Then, doing up his jeans, he went to my fridge and got a beer.

Graham never used that fridge. Graham had never even been in the kitchen like it was now.

But Hound had, repeatedly.

He was in this with me.

He was in this with me.

And we were going to make this happen.

We were.

Even if it killed me.

CHAPTER FIFTEEN

TOTAL WINNER

Keely

I WOKE THE NEXT MORNING to Hound moving me to my belly.

I'd barely opened my eyes when he yanked my hips up so I was on my knees.

"Baby?" I called sleepily.

"Morning fuck," he grunted.

That worked for me.

And it was good it did.

Because Hound didn't hesitate to proceed with giving me just that.

⸻

"OKAY, BOYS FIRST, FAMILY MEAL as soon as. Then I'll tell Bev."

I was in the kitchen mainly putzing around, because Hound was making me breakfast.

He just started right up doing that after we came down.

I didn't say anything.

The time to get into him losing Jean, and how he was coping with that, was not prior to breakfast after we'd made up in a way that meant we weren't hiding in his apartment anymore and we were going to be putting it out there, to possibly volatile reactions.

I'd get into that when I had him lazy and sweet and in a good headspace so he could deal, probably when he was naked after I'd made him blow with my mouth.

"No Bev," he declared.

I looked from preparing my travel mug of coffee to him standing at the stove beside me.

"What?" I asked.

"No Bev," he said to the dual skillets he had going, eggs and, now without Jean and the nixing of pork, the addition of bacon. "She's got a big mouth."

"Uh, Hound, baby, she's Bev. She'll get this is big. She'll be happy for us because she loves me, she loves you. She's also Chaos." Or she was, she was cutting ties and it might be time but still, once Chaos you never really stopped being that. "She'll know to keep her mouth shut about this until we've dealt with the fallout."

He turned just his head to me.

"No Bev, babe. Too risky."

I turned my full body to him.

"Right, honey, we've had this conversation. The brothers will totally understand, after they get their heads around it, why we kept the beginning of us from them. Bev, on the other hand, will totally be pissed at me if she finds out those boys heard before she did. That I kept it from her. And she'd have reason. She is not gonna be a problem. She's gonna be an ally. Someone I can talk to about it. Someone who'll get it. But now you need to get what she means to me and that I simply cannot do that to her. Me saying she'll be pissed is about her actually being hurt. If the tables were turned, I would be too."

I got closer to him, slid a hand along his waist to his back and kept talking.

"She's gearing up to take a huge step back from Chaos, and by that

I mean move on from the Club. This guy might not make her happy but he loves her, spoils her, and he's going to take care of her. And I think maybe she's thinking that eventually all of that will make her happy. So she won't slip up and share anything, because she's not going to be keeping her finger on the pulse of Chaos in order to keep Boz a part of her life. She's letting go."

"He's such a dumbfuck," Hound muttered.

"Won't get any argument from me," I muttered back.

"Right. Then boys first and then you can tell Bev," Hound declared.

I smiled up at him.

He bent his neck to touch his lips to mine.

I went back to my coffee.

And that was when Hound laid it on me.

"Jag had no business putting himself forward to become a recruit for the Club."

My heart skittered at his words and I turned my head to stare at him.

He took bacon out of the skillet and put it on a paper-lined plate.

And kept going.

Briefly.

"Did it for us."

"Sorry?" I asked.

He reached into me and I swung back so he could open the cupboard to pull down plates, saying, "He needs to focus on school. The brothers will let him do that because he's Jag. He's Black's. Normally, they'd put him off. Tell him to hang around, get to know the boys and re-approach after he'd got his degree. It wasn't that he already knew the boys. It was that he was a legacy. I didn't get it when he called me, said he wanted to start earning his patch, especially since Dutch isn't close to havin' his yet. He shoulda waited until that happened too. Knowin' he knew about us, now I know he wanted as in as he could get so he could take our backs when we came out to the Club."

I was back to staring at him.

He'd said all this while scooping out eggs, laying out toast and bacon and he offered me my plate, which I took automatically when he went on, "Not sure he gets a recruit don't have say in dick. The brothers lose their minds, Dutch and Jag try to get in there, that won't go good for them. Black's boys or not. But it was a fuckuva solid they engineered for us in order to try to take our backs."

"It's because of the cut and the bike," I said softly.

"Hit the table, baby," he replied, also softly.

I grabbed my coffee mug and moved to the table.

Hound nabbed his plate and mug and followed me.

After we sat down and were digging in, Hound, with mouth full, agreed with me.

"It was. They saw your car at my place, knew I was fixin' it up 'cause I had you there. Not dumb, either of them, you're never around and they know you were with me, they knew we wouldn't start anything unless it was somethin' real. Then you say you wanted to let those go, they got the clue. So they moved to make sure we had as much firepower as we could get with the Club. Good boys. Good men. Love their ma. Backin' me. Means a lot."

I had egg on a triangle of toast held aloft and my eyes on him.

But my mouth was saying, "Oh my God. I think I'm gonna start bawling."

He sucked back some coffee, turned his eyes to me and smiled big.

"Serious as shit, Keekee, you become one of those cryin' and carryin' on women, I'm gonna have to think of dumpin' you again."

That got me over the need to burst into tears.

"We're not quite at the point where we can joke about that, Shepherd Ironside," I snapped.

"Did I fuck you awake this morning?" he queried.

"I was kinda, sorta awake by the time you started fucking me," I retorted.

"But mostly, you were still asleep when you took my cock."

I decided just to glare.

"So I'd say we're totally at the point we can joke about that," he decreed.

I took an angry bite of egg and toast and shot back with a full mouth, "Now's the time for me to think of dumping *you*."

"Babe, how long was I at you on this table before you went for me?

About a minute? You missed my dick. No way you're dumping me."

"Would you like me to throw eggy toast at you this morning?"

He grinned. "Feel like bawling?"

I did not.

And that made me more irritated.

"You're an asshole, Shep."

He just kept grinning and resumed eating.

I stared at him, unable to remain annoyed because Hound was sitting at my kitchen table, eating breakfast after he spent the night with me.

He was also grinning just a week to the day after he'd walked in and found his Jean bug had passed away.

I'd done it, times two.

I'd won my man.

And even at a rough time in his life, I was making him happy.

So I let it go and ate the delicious breakfast he'd made me.

I WAITED UNTIL MY LUNCH hour to phone my oldest boy.

He answered right away.

"Yo, Ma."

"Hey, Dutch. How's Jagger?"

"He puked three times cleaning up his own puke and another cleaning up some biker groupie's puke, and now he's passed out on the couch on that biker groupie."

Visions of Jagger in his little boy pajamas gleefully pushing himself along with his feet on his mini-motorcycle on Christmas day danced through my head juxtaposed with him passed out on a biker groupie.

This did not compute and made *me* want to puke.

I powered past that.

"Too much information, boy," I muttered.

Dutch started chuckling.

"He gonna rally?" I asked.

"For what?" he asked back.

"I want you boys over tonight for dinner."

Dutch was silent, contemplating this.

He'd been this way since he was a little boy. Except for a time in his early teens when he'd taken to various acts of douchebaggery, which pissed me off and scared the shit out of me, he thought shit through.

It was hell getting a wish list for Santa out of him. He did three or four drafts before he gave me the final.

As was our way, I waited while he contemplated this.

"We gonna do the handovers?" he asked quietly.

He meant were they going to get their father's things.

We weren't doing that.

It was me who was contemplating on that.

I wanted Hound there.

And Graham's bike hadn't been touched so it probably would not start right up. So they were going to have to handle that.

But before it was touched and when Black's cut was handed over, I wanted some kind of ceremony.

I didn't know what that was.

I just knew both boys would be there and I wanted to be sure they were okay, as was Hound, that Hound would be there too.

"No, and no questions," I replied. "Do you have plans?"

"Nope."

"Do you know if your brother has plans?"

"Chaos owns him now, and he can be all about Jagger but he's not that stupid to make plans after he was taken on, so probably not."

"Good. Six thirty. I'm making fried pork chops."

"You should have led with that."

I smiled. "See your asses there when you get there."

"Yeah, Ma. Later."

"Later, Dutch. Love you, kid."

"Back at you."

We hung up and I called Hound.

"Yo, baby," he answered.

"The boys are gonna be over tonight for pork chops. Six thirty," I told him.

"I'll be over earlier, help you cook."

"Cool, honey, thanks."

After saying this, suddenly, I got freaked.

And freakily, over the phone, Hound read it.

"Babe, they're good. They're cool. It's gonna be fine."

"I kinda know that, but having them say they want us together and having them *see* us together are two different things," I replied.

"Are you gonna spend the next six hours winding yourself up about this to end up fuckin' it up?" he asked.

"That would not be the optimal scenario."

He sounded like he was smiling when he said, "No. It wouldn't. So stay cool, mama. This is gonna be the easy part. The awesome part. Don't make it hard. We got enough of that on the horizon."

"Awesome, Shep. Thanks so much for reminding me of that," I muttered.

That was when I heard another man in my life chuckling over the phone.

Waking up alone in my bed for nearly eighteen years, I'd felt like I'd done it a loser. It wasn't until I clapped eyes on my boys every day that I knew that wasn't exactly true.

Hearing first Dutch, then Hound laughing in my ear in the expanse of about five minutes, I knew now I was a total winner.

"You good?" he asked.

"I'm a badass biker bitch. Of course I'm good," I answered.

That had him howling with laughter.

Yep.

I was a total winner.

"See you around five thirty, six. Yeah?" he asked.

"Sounds good, babe. See you then."

"Right, baby." Soft and sweet. And softer and sweeter, "Love you."

I blinked.

I slowly opened my mouth.

But I heard the tone that said he'd disconnected.

Love you.

Had he disconnected because he realized he'd said that?

Love you.

Or had he said it because it was so natural to say it, he just disconnected.

Love you.

He loved me.

Hound loved me.

I knew he loved me but he just *told me*.

"Oh my *God*," I breathed.

I pulled my phone from my ear, my finger poised to dial Bev, and then I realized I could not.

"Shit," I hissed.

"All good?" I heard asked and looked at one of the teachers sitting at another table in the staff lounge having his lunch.

Keith Robinson.

He was one of the ones I really liked, but I didn't know all that well (that last part being how I knew all of them). He seemed totally cool. The kids adored him. I even had one hardcase who skipped school but came *back* just to hit his class.

"My new man just told me he loved me for the first time," I blurted.

Okay, I couldn't believe I just blurted that.

But Hound just told me he loved me.

I had to tell somebody!

Keith's entire handsome face lit with a smile.

"Right on," he replied.

"He's loved me for eighteen years." I thought on that and added, "Maybe longer."

Keith's brows drew together. "That took a while to say."

"I was married to his brother. He died."

"Sorry," Keith murmured. "Rough. Really sorry, Keely."

"It's okay. It was a long time ago," I told him.

"I'm seeing it's not that easy for him to make that play, your husband was his brother," Keith remarked.

He could say that again.

"They were biker brothers," I explained. "They belong to the same motorcycle club."

Somehow, he completely got it. "Right then, probably *really* not easy for him to make that play."

"The Club doesn't know yet," I shared.

"Likely strategizing that communication is akin to planning the raid when they found Osama Bin Laden," he joked.

"You got that right," I agreed.

He gathered his sandwich, bag of chips and drink and moved to my table.

"Know a guy in a club," he shared once he'd settled. "Good man. Good club. What I know is that kind of brotherhood is a deeper one than any. If your man loves you, they'll want him to have that and they'll come around."

"I hope so," I muttered, looking at my burrito and thinking maybe I should pack my lunch because Keith's mammoth homemade shaved roast beef sandwich looked way better than my microwave burrito.

"You doubt it?" he asked.

"My man, my husband, I mean, he was, well . . . he was more beloved than most by those guys."

"And your new man, they're not fond of him?" Keith teased.

"Graham, my old man, he was the glue of the Club. Shep, my *new* old man, he's their shield."

"Sounds like you have good taste," he replied.

I gave him a small grin. "Yeah, I totally do."

"It's gonna be fine, Keely," he said gently. "And just to say, don't know you all that well, but do know the woman I find myself separated from during lunch a lot of the time for, I don't know the last four or five years, is not the woman I'm sitting with today. So I'm thankful to this Shep for pulling out the woman who'd reach across that separation to me finally and give me a bit of yourself. It's an honor. Thank him from me."

"Oh my God." I stared at him. "Now *you* are gonna make me cry."

He looked concerned. "You've been crying a lot recently?"

"I've been grieving my dead husband for nearly two decades, let my life slip away, then decided to take a shot on jumpstarting that life, doing it with Shep. Lost a woman who came to mean a lot to me in the expanse of a weekend. She died in her sleep last Monday. Almost lost Shep because I was playing to win but I failed to tell him the booty was me. And tonight, we're telling my sons, who he helped me raise, that they finally got the stepdad they always knew was just that, we're just making it official."

"So you've been crying a lot recently."

"Yeah, or on the verge," I confirmed.

"Let those tears loose, Keely," he advised. "Because I'm thinking those days are gonna be over for you soon so you might as well let them out when they come now. When the reasons for them disappear, you can look back at them fondly."

"Stop being awesome," I demanded.

"That might be tough but I'll give it a shot," he returned, lips twitching.

He bit into his delicious-looking sandwich.

I bit into my floppy, tired-looking bean burrito.

Once I swallowed, I asked, "Who's the guy you know and what club is he in?"

"His name is Carson, goes by Joker in the club. And it's Chaos, the men behind that custom car and bike business and auto supply store on Broadway."

That got him a huge smile. "That's my man's Club."

And I got a return huge smile. "Then maybe we'll see you at a hog roast. Joker has been asking us to come for months. But my wife and I had a new baby and she wasn't wanting to get a sitter. But the time is coming she needs to give Dora some space, and get some herself, so maybe we'll see you at one."

"I hope so," I replied. "And I contributed to the pot when it went around to get you a baby gift. Was so happy for you guys. Everyone was."

"Not as much as us," Keith told me.

"Yeah. Kids are da bomb."

"They absolutely are."

We talked about Dora. We talked about Dutch and Jagger. And when our lunch breaks were done, Keith walked me back to my office before he went to his classroom.

I watched him go, thinking that suddenly, I had a new friend and we had something in common.

And oddly enough, that was kids . . . and Chaos.

I'd worked there years, but also when I was in my other jobs, when I was volunteering, when I was at school, and just in life, I had not opened myself to making a new friend since Black died.

I had not opened myself up at all.

I was about Dutch, Jag, anger (at both Graham and my asshole families, but also just at life) and grief.

Oh yeah, I was going to tell Hound I made a new friend and express Keith's gratitude that he got the same.

Because Hound gave me that.

Sure, I walked up to his door to get in his face and make the first play.

But Hound walked down that hallway then dropped to his knees and went down on me.

And now here we were.

Here I was.

So perhaps we would not be sharing widely how it all started.

That said, I didn't think ever in my life there was anything as amazingly beautiful and scorching hot as watching my biker badass drop to his knees and bury his face in me.

So being his biker bitch, that kind of start *so totally* worked for me.

AT SIX TWENTY-FOUR THAT NIGHT I was a nervous wreck.

This had to do with the fact that the boys were showing imminently and there I was, in my kitchen, making pork chops, mashed potatoes and buttered, real bacon-bit covered green beans with Hound.

This also had to do with the fact that just hours earlier he'd told me he loved me, had not given me the chance to return that sentiment and now . . .

Now . . .

Now I didn't know what to do.

I loved him, but could I declare that love to him before my sons arrived to eat their first dinner with us as a couple?

I mean, we didn't need to be fucking on the kitchen table (again) when my boys walked in the back door.

"Keely, *chill*," Hound growled.

He was at the stove, manning the pork chops.

I was at the KitchenAid mixer, squeezing roasted garlic cloves into the boiled potatoes.

The kitchen table was set. It would be nice to eat in the dining room but there wasn't an odd number of people that would make even seating unless all ten seats could be taken.

Anyway, I figured the kitchen table was more homey, intimate and familial instead of formal, so I went with that.

The green beans were ready to blanch. The buttery, bacon-bit goodness ready to toss them in. The rolls were warming in the oven. I'd bought a pistachio mousse cake from LeLane's on the way home from work (both the boys' favorite, if I didn't make the cake that was).

It was all under control.

And I was still a wreck.

"They're almost here," I told him.

"Chill," he told me.

"What if it goes bad? What if they, like, realize you're spending the night? Or what me spending the night with you means? That you're banging their momma? What if they get weirded out by that and that turns protective or mean and—"

"Chill," he interrupted.

"It's weird!" I cried. "They've never had to face something like that."

"We both know neither of your boys are virgins," he stated.

"Ugh," I grunted.

"And unless they're under the impression they're the second *and* third coming, they've put it together their momma got her cherry popped a long time ago," Hound went on.

I was right then regretting running my mouth.

Hound moved to me, yanked the spent garlic out of my fingers, tossed it on the counter, hooked my neck with his arm and yanked me into his body.

"They might dig me but they love you, baby, down to their bones," he said softly. "They want you to be happy. They been waiting a fuckuva long time to see that happen for you. This is gonna go great. So . . . *chill.*"

I put my arms around him even as I declared, "You know, it's really, *really* annoying how totally, *totally* awesome you are."

Hound gave me a look.

Then he threw his head back and busted out laughing.

I smiled up at him, loving that look on him best of all.

The back door opened.

Oh shit.

Hound's laughter turned to chuckles as I twisted my neck still in Hound's hold to look at the door.

The boys were both through and staring at us.

"Yo," Hound greeted.

Dutch's body jolted.

Oh man.

Jagger blinked.

Shit!

"Yo," Dutch said.

"Thank fuck, the smell of pork chop grease. Been queasy all day, just what I need," Jagger declared, moving toward the stove.

"Did you roast garlic, Ma?" Dutch asked me, going to the fridge.

"Of course," I whispered, not quite understanding what was happening.

"Hound, got beer?" Dutch asked.

"Could use a fresh one," Hound told him, bending to run his lips along my cheekbone before he let me go and moved away.

"Jagger, you want a beer?" Dutch asked.

"Please, God, if you say beer one more time, I'm punching you in the mouth," Jagger groaned from the stove.

Hound had made it to him, so he clamped a big hand on the back of Jag's neck, swaying him back and forth.

"Still hangin'?" he asked.

Jagger twisted his neck to look at Hound. "Is it entirely necessary to take a shot of tequila after each and every brother takes his shot of tequila?"

"Can't be Chaos if you can't hold your liquor, son," Hound replied.

Right.

What was happening?

"Uh . . ." I mumbled.

"Ma," Dutch called. Having moved across the space, he was handing Hound who was disengaging from Jagger his fresh one.

I turned my gaze to him.

"You want beer or you got wine?" he asked, twisting off his own beer top.

"Wine," I peeped.

"Need it topped off?" Dutch offered.

I shook my head slowly.

What I needed to do was glug it from the bottle.

After I took a shot of tequila.

"Grab those beans, Jag, throw 'em in the water," Hound ordered then looked to me. "Babe, that thing probably mashes potatoes a lot easier if you turn it on."

Both my sons emitted low chuckles.

I just stared dazedly at my man.

"Right," Hound muttered. "I'll turn it on."

He moved into me, reached around me and the KitchenAid started whirring.

"What's happening?" I asked quietly before he moved fully away.

He lifted his brows.

"Ma, serious, Hound does his shot with Jag, hornin' in there to do it first, then he takes off on his bike like the devil is chasin' him. Next thing we know, you're callin' a family dinner when we all haven't sat down to dinner since Christmas. We figured it out," Dutch proclaimed. "You guys pulled your heads outta your asses. Now it's pork chop time."

"You had her pork chops?" Jag asked Hound.

"Not fried ones," Hound answered.

"Man, you are gonna lose your *mind*," Jagger told him.

"Jag, Ma got a pistachio cake from LeLane's," Dutch shared with his brother.

"God, I hope like fuck the pork chops work on my hangover so I can eat half a' that thing," Jag murmured.

"Since I'm eatin' the other half, what are Ma and Hound gonna eat?" Dutch demanded to know.

"Neither of you men are eatin' half a' shit," Hound proclaimed, tossing an arm around my shoulders and pulling me away from the counter. "Jag, get a drink. Dutch, man the potatoes. Your mother needs to sit down before she teeters over, so it's up to us to serve up. Get on it."

Before Hound could push me in the chair he pulled out, Jagger was there, slinging his arm around the shoulders Hound's arm just vacated.

"Jeez, you look like you just got sucker punched in the nose by Anthony Joshua," he observed. Then he gave me his sweet boy grin and lowered his voice. "It's all good, Momma. Chill. Yeah?"

"Yeah, sweetheart," I whispered.

He shoved me down in the chair.

Hound brought me my wine.

They moved around, dealing with shit while I sipped.

Chairs scraped.

Before they started passing stuff around, I called, "Halt!"

Three sets of beloved male eyes turned to me.

I looked from Hound to Dutch to Jagger, saying, "Okay, boys, making this official, even though that's unnecessary. Your momma and your Hound have finally got their heads outta their asses and we're doin' this. And I mean we're *doin' this*. For now, we're keeping it from the Club. We'll share when that's gonna change. But we're taking time for ourselves first and to be with you boys." I lifted a hand Dutch's way, as usual, my potato boy had put the bowl in front of his plate. "Now pass the mashed potatoes."

Dutch shot me a grin.

Jagger punched Hound in the arm.

I took the potatoes as they started passing the other stuff.

I felt Hound's gaze after I picked up my knife to start sawing into my chop.

I lifted my eyes to his.

And there they were.

Hound's eyes across from me at my kitchen table.

My biker and my boys all around me.

A dream I'd lived once, but it died when the blood of its most important component ran free across a pizza place parking lot.

And here I had it again.

I love you, I thought.

I love you, those eyes replied.

I smiled at him.

His mouth got soft.

Then I picked up my fork and started sawing.

"THIS ISN'T THE TIME TO get into it."

"Jag—"

"But if we don't take this time to get into it, that time is gonna pass, we'll never get into it, so we gotta get into it."

We were still at the kitchen table.

The meal had been decimated.

It worked wonders on Jag's hangover.

All three of my boys had hefty pieces of cake and then seconds.

Now Jag had something to say that Dutch clearly didn't want him to get into.

I felt a nervous prickle in my belly as Jagger finally pinned Hound with his gaze, but the question came out low and mellow when he asked, "Why'd you keep Jean from us, man?"

Shit.

"You're right, honey," I piped up, aiming this at Jag. "This isn't the time to get into that."

"Yeah, Jagger," Dutch growled. "Shut it."

"Dutch, appreciate you've got a mind to me," Hound rumbled. "But Jag, you got somethin' on your mind, you don't act like a dick about gettin' it out there, you put it out there."

Dutch shot me a look.

I gave him a just-let-it-happen nod and turned my attention to Hound.

"And this needs to be said because it needs to be understood. Before anything gets any further and thoughts wander, I'm gonna lay it out there like it is," Hound declared.

Yep.

Shit.

Hound kept pronouncing.

"Most important, it isn't lost on you boys that I had feelin's for your ma for a while. You know that, it's now where it is, you were right. That's what it was. But if you ever get it in your heads that was why I had all the time in the world for either of you, push that shit out because that's not only not true, it'd piss me off it even crossed your minds."

Now all of us were staring at Hound.

"It started because of my love for your old man and my respect for your mother. It took about a week before you both earned what you got from me, what you have from me, what you'll always have from me," Hound told them. "I did what I could in the part I played to raise you like my brother woulda done if he wasn't gone. That was for Black. But me doin' it was all for you."

Fucking hell.

I was *definitely* going to start crying.

"Place in my heart, Hound," Dutch murmured. "Always."

Start crying like a ninny!

"Yeah, Hound," Jagger mumbled. "Always."

Damn it!

"Jean was mine," he said.

Oh boy.

I swallowed.

"I get you both got me in your hearts, you didn't have to tell me that. And I get you feel betrayed I kept somethin' that meant something like Jean did to me from you, knowin' I know what you feel for me, how I feel about you. But she was mine."

"I don't get that," Jagger said quiet.

Hound gave it to him.

"Did a lot in my life, son, some good, but there was bad. The worst kinda bad there is. You do what you feel needs to be done, do it without hesitation, do it even with pride, but it scores marks in your soul and you feel those marks. You can let them bein' there take you over and make you think that's all you got in you. Like you boys were, like helpin' your mother out was, Jean was proof that what I got under those marks is still good and pure and right. No way she'd take me into her life the way she did if I wasn't the kinda man who deserved that trust, her time, the love she gave me."

I had to swallow again.

"Now," Hound continued, "she's gone and I'm seein' I was selfish with that. Jean wanted to meet your momma and I let her do that, and she loved having time with your ma. She woulda loved you boys. I wished I'd a' let you have her, but I wish more I'd a' let her have you. I didn't. I gotta live with that. But at least she died knowin' your momma, knowin' I had her, knowin' she had you boys to give to me, so knowin' that I had you too. So I'm hangin' on to that."

When he was done talking, no one said anything.

I was going to jump in but Hound got there before me.

"You feel me on that, Jag?" he asked.

"Yeah, Hound," Jag answered.

He swung his head Dutch's way. "You feel me, Dutch?"

They gave each other an intense look I didn't get before Dutch replied, "Absolutely, Hound."

Then Hound looked to me. "You okay, baby?"

I was not.

I could barely see him with the tears swimming in my eyes.

But I nodded, looked between my sons and said in a trembling, husky voice, "You guys would have loved her. She loved Hound like he was her own boy. And she made him not cuss and take his boots off before he put his feet on her coffee table. It was hilarious."

Hound shot me a sweet grin.

"Seriously?" Jag asked.

I looked to him, sniffed and nodded.

"She a ballbuster?" Jagger asked Hound.

"She was a proper biker grandma," I told my son.

Jagger guffawed.

I grinned.

"Ma makes us take our boots off before we put our feet on the table," Dutch told Hound.

"I know, son. As it should be," Hound replied.

Okay.

I was at my end.

"Oh my God!" I exclaimed. "Someone either pass me the bottle of wine or cut me another piece of cake. No! Both!"

Hound smiled at me.

Dutch grinned at me.

Jagger grabbed the knife on the plate and sliced into the cake (I knew he was being helpful but also doing this so he could get icing and pistachio mousse on his fingers so he could lick it off).

He did this muttering, "Bitches."

"We're about to have a no cussing rule in momma's house," I warned.

Jagger shot me a smirk.

I understood that smirk.

My sons were of Chaos and now just Chaos.

From the time they understood the words, I had a no cussing rule that ended when Dutch hit seventeen, he cursed better and more prolifically than his father (and Hound) and I gave up.

No way I could enforce it now. That had long since left the building.

Dutch got up to get the bottle of wine.

Hound adjusted to the side, stretching his long legs out toward Dutch's side of the table, crossing his ankles, and asked Jag, "You talk to your profs about makin' up the day?"

"Yeah," Jag said, turning to his side and stretching out his long legs toward Hound. "Emailed this afternoon. Told 'em I got some twenty-four-hour flu. It's all good."

Dutch put the wine on the table, sat and then shifted in his seat, stretching his long legs out toward me. "Joke says, after he finishes this build, he's gonna let me in on the next one."

"Lucky," Jag grunted.

"Do your time, son, do your time," Hound murmured, like a biker lullaby.

I poured wine and ate cake.

And I kept my legs right under me.

The better to take it all in, the dream unfolding around me.

A total winner.

CHAPTER SIXTEEN

I'LL DO ANYTHING IT TAKES

Keely

T HE NEXT MORNING, I SAT cross-legged in my bed, having pulled Hound's tee over my head after we'd done our business and he'd gotten up to use the bathroom before I hit it to take my shower before work. I was sitting facing the bathroom.

He came out, naked, his amazing tats on display, his thick, gorgeous cock still kinda hard, his beefy fur-covered thighs too much of a distraction (so I refused to focus on them), his eyes directed right at me.

"You got the twenty-four-hour flu too, babe?" he asked on a lip quirk.

"I love you."

He stopped.

Dead.

"You said it yesterday," I continued. "You didn't give me the chance to reply. And so we're open, it's out there, you get it, you know, I loved you before I came to your apartment that first time. I loved you, which was the reason I went to Black's grave to let him know he was going to have to deal. I spent a lot of time thinking about it and I started to fall in love with you years ago, when you laid it out about Dutch joining Chaos and that I needed to sort my shit. But every day I've been with you, I've fallen more and more in love with you in a way I think that's going to happen, I hope, until the day I quit breathing."

He stood there, staring at me, body frozen, face frozen, giving me nothing.

"I said, or started . . . a while back, in your bed, I started to tell you," I went on. "I said, 'You're the . . . ' but I didn't finish because we weren't there, well *I* was there, but you weren't there yet so I wasn't sure you'd believe me. If it would be giving up too much when I didn't have you in that place I needed you to be. So I'll finish it now. What I was going to say was that you're the best man I've ever known, Hound. I've had twenty-one years of watching the kind of love and loyalty you give to the people you let in your heart, and I want there not to be another day, another second, where you live not knowing what an honor I feel it is that you gave me a place there."

He made no move, no sound, not even a facial tick.

Um.

Okay.

What on earth did that mean?

"Hound?" I called, beginning to get freaked.

All of a sudden, he was a blur of movement. Then my hair was flying, a drifting cloud all around me, and my arms were forced up as he tore his tee from me.

After that, I was back in the bed with Hound kicking my legs apart with his knee.

"You got the twenty-four-hour flu," he growled, his body coming down on mine.

Not frozen, not giving me nothing.

His blue eyes were burning straight through me.

"It's going around," I breathed.

"Yeah," he grunted, then, even though I didn't even notice him getting hard again, he'd done it because he entered me.

Filled me.

Became a part of me.

Physically.

He was that already.

He had been for a long time.

And would be.

For always.

"Wow," I whispered, rounding him with arms and legs.

"Yeah," he groaned, thrusting.

"I take it, you, uh . . . *absorbed* what I just said."

He drove in, stayed in and *ground* in (another wow), gritting, "*Yeah.*"

I put both hands to his stubbly cheeks. "Love you, baby."

He stopped grinding and closed his eyes.

"Love you," I repeated.

He opened his eyes and he didn't say it back.

He didn't have to.

Those expressive eyes he'd kept closed down on me for so long to hide the way he felt for me were open and sharing, no . . . *shouting* just what he felt, and how deep it ran . . . for me.

Then he kissed me and started up again fucking me.

That twenty-four-hour flu was a killer.

I stayed in bed all day.

IT WAS THE NEXT EVENING and I was just about to turn down Bev's street.

"Make sure she gets the message it stays between her, the boys, you and me," Hound voice sounded throughout my car.

"I think I got that," I replied, hitting my blinker.

"When you leave, text you're on the way," he ordered.

"Affirmative, cowboy, but where will I be on my way to?" I asked.

"Where else?" he asked back.

"Well, you've got a pad and I've got a pad so whose pad are we crashing at tonight?"

"Fucking then crashing," he amended.

I made the turn, grinning.

I hadn't had the longest, driest spell in history, but I was sure it was up there.

Still, it was clear Hound was dedicated to eradicating it in a way I might someday (soon) wonder if it even happened.

"Fucking and crashing," I agreed.

"Your car sits under threat of being stripped or disappearing altogether and being dismantled at some chop shop every night you park it outside my place. So yours."

"You leave your truck and bike there," I reminded him.

"My truck has a Chaos badge in the back window and my bike is known to be my bike so if any motherfucker even looks at either funny, especially my bike, they know they better take a selfie so they'll remember what they looked like before I rearranged their face."

"God, it turns me on when you're badass," I moaned, semi-teasing, semi-totally-serious, driving down Bev's street.

"Smartass."

"No, really."

"Text me when you're on your way, Keekee," he demanded.

"You got it, honey. See you later."

"Her. The boys. You. And me," he stated.

I rolled my eyes and turned into Bev's drive.

"Later," he finished.

"Later, Shep."

I heard my radio come on just in time for me to shut the car down.

I turned to grab my purse, the bottle and the bag of stuff I'd gone out to get after work that day, threw open my car door, folded out and moved up Bev's walk.

She lived in a one-story, two-bedroom in Englewood close to the brilliance of El Tejado and Twin Dragon, some of the best of south of the border and Chinese cuisine you could get in Denver.

It was also very close to Ride.

It was the area I'd always thought of Hound living in, one of those simple, not too old, definitely not new, on-a-big-lot, tidy houses close to good food . . . and Ride.

Bev and Boz had bought that house together and eventually they'd fought bitterly over it when she'd realized he wasn't going to reconcile with her, even though he'd been in the wrong and she'd forgiven him. He wanted a pad close to Chaos. She'd probably partially wanted the same thing but mostly she wanted their life to start up as it was when Boz came back.

It was just that he never came back.

I wondered if she'd ask her insurance salesman to move in with her. I didn't remember but I thought he lived in a bungalow in Platte Park. Or maybe it was Washington Park. His kids were both mid-teens and lived part-time with him. He'd probably want to stay put.

I just couldn't imagine Bev moving.

She had the door open before I got to it and I smiled big.

I held up the bottle and announced, "Sofia sparkling rosé, because Coppola is a freak of nature, the man has the chops to make a damn fine film *and* a damn fine wine and we're using that second talent to celebrate impending happiness." I dropped the bottle and lifted the bag. "And spoiling the surprise, the sexiest damn teddy in the Denver metro area, edible body glitter, paint *and* massage cream, because if the man can't find it with his fingers, we'll get him there with his mouth."

Bev gave me a look through her opened storm door before she busted out laughing.

This meant I came through, gave her a kiss on her laughing cheek and did both smiling.

She took the stuff from my hands.

Like her home was my home, as I always did when I hit her pad, I tossed my bag and jacket on her couch as I made my way fully in.

She went right to the kitchen, and by the time I hit it, she had her head in the fridge. She came out with a bottle in cellophane and lifted it up, my bottle in her other hand, and they were identical.

"Great minds think alike!" she cried.

"*Gurrrrl*, I shoulda Ubered," I told her.

"We shoulda done this not on a school night," she replied, putting my bottle in and keeping her bottle out, starting to take off the cellophane.

For a special night, even though I'd never done it (before yesterday), I would have called off work for Bev. Since I took off yesterday to have a fuck festival with Hound after my declaration of love (he celebrated mine *way* better than I celebrated his), I couldn't.

But I could go to work hanging. It'd been years since I'd done that too. In fact, I didn't think I'd ever done that since I'd been at the school.

It was now time to learn if I still had it in me to ride out a hangover.

Best part, if I got trashed, by that time, Bev would know about Hound and he could come and get me.

We hadn't had drunk sex yet.

Trashed it was.

"Uber doesn't mind I leave my car in your driveway and you probably won't either. I should have brought two bottles," I said.

"We'll call Dutch and tell him to bring us another one. I'm pretty sure waiting on old ladies, even de facto ones like us, is part of recruit duties," she returned right before the cork popped.

"I'm on glasses," I declared and headed to her cupboard that held them.

"I'll pour," Bev cut me off on my way. "I made one of those charcuterie boards. Tad taught me how and I've decided to do that at least five nights a week. All you do is open a bunch of jars and packets of different kind of salamis, cut some cheese and *voilà*! Dinner!" She jerked her head to the fridge. "Go grab it."

I grinned at her and headed to the fridge, pulling out the big wooden board filled with meats, cheeses, pickles and olives she had in there.

Bev got the wine sorted and cut up some wedges of store-bought but fresh-baked bread, and we sat at her cozy kitchen table because she didn't have a dining room and we usually camped out there because, as I mentioned, it was cozy. It was also closer to the fridge so we could keep our champers chilled.

I dug in.

She didn't touch the food.

She yanked out the black teddy from the bag. It was made of mostly see-through mesh that melded with beautiful lace around a *very* plunging deep vee at the breasts (that *very* meaning it went all the way down to your midriff and opened all the way across to barely cover your nipples), had little ruffles along the hips and at the ends of the three-quarter sleeves.

We were sisters so I had no problem buying the same thing for me to wear for Hound. Except, in order not to make it gross, mine was red.

"Holy crap, Keely, this is beautiful," she said reverently, stretching out the mesh to see the shape of it.

"I'll buy you a white something-or-other for the big day," I told her. "That's for fun now."

Her pretty blue eyes slid to me.

She'd changed over the years, her girl-next-door beauty maturing into woman-that-had-been-around-the-block beauty, but it was still beauty, and I'd watched as she'd done it.

She dyed her hair almost the exact blonde it used to be, maybe a shade darker. She still wore it long, with a tease at the back and flippy bangs that brushed her lashes. She had a few lines around her eyes, like I did. A few around her mouth, like I did not.

She'd probably put on fifteen, twenty pounds since we traipsed around the Compound in frayed-edge, jean miniskirts or skintight jeans with slits in the knees, or, if it was a special occasion, spandex pants that had wide laces up the sides showing skin, these coupled with tees slashed down to our tits or tanks so tight, you couldn't miss it if the day was cold.

But even back then, she'd looked like she was in costume.

She'd always looked more like the retired cheerleader, current banker's wife who shopped at Nordstrom and sipped wine while her husband had his scotch while they watched *Shark Tank* on Friday evenings.

Or, maybe, the wife of an insurance salesman who was so happy she was wearing his ring, it was him that went out and bought bridal magazines for his forty-something second chance at love.

"I should have been more supportive from the beginning," I started. "I should have immediately helped you plan a course to finding your happy."

"I told him I was done with Chaos," she proclaimed.

I stared and then did what Hound did a lot.

A slow blink.

"Sorry?" I asked.

"I thought he was going to start crying," she told me.

My back started to go straight and she reached an arm out across the table to me.

"Not like that," she said quickly. "He wasn't being like that. He knows all about my past with the Club. About Boz. He doesn't care. He doesn't have a judgmental bone in his body. But he probably knew better than I did that I was holding on in the lame way I was to the life I'd had there in order to hold on to Boz. When I said it was done, he knew I was done with Boz."

I put my hand out and took hers. "It wasn't lame."

"It was lame."

"Beverly—"

"*He* cheated on *me* and then he made *me* feel like I was unfaithful to him because I wouldn't get it. And you know what? That's cracked. For years I kicked myself for making a big deal about it, but he put *my* cock in another woman. I wasn't cracked. He could give me the biker lifestyle spiel until the day he died." She pulled her hand from mine but not her gaze. "But I knew better. High's back with Millie and it's like the years in between didn't happen. Shy nearly renounced the Club to have Tab. I swear to God, I melt a little every time Lanie walks into the room, the way Hop looks at her. And Naomi was a screaming bee-yatch and Tack might have thought about it, but he scraped her off before he had his fun. But then he found Tyra and the man walked through a hail of gunfire to save her life. It isn't the lifestyle. It's Boz."

She took a sip of wine from her flute, looking away for a beat, then she looked back at me.

And when she did, I held my breath at what I saw in her eyes.

"I think Tad would walk through gunfire for me," she whispered. "He'll never be in the position to do that but I honest to God think he would, Keely. And I've been thinking on it since our phone conversation and I think that's why I said yes. I think I'm whacked because I started to fall in love with my fiancé after he proposed to me."

"And I think I'm beside myself with glee that's happening for you, babe," I replied softly.

She shot me a grin.

I lifted my glass up between us.

"To the magic of edible glitter dust and budding love," I toasted.

"To hot-as-fuck teddies working wonders and best friends forever," she toasted back.

We grinned at each other like goofs.

Then we clinked and drank.

Before she put her glass down, she exclaimed, "Shit! I forgot the fancy little knives. Hang tight."

She dashed to the counter.

I didn't need a fancy knife to shove a sliver of prosciutto in my mouth and I proved it by doing that.

"Okay, I said I was out of it," she started before she turned back with the baby cheese knives in her hand, "but old habits that aren't exactly old, since I haven't yet gone cold turkey, are hard to break. In other words, I'm talking Chaos gossip. So what gives with you dogging Hound at that old lady's funeral? Everyone is gabbing about it."

I nearly choked on prosciutto.

Bev slid back into her seat and shoved knives into cheese even as she looked at me. "You okay?"

I pounded my chest, grabbed my glass and pushed out, "Yes," before I took a sip.

"The old ladies are pissed, Keely," she shared. "Everyone knows Hound has a soft spot for you. You show at that funeral and take off without giving him a hug?" She grew cautious. "I mean, I know . . . well, I guess I figure it's about cemeteries, and well, no one likes them but you have more reason not to."

"Bev—"

"But Elvira saw and she got ticked and she's winding up Tyra and Lanie and Tabby and even Carissa, who's sweet as sugar."

"Elvira?" I asked.

"She's a Club adoptee. I don't get it. She was the black lady sitting in the seats by the casket with that smokin' hot black dude. They just got engaged. He's a cop."

Even though I only had thoughts (and eyes) for Hound and Jean at the funeral and didn't see any black lady with her smokin' hot guy, I did another one of Hound's slow blinks on learning that anyone having anything to do with a cop was adopted by Chaos.

"She's a long story," she finished.

I asked another one-word question.

"Carissa?"

"Joker's old lady."

"Ah," I mumbled.

"Millie defended you, according to Lanie, but they figure with the time in between," she shrugged a shoulder uncomfortably, "you should have . . . well, I mean, it's Hound. How many old Jewish women has he been lookin' after? Everyone was floored she even existed. They thought you could suck it up and show him some love."

I was showing him some love all right.

"Bev, honey—"

"Not to come down on you but I also thought it was kinda uncool," she kept going hesitantly.

"Bev—"

"I don't want you to think I'm a bitch but he's always had your back."

"Bev, let me speak."

She shut up and stared at me.

"Okay, I need you to brace. I mean, hang on, sister. Seriously," I warned.

She kept shutting up but now was staring at me intensely.

Shit.

Okay.

She would get it. She'd be on our side. She'd be for anything that made me happy.

Just do it, Keely!

"Hound and I are together," I announced. "We've been together a few months. The boys know. My boys that is, Dutch and Jagger. We were having a rough patch when Jean died that was really rough. I think we'll have a lot more rough before it's done, just not that kind. He loves me and I love him and we're committed to this. Like *committed*. He's my future. I'm his. He makes me happy. He lost Jean and I'm not certain he's dealing but we just got back together and made the decision to tell everyone, come out, so I'm letting us settle into that before I take his pulse on Jean. But we're not telling the Club. Not yet. Just you. And the boys. They're ecstatic. And, well . . . so am I."

She just kept staring at me intensely.

"I really am, Beverly," I whispered. "And it's bad timing, I get that, after I wasn't all that supportive of you making a decision in your love life I wasn't sure about. But that was a lot about you bursting into tears and babbling about Boz for fifteen minutes after you told me you said yes to marrying another man. I'm all in with Hound. I've talked to Black. I don't know if he'd understand but it doesn't matter. I'm in love with Hound and he loves me fierce, babe. So *fucking fierce*. And that's all I'm letting in right now."

Like Hound was when I told him I loved him, my best friend sat there unmoving and unspeaking.

"Bev, I really need your support in this. The brothers are gonna—"

I didn't get that all out.

I jumped in my seat when she let out a war whoop and burst out of her chair. Doing an arms and legs spread cheerleader leap in the middle of her kitchen, she then half-skipped, half pranced in a circle, almost like a Native American dance without the offensive slapping her hand to her mouth, but definitely making unintelligible sounds of sheer jubilation before she stopped suddenly.

She whirled to me and threw out an arm, finger pointed at me.

"I *knew it!*" she yelled. She raised her arm and hacked it down with finger pointed toward me again. "I *love this!*" She brought both hands in front of her and clapped repeatedly, fingers pointed straight up. "He has been *so into you* for *so long*. And he's *such* a *good guy*. Okay, he's a little bit loco. Maybe a lot loco. But he's still *such a good guy*. This is *so fucking AWESOME!*"

She screamed the last.

I opened my mouth to say something, the smile on my face so big it hurt, when she rushed the table and the smile died fast when I jumped in my seat again after she slammed a fist violently on the table, making everything on it jolt and wobble. In fact, three olives rolled off her charcuterie board along with a pickle, such was the violence of her hit.

"If *any* of those motherfuckers does *dick* to make this hard on you two, I'm gonna *lose my mind*," she shrieked. "One last thing I'll give Boz is a striping if he even *thinks* of pulling any shit with Hound about this.

I'll even butt up against Tack!" she shouted.

Uh-oh.

Biker cheerleader Beverly going up against Kane "Tack" Allen, president of the Chaos MC who got his title by means of executing the last one?

Shit.

"Bev, babe—"

"They're gonna make him stand the gauntlet, and you know it, girl."

It was then, *I* froze.

"And if they go through with that shit," she carried on, "I'm gonna burn down the Compound my damned self."

I was thrilled with her excitement. Absolutely.

But I was stuck on what she'd said.

Black had told me about standing the gauntlet years ago when Chew had slept with Crank's ex-wife and Crank had demanded a vote from the brothers, wanting Chew to stand the gauntlet.

The brothers did not vote this to happen seeing as first, Crank was a fucking asshole and most of the brothers hated him and were making maneuvers to get his ass out. And second, because Crank doing that to Chew proved what a fucking asshole he was (well, some of it) because he shouldn't call for anything that extreme to make a brother pay penance for sleeping with a woman Crank himself scraped off.

As in, legally.

He'd been the one who had dumped her and filed for divorce. Not only that, he talked trash about her any time she was brought up in a way you'd think he'd hated her, so Black nor I ever got why he'd gone balls to the wall about Chew fucking her.

"Keely?" Bev called.

My dazed eyes went to her.

Shoulders slumped, she slid into her seat.

"You hadn't thought of that?" she asked.

"I knew that they wouldn't be . . . wouldn't be happy and that Hound would face that displeasure, but . . . the gauntlet?"

Bev sucked in her lips and bit them.

I didn't know if they'd ever made anyone stand the gauntlet. It wouldn't be something they put out there if that decision was made.

That would be brothers only. It could have happened when the Club was sliding toward the hellmouth that was Crank and fighting desperately to pull themselves clear before they went into freefall. Everything was insanity back then.

But I did know what the gauntlet was.

They didn't run it, oh no.

They *stood* it, or to my way of thinking, they were forced to stand it so they could be forced to *withstand* it.

In other words, if a brother did something that the other brothers felt he deserved to pay penance for, they didn't pile shit on him for days, weeks, months, making him eat it until they felt he'd paid their price.

They got shit done and quick.

This was by tying that brother's dominant hand behind his back and making him fight every single brother for a round of five minutes. There was no break for the brother doing atonement in between. Once that five minutes was done, the next brother came right in. If he went down, they pulled him up. If he became unconscious, they threw water on him until he was sentient, or at least standing, and then they went at him again.

Once the last brother threw the last punch, it was done. Amends were considered made. And all was forgiven, if not forgotten.

"They wouldn't do that to Hound," I said quietly.

Bev made no reply.

"Not Hound. They wouldn't do that to Hound."

She finally said something.

It was, "Girl."

And that was it.

That meant she thought they'd do it.

To Hound.

"I couldn't bear it if they did that to Hound. Not Hound. Not at all. But definitely not because of me," I told her.

She leaned across the table toward me.

"Don't," she hissed.

"Beverly—"

"He'll do it, he'd stand through it, and he won't give a shit," she declared.

He would.

He'd do it and he wouldn't give that first shit.

For me.

My voice was getting higher. "I don't care! They can't do that to Hound because Hound is *Hound*."

"And Black was Black," she said gently.

"So?" I snapped. "They can't see past that to see Hound's happy? I'm happy? It has not one fucking thing to do with them, and they can't act like they're having a little tizzy for a day or two and then get over it?"

Her lips ticked up but she said, "Not sure any of those men have 'a little tizzy' in them. More like the different levels of the wrath of hellfire when they get pissed."

"Well, they can just get over it," I bit out.

"Keely—"

"They fucking *can*," I sneered. "I swear to Christ, Bev, if they put my man through that for doing nothing but falling in love with me, I'm done with the Club. Hound will stay in it. Dutch and Jag will patch in. But I'll be *out*."

"Keely," she whispered, blue eyes big and horrified.

"And I'll tell each and every one of them just that if they even *think* about making him stand the gauntlet."

"You need to stay out of this and you know it, babe," she advised gravely. "It'll be a brother thing."

"Excuse me? The man I pick to drive his cock in me is a brother thing?" I asked sarcastically. "I don't fucking think so."

"Keely, you know how it is."

"I know how it's *not* going to be and that is the fact they are *not* going to make my man stand the gauntlet for falling in love with me. Not after all he's given to the Club. Not after what he gave to Black. Not after how he took care of my boys. Not after all he did for me. No way. No fucking way."

With that, on a slash of my hand, I grabbed my champagne flute, almost committing the sacrilege of spilling some Sofia, before I put it to my mouth and swallowed the whole damn thing.

When I put it down, Bev was already up, going to the fridge to get the bottle.

She filled my glass and set the bottle on the table, her gaze on me.

"You know I got your back, babe," she said softly. "You also know that doesn't mean dick."

"Thanks, Beverly. And you'd be surprised. Those men love you. And it seems to me from what Hound's been telling me, they might live their lives and do their thing and they don't give a shit what anyone thinks but they do care what the brothers think, and from what I've heard, they now also care what their women think. And you're still considered Boz's so you have more loyalty from that Club than *you* think."

She looked like she'd fallen into a weird trance.

So I called, "Beverly."

She snapped out of it and came back into the room, her eyes clear, so clear, they were almost sharp and . . .

Fuck.

Dancing.

She swiped up her glass and lifted it toward me. "You're right, sister. Love is in the air and fuck it. They don't think snatch has a say? They don't think our feelings matter? Whatever. We'll just keep on keepin' on, and in the end, be happy."

I ignored the earlier look in her eyes, lifted my recharged glass and again we clinked.

She gulped hers all down.

I only drank half of mine.

She put her glass to the table, grabbed the bottle, started her refill and said, "Gotta keep up with my girl."

I shot her a smile that I hoped wasn't shaky and replied, "Abso-fuck-ing-lutely."

IN THE END, WE GOT trashed.

So in the end, I had to call Hound to pick me up.

Also in the end, I nearly burst into tears when Hound showed at Bev's door and she threw her arms around him, shoved her face in his chest and shouted, "You and Keely! This makes me *so happy!*" then dissolved into sobs.

I managed not to burst into tears when Hound's arms slowly wound around her, he looked over the top of her head and raised his brows, giving me a "Please kill me" look.

It was then I had to stop myself from laughing.

Needless to say, getting in Hound's truck with Hound, the first time I'd ever been in his truck with him alone, the first time I'd ever ridden beside him without the boys with us, and it coming to me I'd never been on the back of his bike and couldn't until we told the brothers, I started to dive into my head.

This being, diving into my head angrily.

Because Bev was right.

Those men practically worshipped Black.

So they'd make Hound stand the gauntlet to have me.

I was so into my head, thinking these things, I didn't notice that I didn't speak all the way home.

Or all the way up to my front door.

Or all the way up to my room.

All this last with Hound following me.

"Everything good with you and Bev?" Hound asked carefully when we both hit the room.

I shot him a glare. His brows went up. And angrily, I went to the shopping bag I'd left on the armchair, which looked like it was covered in shaggy sheepskin, that sat in the seating area of my huge bedroom.

With my back turned to him, I tore off my clothes, all of them. Then I yanked the teddy out of the bag, bit the tags off with my teeth, and molded it on, adjusting it around my not-as-abundant-as-Bev's-boobies so it gave them some lift and squeeze.

I turned to Hound, slammed my hands on my hips even as I jutted one out and demanded, "Well?"

That got me a new look from my new, expressive Hound. One that shared he wanted bad to bust a gut laughing at the fact I'd just angrily slid on a teddy, at the same time he wondered how pissed I would be if he ripped that brand-new teddy clean from my body.

It was a freaking *awesome* look.

"Do you like it?" I asked when he said nothing.

"I'm not sure how one second, I could be worried you got into it with your girl and the next minute I'm so hard I think my dick's gonna split in two at the same time I wanna laugh my ass off 'cause you're so damned cute. So yeah, I like it, but answer me. You and Bev okay?"

"First," I brandished an arm down my front like I was a model calling attention to a shiny car on a podium at a car show, "Happy day after I told you I love you day."

That got me another new look from Hound.

One that said he thought I was damned cute and he loved me . . . *fierce*.

I had to ignore that so I could stay on target with what I had to say.

"Second, if the brothers make you stand the gauntlet, I'm done with Chaos," I leaned toward him dramatically, *"forever."*

His face softened, registering openly his understanding.

"I see the old ladies got together and got their panties in a twist," he muttered.

"I'm being very serious, Shep," I warned.

"Baby, on your knees at the edge of the side of the bed. Now."

That took some of the anger out of me mostly because you couldn't be angry when you were in the throes of a mini-orgasm.

I went to the bed and did as I was told.

Hound didn't waste time coming to stand in front of me.

He also didn't waste time making new adjustments to the neckline of my teddy, gliding it over my nipples to expose them in a move that felt so good, my lips parted and I felt a rush of heat between my legs. He then put his palms to the bottom sides of my breasts and shoved them up and in.

"Better," he murmured.

"Hound."

His gaze went from my tits to my eyes but he kept his hands where they were.

"They might make me do it," he whispered.

A frisson of fear moved through me and I put my hands to his abs.

"Baby," I whispered back.

"And I'll do it. To have you and have my brothers, I'll do anything, but Keekee," his thumbs slid over my nipples and again my lips parted as I swayed into his hands, "bottom line, I finally got you, I'll do anything it takes to keep you."

I slid a hand up his chest and guessed, "You knew this was a possibility."

"Yup."

"It's not fair."

"It's the way it is."

"It isn't fair," I pushed.

"It's how much you're worth it to me," he returned, and I swayed deeper into his hands. "I almost want it, Keekee. That shot to prove to them where I'm at with you. To show Black I deserve you. They decide that's where it's gonna be, I'll be all in."

I curled my fingers around his neck. "But what if I don't want it?"

"You know the man I am, the men they are, what this is and how it's gotta be." He dropped his head to rest his forehead against mine. "It'll be their last act of loyalty to Black. They gotta give you up too, Keely. They gotta give you to me. If they can't find it in their souls to do that without makin' me bleed, then I'll give that to them too."

God, he loved his brothers.

And man, did he love me.

"I won't like it."

"Wouldn't suspect you'd want your man beat to shit," he said with amusement, lifting his head from mine.

"I know this is just another day in your life, your world, you get how it goes," I told him, squeezing his neck. "But I want it understood, I don't like it."

"I need you at the hog roasts at my side," he returned. "I need you on the back of my bike on our rides. I need to fuck you in my bed at the Compound. I need you in Chaos with me, Keekee. It's noted you don't like this might happen. But I don't want you pullin' outta Chaos because your man is Chaos, and to be at my side, I want you a part of everything that makes me."

Fuck, I had to give this to him.

"Okay," I grumbled. "But I still don't like it."

One of his hands slid from my breast down my ribs, my belly, he bent into me so he could trace the outside of the teddy between my legs, and then he pushed it aside and glided one finger inside me.

Well, there you go.

Hound found a successful way to end a conversation he was done having.

I arched into his chest, breathing out, "Baby."

"Fuck, I don't know how to fuck you in this, don't wanna take my eyes off all a' you," he growled, sliding his finger out and then going back in with two.

I wrapped both of my hands around his neck and held on.

"Use my neck to lean back, baby, I wanna watch you in that thing takin' my fingers."

I did as told.

His eyes roamed down me and locked between my legs.

I slid my thighs out wider.

"Jesus, so fuckin' slick. I'm coated thick and you're still runnin' down my wrist."

I whimpered.

He looked at me face. "You gonna give me a day after the day after you said you love me present?"

I fucking was.

"Absolutely."

He grinned.

It was predatory, feral.

My hips jerked against his fingers.

"Ride that, Keekee," he growled.

I rode his fingers in my teddy, my breasts exposed, pushed up by the tight lace and mesh, and Hound watched me and kept watching me until I exploded for him, crying out, bucking on his fingers at the same time grinding into the thumb he was using to rub my clit.

I barely got over it when he yanked up the material tight between my legs. I moaned as it dragged hard against my clit. And then I was turned, pushed down with cheek to my comforter, my thighs pressed farther apart, my knees still at the edge of the bed, and Hound was inside me.

"Love you, baby," I breathed.

He pulled the material again, this time at the back, making it drive up my crease.

Yes.

"Yeah," he grunted.

"Fuck me, honey," I begged, slamming back into his thrusts.

Hound's fingers seized the material at the front between my legs and yanked the teddy taut against my clit and kept doing it as he took me from behind.

"*Yeah,*" he grunted.

I came up to my hands and he mounted me, chest to my back, one hand rhythmically tugging hard at the material, one hand covering my tit and pulling at my nipple, his cock pounding.

He took me there again and straightened away only to drive two wetted fingers up my ass, and then he took me there again.

Only then did he go there with me, the muted thunder of his roar as he shot deep making me quiver all over on my hands and knees in front of him.

He couldn't have been over it when he pulled out, flipped me to my back and leaned into a hand beside me in the bed, arm straight, other hand covering me between my legs.

"You still drunk?" he asked.

"Mildly," I answered.

"I want my cum in every part of you that can take it tonight, Keely."

I didn't have to be drunk to be down with that.

I reached out an arm to curl my fingers around the back of his neck and used his solid strength to pull me off the bed so I could put my face in his.

"Then give it to me, Hound."

His snarling growl sounded and kept doing it even as he kissed me.

It was then he followed through with his plan.

I went to work the next day with a slight hangover, still feeling my man's cock up my ass and in my pussy.

And I learned, happily, I could still tear life up, move on to the next day and get the job done.

CHAPTER SEVENTEEN

GHOSTS ARE RISING

Keely

IT WAS FRIDAY MORNING.

I was at the kitchen table and Hound was on the phone with what sounded like Tack.

He was still making breakfast for me every morning, and this was evidenced by the fact that he'd just slid my plate in front of me.

He was branching out.

Cheesy scrambled eggs, toast and sausage patties.

I grabbed my fork and knife and dug in, but did it feeling funny.

Hound had woken up beside me every day since Monday.

And every day, he got up with me when he could easily stay asleep in bed and he didn't do it just to fuck me.

He made me breakfast.

We were good. The boys knew and were happy for us. Bev knew and was happy for us. We had an understanding of the worst that might come when we told the brothers and we also had an understanding of how we'd deal with that.

But I'd come home from work the day before to Hound's truck in my drive, his bike behind it and a massive duffle filled with Hound's clothes in my bedroom.

I had not asked him to kinda, sorta move in.

I did not mind he'd kinda, sorta moved in without my invitation.

What concerned me was, as far as I knew, until both his modes of transport hit my driveway and that bag hit my bedroom, he only went back to his place to change clothes.

Before the night was done, he moved his bike and truck through the gate at my back fence into the enclosed area, which Black had built for our park model camper he'd bought for when we hit rallies. I'd sold it a few years after his death to Arlo, and that space had gone empty since.

Until now, it became where Hound could park his rides so they wouldn't be seen sitting overnight at my house by anyone who we might not want to see them who also might pass or stop by.

The hiding had to end and I was all for that, I just wasn't all for how that might have to come about (at all).

And we'd agreed not to take this slow so he could move all his stuff to my place, I didn't care. I'd even get rid of the old furniture that used to be in our living room, which I'd moved down to the basement when I'd renovated so the boys could have a place that was their own when they got to the age they needed that. Hound could put his kickass new shit down there.

What concerned me was that it seemed he was avoiding his space and it might not be the greatest, but it was where we started, it was his, and I liked being there with him.

What I didn't like was that I knew he was avoiding it because he was avoiding memories of Jean.

"Knight's not gonna take it that far, not with a woman, and as much as she's an asshole, Turnbull's still got a vagina," Hound said into his phone, coming back to the table with his plate.

He sat down at corners with me and grabbed his fork.

But I was stuck on the name he said.

Turnbull.

I knew that name.

I hadn't heard it said in years, but then again, I hadn't heard anyone mention Chew in years. But it seemed with that he might somehow be back, and that somehow was not in a good way, as any way a total dick like Chew could be back.

I couldn't say I hated Chew in the beginning.

I could say I hated him in the end.

"I know our patch is still clean," Hound went on. "But I think we may need to back his play. He stayed outta it for us. Now he's in it, we need to get back into it with him."

He listened and ate. I just ate because he was silent and there was nothing to listen to.

Then there was.

"Yeah," he said on a sigh. "Another meet. Doin' that so much, might as well put cots around the table so we can sleep." Pause before, on another sigh, this one heavier, "Right. Yeah. I'll be there. Later."

He put his phone down and sank his fork in his sausage patty.

"Everything okay?" I asked carefully.

"Club shit," he muttered, shoving sausage in his mouth.

There was a lot of bad that Hound had to deal with coming after Black.

At his clear indication we were not going to talk about his phone call, a calm, sweet feeling settled low in my belly that there was something important, something good that he'd have, coming after Black.

I knew the golden rule when it came to Club brothers and old ladies, and this was not just Chaos. There was a lot that could be negotiated over time between hardcore bikers and their women, and in that lot, it was the old lady who had to make the decision if she was going to put up with it or not.

But I knew the golden rule.

If there was club business happening and a biker babe's old man didn't share, it was not hers to have. She didn't wheedle, connive or nag. She kept her mouth shut and sucked it up, however that business affected her man, and in turn her, and without comment, she was there for him.

If she was smart, but mostly if she was loving, she proved with actions over time that he could trust her. And if he learned that, he might give her a little bit, he might give her it all. And they might have discussions about it, he might ask her advice, or if she turned stupid, there might be arguments.

But if he eventually gave her that trust, the one thing she couldn't do was know what was happening with the club then stick her nose in it with the brothers.

She might have some influence but that had strict boundaries, behind the doors of the home she shared with her old man. Outside, especially on club turf, she had her man's back, she had the club's back and that was most assuredly *that*.

I knew Chaos had troubles and I had a feeling Hound trusted me. However, with my history, he was not sharing, more than likely because he was protecting me. I lost my mind after Millie had been taken and I went to the Compound to speak what was left in it. He didn't want a repeat of that, not because I was so angry, because he understood the hurt and fear that lay under that.

I'd need to take the time to turn that around so I could do my bit to be the part of his life that was the calm to whatever storm Chaos had found themselves in, taking Hound right along with them.

The way I could do that now was not to push him about whatever was happening, just let it be and not have any reaction to knowing it was happening.

So I did precisely that.

I also changed the subject, but unfortunately it was to one that might be almost as sticky.

"Bev called yesterday and said she'd like to have a family dinner with the boys and her fiancé. And by family, she made it clear she means you too."

Hound turned his attention from his plate to me and I quickly went on before he could refuse this suggestion and do it with extreme prejudice.

"She's excited for us. She's falling in love with this guy, kinda after the fact, but she is. And I wasn't really supportive of it all while it was happening. She wants me and the boys to meet him, and she wants you to do that too. She wants him to be deeper in her life, which means knowing the people she loves. This guy is an insurance salesman. He'll never rub up against Chaos—"

"Set it up, babe, but do it here. You have a dining room table, Bev doesn't, and no offense to the woman, but she isn't near as good a cook as you. Tomorrow night. Or Sunday. I'll talk to the boys."

I stared at him.

He kept eating.

"You, well . . . you said her, the boys, you and me only and now we're bringing in Tad," I mentioned quietly.

He grinned at his plate, shaking his head, muttering, "Tad."

"It's the man's name, Shep," I told him.

He sat back in his chair, nabbing his coffee mug, aimed his grin at me and stated, "An insurance guy named Tad."

I felt my eyes narrow. "You'll be nice to him."

"Sure," he agreed, taking a sip of coffee.

"And you won't talk about insurance people fucking folks up the ass," I demanded.

"I'll do my best not to work that into conversation," he joked.

"Seriously, Hound," I snapped.

"Chill, Keekee. It'll be cool," he returned.

That was what I didn't understand. That he was "cool" with this when he'd been so adamant it was only the boys, Bev, him and me.

Therefore I got into that. "So now explain why you're all good with Tad showing, because that kinda freaks me."

"Babe, he's an insurance agent," he said in explanation, which was not a full explanation.

"Yes," I said back and did it slowly.

"First of all, he doesn't know any of the guys. Second, he's probably never gonna know any of the guys, except me but only 'cause a' you. So like you said, he's never gonna run into Chaos and if he does, I'll tell him to keep his mouth shut and that'll probably not only make Tad's mouth stay shut, it'll probably tighten his sphincter so he might not be able to take a shit for a week."

"Don't threaten him either, Hound," I warned irately.

He gave me a big smile. "Jesus, Keekee, you think I'm gonna back this guy into the wall of your foyer with a hand at his throat the minute he strolls in and tell him I'll serve him his balls for dinner if by some extreme off-chance he runs into any biker in the Denver Metro area and says, 'Hey, by the way, did you know that Hound guy is bangin' that biker babe named Keely?' Christ. Give me some credit, woman."

As this was something he wouldn't do, nor would Tad (I hoped), I nodded.

"Just . . . try not to be too naturally badass," I said. "And warn the boys not to be too badass either. I think Beverly likes his sphincter working properly."

Hound's brows went up. "She give it to him up the ass?"

"No!" I snapped. "Well, I don't know. She shares, but she hasn't shared that."

"Maybe you should get her a strap-on for her bachelorette party. One a' them's gotta have a dick, and when it's his turn to give it he might find it handy."

I reached out and punched his arm.

He started chuckling.

Since he was in a good mood, right or wrong, I didn't know him well enough as we were now—Hound, my old man, Keely, his old lady—but I decided to go for it.

"You don't have to make me breakfast," I announced.

I found out it was wrong.

His humor vanished, he set his coffee down and he bent back over his plate.

"Shep," I whispered.

He stayed bent over his plate and turned just his eyes to me.

"I need to make you breakfast," he stated low.

Okay, that was where he was at and right now, that was where I had to leave it.

I nodded.

"Okay, baby," I said gently. When he looked back to his food, I finished, "Love you."

He grunted at his food.

I took that as "love you back."

Taking us out of those dark waters, I declared, "You don't have to share what the Club's into, but, you know, now that you're rubbing up against Chew again, next time you see him, tell him I told him to go fuck himself."

I went immediately still because Hound went so still, the air not only in the kitchen but also I figured in the entire house (and maybe down the block) went still.

I watched as, slowly, he turned his eyes to me.

"Chew?" he growled.

"I . . . uh . . ." I started then stopped.

It was not done to renounce the Club. If you became a member of a motorcycle club like Chaos, it was a lifetime commitment.

Chew had renounced the Club.

This was not a popular decision, generally.

In the end, however, I sensed the men were happy he made that choice.

This was because the man Chew proved himself to be when he didn't vote for Crank's execution, thus solidifying Tack's takeover, and renouncing the Club rather than being in it when Tack was leading them to clean was even less popular. The reason Crank's reign was finally brought to an end was all the reason every brother felt Chew should get his shit in line.

It wasn't that every man lost respect for him, how deep he fell into the shit Crank stirred up, how dirty he got and how much he enjoyed it.

It was that they all hated his guts and were happy to see the back of him, would have burned the Chaos emblem off his back if he'd done that first thing to earn it, and since then, even if I wasn't deep into the Club, I'd had an informant named Beverly, and I hadn't heard his name mentioned once.

We'd obviously never had the conversation, but I didn't have to have it with Hound to know where he fell on the scale of how deeply he hated Chew's guts.

But even if that was in question, his reaction to me mentioning Chew would have told me the depths of his hatred rang the bell at the top with a very loud *clang*.

Hound straightened from his plate but did it turning his body toward me and putting his forearm and elbow on the table in a way that put him right in my space.

"Why'd you mention Chew?" he asked.

"Your phone call," I answered.

"What about my phone call made you mention Chew?"

"You said the name Turnbull."

Oh shit.

I could actually see the muscles in his neck, shoulders and chest getting tight, making him look like he was growing, expanding, filling the space physically and not just with his enraged vibe.

"Explain," he gritted between his teeth.

"It was . . . I . . ." I began.

And then I remembered why he wouldn't remember.

It was also dawning on me just how important this was.

I leaned into him, cupping my hand over the top of his fist on the table and holding on tight.

"Do you remember when Crank was pulling that shit, wanting to show the world a different face of Chaos, pretend out there, but especially to the cops, that Chaos wasn't what he was making you?" I asked.

"No," he bit off.

No, he wouldn't. Because, like most of the boys, he didn't buy into Crank's bullshit. He just ignored it.

"Well, he did. He signed the Club up to do some stuff at the schools with kids. Road safety. Awareness of your surroundings. How to deal if a stranger approached. The people at the schools thought it was great when bikers volunteered. Thought the kids would listen to bikers. But when it came down to actually doing it, mostly it was the old ladies getting tricked out in biker bitch gear and heading over. Except Black, Dog, Tack and Hop were all in. And . . ." I squeezed his hand. "Chew."

"And?" he practically barked.

I nodded and continued swiftly. "I figured out why Chew came when I noticed him flirting and playing with some of the moms, especially the single ones. And he got tight with one. I know he took her out because Black and I saw them together at The Blue Bonnet. She had a little girl. Kind of a handful. Lots of attitude. Her name was—"

"Camilla."

At the way he said that name, and the fact he knew it, I shut up.

Hound's hand was gone from mine and his chair was scraping against the floor as he threw it back while rising from it, tagging his phone from the table.

I tipped my head back as he bent to me, pressed his lips to mine hard and pulled away saying, "Gotta go."

"Chew's back, isn't he?" I worried. "And it's not good."

He grabbed me at the back of my head and got in my face.

"You do not worry," he growled. "Now I gotta go." He touched his mouth to mine and then muttered, "Love you."

And with that, putting thumb to his phone and then his phone to his ear, he snatched his cut off the back of the chair closest to the door where he'd put it the night before, and he was gone.

"Okay," I said, staring at the door. I took a deep breath and finished, "Shit."

THAT EVENING, I WAS IN my closet, making room and finding places to put Hound's clothes, when he walked in.

His eyes went direct from me, to me hanging a pair of his jeans on a section of closet that was two bars, high and low.

There were several of these sections around. But the bar atop where I was putting his jeans held my stuff (as did all the other ones). The bar under it had ten pairs of faded jeans, a black, long-sleeved shirt with bib panel that was so hot I wanted to ask Hound to try it on for me, and four plaid flannel shirts all in the dizzying arrays of grays mixed with black, or black mixed with grays.

His attention came back to me.

"This is your section of the closet," I shared, pointing at it. I moved to the space beside it, indicating a set of drawers, primarily the third one down. "Underwear, socks and wife beaters. The one under that, your tees."

His now-expressive face changed but I quickly lifted a hand, palm out his way.

"Before you fuck me on the floor of the closet to thank me for putting your clothes away and what that means, first, bring the rest of them. Second, if you're blowing off the apartment, there's no reason to blow money paying rent there, so we'll get the boys over here to get rid of the shit in the basement and move your new shit down there. That can be your biker sanctuary. Third, we *will* be talking about Jean, and soon, baby, because you're worrying me. And last, Tad and Bev are coming over for dinner on Sunday night so one of us needs to text the boys to get their asses here."

He didn't move.

"I'm done," I informed him. "So now you can fuck me."

He studied me closely.

Very closely.

So closely, I got a little freaked.

But I understood why he did it when he began speaking.

"The man behind kidnapping Millie is a guy called Benito Valenzuela," he declared.

I pulled in breath.

It was happening already.

Hound was going to trust me.

Right there in my closet, I was officially becoming his old lady.

I felt a tingle of happiness even as I braced.

He kept going.

"He's a lunatic. Psychopath. Sociopath. I don't know the difference but he's probably both. He makes pornos, runs girls and deals drugs. He wanted Denver and Chaos is in Denver so he was pushing to take our patch. We been rubbing each other the wrong way for a long time. Not long after he kidnapped Millie, he disappeared. And a woman, his woman, or we thought he was banging her, but whatever she was doin' with him, she had a place in his operations. Now she's taken *his* place. And her name is Camilla Turnbull."

"Oh my God," I whispered.

Hound ignored my whisper and kept talking.

"Chew is either behind Valenzuela's maneuvers or he's behind Turnbull pushin' her way in, getting close and then taking him out so Chew can take over. One way or another, it's Chew who wants Chaos. And if Valenzuela got dead after the Millie shit, it would make sense because only Chew would retaliate for one of his men doin' something that stupid and doin' it to an old lady. But mostly, doin' it to Millie."

He was right. Chew had loved Millie. In fact, I thought back in the day that Chew had *loved* Millie. It was just that she was High's in a way that she was *High's* and that would never change, this being proved because even when that did change, it never actually did and they were back.

"So what does this all mean?" I asked.

"Either Valenzuela knows he fucked up, the big man is pissed, that big man bein' Chew, and he's on the run, or they made their move and he's dead. That only matters if he's on the run and he finds himself the firepower to come back. What matters now is that our real enemy knows us in a way he *knows us*. Most a' the shit we did, the statute of limitation is long past. Some of it doesn't have a statute of limitation, and if he doesn't know where the bodies are buried, he can guess."

"Oh my *God*," I breathed, understanding what that meant, particularly for my man. The happy tingle was long gone and the only way I could express the very different tingle that took its place was to whisper, "Hound."

"Tack's dealin' with that tonight with me and some brothers. The recruits won't touch this, 'specially Dutch and Jag will not be layin' hands on the bones of the men who took out their daddy."

A chill slid over me.

"God. Hound."

"I need you solid with this, Keely, 'cause ghosts are rising and I finally got you, I am *not* fuckin' losin' you to more of Crank's fuckin' *shit*."

He wasn't ever going to lose me.

But right now I could tell he was losing *it*.

So I went to him immediately.

I curled my arms around him in his cut, pressed myself close and tipped my head back to look in his eyes.

"You won't lose me," I assured him.

"We all put bullets in him and the man still won't die."

I slid my hands under his cut and started to stroke his back over his tee soothingly, murmuring, "Honey. This is not Crank. Crank is gone. This is Chew."

"He was Crank's boy. Like a fuckin' lapdog. Pantin'. The deeper Crank pulled us under, the more the rest of us choked on shit, but for Chew, it made him freer to breathe."

"It's over," I reminded him.

"It's not over," he bit out. "Evidenced by the fact I gotta meet up with Tack, Dog, Brick, Boz, High and Hop and go dig up his motherfuckin' bones and take them somewhere to put lye on 'em."

I beat back a shudder and fisted my fingers in the back of his tee. "We're talking Chew here. Remember that," I urged strongly. "That man cannot take on Chaos. He can't outthink Tack Allen. You got this."

"He's managed to dick with us for a really long time without a single one of us knowin' shit, Keely."

That seemed to be true.

I pressed my lips together.

I unpressed them to say, "You all . . ." I yanked his shirt out then pushed it back, digging my fists into his back, *"have this."*

He finally lifted his hand, put it on my crown and slid it down the length of my hair before he went back up and cupped the back of my neck.

"The good part, we know what we're dealin' with," he said. "We didn't before. Tack has what he needs now to do his thing. And that came from you."

I nodded.

"But I had to lie about how I got that shit," he told me.

"Yeah, probably not the time to tell them I gave you this info over breakfast, or your second breakfast because your first one was eating me."

Finally, some of the ferocity went out of his face and his mouth softened.

"Can I ask why you didn't put lye on them before?" I requested curiously.

"Brother vote, they rot slow in deep graves, forgotten."

That seemed a perfectly sound decision to me.

Too bad circumstances circumvented it.

I pressed closer. "I'm sorry you have to deal with this tonight."

His eyes drifted to his rail of clothes and back to me. "Yeah, my woman moves me in, other ways I'd like to spend the night."

I smiled up at him. "Later. Now get this done."

He nodded. Bent. Touched his lips to mine.

"Later."

I gave him a squeeze and let him go.

He took his time untangling his fingers from strands of my hair that didn't want to let him go, and then he started out of the closet.

"Baby?" I called before he disappeared.

He turned back.

"Are Dog and Brick back?" I asked.

He nodded. "Dog, yeah. He and Sheila are back and stayin' back. Brick, no. He's back to help us see the end to this shit but he's got a woman on the western slope. Her name is Stella. Apparently, she's the shit and treats him like gold. Dog likes her. Sheila thinks the world of her. Brick's finally found it, Keekee. He'll go back to her. They're gettin' hitched the end of the summer."

That made me happy. Brick had a soft heart but got it trampled way too often by women who took advantage of it. If Dog liked her, this was good. This meant she was worth having Brick.

"See?" I asked quietly. "It's all good. It's all gonna work out. All the brothers are finding their way to happy."

He studied me a second, did it intently, I weathered it easily, enjoying what was working behind his eyes, especially since it was working there at a time when he was going to walk out of my house to do what he had to do that night.

In other words, standing there solid for my man, I gave him some calm before he had to hit the storm.

Finally, he said, "Yeah."

"Love you, Hound."

He dipped his chin to acknowledge that.

It was what was in his eyes that gave that back.

Then he disappeared.

IT WAS LATE WHEN HOUND returning to bed woke me up.

I turned into him and nuzzled his throat with my face, murmuring,

"All good?"

"Yeah, baby. But I'm wiped. Go back to sleep."

"'Kay," I mumbled, nuzzling all the rest of him with all the rest of me.

I fell asleep pressed tight to his side, Hound on his back, one of my legs tangled in both of his, feeling his hand flat and warm on the small of my back.

Hound

HOUND DID NOT FALL ASLEEP.

Hound held his Keely to his side and stared at the dark ceiling.

He did this because Hound, Tack, Hop, High, Boz, Brick and Dog went right to where the bones were buried.

They'd dug them up.

The problem with that was . . .

Those bones were gone.

CHAPTER EIGHTEEN

THEIR BLOOD RUNS CHAOS

Keely

"OH MY GOD!" I SNAPPED. "If you don't quit eating that, Jagger, I'm gonna kick your ass."

I barely finished saying that before Hound strolled up, reached between me and Jagger, nabbed a chicken tender off the mound on the plate beside me at the stove and bit off half of it.

"Seriously?" I asked my man.

He gave me a closed-mouth grin while chewing and swallowing, before saying, "Babe, you bought four packets of chicken tenders. Each pack had to have four breasts in it. There's six of us eatin'. You've been fryin' chicken for almost an hour. Unless this guy is a Saskatchewan, he's not gonna eat twelve chicken breasts worth of chicken tenders. So, chill."

Needless to say, it was Sunday evening.

Time for dinner with Beverly and her guy.

I squinted my eyes at Hound. "If you don't quit telling me to chill after you've annoyed me, Shepherd Ironside, you'll be *wearing* this chicken and we'll have to serve Safeway stuff to Bev and Tad."

"I still can't believe Aunt Bev's man's name is *Tad*," Jagger said under his breath, getting my attention.

"He probably can't believe your name is Jagger," I shot back.

"Yeah, but I'm named after a Rock God and he's named a word that means," he smirked, *"little bit."*

"Fitting," Dutch mumbled, joining us, reaching in and grabbing his own tender.

I made to smack his hand with the tongs I was holding, missed, but did this seeing the error of my ways that I announced Tad had a little dick in the Compound.

Shit.

I pointed the tongs at each of my boys. "Not a one of you mentions his member."

"Or lack of," Jagger joked.

I skewered him with a glare.

"Christ, woman, we're not gonna talk to the man about his cock, not the first time we meet him, not *ever*," Hound declared.

"Ma, *unwind*," Dutch said. "Aunt Bev is the shit. We love her. We got her back. Tonight's gonna go awesome."

Dutch would be awesome.

Jagger loved his Aunt Beverly and would try to be awesome, he also might fail.

I had never been with Hound in a social situation that didn't involve pool tables, a hog turning on a spit, copious drinking and at least fifty other people. He loved me. I loved him. He gave amazing orgasms. He could be sweet. He could be funny. He made great eggs.

But he could also be a lunatic.

A knock came at the front door.

Shit.

"I got it," Jagger said, moving off.

Not my first choice.

"Jag!" I called. He stopped and turned around. I did the thing with the tongs again between all of them and said, "All of you. Button up the badass. We're just your normal, average family of mechanics and a truancy officer, the mechanics working at a custom car and bike garage with auto supply store that happens to belong to a motorcycle club made up of vigilante bikers. Hide that last part."

"Yes, ma'am," Jag said, lips twitching and also again moving to the front door.

"You think Aunt Bev is as whacked out as you right now?" Dutch asked.

I turned to the skillet to flip chicken. "I think your Aunt Bev is right now quaking in her boots."

"Keekee," Hound murmured, drifting his fingers across my shirt at the small of my back in a way that sent a shiver up my spine. "We've got this. For Bev."

I caught his eyes over my shoulder, saw he was serious and finally relaxed.

I nodded. "Thanks, babe."

Dutch nabbed another tender.

I looked to the ceiling.

"Uh, they're here," Jagger said, weirdly tentatively.

I turned to the door to the kitchen to see Jagger moving in, Bev moving in behind him, and then my mouth dropped open when Tad moved in.

Tad was not what most minds would conjure up when you were told of a man named Tad.

Tad had to be six foot four (at least) and I wasn't sure Tad's shoulders could fit through the doorway to my kitchen, and it was a double-wide door. Tad also had a thick shock of black hair with little flecks of gray in it that was flowing back from his forehead in a way that had to be styled at the same time it looked natural. His tree trunk legs were encased in faded jeans. His broad chest was covered in a vintage AC/DC T-shirt. And his face was the chiseled magnificence that occupied every breathing woman's wet dreams.

I now understood why Bev didn't care he had a little cock.

He also had incredibly long fingers on beautiful hands that he could be taught to use in amazing ways, but regardless, I could just look at him and have an orgasm.

"You might wanna shut your mouth, baby," Hound whispered in my ear.

I started.

Then I shut my mouth.

"Seems he *is* a Saskatchewan," Hound kept whispering.

I elbowed him in the side.

"Tad, right?" Dutch asked, moving forward, hand up. "I'm Dutch, Aunt Bev's nephew-not-by-blood."

"Dutch, nice t'meet you." His rolling, silky, deep voice slithered through the room.

I bit back a moan.

Okay, all he would need to do was talk dirty to me.

"Tad," he introduced, taking Dutch's hand. "Probably figured I'm Beverly's fiancé."

"Yeah, man, happy for Aunt Bev, happy for you," Dutch murmured, shaking his hand.

They broke off and his eyes came to me. "You must be Keely. Beverly talks a lot about you."

He walked my way, hand up, and I was so mesmerized by his jade-green eyes, I didn't put the tongs down at first. In the end, I transferred them to my left hand and felt my right engulfed in the strength of his.

Oh yes, he could be taught to use those hands.

"Yes, uh . . . Keely," I murmured. "Really great to meet you, Tad."

He gave me a movie star smile.

I bit my lip.

He let me go to turn to Hound. "And you're Hound."

"Hound. Shepherd," Hound said, taking his offered hand. "Whatever you're comfortable with, friend."

"Right," Tad said on a less megawatt smile, but even less megawatt and not aimed at me, I appreciated it.

"Hey, girl." Bev moved into me.

I gave her a hug and whispered in her ear, "Why didn't you tell me he was gorgeous?"

She shifted back but didn't let me go and gave me a confused look. "I thought I did."

Maybe she did. Maybe the penis size information just shoved it out.

"We gotta talk," she said low.

I looked in her eyes.

Then I declared to the room. "I'm done with my boys stealing chicken so you're all kicked out. Tad, sorry, you too. Shep, honey, get Tad a beer or . . ." I verbally stumbled. "Sorry, Tad, do you drink beer?"

Another movie star smile. "I drink beer, Keely."

"Great," I replied, then looked to Hound. "Pop one open for our guest, babe. And wrangle these boys out before I flour and fry the next hand that reaches for a tender."

Hound shot me a grin, got Tad a beer, the boys grabbed theirs and they took off.

I watched until they disappeared into the living room, leaning back from the stove to do it, and when they were out of earshot, I whirled on Bev.

"He likes AC/DC?"

She again looked perplexed. "Keely, girl, he's not a dud. He likes rock 'n' roll. He likes beer. It's not like he curses every other word but he doesn't have a stick up his butt. He's got a bike. Actually, he has two."

I gave her another slow blink.

I'd thought he was a wimp.

That might also have to do with the penis size information, but probably more had to do with the insurance salesman information.

Well, it just went to show you, no matter which way you rushed to judgment—bikers shoved into stereotypes, biker babes shoved into stereotypes, insurance salesmen shoved into stereotypes, etcetera—you just shouldn't.

"Neither are Harleys," she shared. "One's a BMW, and I know it's practically blasphemy to say this, but it's seriously hot. The other is an off-road Ducati. Before me, he was gone a lot on the weekends he didn't have his kids because he was off-roading. He's a total adrenaline junkie."

I should not be surprised about this. Bev was a biker babe.

She'd just switched brands.

I felt my shoulders droop because all that was that man, and the more that I'd learned that was all good for Beverly, was not all he could be.

"Sister, look at me," Bev called.

I turned to her.

She got close. "Okay, well, the teddy worked."

I stared at her, hope bubbling up inside me.

"Or, maybe it wasn't the teddy," she carried on. "Maybe it was my newfound knowledge I was falling in love with him. We, uh . . . this last week, we uh . . . kinda . . . sorted shit out."

"How?" I breathed.

"Well, after the first time it went stratospheric . . ." she began.

Stratospheric?

Oh my God!

She kept going, "He had a chat with me and told me how relieved he was that I, um . . . well, showed him I knew what I was doing in that department."

She knew what *she* was doing?

Now I was perplexed.

"What?"

"The bad sex, babe, it was on me."

I said nothing.

"I was so wound up, hung up on Boz, had my head all messed up. He was gentle about it but he said he was meaning to talk to me about it for a long time, he just didn't know how to bring it up. But when I came out of the bathroom in that teddy, all glittered up in a way he could lick it off, things got going." She grinned. "It heated up *great* and it was *amazing*. He knows where a clit is," she rolled her eyes in ecstasy, "girl, does he *ever*. And he might not be well endowed but he likes when I suck him off and doesn't mind fucking me with my vibrator while he's eating me while I'm doin' it. And we'll just say there's something good about being able to take *all* of a man in my mouth and how hot it is when he shows his appreciation. And get this."

"What?" I asked breathlessly when she didn't go on, however, I was kinda wondering if Hound might get into doing the eating me/vibrator gig.

"He was totally into the vibrator thing. And the glitter thing. And the edible massage stuff thing. So he says the next basket he's bringing, his secretary is not putting it together. He's gonna make me a sex basket, and he said if I want, he'll pick me out a huge dildo. He says when I'm in the mood for that, he can use it and otherwise multitask."

"Oh my freaking *God!*" I cried softly.

"I know, right?" she agreed.

"I've known him for all of about ten seconds and I already know there's so much more to that man than having a small dick. I'm glad you're learning it," I shared.

"Me too. It's weird to go average, but I'm sure getting used to it. I think he guessed that Boz was packing, and I was missing that, but for Tad, seein' as I was used to taking as much as I could get of twelve inches down my throat, his seven isn't an issue *whatsoever*. So he gets the good part of that kinda training."

And that got her another slow blink.

Tad's *seven?*

Seven?

That wasn't small. It wasn't even average!

"Tad doesn't have a tiny dick?" I asked.

"Well, relative to Boz's giganto one, he does. And relative to Tad's giganto size, he does."

Another slow blink as something else she said sunk in. "Boz has *twelve inches?*"

"Girl, why you think it took me so long to get over him?" she asked.

Things were beginning to come *very* clear.

And one of those things was that I might not be able to look Boz in the eye ever again.

"And . . . and . . . you can deep throat seven inches?" I asked.

"Sister, I think Tad nearly took my ring off my finger to return it so he could get a bigger one after I got into the swing of things and took him all the way to the root."

Well, one thing was for certain, unless my definition of the girl next door was way off, that vision I had about Bev for decades was gone forever.

Though, cheerleaders might have that talent, I wouldn't know. I was never a cheerleader.

"So Tad . . . he's . . . he's just . . . just . . . all-around *perfect?*" I stammered.

She grinned a small but exceptionally happy grin and whispered,

"Yeah."

"That is *so awesome*," I whispered back, grinning my also small but exceptionally happy grin right back at her.

"You know what's more awesome?" she asked.

I couldn't think of anything more awesome than Bev having a new biker guy that hot who liked AC/DC, loved her, had a more-than-healthy-sized dick and knew how to give it to her that good in the bedroom.

"What's more awesome?" I asked.

"He loves *me*. Not my blowjobs. Not my pussy. *Me*. He had no doubts we'd get there. He fell in love with the woman I was and the promise of what we could have if I gave all of myself to him. He never gave up on me, and that, babe, *that* is definitely more awesome."

I found her hand and squeezed it.

"You're right, Beverly, that is *way* more awesome," I replied. I got closer to her and asked, "So, how you doin' on that road to happy?"

"Uh, did you *see* my man?"

I gave her a big smile. "I saw him. Don't be mad at me because I also had a mini-orgasm when I saw him."

"I'm not mad, sister, I'm proud. Because that's *my man*."

I giggled so I wouldn't cry.

She squeezed my hand and giggled with me.

"Men!" Jagger shouted from the doorway. "Warning, the estrogen has been let loose in the kitchen. Enter at your own risk. I'll get us a good supply of beer so we don't have to expose ourselves too often."

"Shut it, Jagger," I threw over my shoulder at my son.

He shot me a grin but went right up to his aunt.

He then kissed the side of her head before he said, "He's the shit, Aunt Bev. You have my approval."

"Thanks, Jag, that seals the deal. I was holding back but I'll start looking for wedding venues now," she teased.

He saluted her walking away, heading to the fridge.

"Now," she rubbed her hands together, "Keely's Buttermilk Goodness Chicken Tenders. I told Tad I hoped that was what you were making. He's gonna love 'em. Now I just gotta hope you made your potato salad too."

I did.

It was Hound's favorite.

"I wish you women wouldn't call Ma's chicken that. It makes me think I'll turn into a girl if I eat it," Jag put in, heading back out of the kitchen with four beers, even though Tad's was just opened so they only maybe needed three.

"You might wanna check your junk, sweetheart, since you've had your share already," I called to his back.

He walked out, shaking his head.

I turned to my girl.

She had that hot guy.

At long last, Brick had some woman who did him right.

High and Millie found their way back to each other.

Little Tabby Allen was all grown up and making babies with a man who loved her so much, he'd pick her over his Club.

Tack finally had a woman in his life that he wanted right there.

And I had Hound.

So Chew was back.

The likes of Chew couldn't bring down this goodness.

No way.

No how.

It burned bright and it was going to burn him right up.

Men like Chew didn't win.

Men like Hound and High and Tack and Hop and Dog and Brick . . .

They were winners.

"YOU WORE A PURPLE BANDANNA."

"I didn't wear a purple bandanna."

"You totally wore a purple bandanna. *Ma's* purple bandanna."

"*I didn't wear a purple bandanna.*"

"You wore your mother's purple bandanna, son."

We were at the dining room table. We'd pulled away the chairs we weren't using and there was a lot of room but it still felt nice and intimate and I loved that it wasn't just Dutch and Jag and me at Christmas or Thanksgiving, most of that long table empty. I loved that instead it was filled with people I adored and the detritus of a meal I'd made them that they'd devoured.

It was after dinner but before dessert. We were giving Jagger shit. It was annoying him but he'd always been a good sport, not one who could dish it out and not take it.

I loved that too.

"Aunt Bev, will you and Tad adopt me?" Jagger asked Beverly.

"Tad's daughter is sixteen and she's a knockout and you're a dawg, so . . . no," Beverly answered.

Jag looked to Tad. "Your daughter is a knockout?"

"Son," Hound murmured warningly.

"Yeah, Jag, she's also gonna remain untouched until she's thirty-nine so your best bet is to put her outta your mind," Tad answered.

"I hear you, man," Jag replied on a knowing nod. "I hope I don't have girls. With my superior genetics and taste, which means I'm gonna score me a hot babe, I'll have to buy, like, ten guns."

Hound caught my eyes across the table and shook his head, his lips twitching.

"Speaking of that," Tad began, "Thursday good for you boys to go to the range?"

"Good for me," Hound said.

"I'm in," Dutch said.

"Totally," Jagger said.

"Are women not invited to this outing?" Bev asked.

"Baby," Tad said sweetly, and I felt gooey *for* Beverly just listening to how he said it. "Bonding over bullets is a brotherhood type of thing. And anyway, last time we went to the range, you got a case down your shirt."

Spent shells burned like hell.

"Ouch," I said in sympathy.

"Leave it to me to wear cleavage to the firing range," Bev replied to me.

"It wasn't the shirt I had a problem with," Tad muttered.

Hound and Dutch chuckled.

Jag guffawed.

A knock came at the door.

All my happy, gooey goodness of food and family and friends and love in the air flew right out the window when my panicked eyes hit Hound.

All the people I knew who would show at my door were at this table.

Except people that belonged to Chaos.

Hound was scowling toward the door.

"Shit, fuck, shit," Jagger mumbled.

"I'll get it," Dutch said, pushing back his chair.

"No, honey, no," Bev put in, moving faster than my boy. "I'll get it."

Her gaze darted to me and then she scurried to the door.

"Do I need to follow her?" Tad asked, his silky voice alert to the vibe.

"Should you hide in the kitchen, Hound?" Jagger asked.

"I'm not hidin' in the fuckin' kitchen," Hound growled.

"Right, I get something is going on," Tad also growled. "So do I need to follow my woman?"

"She'll be good, Tad," I said softly.

Tad had no chance to relax.

None of us did.

"No! You don't get to do that!" Beverly shouted angrily.

Tad was out of his chair like a shot.

So were Hound, Dutch and Jag.

I came a lot more slowly so I was still climbing down when my eyes fell on the six people that stormed into my dining room and I felt the entire room freeze, including me.

I had not seen a single one of them in years.

And I wished I was not seeing them then.

"What the fuck?" Jagger muttered, having come to a stop behind me.

"They pushed in, Keely, I couldn't—" Bev was saying, rounding them as she came into the room.

"That," Graham's father spat, pointing at Jagger. "That right there. That language. That's why we're here."

"Simon," Graham's mother whispered, reaching out a hand to his forearm to pull it down.

I stood immobile, not believing on one of the handful of good nights that I'd had in eighteen years, good nights that would be remembered as one of life's best, that these people were in my living room.

Graham's parents and sister.

My parents and sister.

"So, Keely, your mother talked to Dutch last week and he shared that Jagger, too, has joined this gang," my father stated accusingly.

I should never have allowed them into my sons' lives.

After what they'd done to Graham and me, I should have *never* done that.

"Get out," I said.

It was strangled, barely above a whisper, which was not the only reason why not a one of them listened to me.

"So now we're here to do an intervention because we cannot *believe* that you married a man who was messed up in something like that, learned your lesson the hardest way that could be learned, and now you're allowing your sons, my *grandsons*, to make that same mistake," my father went on.

"Dutch, Jag, you don't want this to get ugly, you get these people outta this house," Hound warned.

Tad waded in, moving toward them. "I think that—"

"You get another step closer, we're calling the police!" Graham's mother shouted, panic in her voice, clearly mistaking Tad's AC/DC tee, taking it as indication he was a spawn of Satan member of a motorcycle gang.

"You can't call the police when *you* are the ones not welcome in a home," Beverly snapped.

"Our grandsons are here," my mother snapped back, swinging an arm toward my boys.

And, I noted, but was not surprised that she did not make mention of the fact that her daughter was also right there.

"God, Keely," my sister Tierney said disgustedly. "When are you gonna get yourself together? This is insane. You're so disturbingly messed up. Both your boys in that gang? I swear, Mom nearly had a heart attack when she learned. She wasn't even over Dutch getting into that insanity. Now you allow Jagger to get involved too?"

"Like we said, this is an intervention," Sarah, Graham's sister put in. "We've left it too long. We should have gotten involved long ago, before we lost Graham to that mess. But now, we can't allow this to carry on."

"Keely—" Hound growled, and he said more.

I just didn't hear him.

"You can't allow?" I asked quietly over him speaking.

"Can't allow, won't allow, take your pick. But I'm not losing my grandchildren like I lost my son," Simon declared.

"You lost your son before his throat was slit, Simon," I spat.

Graham's mom, Blair's face drained of color as her hand inched up to her throat and she stared at me like I'd connected a punch to her face.

I should feel that. As a mother, I should feel that.

But since that woman missed her son's wedding, was not there when either of her grandchildren were born, and didn't show at Black's funeral, for Blair, I felt nothing.

"You didn't accept who he was before he found Chaos," I kept at Simon, ignoring Blair. "You definitely didn't accept him after he found Chaos, you disinheriting him clear indication of that. You didn't accept him or me when we found each other. You continued not to accept either of us or our boys when we had them. And you didn't step in when my babies and I lost him. So your legacy of loss is not on Graham, Simon. It's on," I leaned his way, *"you."*

"All right, you guys," Dutch said, and I heard him moving around the table. "Jag and me'll walk you out to your cars and we'll make a time to talk about this later."

"I'm not talkin' about dick later," Jag bit out.

"Jagger, sweetie—" my mom started.

Sweetie?

Sweetie?

For some reason it was that that made me see red.

Because when had she earned the right to call my son *sweetie*?

Was it when she made him cookies?

No, because she'd never made him cookies.

Was it when he was being adorable after getting a birthday or Christmas present he especially wanted?

No, because she'd not been with him for a single birthday or Christmas.

Was it when she blew on scrapes on his elbows and knees the many times he'd gotten them?

No, because she was never around when he got into scrapes.

Not even when he suffered the worst scrape of all, when his father was scraped out of his life.

"Shut your mouth," I clipped, and she reared back like I came at her physically. "And get out of my house."

"You want *us* out, but these guys," Sarah sneered, indicating Hound and Tad, "are welcome. Right? Are they ones that got my brother's," she leaned toward me, her face twisted, "*throat slit*, Keely? *They* can sit at your table but *we* can't be in your home?"

"Jag, Dutch, deal with this," Hound ordered, and I could tell he was barely reining it in. "*Now.*"

"Come on, guys," Dutch tried gently. "Let's get you outside."

I ignored all this.

"Yes," I said to Sarah. "Absolutely. Although Tad is Beverly's fiancé and sells insurance, Hound is Chaos and yes. He's welcome at my table. Because he earned his place there by being *here*," I pointed to the floor, "for me *and* my boys. You, on the other hand, didn't even meet them until Dutch had hit double digits."

I knew I hit true with the look in her eyes but still Sarah curled her lip and opened her mouth to speak, but I got there before her.

"If you speak one more word to me, Sarah, I swear to fuck I'll scratch your goddamned eyes out."

Sarah gave me a brave look but I could tell she thought I'd do it with the way she braced like she was about to run.

"I cannot believe I'm hearing my own daughter speak this way," my mother whispered in horror.

"You can't?" I asked her. "So, when did you earn my respect, Mom? When did any of you earn my respect?"

I indicated them with an out-flung arm but ended it jabbing a pointed finger her way and kept speaking.

"But we'll start, specifically, with *you*. Was it when you came to me on my wedding day to tell me my father was thinking of never speaking to me again and you'd be forced to do the same if that was his decision if I married the man I loved, who I then gave babies? Or was it when you both carried out that decision? Or wait. Was it when you came to me in my sorrow and grief after we all lost him and held me and told me this was terrible, it was awful, you wished I wasn't experiencing the crippling depths of pain I was experiencing but you were there for me? Or was it when you were actually there for me, my sons, helping me to find reasons to get out of bed every day and make sure they were bathed and fed and got the Halloween costumes sorted that they wanted? No? Those last things weren't you?" I asked sarcastically. "You're right. They weren't. You were nowhere near me and my boys."

Before my mother could reply, I turned eyes to Simon and Blair.

"And *you*," I hissed. "He was *your boy*. And you didn't even show at his wedding. You also didn't show at his goddamned funeral. And you think you have any right to be standing in the home he provided for me and our sons?"

"I do," Simon returned arrogantly. "Because your sons have *my* blood in them."

"Their blood runs *Chaos*," I snapped. "If I did one thing right by my boys, if I did one thing right by my husband, I made it so they were raised with all the love and loyalty and goodness and light that their father gave them, that their father wanted to keep hold on, and by God, I did just that. What they did not get is they are not pompous, critical, holier-than-thou assholes like *you*."

"We're not getting any younger, Keely. Those boys are in line for trust funds and if you allow this to carry on with this gang," Simon fired back, "we'll be forced to do what we did with Graham and make different arrangements."

"Do it."

I went solid at Dutch's voice.

Obviously, when the time came that my family and Black's had wanted to re-enter my sons' lives, I'd put them off until my boys were old enough to make the decision (at ten and eight, precisely), and I left it up to them.

As for me, they made no effort to make amends with me, but it wouldn't matter. These people had killed anything that was left that they had from me when they'd let all of us deal with our loss on our own. And I had never been a shrinking violet (one of my problems, according to my mother), so I made that known.

But I felt it was my sons' decision, so I let them make it.

Both of them had wanted that piece of me and that piece of their father.

They still held distant. It wasn't like they didn't get it, how all of these people had let us swing.

But they'd let them in.

Dutch more than Jagger because he had that kind of heart. He had that part of his father. He tried to learn everyone's perspective, and even if he didn't understand it, he did his best to accept it.

Jag was like me.

He could hold a mean grudge.

But he'd followed his brother. I just got the sense he never fully committed to it.

As ever with my boys, I was not wrong about Jag.

And as ever with these people, right that moment with Dutch, they were letting sheer beauty slip right through their fingers.

"Do you think we want your money?" Dutch asked.

"Son—" my father started.

"I'm not your son," Dutch returned harshly, coming to stand at my side but partially in front of me. "I'm a man called Black's son, and I'm a man called Hound's son. I'm a son of Chaos. And it's obvious that you people didn't learn anything the first time around. So we'll just cut our losses here so everyone can get on with their lives, but mostly so you don't drag Ma through your crap *again*."

"You don't understand, honey," Tierney tried. "Your father was—"

"My father loved my mother and he loved me and he loved my brother and he loved his Club and he woulda loved all of you," Dutch jabbed a finger angrily toward them, "if you'd have let him."

"We're your family, we were his family, and—" Blair started.

"Has it occurred to you, Grandma, maybe *why* Dad went lookin' for another family?"

Excellent point.

She appeared struck and not in a good way.

Hmm, at least it seemed Blair got his point.

Dutch wasn't done.

"Do you think that hasn't occurred to me? To Jag? Do you think after all this time we don't know who our family is? Do you think, even at *fuckin' five*," he bit out that last, cursing in front of his grandparents, which shocked even me, "I didn't know you left her swingin' in the breeze when her life crashed down around her? With that and all the nothing that you gave her that came after, did you honestly think you could walk in here and we'd let you get up in her face? If you did, I have one question for you. What in the hell is the matter with you?"

"Dutch, do not talk to your grandmother that way," Simon ground out.

"And Simon, get the fuck outta my house," Dutch returned.

They all, every one of them, reared back.

Personally, I wanted to start clapping.

Jag came up on my other side, partially in front of me.

"You heard him," Jag bit. "And just for the record, I don't give a fuck about your money either. And I was over your bullshit judgment ages ago. It was just that Dutch thought I should give you a shot. You had it. You took it. You blew it. Now you can get the fuck out, but before that . . ." he turned his attention to Tierney, "my mother is not messed up. She married a man she loved because she knew her own heart and she had the strength of will to face losing everything she'd known all her life to follow it. And then she lost him. She still gave us her, a nice home, got her goddamn masters, and when Dad's Club made it so she wouldn't have to work even a day in her life, she still showed us the importance of making your own way. So newsflash, Tierney, your definition of messed up is messed up. You wanna see it straight, look at your sister. You wanna see a mess, look in the goddamned mirror."

Tierney's eyes got huge and hurt.

I pressed my lips together so I wouldn't smile.

"We—" my father began.

"I have absolutely no clue what's going on," Tad broke in at this juncture with his smooth, beautiful voice. "But from what I've heard, it boggles the mind you folks can stand in this lovely home your daughter created and look at this strong family she made against what sounds like pretty extreme adversity, some of that being you, and not feel anything but pride. However, since you can't, I will give you this one warning that you need to take this immediate opportunity to leave or I will personally be seeing each of you to the door. And if I have to put my hands on you, I don't care which gender you are, I'll do it."

Okay.

Official.

I *loved Beverly's new man.*

My mother made a move toward me.

And suddenly, Tad was right there in front of me.

Dutch moved forward to stand beside him.

Jag went to his other side.

But Hound walked determinedly across the room, so determinedly, Sarah and Blair had to jump out of his way, and he disappeared in my foyer.

I heard the front door open.

"I'll allow you to stretch the definition of immediate to *now*," Tad rumbled.

Hound appeared in the opening to the foyer. "The door is open. Best be using it before things get any uglier."

With looks through Tad and the boys at me, all of them started moving.

Hound stared them down as they passed him, so as best they could in the narrow space he gave them, they gave him a wide berth.

Tad followed them.

Dutch and Jagger followed Tad.

"You boys stay with your mother," Hound ordered.

My sons stopped moving.

Hound and Tad disappeared.

Beverly tagged behind and I lost sight of her in the foyer.

"Get back to your girl, baby," I heard Tad say softly.

Beverly reappeared.

She went direct to Jagger and put her arms around him.

This was probably because I was approaching Dutch, and when I made it to my boy, I slid my arms around him, my front pressed to his long, lean side.

His arm curled around my shoulders.

It took some time and that time included us hearing car doors slamming, vehicles starting and pulling out through the still-open front door.

But once those sounds ended, Hound and Tad came back.

Hound barely hit the room before his beautiful blue eyes moved between my sons and he declared gruffly, "I've never been prouder in my life of you two boys than I am right now."

It was then I knew why he didn't barrel in to take the situation in hand.

He was waiting for Dutch and Jag to do it.

Because he knew they *would* do it.

Shit, I was going to cry.

Hound turned to Tad. "And know you don't need it, but serious as fuck, bud, you got my blessing."

Beverly made a crying, laughing noise and Jag, holding on to her like Dutch was holding on to me, wound his other arm around her when the crying part won over.

Tad gave Hound a nod and then moved to claim his woman from my son's arms.

Hound didn't move.

But his gaze was locked on me.

"You good?" he asked.

I nodded shakily.

He looked to Dutch. "You got her?"

"Yeah, Hound," Dutch answered.

And he did.

My oldest boy did.

He always had.

I held him harder.

"Fuck," Hound whispered.

Then he came at us and he rounded us both in his arms.

Tight.

Jag pushed in and we became a huddle.

Beverly shuffled Tad over and we made room for them and it was Tad who was adopted into the Black/Ironside clan.

Through the wide chests of four men, Bev caught my eyes.

"I really need tequila," she whispered.

"Probably the second most precious thing I've heard you say, sweetheart, after 'yes' when I asked you to marry me," Tad joked.

I started laughing.

Jag started laughing with me.

Dutch joined in and then Bev and Tad did too.

Hound did not laugh.

He was looking at me telling me he loved me and he was proud of our boys.

I looked back at him telling him the same thing.

Then I broke out of our huddle to go get the tequila.

CHAPTER NINETEEN

WEIRD

Keely

THROUGH THE MIRROR, AS I was brushing my teeth the next morning, I watched Hound skirt my tub in the middle of the room on his way to me where I was at the sink.

It was the first day we'd woken up in my house where we didn't wake up and then fuck, if not immediately, almost immediately.

This was because both my boys found reasons after the drama to spend the night.

Hound had no problem with this and I knew it wasn't because he thought that they didn't think Hound had this, taking care of me after a big, emotional drama.

It was habit, my boys taking care of me.

And Hound was totally down with that.

"Christ, woman, I got no fuckin' clue how you don't get a headache standin' in this room for more than two minutes," he muttered, reaching in front of me to get his toothbrush.

I grinned in the mirror and kept brushing.

"You got more shit on the walls in this one room than I got in my entire house," he gave me crap.

I spit, rinsed, and with water dripping down my chin, I replied, "It's awesome," before I grabbed a towel and wiped my face.

"The floor alone makes Willy Wonka's interior designer look sane," he returned.

I tossed the towel by the sink and started giggling.

As I did this I noticed that Hound looked slightly amused but mostly intent.

So I quit doing it, leaned into him and wrapped my arms around his bare waist (Hound was not one for clothes if he could get away with being naked, and in my bathroom first thing in the morning, or any time he felt like it, he totally could do that).

"I'm okay," I shared.

It felt like he was examining me before he found what he was looking for and said, "I'm not. I think I pulled somethin', not landin' a fist in Black's dad's face."

I pressed my lips together.

"And his sister's," he went on.

I pressed them together harder.

"And *your* sister's," he kept going.

"They're gone," I reminded him.

"They're a bunch of motherfucking twats. They were that years ago. They haven't changed a stitch. I know the boys talk to them but they never shared if that got tight or not. Seemed not last night. But, babe, they gonna feel this?"

I shook my head. "I don't know but I don't think so." I gave his waist a squeeze as well as a shake. "What I do think is that this was gonna happen. I should have thought about it and prepared them for it once they started up officially with Chaos. But they've been so far out of my life for so long, I didn't give them that first thought."

"We'll keep an eye," he muttered then said in his normal voice, "You gonna keep your tits pressed to me while I brush my teeth or what?"

"Would you have a complaint if I said I was?" I asked.

"No, but I'd tell you to lose the robe so I could get the full benefit of that if you do," he retorted.

I started giggling again.

He bent and gave me a kiss that included a thrust of the tongue.

Call me crazy, but after beer and tequila and a night's sleep, Hound still tasted awesome in the morning.

When he was done, I tipped my head to the side and asked, "Did you know Boz has a giganto dick?"

Hound immediately went from looking morning-just-tasted-my-woman content to looking sick.

He also did not answer.

So I kept talking.

"Apparently, Tad is well endowed too. It's just that Boz is seriously *well endowed* so Bev didn't have the right measuring stick for comparison, as it were."

"Do we need to talk about this?" Hound asked.

"It's not like you're not lookin' good down there too, baby," I assured him. "Though you're a winner in terms of formation and girth."

"Seriously," he growled, "can we *stop talking about this?*"

And again, I was giggling, but through it I said, "Sure."

"Obliged," he grunted and reached for the toothpaste.

I moved out of his way so he could brush his teeth.

A little later, he moved into the shower so he could shower with me.

Fortunately, water drowned out a lot of noises.

So it was delayed, but our morning fuck was still awesome.

HOUND SLID A PLATE FILLED with a stack of buttermilk pancakes and rashers of bacon in front of Dutch, who immediately looked from Hound, to it, to me, as Hound moved back to the stove.

I gave my son big eyes.

His eyes narrowed on them.

"Jag, you want four, like Dutch?" Hound asked the stove.

Jagger kicked my foot under the table.

I moved my big eyes to him.

He gave me big eyes back.

"Uh . . . yeah, Hound," Jagger answered.

I forked into my pancakes.

"You'll start with two, like Dutch," Hound muttered to the skillet.

"You . . . uh, you guys eat this big a' breakfast every morning?" Dutch asked.

I looked up from my plate and gave him bigger eyes.

Hound grunted.

My foot was hit again by Jag's.

"What the fuck is goin' on?" Jagger mouthed at me.

Dutch tapped his plate with his fork and my gaze went to him.

"Yeah, Ma, what the fuck?" he mouthed.

"What the fuck what?" I mouthed back.

"Why are you being weird?" Dutch asked silently.

Jagger kicked my foot under the table yet again and I looked at him.

"And why is Hound cooking?" he also asked silently.

"Just eat it when you get it," I answered, yes, silently.

"Jesus, hope you three don't get yourselves in a situation where it's actually important you gotta communicate without communicatin'," Hound remarked, and my gaze flew to him to see his back was turned to the skillet where two fat pancakes were rising and bubbling, batter-side up, his arms crossed, the pancake turner sticking out at his side.

"Um . . . Ma was just bein' weird and uh . . . we've never had breakfast with you two and, well . . . you're cookin'," Jag pointed out.

"Men cook, Jag, they wanna eat anything other than Arby's," Hound answered.

"Right," Jag mumbled.

"I know your mother taught you how to cook," Hound continued.

"Yeah, she just doesn't go weird when I'm at the stove," Jag replied.

Hound looked to me.

I tried a casual shrug.

"Jesus, we know you guys are boning. You don't have to be weird about it," Dutch put in at this point, sounding exasperated . . . and pained.

My eyes got so huge I felt they might pop right out of my head.

"Gulk, I might get sick before I eat pancakes," Jagger gagged.

"Okay, this we're not talkin' about," I declared.

"No, we absolutely fuckin' are not," Hound stated, all steely.

"Okay, then don't act all weird at the breakfast table when we already know you got your bang on," Dutch returned, *to me*.

Jag threw himself against the back of his seat and tipped his head to stare at the ceiling, requesting, "Somebody kill me."

"It's not that," I told my eldest.

"We're not four, Ma. You came down all dreamy and Hound came down lookin' like he just ate a really good steak," Dutch, unfortunately, carried on.

Hound grunted again but this one sounded amused.

After I shot him a glare, he got it together and asked, "Did you not hear us say we're not talkin' about this?"

"What I'm sayin' is, just do your thing. It isn't weird unless you *make* it weird by *actin'* weird," Dutch shot back. "Christ, Jag's fucked girls in practically every room in this house and he doesn't act weird."

Slowly my eyes turned to my youngest, who I saw was scowling at his big brother.

"Like I didn't catch Dinah goin' down on you, curled on the floor while you were sittin' at this very table," Jag clipped at Dutch.

Dinah.

She'd been one of the good ones.

And there I was, sitting at a table where my son sat to get a blowjob.

Of course, he was also sitting at a table, precisely in the spot where his momma got gratifyingly banged by his stepdad.

I couldn't hack it.

"Oh my God!" I yelled. "Everybody, stop talking!"

"We'll stop talking when you stop being weird," Dutch shot back.

"I'm not being weird," I retorted.

"You're bein' weird and we're, like, just about as glad as we are grossed out you're gettin' some, with Hound gettin' some too, from you, so you can just relax," Dutch returned.

"I'm not being weird about having sex with your stepfather!" I shouted.

"It's the way of the world, Ma, get a grip," Dutch fired back.

"I know it's the way of the world so I wasn't even thinking about that until *you* brought it up. I'm being weird because Hound made Jean breakfast every morning and now he's making me breakfast every morning and today he's making *all of us* breakfast in the morning and I'm worried sick he's not dealing with the loss of a woman he loved very much!" I bellowed.

Dutch shut up and slid his eyes to Hound.

Jag looked over his shoulder at Hound.

I turned to glare at Hound but only because the glare was meant for Dutch, and I was too embarrassed and upset to stop glaring when I also looked at Hound.

Hound was looking at me.

"Babe," he said softly.

"Well, I am," I snapped.

"Jesus, Ma," Dutch bit out, and I looked at him to see him glowering at me.

"Yeah, Ma, Jesus," Jagger clipped, and I saw he too was glowering at me.

"What?" I asked, totally confused at their glowering.

"Now I'm more ticked you're bein' weird 'cause however he's gotta deal, just let him deal, yeah?" Dutch stated, sounding what he said, more ticked.

"Yeah, a man deals how he deals, you just deal with how he needs to deal, Ma. God," Jagger put in irately.

"Are you two ganging up on me because I'm worried about Hound?" I asked in order to see if I had this situation straight.

"Yeah," Dutch answered immediately. "Just, you know, be, like . . . supportive and shit."

"Yeah, and not weird," Jagger put in. "That's not supportive. It's just weird."

"I am being supportive and shit," I returned sharply. "Hound grunts instead of saying, 'I love you.' When a man expresses an important emotion like that through a grunt, you gotta feel your way with supportive . . . and shit . . . when he loses someone he cares about as much as he cared about Jean."

Dutch looked at Hound. "You love Ma?" he asked.

"Son," Hound said, but that one word also said, "That's a stupid fucking question."

"Hey," Jagger put in, now all smiles. "Cool."

Hound just gave Jag an amused look and turned to flip pancakes.

"Just to say," Dutch began in an I'm-about-to-instruct-you tone of voice, his attention again on me, "men like us are not wordy. If you get that a grunt means 'I love you,' leave it at that."

"Yeah," Jagger agreed. "Seriously."

"I did leave it at that," I told them.

"Well, keep doin' that," Dutch encouraged.

I lifted my hands up and to the sides, one holding a fork, one holding a knife, both dripping maple syrup. "Am I really sitting at my own kitchen table with my two sons instructing me on how to conduct my relationship?"

"Yeah, you really are," Dutch answered without hesitation. "'Cause Hound's like us, and Dad's been gone awhile so you need a refresher."

"Just to say, he may grunt," Jagger put in, "but you should tell him you love him back and use your words."

"I do," I told Jagger heatedly.

He nodded at me like he was encouraging a small child and repeated his brother's words, "Keep doin' that."

It was then, a continuous low, rolling noise coming from the stove caught my attention and I looked that way to see Hound's shoulders shaking.

He was laughing.

"This is not fucking funny, cowboy," I snapped.

He flipped Jagger's two pancakes on a plate that already held four rashers of bacon and turned to me.

"Jean would be laughin' herself sick, listenin' to this shit. Her face all screwed up, wrinkles all movin' in. I'd lose her eyes but get her teeth, she'd be laughin' so fuckin' hard," Hound declared. "That is, after she read you all about talkin' about bonin' and bangin' at the kitchen table, or anywhere," he amended.

The room went silent.

Hound kept his eyes to me as the humor slid away. "I miss her. I'll never stop missin' her. It's a pain that runs deep and will never die, I'll just get used to livin' with it. She's the reason I got up every day to face that day, baby. Now you're that reason. She'd feel joy knowin' I have you for that reason. So let me have that reason and stop worrying."

"Okay, honey," I whispered.

He gave me a long look, took in the look I was giving him and nodded.

"And boys, listen up," Hound kept going, his gaze moving between my sons. "Your mother doesn't need a refresher. She knows how to take care of her man, and if you were payin' closer attention to her than you were havin' a mind to me that I know, 'cause I know my boys, also has to do with you bein' worried about how I'm copin' with losin' Jean, you'd have seen it. But just to say, here on out, you best watch how that flows from your ma to me because that's what you'll be lookin' for when you find the one you wanna make your old lady. You hearin' me?"

"Yeah, Hound," Jag mumbled.

"Totally," Dutch said.

"I love you," I piped in.

Hound looked to me and grunted.

Then he moved to put Jag's plate in front of him.

He went back to the stove to pour more batter.

I smiled at my pancakes.

"Man, I'm totally coming back every morning," Jag said, digging in to the butter to prepare his pancakes.

"Come later," Hound said. "Your mother and I get down to business in the morning. We don't need interruptions."

Jag's hand arrested in spreading butter, he started to look sick and mumbled, "I think I just lost my appetite."

Dutch, on the other hand, busted out laughing.

I looked to my man.

He was smiling at the skillet.

His family was around him.

He was happy.

And I knew he was right, Jean would be happy for him.

So I forked back into my pancakes.

Just as happy.

THAT EVENING, SEEING AS I was in the garage, staring at Black's bike, not in my seemingly sound-proofed house, I heard Hound's bike as it pulled in at the back and the roar of the engine cut off.

I kept standing there, staring at Black's bike like I was mesmerized, so my phone beeping in my hand with a text made me jump.

I looked down at it.

The text was from Hound and it said, *You said you were home. I'm home. You're not. Where are you?*

He was home.

Home.

I let a smile drift across my lips before I texted back, *In the garage, babe.*

About one minute and five seconds later the back door opened, Hound prowled through but his gait slowed when he saw me standing by Black's bike.

He looked at me, the bike, me and asked, "You okay?"

I nodded. "I'm trying to figure out the ceremony."

My expressive Hound had appeared watchful and wary as he approached me, but now he looked perplexed.

"What ceremony?"

"The Give Dutch Black's Cut Give Jagger Black's Bike Ceremony," I told him.

He stopped close to me and started staring at the bike.

"You have any ideas?" I asked.

His gaze came to me. "Hand Dutch Black's cut and pass off the keys to Jag."

"That's not a ceremony," I pointed out.

"Okay. Then crack open some beers after you do that."

I grinned at him, shuffled the foot of space I needed to get to him and then leaned against his side, putting my head on his shoulder.

He slid an arm around my waist.

I did the same to him.

We both stared at Black's bike.

"It hasn't been started up since Graham shut it down. I'm not sure it works," I muttered.

"Jag'll get it goin'."

I took my head off his shoulder and looked up at him. "Will you do that? So Jag can just fire it up and ride away?"

I didn't even get all the words out before I felt his loose body get tight and his expressive face close down.

Okay, apparently, that was the wrong request to make.

"Sorry, that's . . . sorry, obviously I shouldn't have asked," I whispered.

"I got his woman, not touchin' his bike," Hound replied.

Well, I wasn't *exactly* Black's woman, considering I was now Hound's. But that was a conversation for later.

I nodded, fast. "Yeah, yes, honey, I get it."

"I hear you wantin' Jag just to be able to fire it up and roll on out but he'll like lookin' it over. He and Dutch can do that together. Won't take much. But they do that together, that'll be something else they'll both have."

I kept nodding. "Yes, that makes sense."

"And I won't be there for that," Hound declared.

I turned so my front was pressed to his side and wrapped my other arm around him. "I get it, when they work on it, get that bike running again, that they do it on their own. I get that, but whatever ceremony I come up with I think you should be there."

"I'll be there, if you bring all the brothers in, but not just me, Keely."

"Just you, Hound," I pushed. "You and Dutch and Jag and me."

"And Black."

"Baby," I said carefully. "It's about moving on from Black."

"No, Keekee, it's about you lettin' him go in that way and givin' him to your boys. And I got no place in that."

"You do," I pressed.

"I don't, babe. That's about your family."

"You *are* our family."

"I hear that and I love that, babe, but this is something else."

"If it is, then who was at my back when I went to the morgue to identify him?" I asked.

Hound had no response to that.

"Who was in my living room when you all came to tell me you took care of Crank?" I went on.

"Kee—"

"Who stood on my back walk after he took out the man who took my husband from me, the man who took away my sons' father?"

"That isn't—"

"And I know I don't have to get into all the other times you've been there for me. For the boys. For *Black*."

"Keekee," he murmured.

"He was ours. And he was yours. And now you're ours," I reminded him.

He turned fully toward me, lifted his free hand to cup my jaw, bending his neck so his face was closer to mine, and he spoke.

Gently.

"All right, baby, like you share how shit is between you and Bev, I'll share how shit is between me and my brothers, one of those brothers bein' Black. I know you know what that cut meant to him. I know you know what this bike meant to him. I also know you know what you and Dutch and Jag meant to him. Those are his and his alone. I've staked my claim now that he's gone but this thing that you're doin' with those things that were not his, but *him*, I can't be a part of that."

"The boys will want you there," I asserted.

"The boys will get it immediately that I'm not. It's you who has to understand why I can't be there," he refuted.

I stared up at him and it sucked, but the truth of the matter was, he was right.

I dropped my head and did a forehead plant in his chest.

His hand slid from my jaw to the back of my neck.

"You do the handovers, Keekee, the boys are gone and they've taken their pieces of their old man with them, you call me and I'll come to you right away, yeah?" he asked quietly.

I nodded, my forehead rolling on his chest.

He changed the subject, thankfully.

"Now, got Jean and my places paid for until the end of the month but I'll tell my landlord I'm clearin' out both. Need your help with Jean's stuff, babe. And the boys. Most of it can go but it's not gonna be easy, siftin' through it so gotta ask you, all a' you, to be there with me."

I tipped my head back and promised, "We'll all be there."

He gave the back of my neck a squeeze then moved his arm so he could wrap it around me with the other one.

"We'll get rid of what you got down there and move my stuff in your basement. Then I'll be all the way in."

Yet another ceremony of letting go of the material remnants of someone important and moving on, holding tight to only memories.

But at least in the end, I'd totally have Hound and he'd be all in with me, so we'd be all set to make new memories.

I nodded, giving him a happy squeeze, but saying, "And we need to talk to her rabbi about moving the mezuzah to my house."

"Say what?" he asked.

"I don't know the way it's supposed to go. So we need to ask how we're supposed to do that. Move that piece of her here to be with you because that part of her needs to be with you."

"Right," he murmured, melancholy hitting his eyes so I held him tighter. He powered through it and muttered, "Seems when we said we didn't wanna go slow, we were both all in with that."

I gave him a small smile.

He bent his head and kissed it.

He didn't go very far when he pulled away.

"Saw your panic last night when there came a knock on the door," he noted.

Oh Lord.

I wasn't sure I was ready for this particular change of subject.

"Shep—" I tried.

"We're all in with doin' shit fast, the brothers gotta know."

Shit.

"I'm not ready for that," I shared.

"I dig that and you were right when you said that the brothers are gonna get it, we kept it from them in the beginning. They might not get it so much Dutch and Jag know, Bev knows, the boys got their pieces of their dad, and I'm moved in. Shy and Tab kept things on the down low and that did not go over too good, a brother startin' shit up with his brother's daughter and not sayin' dick about it to anybody. What's happenin' here is gonna be even less popular so it might be good to get the bad shit outta the way so the brotherhood can start to heal and you don't gotta live with that hangin' over your head."

And it sucked yet again that he was right.

"Can we have a little more time?" I asked.

"You can have anything you want, it's in my power to give it to you, baby. You wanna keep it just us for twenty years, I'll be down with that for you. But I got a feeling you wanna be on the back of my bike close to as much as I want you there and that cannot happen until we bring Chaos into our lives."

My lips quirked in a not entirely amused grin at his wording and when he saw them do that, Hound's did the same.

"Just a little more time," I whispered.

He nodded and sealed that when he again dropped his head and touched his lips to mine.

And again, when he pulled away, he didn't go far.

"That ceremony, Keekee," he said softly. "My advice, make that all you. Don't make your boys watch you let go of their father again. Whatever you gotta do to make it okay you hand over the last of what you been holdin' onto of their dad that isn't in permanent residence in your heart, do it on your own. When you give that cut to Dutch and those keys to Jag, do it as their mother, not their father's widow. You do that last, they won't want to take it from you, and it's time they take hold of Black's legacy. You understandin' me?"

"You're very wise, Shepherd Ironside," I whispered.

"I'm a man who wears the same patch Black earned and if it was me under dirt and those boys had my blood in their veins, that's what I'd want, Keekee. When you let go of me, I'd want to be alone with you. And when you gave me to our boys, I'd want it to be about them."

God, I loved it that he understood.

God, *God*, I *loved* it that he understood *everything*.

I stared into his eyes and felt the first tear fall, gliding a cold trail of wet along my cheek.

Hound didn't try to catch it.

Or the one that came after it.

Or the one that came after that.

Or any of the others that silently followed.

He stood with me in my garage next to my dead husband's bike that had been sitting in the exact spot he'd put it in nearly eighteen years ago and watched me as he held me while I shed more sorrowful tears for the brother he loved, tears that mingled painfully with joyous ones for finding the brother Hound was who I loved.

Only when I sniffed did he move his hands to the sides of my head and swipe his thumbs over both my cheeks.

"You need me to go?" he asked gently.

God, *God*, I *so totally loved it* that he understood *everything*.

I nodded and said nothing.

"You text when you want me back."

It wasn't an order.

It was a request.

So I nodded again.

Hound then moved in, pressing his lips to my forehead, holding my face in both hands.

I closed my eyes and he kept his lips there for what seemed like days, weeks, years before he pulled away, I felt the pads of his fingers dig in, and then he walked away.

I opened my eyes and stared at the Chaos patch on the back of his cut.

I kept staring at it, seeing it in my mind's eye even after he closed the back door to the garage behind him.

In that moment, I didn't have to think about it, dream something up.

In that moment, I just knew.

So, in that moment, I followed Hound's steps, steps I'd taken time and again over the years, steps my sons had taken, steps their father had taken, steps Hound would take, and I walked to my house to get everything ready.

❦

IT WAS MELODRAMATIC.

I didn't care.

It was totally over the top.

I didn't care about that either.

It was cold as shit in my garage.

I didn't even feel it.

I sat in my spandex pants with the crisscross laces that showed skin all the way up the sides of my legs, the tank I'd dug down deep in a drawer to find that was cut way low and laced together loosely at the tits, high-heeled black boots with a lot of buckles on them that I hadn't worn in years, my purple bandana wrapped around my crown, tied in the back, my hair flowing out from under it.

I also wore Black's cut.

I was vamped out, lots of makeup around my eyes, on my cheeks, tons of red lipstick.

All around Black's bike was a circle of candles I'd lit, the only illumination to the space.

I had a bottle in my hand, primo tequila, the good shit, and around its neck was a ring of red from my lips.

I was astride Black's bike.

"We didn't have a lot of time," I said to the tank. "But the time we had, we tore it up, baby."

I bent over, pressed my red lips to that tank and did it hard.

Then I dismounted. I found the top, capped the bottle of tequila and set it aside. I took off the cut and folded it, arms in, Chaos patch up, and set it on the saddle. I reached into the pocket and pulled out the red bandana I'd stuffed there, wound it in a cord, tied it at the ends and set it on top of the cut.

I took off my own bandana and did the cord thing, but I tied that to a grip on the bike.

I'd already put the keys in the ignition.

I blew out the candles and kicked them to the back of the garage, getting wax all over my boots and all over the floor of the garage.

But I didn't care.

I then grabbed the bottle of tequila and walked outside, then into the house, up the stairs, right to my bed where I had clothes spread out.

I took off my tank.

I took off my boots.

I took off my spandex pants.

I folded them all carefully and shoved the clothes with the boots in a bag of stuff ready for taking to Goodwill, the bag of stuff I'd dug through all my things while I was preparing for the ceremony and filled full with the Chaos Keely of yesteryear.

I went to the bathroom and cleaned off my makeup, scrubbed away my lipstick.

I walked back into the bedroom and put on my ripped, faded jeans.

I put on my socks.

I put on my cowboy boots.

And I tugged on my long-sleeved tee with a different ragged slit down the front that didn't go very far or gape so wide it needed laces.

I pulled my long hair out of the back and then lifted it up to put on my choker.

I slid in some earrings.

I put on my blanket coat.

Then I grabbed the bottle of tequila, my purse, went out, nabbed one of the candles and got in my car.

I drove to the cemetery.

In the dark, I walked the oft-traveled path to Black's grave.

I set the candle on the base of his gravestone and lit it.

I set the bottle of tequila next to it.

And I looked down at my man.

"I'm on an errand. I'll be back for a longer visit. So now I gotta say I'll see you later, baby. Love you," I whispered.

I blew him a kiss, shot him a smile, turned right around and walked back to my car.

I got in and drove to Target.

Perusing my selections, I bought two new to replace the old.

One in the stars and stripes and one in navy.

I selected these because, on different occasions, I'd seen Hound wear the same of both (most often, the navy).

At the register, I didn't accept a bag.

I just shoved the new bandanas in my purse.

When I cut the ignition of my car in my garage, I looked to the bike beside me with the patch stitched to leather sitting on it and pulled out my phone.

In a group text to my boys, I said, *Did my goodbye thing with your dad. The cut and bike are in the garage, ready whenever you're ready. All I ask is that you come together to get them and you work together to get your father's bike running. I love you.*

By the time I got upstairs, I had two return texts.

Love you, Ma. Forever. Always. Dutch.

Bottom of my soul, Ma. Jagger.

They were pains in the ass.

But Black and me made *such good boys*.

I put the glass of wine I'd poured myself on the nightstand, took my coat off, threw it and my purse on my sheepskin chair, took my phone to my bed and climbed in.

I bent my head to it.

Come home, baby.

HOUND WAS HOME IN TEN minutes.

BLACK'S BIKE AND CUT WERE gone by the time I got home from work the next day.

CHAPTER TWENTY

CAN'T REIN THAT SHIT IN

Keely

I WAS ON MY BED with my laptop searching through vacation destinations, because I was on Spring Break with nothing to show for it but spending hours going through Jean's stuff, donating most of it and getting rid of the shit in our basement by donating all of that, none of this all that fun, even if I did it with Hound and the boys.

So the minute summer break hit, Hound and I were going somewhere *awesome*.

Therefore, I was on my bed when Hound walked in wearing jeans that I found confusing because I loved them so much, I wanted to take them off him. His feet were bare. His torso was covered in a skintight wife beater that did fabulous things for his wide chest and awesome tats, showing enough your mouth watered thus making you want to witness it all. The top of his hair was pulled back in a little ponytail at the back of his head, something I also found confusing because it made him look cool and badass at the same time I wanted to yank it out and bury my fingers in his hair.

He was also carrying a laundry hamper full of folded clothes toward the closet.

I'd put a load in the dryer what was apparently a little over an hour before.

Watching this, I was pretty sure my mouth had dropped open but I was too in shock to notice if that was actually the case.

Hound had been living with me now for three weeks. He was all in. His and Jean's apartments (mostly) were all cleared out. We didn't have a lot of time in but we had some time. He made us breakfast every morning. I made us dinner every night. We slept together, woke up together, touched base during the day, and in that time, I'd had occasion to do a load or seven of laundry.

Hound had said nothing but he was a dude. Dudes didn't thank you for things like having clean jeans. They just thought clean jeans miraculously made their way from the floor to a hanger for them to grab.

But as I had this thought it occurred to me that Hound's jeans didn't even hit the floor. They hit the hamper. As did his shorts, socks and tees.

He was categorically a dude.

He was also categorically a biker.

Ditto with a badass.

And last, a bachelor for thirty-nine years.

He'd said to me (and he was being nasty because he was pissed but I figured there was a modicum of truth to it) that he got rid of women when they started dragging on him. The truth part of that was that I knew in all his years he had never gotten serious with a woman at all, much less lived with one.

This was probably because in all those years, he'd been in love with me.

That would have been sad if he wasn't right there with me, which was some serious happy.

But still.

Where did he learn, when the dryer was done, to fold and bring up laundry?

He walked out of the closet and looked to me. "Gonna get a beer and park it in front of the TV. You gonna come down?"

"You folded the laundry."

He stopped on his return journey to the door and shifted to face me.

"Yeah," he said. "Now you gonna come down or do you want me to bring you a beer up here and we'll catch some tube in bed?"

"And you brought it up. Like, folded, in a hamper, to the closet."

He looked to the closet then back to me.

"Yeah," he said slowly.

"You also put your clothes in the dirty clothes hamper," I went on.

"Where else would I put them?" he asked.

"On the floor," I answered.

"They don't belong on the floor," he returned. "They been worn, they belong in the dirty clothes bin."

I did a slow blink.

Hound started to look aggravated.

But if I wasn't mistaken, he also looked kind of hurt.

"So, here we are," he said quietly.

"Where?" I asked cautiously, due to the possible hurt look.

"Black left his clothes on the floor."

My back went up.

We were not going to go there. Not right then.

And I had to make it so it was not ever again.

"Yes, he did, until I broke him of that habit," I shared then went on to what was important. "But this isn't about Black. And I think it's crucial at this juncture to state that there's nothing about Black when it comes to you and me. Except for the love we share for him, that's all the part he plays between you and me. If I'm talking to you, it's about *you*, or you and me, and not about Black. Not *ever* about Black."

He looked somewhat relieved.

But still irate.

He didn't hesitate to explain the irate.

"So why you lookin' at me like I'm a freak?" he demanded.

"I'm not looking at you like you're a freak."

"Woman, you're lookin' at me like I'm a freak."

Since I didn't know how to change a look I was sure I wasn't giving him, I did my best to rearrange my face and shared, "You're a biker."

"Bikers clean their clothes, babe."

"Your place was a sty when I first started it with you," I reminded him.

"I wasn't tagging hot chick pussy on a regular basis at my pad when you first started it with me."

That was a good point.

"But the pussy I tagged wherever I tagged it, I tagged it wearin' clean clothes, that is before I took 'em off," he continued.

"It's just . . . you were a *confirmed* bachelor . . . until me."

"I was. I'm also a man who's now livin' with a woman and I might spend most my time with men and have my own dick, but most those men have women. I hear them talkin' and bottom line, I'm just not stupid. So I'm not gonna move in with my woman and court her gettin' up in my shit 'cause I leave my clothes on the floor or hear the dryer go and don't unload that fucker." He flung an arm toward the closet door. "But you're puttin' that shit away. I don't know where your crap goes, and if it was up to me, I'd shove all my shit on a shelf or in a drawer and not bother with hangers."

"So you absorbed being a good partner through your Chaos brothers?" I queried skeptically.

"Maybe, but more, I kinda like you and I definitely like tagging your pussy so I also might want this to last awhile. And you got somethin' good, you put work into it to keep it that way. It's no skin off my nose to fold some clothes and haul them up the stairs so that's what I did. Though, not sure I'll do it again, I get shit about doin' it."

Oh no.

We weren't going there.

I hated folding laundry.

Hell, I hated *doing* laundry.

"I'm not giving you shit."

He lifted both hands to his sides before he crossed his arms on his chest, making his tats dance, thus making them even *more* awesome, asking, "So what is this?"

"I was just surprised." Before he could say more, I added, "In a *good* way."

"If it's in a *good* way," he retorted, "don't bust my chops."

"I'm also not busting your chops."

"Doesn't seem that way from where I'm standing."

Okay, I needed to get this under control, pronto.

"Shep, I was just surprised. It took Dutch and that other recruit three hours to clean your apartment. It doesn't take me that long to clean this entire house."

"That other recruit is called Chill," he educated me.

"Chill," I murmured.

"And just to say, we're not in my apartment, which we've had this conversation, but I'll say it again, it was a shithole and the only reason I fixed it up was because you were there."

"And thank you for that."

He didn't comment on that.

He went on with what he'd been saying. "Now we're in your house."

"*Our* house."

"Your house, Keely."

Oh boy.

"You live here, Hound," I said quietly. "So it's *our* house."

He stared at me.

This lasted some time so I asked, "Do we need to have a conversation?"

"No," he answered.

"Are you sure?" I pressed.

"If I wasn't sure, my answer would have been 'I don't know,'" he returned. "That wasn't my answer. My answer was *no*."

"You jumped right to the conclusion I was thinking about Black when I made a comment about you bringing those clothes up," I pointed out carefully.

"He was the last man you lived with," he pointed out right back, though not carefully.

"A long time ago, honey," I said.

"Doesn't change the facts," he retorted.

I was right.

Oh *boy*.

"So we *do* need to have a conversation," I whispered.

"Keely—"

"I'm yours," I declared.

"I know that," he gritted.

"You're mine," I went on.

"I definitely know that," he bit out.

"So you *definitely* know you're mine but you only just *know* I'm yours?" I asked.

Taking his arms from his chest, he planted his hands on his hips and looked to the ceiling, muttering, "For fuck's sake."

This wasn't going to happen, stuff like this coming between us, so I made the decision right then that we were going to change things so it *wouldn't* happen.

And they were going to change in a big way, and that big way would be permanently.

"We're moving," I decreed.

His eyes came right back to me. "Say again?"

"We're moving. We don't need four bedrooms for just you and me. Too much history here. And the boys are both gone in a way I know they're *gone*. They'll get it. They're on the path to building their own lives. But you and me, we need a fresh start."

Something chased across his face before it blanked.

And that something was not good.

Shit.

"What?" I asked.

"Babe, how 'bout we come out to the brothers before we get into real estate," he suggested.

"What was that look that you just blanked?" I pushed.

"What look?"

Oh no he didn't.

He wasn't going to lie to me by hiding from me.

"What were you thinking when I said we need to move?"

"I was thinking I just moved a bunch a' shit outta my place to make room for the shit you moved into my place and then I moved a bunch a' shit outta *two* places to clear out Jean's and move in with you, so I'm not real hip on talkin' about movin' a bunch *more* shit someplace else."

This answer made sense.

He was still hiding from me.

"That's not it."

Hound started getting impatient. "That *is* it, woman."

"Talk to me, Shep. We said we'd be open and we need to be open. What was it you thought when I said we should find our own place, get a fresh start?"

I mean, did he want me to keep this place because Black gave it to me?

That'd be sweet, but unnecessary. I had what I needed from Black and always would.

Or did he want me to keep this place for the boys, thinking that it was their home and they might get pissed if we got rid of it?

This was something that was also sweet, but unnecessary. Or I hoped so. We'd have to talk to the boys.

"Keely, just drop it," he muttered, taking his hands from his hips and looking like he was going to walk out of the room.

"Don't walk away from this conversation, Hound," I snapped, and he stopped moving to lock eyes on me.

"We need to be careful here, baby," he said warningly.

"I know," I agreed pointedly. "What are you holding back from me?"

"Babe—" he started like he was going to keep trying to blow it off.

"Please, don't keep anything from me. If something's bothering you, talk to me."

"Right now, my woman getting up in my shit to push me to talk to her is what's bothering me," he clipped.

I stared into his eyes then turned mine to the laptop while I reached out and slapped it closed, shutting away websites about fabulous vacation destinations.

Then I pushed off the bed and murmured, "I'm gonna take a bubble bath."

"Babe," he growled.

I kept walking toward the bathroom.

"Keely," he called irritably.

I was at the door to the bathroom when he spoke again.

"Got two boys."

I turned to him.

"That aren't mine," he finished.

So it was about the boys.

"They are," I whispered.

"They are and they aren't and it's the way I lived my life, my choices that I didn't make a kid of my own. Now I got you and you're right. We should move. We should move because it's always gonna be the house Black bought for you and that'd eventually get under my skin," he admitted. "And we'll get on that after other important shit is sorted. But you said you and me don't need all this space. The boys have moved on. And it just dug in that you and me don't need all this space."

We *didn't* need this space. We were just two people. I knew he'd long since broken ties with his family. He was standing in the room when I'd irrevocably broken ties with mine. It wasn't like we were regularly going to have out-of-town guests (though my family, and Graham's, lived in town . . . still).

Except . . .

I didn't make a kid of my own.

Oh God.

I stared at him.

"You want a baby," I said quietly.

"Never thought about it," he grunted.

"But now, you're thinking about it."

He said nothing.

But now he had a woman.

Now he had a home with a woman.

A woman he loved who loved him back.

And I was that woman.

"You want a baby," I repeated.

"Keely, babe—"

"So we'll have a baby."

It just came right out of my mouth.

Shit.

He went perfectly still.

Every inch of him.

God.

Oh God.

Shit.

He wanted *a baby*.

"Hound," I whispered.

"You'd give me a kid?"

That question was guttural.

Oh yes, he wanted a baby.

"Well, uh . . . my parts still work, I love you, you love me and—"

Christ, I was babbling . . . about having *a baby*.

"You'd give me a kid."

"I'm not twenty-three anymore but my lady parts haven't shriveled up yet, honey," I joked.

"We're not laughin' about this," he declared.

And that declaration was flinty.

"You gotta be sure about this," he decreed. "You don't say that shit to me unless you're sure about this. What it means to you. What it might mean to Dutch and Jag. What it means for us. What it means for me. You just don't throw that out. Not that. Not you and me makin' a baby."

No.

Hound didn't want a baby.

Hound wanted a baby with me.

I stared at him in those jeans and that tank with those tats and his badass hair and his amazing eyes and that look on his handsome face, and for the first time in the years of us being together when we were not and in the past months of us being together in a way we actually were, it was only then I felt the true fullness of the decades of love he'd given me.

It was overwhelming.

And it was *exquisite*.

Plus my boys were gone. On the path to building their own lives. They'd been the only true, long-lasting joy in mine. I still had them but I had them in a way I missed them, because they weren't my little boys anymore.

I could make another one. Another one with lapis-blue eyes and a handsome expressive face who every time I looked at him, he reminded me not only how much I loved him, but how much I loved his daddy and the love we had for each other that made him.

"He has to have your eyes," I whispered.

"*She* has to have your hair."

Oh my God.

Shit.

Oh *my God*.

Hound and me were going to make a baby.

"No cursing rule in this house until she's thirty-three," I said, sounding croaky.

"Get your ass over here," he said, sounding bossy.

"We can't make the baby *now*," I said, sounding panicked. "We have to tell Chaos first."

"We're not making the baby now, Keekee," he said, sounding amused. "We have to tell the brothers and then we gotta move to a different house. Sayin' that, we're gonna practice up real good so when it gets down to doin' it with a purpose, we got it set."

"I think we already have it set, honey."

"We're still gonna practice."

Oh yeah we were.

I got my ass over there.

Hound didn't attack me.

No.

What Hound did was reach with both hands, grab my head, yank me to him and then wrap both of his arms around my head.

He held me to his chest that way.

I'd never been held that way in my life.

There was something poignant about it, profound.

Amazing.

Oh yeah.

Yeah, yeah, yeah.

My man wanted to make a baby with me.

I circled him with my arms and clutched his wife beater in my fists between his shoulder blades.

When we'd stood that way for so long and it was either crack a joke or burst into tears, I made the only decision I could.

"Thanks for partnering up, cowboy, and folding the laundry."

He dropped his face to the top of my head and held me tighter.

"Christ, I fuckin' love you."

I let his tank go and wrapped my arms around him as tight as I could.

"You sure?" he asked my hair gently.

I smiled.

"I'm sure," I answered his chest nearly inaudibly since my face was smushed there.

"Startin' all over again?" he pressed.

"With you?"

"Yeah."

"Then absolutely."

He held me tighter.

I let him, and when I was worried he'd dislocate my nose, I gave him a squeeze.

He didn't release me but he did release some of the pressure, so I turned my head and laid my cheek on his chest.

I saw his tatted arm cocooning me.

And I hoped like fuck our little girl got her daddy's eyes.

"Boys would love a baby sister," I muttered.

"We gotta get on Chaos," he said.

Fuck.

He was right.

My lady parts worked but time was marching on.

Not to mention when those assholes made my man stand the gauntlet, he had to heal up so we could fuck with a purpose and also I had to have plenty of time to hold my grudge against the brothers before I eventually forgave them . . . for Hound.

"So, uh . . . this going fast thing, we're breaking all the records, yeah?" I quipped.

"That's us, baby. Wild like the wind. Can't rein that shit in."

He was so right.

So right.

And anyway . . .

Why would we?

"I love you, Shep."

Hound held me close for a long beat.

Then he grunted.

AFTER I'D TAKEN HIM THERE with my mouth, I slid the tip of my tongue up the underside of his cock and lifted my eyes to his face just as I hit the edge of the rim of his cockhead.

His head came up off the pillows and he murmured roughly, "Up here, baby. Come sit on my face."

I felt a nice shiver but I didn't go up there and sit on his face.

I'd do that later.

Right then, I moved my tongue to the bottom of the lance tatted into the hair between his legs and I stroked it up, up, right to his heart.

I put my chin there and again turned my gaze to him.

He'd shifted his arms so his head was resting on his hands, his attention on me.

"You got Native American blood in you, cowboy?" I asked quietly.

"No," he answered, watching me intently.

"An interest in that culture?" I went on.

"No," he repeated.

"Me," I whispered.

"Yeah," he whispered back.

God, yes, he'd loved me for a long, *long* time.

And I now had that in all ways I could, and I'd have it in more ways when we made our baby.

But the best part about it was that I finally got to give that back.

I lifted up, tracing the lance back down with my fingers, the bow and arrow up, the club down.

"Keekee," he called gently.

I turned my eyes to his.

"It was before, wasn't it?" I asked, but I didn't need to. I just wanted to hear him say it. "Before Black died. Before anything. You've always loved me."

His big hand came from behind his head so he could cup my cheek.

"Always, Keely."

"Cock to your heart," I whispered.

His thumb drew circles on the apple of my cheek. "Cock to my heart."

I smiled at him so I wouldn't get overwhelmed with all his beauty and do something else entirely.

"I'm so glad I stripped buck naked in your living room," I remarked jokingly.

"I think it's safe to say, not as glad as me," he replied, and he was not joking.

I wasn't either when I returned, "No. I'm not sure it's safe to say that."

A beautiful darkness clouded over his face before both his hands were under my arms and he was dragging me up his chest and up even farther.

He planted me on his face, hauled me down to his mouth and I grabbed the headboard as my head fell back when he went at me.

He took me there after shoving two wet fingers up my ass, eating me and fucking me.

After I came down while he worked his mouth gently between my legs, he slid me back down his body and shifted only to reach to the covers and pull them up on top of us.

I rested my weight into him and he curved his arms around me.

"You wanna take a bubble bath?" I asked in a murmur into his neck.

"You'll get my ass in that tub only if I'm unconscious," he murmured back.

I smiled against his neck.

"So bikers don't take bubble baths," I remarked.

"This biker doesn't," he replied.

"Mm," I hummed.

"Jag's birthday is comin' up," he reminded me. "You got plans for that?"

"He always requests my prime rib and twice-baked potatoes with my carrot cake. But I'll ask just to confirm."

"Forgot about your prime rib," he muttered.

And I'd forgotten until then that when Hound had been at my table for dinner, there was the odd time here and there that he'd been at my house doing something, or being there for the boys, I'd asked him to stay for dinner, and he did, but for every one of my boys' birthdays, he'd been at my table.

Various and sundry Chaos men would also be there, with their old ladies or not, depending on how they felt about their old ladies.

But Hound was always there.

And it was then I realized just how much history we shared and precisely how precious all of it was.

I was in a variety of happy glows, including the one that realization gave me, when Hound gave me another one.

"Just sayin', standing order for that on my birthday."

I was going to get to spoil Hound on his birthday.

I could not *wait*.

I snuggled closer to him. "I can do that."

He gave me a squeeze.

I was starting to get drowsy, but before I drifted away, I said quietly into his neck, "We'll tell the brothers soon."

"Yeah."

"Talk to the boys first. Let them know we're coming out. Take their pulse about the possibility we're gonna sell the house," I went on.

"Right."

"We'll see how that talk goes, but it might be too soon to mention the fact we're gonna be looking at expanding the family," I said.

"Agreed," he replied.

"Are you gonna wanna get married?" I asked, and his arms spasmed around me.

I had my answer but he still said, "Yeah. You?"

I nodded, my head and hair moving on his shoulder and chest but verbalized it with a, "Totally."

His arms spasmed again but stayed tight this time.

"In case you didn't get it, I'll say it," I began. "Thanks for folding and bringing up the laundry."

"You don't have to thank me for doin' something that contributes to our life."

Was he for real?

I snuggled even closer.

He was for real. Every inch of him.

Hound's arms loosened but not that much, only so he could trail his fingertips along my sides.

I felt him relax under me and I did the same on top of him.

We were both close to sleep when I murmured, "I can't wait to be on the back of your bike, cowboy."

His arms got tight again.

"Me either, baby," he whispered. "Me either."

I smiled against his skin.

And lying on top of my old man, happy, sated, in love and with so much to look forward to in life it wasn't funny, I fell asleep.

CHAPTER TWENTY-ONE

I WILL NOT EVER FORGET

Hound

"YOU GOT YOURSELF A PET?" Camilla Turnbull asked nastily, her focus on Hound.

Hound didn't move. He just stood in her living room that he'd walked into, following Knight Sebring and his man Rhashan Banks.

She'd been eyeing him up from the minute he moved in. Her four goons had been doing the same.

What she didn't do was get off her ass, which was planted in her fancy couch in the room with a view. Not even to offer Knight a seat.

Knight took one anyway, across from her in a chair.

"Why don't we at least try for civil?" Knight suggested.

She didn't take her eyes off Hound. "We vacated Chaos."

Hound said nothing, just held her gaze.

Knight spoke.

"Chaos requested a rep at this meet, I agreed. They're concerned you're not committed to your retreat from their turf, and I'm concerned you're not committed to your promise to me that you'll deal with your girls in ways I find less provoking."

Her attention finally turned to Knight.

"Now, why would I break a promise I made to the all-powerful Knight Sebring?" she asked bitchily.

"Your current attitude, you honestly expect me to answer that?" Knight asked back, and Hound could sense him losing patience, but he didn't have to sense shit. Knight wasn't hiding it.

"They're whores, Sebring," she returned.

"They're humans, Camilla. If they're at a place in their lives they gotta turn tricks, you run them, why would you make that worse for them?" Knight fired back.

Her upper lip curled in a humorless grin. "They're not all your mother."

"None of them are my mother," Knight bit. "And that doesn't mean dick. You knowin' my history doesn't mean dick. You sharin' you know it when it's no secret doesn't get you dick. But you takin' from this meet that you got attention you don't want means *more* than dick. I'm here. I'm givin' you my time. I'm showin' you respect. You throw that in my face, that'll be a statement you're makin' and I'm not sure you'll wanna know where I take it from there. What I will let you know is this will be the last meet you get so maybe you wanna curb the attitude and make this time useful for both of us."

"How can it be useful for me when the only purpose you have in being here is telling me how to run my girls and threatening me not only with you," she jerked her chin at Knight, then at Rhash and finally moved her eyes to Hound, "but also Chaos, when Chaos doesn't have shit to do with it anymore? You wanted Chaos clean," she said to Hound. "It's clean. Now run along, little doggie."

Hound didn't make a move or a sound.

He just kept staring at her.

She was young. Okay looking. She made the little she had better with expensive clothes and makeup and a good dye job for her hair. He could tell she worked at that body. It was lean to the point it was feral. She probably kickboxed or some shit.

She could kickbox herself unconscious.

He still could snap her neck before she could blink.

"We've wasted our time," Knight murmured, getting up from his chair, doing it getting her attention.

"I told you I'd lay off my girls, I'm laying off my girls," she snapped.

"Not from news I got last night, which prompted me reaching out to make this meet," Knight replied.

Her eyes skidded to one of her goons before they went back to Knight.

The eye skid meant that was news to her.

This little girl didn't have a grip on her boys.

This whole act was show.

But she better get a grip or get the man pulling her strings to sort their shit, because when Knight said she didn't want to know what he'd do if she didn't get things in hand, he wasn't talking shit.

"Perhaps the message hasn't yet filtered through the ranks," she mumbled. "I'll make that happen right away."

"Your boys don't take freebies either, Camilla," Knight added. "Not at all, but definitely not rough ones."

Hound watched her mouth get tight as she listened to Knight give it all to her, but Hound didn't know her so he couldn't read that. Either she was pissed her boys weren't listening to her or she was pissed Knight was telling her how to do her business.

Chew ran Chaos's girls when they had them.

Chew took freebies whenever the fuck he wanted.

And Chew could get rough.

"You with me on that too?" Knight prompted.

"That message as well will be repeated," she said tightly.

"Where's Valenzuela?" Knight asked suddenly.

Hound watched her closely and she didn't miss a beat when she answered, "He's expanding operations elsewhere."

"He comin' back anytime soon?" Knight went on.

Again with the unamused lip curl. "I'm thinking he'd frown on me sharing his travel plans widely, Sebring. He'd especially frown on me sharing it with Chaos's dog in the room."

"He's been gone a long time," Knight remarked.

"He's exploring some exciting opportunities," she returned. "That takes a lot of time."

Hound kept watching her, and for the life of him he couldn't catch anything. Not a flinch. Not a tick. Nothing.

Knight kept at her. "He know you ordered the retreat from Chaos?"

"Of course he does, since he's the one who ordered it," she replied.

No flinch.

No tick.

Nothing.

All Hound could see coming from her was that she was landing truth on them when he knew it was nothing but lies.

"Years of pushin', he gave up easy," Knight noted.

She shrugged. "I've never understood why Benito does half the shit he does. Though I don't question it. He's not a fan of that."

"He's also not a fan of giving women positions of authority in his business," Knight pointed out.

There was more hard than normal behind her, "I proved myself."

Knight gave it a beat. Rhash stood at his man's back while he did. Hound stood four feet away and kept his attention locked on her.

"Do we have more to discuss or can we all get on with our days?" she asked in a prompt for them to get the fuck out, the words sugar sweet and all fake.

Since Hound kept watching her, he only felt Knight and Rhash turn their eyes to him.

"Not discuss," Hound said, and she looked to him.

"It speaks," she said on one of her catty smiles.

He ignored that. She was young. She had no idea with men like him, bites like that had lost their power to sting a long time ago.

"Just say," he went on.

"So say it," she spat when he didn't continue, and Hound thought it was interesting she thought she could play with Knight but she had zero patience with him.

"You tell Chew, he's got a beef with his former brothers, he shows his fuckin' face and communicates his shit. He doesn't hide like a pussy behind a little girl who's playin' a dangerous game that might get her neck snapped."

That's when he saw it.

Surprise and panic cut through her features before she erased it.

Hound wasn't the only one who caught it.

"He wants to come outta the shadows," Knight put in immediately, "you can set that up with me. I'll find a neutral place. He'll have parlay."

She pulled herself together to retort, "I'd be happy to pass on this message if I knew what the hell you were talking about."

But Hound caught it. A little lift of her chin.

She'd been cool and in control. She thought she had a secret.

They knew her secret.

So now she was rattled.

"You need to get smart, girl," Hound advised low. "It seems like shits and giggles until someone's throat gets slit."

"You'd know all about that, wouldn't you, Mr. Ironside?" she hissed.

"Yeah," he told her. "I would."

He said that, and then he walked right out.

He took the stairs, fifteen floors. He did it because it gave him time, not with Knight and Rhashan, to make his call.

Tack answered on the first ring with, "Message delivered?"

"It's Chew," Hound told his brother, jogging down the stairs.

"How'd she handle it?"

"Shook her shit."

"Knight offer parlay?" Tack asked.

"Yup," Hound answered.

"You get anything else?"

"She knows I took out Black's killer."

"Fuck," Tack clipped. "Chew was out of Chaos by then. Only men who knew were in the room, and not a one of them would say dick."

"A room Chew knew existed," Hound pointed out.

"Surveillance?" Tack asked.

"He was a little weasel, obviously still is a little weasel. Coulda been watching. Coulda set up cameras."

"Could have cameras still there," Tack noted.

"Best get boys out there, Tack," Hound advised. "Send Dutch with whatever brother goes. He needs to learn how to find shit like that."

It was too bad Jagger was at school. He needed to learn that too.

"On it," Tack said then went on, "At least we know one thing."

Hound gave him that one thing. "The old ladies are safe."

"Yeah," Tack agreed. "That's a line Valenzuela would cross, but Chew would not."

"Yeah."

"Right. Still gonna keep the women covered. Now I got calls to make," Tack told him. "Later, brother."

"Later."

He disconnected, shoved his phone in his back pocket and jogged down the rest of the steps.

Knight and Rhash were waiting for him outside the building.

"That go the way you wanted?" Rhash asked when he stopped with them.

"Absolutely," Hound answered.

"I didn't get a good feel about that last part," Knight shared, watching him closely.

"It's in hand," Hound lied.

"I hope like fuck it is, man, 'cause this shit was annoying. Now it's twisted and nasty and the time comes Chaos is forced to take a turn they don't wanna take, a path that's dark might hit pitch when your whole Club falls down a deep hole you can't dig your way out of," Knight declared.

Hound hoped like fuck that didn't happen too.

"Who woulda thought we'd miss dealin' with the psychopath that was Valenzuela," Hound muttered, looking from them to scan the street, wondering if Chew was there keeping an eye on his girl.

"You might consider bringing Lee in on this," Rhashan suggested and Hound turned his attention back to the big black man. "Ferret this fucker out."

Lee, as in Lee Nightingale, a top-notch private detective with a team of the same, all of them covering skillsets that were extreme, all of them scary-good at what they did.

And all of them were allies.

"Nightingale and his boys got skills, but we now know this is Chew. So this is Chaos. It started with Chaos. It'll stop there," he replied.

Knight nodded understanding, but Rhash gave him a look, because he didn't.

Hound got Rhashan's reaction.

The faster this shit could end the better and Nightingale could assist in taking it Mach one.

But Chew had once worn the Chaos patch. He'd get the degree of respect he had left, which he'd earned when he'd earned that patch.

When he wasted that, the gloves would come off.

"We all got shit to do," Hound said to them both. Then he spoke right to Knight, "Gratitude for arrangin' that meet."

"Good luck, Hound," Knight replied.

Hound lifted his chin to Knight and then to Rhash.

After that he walked away thinking they didn't need luck.

They needed what they always needed in the never-ending quest of dealing with this shit with the hope of finding an end to it.

Heart.

And balls.

Keely

I STRUGGLED IN THE BACK door with six bags of groceries dangling from my fingers, thinking that when Hound and I moved, we were so totally going to buy a house where the garage led right into the kitchen.

I hadn't thought about taking that trek outside, along the back of the house and up the back stoop, not for years. It was just what I did, laden with grocery bags or not.

Now that my future included something different, I couldn't wait to rush out to meet it.

What I could do was wait about ten more days (or ten more years) for that night.

We were having dinner with the boys to share with them that Hound and I were going to come out to the Club (or Hound was, he wasn't allowing me anywhere near the Compound when he shared that information with his brothers, no matter the fits I'd pitched, and I'd pitched some fits in the two days since we'd made the decision).

It wasn't that I couldn't wait to have dinner with all my boys. I was looking forward to that.

It wasn't even the fact that if that news went over okay with Dutch and Jag, we were also going to share that, once we were out with the brothers we'd be putting the house on the market and looking for something a little smaller.

I didn't get the sense either of my sons were attached to the house. They were attached to me, not the house.

But if I was wrong and one or both of them was, we'd find a way to keep it for them. Rent it out or even let them move in and share it until the time came when the decision had to be made about which one would get it.

So, all that would be all right.

However, that night, Hound also wanted to tell them we were eventually going to get hitched.

I wanted him to officially ask me to marry him before we shared that news with my boys.

At least he'd agreed to that.

Obviously, we were not going to share we were planning on giving them a baby sister.

Not yet.

So that night I figured would go okay.

It was once that was done, the next step was telling Chaos.

That was what I could wait ten years for.

I dumped the bags on the kitchen table and started rooting for the stuff that went in the fridge and freezer, trying not to think about the fact that dinner tonight with the boys was step one of a two-step process with the second step not being a fun one.

In fact, I was back to wanting to postpone this step so the next step wouldn't come and was even thinking I could convince myself that Hound and I could live the rest of our lives in hiding from his Chaos brothers if it meant he wouldn't have to stand the gauntlet.

I knew he could not only handle it, in some badass part of his mind, he felt he needed to withstand it in order to finish the act of earning the honor of calling me his old lady.

It was me who couldn't deal with it, and the closer it came, the harder it was to try to put myself in the place that I could, for Hound, for our future, even for Chaos.

I just didn't know, if it came down to the gauntlet, if I could forgive them.

It was on this thought, and while I was shoving pistachio ice cream in the freezer (Dutch's favorite, and also, I'd found, Hound's) when a knock came at the front door.

I looked that way then moved that way.

It was the Saturday that heralded one last day of my spring break before having to go back to work. Hound was coming home to help me make dinner for the boys, but I didn't expect him back for at least an hour.

We'd make dinner.

Then have dinner and tell the boys.

And the next step . . .

Well, at least we'd agreed on where we were vacationing when school was out. I'd even made the booking at a fantastic, pricey resort in Baja. I was excited about it. When I showed Hound the resort's website and told him we had a booking, Hound had grunted through a smile, which I took as him being excited about it too.

Something else to look forward to.

It was just that before we got there, we'd have to deal with something I did not look forward to.

I sighed and moved through the house to the front door. When I hit the foyer, I saw through the oval of frosted glass that was in my door what looked like two figures, one taller than the other, one a woman, one a man . . . wearing a Chaos cut.

Shit.

Well, thank God Hound wasn't due home for a while.

I peeked through the side of the window, which was a sliver of non-frosted glass.

Millie and High.

Okay.

What?

Why?

Shit.

One thing I knew with my door, if I could see them, they could see me. In other words, I had no choice but to open it.

Which was what I did.

I looked from Millie to High and back to Millie.

Millie looked a little hesitant . . . no, actually wary. High looked like High. Tall, dark, good-looking, and right then clearly acting as a guard dog for his woman.

They hadn't ended things well years before, and Millie had become *persona non grata* for all of Chaos, including me (even though Black had always said, unless we heard it straight from Millie's mouth, we shouldn't judge because we couldn't know for sure what had happened, and again it seemed Black was right).

Obviously, even though Millie and I had exchanged a smile at Jean's funeral, both of them thought I still held that ill will.

"Bev told me you two were back together," I said as greeting.

"Yeah, uh . . . yeah," Millie stammered, pulled it together and said quietly, "Hey, Keely."

"Hey, Keely?" I asked.

Millie now looked a little confused and a lot more wary.

High looked like he was preparing to get extremely pissed.

"I mean, that's it?" I asked. "'Hey, Keely?'"

"I, well—" she started.

"Oh for God's sake, get over here and give me a fucking hug," I snapped on a smile.

The wary slid away, a relieved look hit her face and I didn't wait for her hug.

I reached toward her, grabbed her and yanked her into my arms.

"God, I've missed you," I whispered in her ear.

Her arms around me got tighter. "Me too."

We pulled away but not too far, only enough so we were holding on to each other's forearms.

"You look awesome," I told her, and she did.

She used to be right there with me and Bev in our biker bitch clothes (Millie used to wear High's T-shirts belted at the waist as her form of micro-mini dress, it was shit hot).

Now she was all proper in a beautifully cut tight skirt, high-heeled boots and a slim fitting sweater.

"You haven't changed a bit," she replied.

"I've given the spandex a rest," I told her, and she laughed.

"I hear that," she said.

That was when I laughed.

"Woman, you gonna make us stand on your front stoop for the next hour of gettin' reacquainted?" High asked grouchily.

Since Hound wouldn't be home for a while, in that time I could duck away from them and text to let him know it wasn't safe to come home and he and the boys should hang tight until they heard from me.

So I shot a grin at High, let Millie go, stepped to the side and swept my arm in front of me, indicating they should come in.

"*Beinvenido a mi casa,*" I declared.

Millie smiled at me and walked in. High shook his head and followed her.

Even though Millie took a few steps into the living room, High stopped in the foyer and turned to me.

I thought he wanted me to take his cut or something (which would be weird, he'd been to my house, he knew he could dump it anywhere if he wanted to take it off) and I started to offer that.

He didn't, and I knew this when he said, "My woman gets a hug and you're dissin' me on that shit?"

"You're not a hugging type of guy," I told him because he wasn't.

Way back, he used to be a sweet and affectionate type of guy. But since Millie broke it off with him, he was a surly type of guy. As mentioned, he came to the house, helped out, he wasn't a stranger. He'd loved Black too. And me. And my boys.

But he wasn't cuddly.

"I'm turning over a new leaf," he told me.

I looked beyond him to Millie, who was looking at her man's back with a happy smile flirting at her mouth, and I knew why this leaf was turning.

So I looked back at High and walked to him.

He opened his arms, and when I got near they closed around me, so I returned the favor.

"Found your way home, I see," I whispered in his ear.

"Home found me," he did not whisper back. "Got lucky."

I looked over his shoulder at Millie who now sported a tender, happy look, and at that look I wondered which one of them felt luckier.

"Yeah," I agreed.

He let me go but kept one hand at the small of my back to push me around him and into my own living room.

I guessed it was time to move on from hugging.

"Throw your cut anywhere, babe," I said to him and looked at Millie. "Wine? Beer? Tequila shooters?"

"Wine, whatever kind you have will be great," she answered.

"High?" I asked.

"Beer, babe," he grunted, proving he was Hound's brethren beyond the cut he wore.

"You guys get comfy, I'll bring the drinks in," I told them, thinking this would give me a shot at texting Hound.

"We'll help," Millie offered.

Shit.

"No," I said over my shoulder, seeing her glancing around my living room. "That's cool."

"I haven't seen your house yet, Keely," she replied. "And from what I can see, I want to see more."

Yep.

Shit.

"Come on back then," I murmured.

I heard the distinctive sound of a leather cut hitting a sofa and they followed me back.

I knew when Millie hit the kitchen because she exclaimed, "Holy crap."

I grinned.

"This place is . . . this is . . . holy crap," she went on.

I grabbed the grocery bags from the table and set them on a counter and then went right to the fridge to yank out a beer as well as a bottle of white.

"How many pitchers are there?" she asked.

I looked to my wall that ran behind the stove and farm sink and fed up to a slanted, vaulted ceiling. The entire wall above an area of tiled backsplash was shelves filled with different beautifully but brightly painted pitchers and canisters I'd started collecting even before Graham had died.

"A lot," I answered.

"The fireplace is amazing," she noted.

I turned my attention to the fireplace against the back wall that had a stucco mantel and chimney that was painted a deep, rustic yellow and adorned with decorative plates. It was filled with a wood burning stove that heated the kitchen in the winter in a way it was super cozy and suddenly walking my groceries from the garage to the kitchen didn't seem like a chore anymore.

"Yeah, I . . . actually . . ." I turned from popping the cap on High's beer to High. "Didn't you paint that?" I asked, handing him his beer.

"Yup," he answered, taking it. "With Hound."

Yeah.

He'd painted it.

With Hound.

And Hound could help me paint our new kitchen.

I was back to thinking dragging my groceries from garage to house was a chore.

"I'll grab the glasses," Millie offered. "Where are they?"

"Over there." I indicated the other side of the kitchen with a jerk of my head as High pulled the bottle from my hands in a way I couldn't fight, so I didn't.

"Corkscrew?" he asked.

I shifted, opened a drawer and handed him the corkscrew.

Millie came and set the glasses by him on the counter.

"Take a seat," he ordered, like I was in their kitchen.

Ah, Chaos.

It was going to suck, having to hate them for as long as it took me to get over whatever they did to my man, because they were often just plain lovable (even if it was sometimes in an annoying way).

"We can take a tour later," Millie declared, right then taking my hand and guiding me to my kitchen table.

We sat.

A cork popped out of a bottle.

I watched High start to pour but looked back to Millie sitting at corners to me as she put her hand on mine on the table.

"How are you, Keely?" she asked.

There was something weighty about that question that I wasn't sure I understood.

"I'm good, babe. Though I'm sorry I didn't reach out earlier when I heard you guys were back together, especially after what went down a while back, and definitely after seeing you at the funeral. Things have just been . . ." I hesitated before I decided it was safe to finish, "a little crazy."

She nodded her understanding but did it watching me very closely.

When she said nothing, I carefully asked, "You?"

"I'm, uh . . . well, I'm . . . that is," her hand squeezed mine, "I was so, so sorry to hear about Black, honey."

Oh. Okay.

She'd been gone for a long time. The news might even be relatively new news to her. And like everyone, she'd loved Black. And as with everyone, Black had loved her.

"Thanks, Millie, that's sweet, but it happened a long time ago," I told her softly. "I'm more interested to know how things are going with you after what happened a few months ago."

"I'm fine, it's good. I mean, it took a bit to get there because that was, well . . . not fun."

I figured, getting kidnapped and watching two men get murdered, that was the understatement of the year.

Before I could mention that, she carried on, only mumbling, "But, um . . ." before weirdly her eyes darted to High and back to me like she was nervous.

I put this down to High approaching with our filled wineglasses (though I still didn't get the nervous part). He set them in front of us and then pulled out the chair at the head of the table, next to Millie, down from me, where I used to sit but now where Hound sat.

He sprawled out like he paid the mortgage.

I nearly laughed.

Seriously.

Chaos.

It was then I noticed the look on his face, and I wasn't feeling like laughing anymore.

It was my eyes that were darting between High and Millie then.

She was nervous.

And he was vigilant.

Disturbingly so.

"What's going on?" I asked slowly.

"Okay, uh . . . I just . . ." Millie stammered, looked to High, to me, to High, and I felt my body start to string tight.

Before I could ask again what was going on, High asked his own question.

"You okay?"

"I already answered that, and I was, until you two showed and my reunion with Millie got weird," I answered.

"Jag's ridin' Black's bike," he announced.

I relaxed.

They were worried about my state of mind now that my son had my dead husband's bike.

That I could handle.

"Logan!" Millie snapped.

"What?" he asked her.

"You could have led into it," she told him.

"Like you were doin'?" he fired back.

"I was getting there," she returned.

"When, next week?" he asked, but it was a sweet tease.

She moved in her chair in a way I knew was her kicking him under the table.

He didn't mind, and I knew that when I saw him grin at her.

And I sat there watching them, my tension gone, tickled freaking *pink* that they had this back again.

"You guys, I'm fine," I cut in on a smile and got both their attention. "It was just time. Time to let go. I had my little ceremony with Black and then gave Dutch his cut, Jag his bike, and . . ."

I trailed off because High had been watching me while listening to me but his attention turned to the back door.

My attention was turned from him when Millie asked, "Ceremony?"

"It was kinda . . ." How to explain it? The way Hound put it came to me. "All I had left of him that didn't have a permanent place in my heart. And the boys are both earning their patch. Since they are, I know now that they would get the significance of getting those things of their father's. So the time was right, I held a little ceremony and then gave my boys their father."

"Yeah, I get it," Millie replied. "But, Keely, honey, that couldn't have been easy."

"I took a long time saying my good-byes, babe," I told her gently. "Really, I'm o—"

I was interrupted by the back door being opened.

In a flash, my entire body was tight as a bow, so I felt it in every inch as I twisted in my seat and watched Hound walk in.

I hadn't heard him pull in at the back, but High had.

And since he pulled in at the back, he wouldn't have seen High and Millie's ride at the front.

Maybe it was time to get my hearing tested.

Damn.

Hound saw High first, then Millie, then me.

He stopped dead for just a beat before he stepped fully in and swung the door closed behind him.

He said nothing.

I said nothing.

High and Millie said nothing.

The air in the room was thick.

I knew that at least High knew that Hound looked after me all these years.

I also knew that High probably knew that in all that looking after, he'd never just let himself in the back door.

Furthermore, we couldn't lie.

He was coming out to the Club soon, maybe even tomorrow. He couldn't lie to High and Millie now and then tomorrow tell all the boys he was with me, we were living together, moving to a new house together, eventually getting married and building onto our family . . . together.

Shit!

What did I do?

"Brother," Hound grunted.

"Brother," High growled.

Hound moved in and I held my breath.

"Millie," he greeted.

"Hey, uh . . . Hound," she said hesitantly, definitely not knowing what was going on but also definitely feeling the vibe.

Hound shrugged off his cut, and I now felt every inch of skin tingling with adrenaline-fueled panic as he made it to me, tossed his cut to rest along the back of my chair like he normally did every time he came home and took it off.

Then he bent down to touch his mouth briefly to mine.

The air in the room became stifling.

He lifted away but an inch.

"Hey, babe," he murmured.

I stared into his eyes.

They were determined.

This was his home.

This was where me made me breakfast and I made him dinner. Where we went to bed together and woke up together. Where we fucked and where we cuddled and where we hung out with beers in front of the TV.

And I was his woman.

No, he was not going to lie.

He was staking his claim.

"Hey, cowboy," I whispered.

He straightened and aimed his gaze right at his brother.

I also aimed my gaze at High.

High's face was made of stone.

"We're together," Hound announced. "We been together for months. We're stayin' together. Buyin' a house together. Gettin' married. Makin' a baby girl together."

Holy *shit*!

He was going all in with the baby girl and everything!

My heart leapt right up into my throat, filling it so full I felt like I was choking.

"We took our time, dealt with our shit, made sure it was solid," Hound went on. "Dutch and Jagger know. Bev's Keely's girl, so she knows. Tomorrow, I was gonna share it with the brothers."

"Coincidence me sittin' here while you walk in like you own Black's house, touch Keely like she's your property, and suddenly you're gonna tell the brothers tomorrow, man," High said tightly, this not doing anything to alleviate my strangled feeling.

"Yeah, coincidence or bad timing, whatever way you wanna look at it," Hound replied.

"I look at it as bullshit," High returned.

Oh no.

"Logan," Millie whispered, and I knew by the tremor in her voice she was up to speed on the shit show that had just begun.

"It's not Black's house."

That was me, and High's angry eyes cut to me.

"His money that bought it," he bit out.

Oh boy.

Now I was getting angry.

"That's true but—" I began.

"His money that kept it," he spoke over me.

"Perhaps mostly, however—" I tried again.

"His house," High gritted in conclusion.

"You interrupt my woman again, High, we'll be outside havin' words," Hound growled.

Okay.

Shit.

No.

High slowly got up from his chair.

Millie got up from hers as he did, and she didn't do it slowly.

Fuck!

"Men—" I started.

"Logan—" Millie began.

"Those words'll come at the Compound. We're callin' in the brothers," High decreed.

Absolutely *no*.

I shot out of my chair and slammed my fist on the table.

"*No!*" I shrieked at High.

"Low, let's go into the other room and have a quick chat," Millie said urgently to her man.

Having made her way the short distance to High, she put her hand on his chest.

But High's eyes never left Hound.

"You trailin' me or am I trailin' you?" he asked my man.

"You sayin' you won't ride at my side?" Hound asked back.

"I'm sayin' we got shit to sort with the brothers," High returned. "But I'm not on my bike, Hound. This goin' down, even if I was, I still wouldn't ride at your side."

Right.

That did it.

I'd had enough.

"And *I'm* saying we knew this was going to happen and Hound is all in to pay whatever price you all have absolutely no right whatsoever to require of him," I snapped. "But I am *not*."

"Baby," Hound whispered, his hand coming to the small of my back.

But my gaze never left High.

"If Black was standing in this room, Hound wouldn't be standing in this room. But Black hasn't stood anywhere in *eighteen years* and I can't even in my wildest imaginings think that he wouldn't have wanted me to move on a long, *long* time ago and find my way back to happy," I told High.

"He would never want you to do that with a brother, Keely," High bit out.

"He would have wanted me to be happy whatever way I was genuinely happy, including finding that by falling in love with one of his brothers,"

I shot back.

"You think that then you didn't know your man very well," High retorted.

Oh my God.

He didn't just say that right to my face.

"Logan!" Millie snapped.

"How dare you," I whispered.

"We're takin' this to the Compound," Hound announced.

I looked up at my man. "No you are not. We're having dinner with our boys and telling them this shit has gone down, and tomorrow you can do what you planned to do." I turned again to High. "You and your brothers are just gonna have to wait."

"It doesn't work like that, Keely," High returned.

"Logan, you need to step into the other room with me," Millie hissed.

High didn't move.

I leaned into my hand on the table, fingers spread out, putting my weight into the pad of each, and I stared right into High's eyes.

"You owe me this," I said quietly.

"Keely, babe," Hound murmured.

I kept direct contact with High's gaze.

"Your shit took away one man, I'm claiming another. You *owe me this*, Logan Judd. And you fucking *know it*."

"Low, take a second," Millie urged, "and listen to Keely."

"But more," I went on, pushing up from the table and stabbing a finger in his direction, "*you* owe *Hound* this, and you know that too."

A muscle ticked in High's cheek.

He knew that.

Oh yeah he did.

"I love him and he loves me," I said softly. "He makes me happy. I haven't been happy, truly happy, since I lost Black. Now I am. And I make him happy too. *I make your brother happy*, High. When was the last time you knew down to your bones your brother was happy?"

I waited for a response to that question.

None came.

So I kept at him.

"He'll withstand whatever you force him to do and he'll do that because he loves me. He'll do that because he loved Black. And he'll do that because he loves *you*. Now how much love do you have for him, High? That's the question. You've known the man standing at my side for decades and you know the loyalty he has. The depth of love in his heart. The lengths he'll go to for his brothers. You know all of that. What he's going to learn is how deep all that flows back *to him*. And when he learns, I'll learn it too, and if you take that in the wrong direction, I'll never forget, High. I'll do my duty as an old lady and I'll find a way to forgive. But I will not *ever* forget."

I watched High's jaw flex through his thick salt and pepper stubble then I turned to my man.

I lifted a hand and curled it around the side of his neck, getting his attention as he dropped his gaze to look at me.

There was determination there still, I could see.

That was mingled with the love he had for me that was always right there, at the surface, all for me.

"You do what you need to do, baby," I told him. "If we're having dinner, I'll get on that. If we're not and it comes time you need me, I'll be there. Or when you come home, I'll be waiting."

He nodded.

I gave him a squeeze, got up on my toes, touched my lips to his then rocked back and let him go.

I turned, snatched up my wineglass and walked to Millie.

She took her hand from High's chest and turned to me.

"Wish we had more time to catch up, but we will, babe," I said. "Just know I'm glad to have you back."

I bent in, touched my lips to her cheek, pulled away, slid my glance through High and then walked out of my kitchen, to the stairs and up to my room.

Sitting in my sheepskin chair, I waited and I hoped. The hope part was hoping that Hound would come up, tell me we were having dinner with my sons, meaning both he and I would have time to prepare for what was to come.

I heard nothing except doors closing.

I waited some more.

When Hound didn't come up, I went down.

My heart clenched then warmed when I saw that all the groceries had been put away.

My man, my biker, my Hound . . . always so good to me.

My heart just clenched when I saw the note on the kitchen table.

I went to it and picked it up.

In Hound's messy scrawl it read,

Hitting the Compound, Keekee. Be home soon's I can.

I closed my eyes, pressed the note to my chest and took in a huge breath.

Then I opened my eyes, dropped the note to the table and went to my phone.

First, I called Dutch.

After that, I called Jag.

And after that, I called Bev.

CHAPTER TWENTY-TWO

GOLD-PLATED LOVE

Hound

"THIS IS BULLSHIT AND I'LL have no fuckin' part of it," Rush Allen spat at his father.

All the brothers were in the meeting room of the Compound, most of them sitting around the table with the Plexiglas in the middle, under which the first Chaos flag ever stitched lay.

Hound was not at the table.

Hound was where Hound usually was during meetings.

Standing at the back against the wall, one boot up against it, his arms crossed on his chest.

Standing down from him was Boz, and down from Boz was Brick.

The rest of the men sat at the table.

"Rush, you weren't—" Tack, at the head of the table, started to say to his son.

"If you say I wasn't a brother when Black got whacked, you know that don't mean dick. He wasn't like my favorite uncle. He was like my second father, and you fuckin' know that shit so you know I sit here havin' earned my patch *and* I sit here as a man who lost Black same's the rest of you," Rush fired back.

"Then maybe we'll listen to you when you got a woman you give a shit about," Arlo put in heatedly.

Rush's attention turned to Arlo. "Is that what it takes, Arlo? 'Cause if you know how that goes, you show me the woman you gave a shit about for more than it took to find some new pussy to sink into."

Arlo's mouth got tight because Arlo had an old lady and had had her for a while. He'd also had his share of other pussy, before her, and since.

Rush looked back to his father. "Coulda gone a lotta ways, you walked through that gunfire to get to Tyra. Blood leakin' out of her, ten more minutes, she'd have been gone. Would you keep your dick to yourself for the rest of your life if you lost the love of your life?"

"That's not what we're talkin' about here," Tack growled.

"So that happened, time passed and Lanie rubbed up against you, you wouldn't think about it?" Rush pushed.

"This isn't about Lanie," Hopper bit, not happy his old lady was dragged into this discussion.

"I'm makin' a point," Rush bit back at Hop.

"We're gettin' your point and it's not the same damned thing," Hop returned.

"It fuckin' is and you know it," Rush shot back. "With those two women, sisters of their own kind of patch, you know it. And you also know, time went by, she wasn't feelin' you but she was feelin' Dad, Dad felt like goin' that way, he wouldn't blink before he took what he wanted."

Hop's jaw bulged as he clenched his teeth, because Hop knew Tack found what he wanted in Lanie (even though he wouldn't, she was slim, and Tack was a tits and ass man), and it meant something even with what she meant to Tyra, he wouldn't blink.

Rush turned again to his old man. "And say a bullet tagged you and we lost you. Tyra didn't even have your ring then and Chaos would still have moved in. We'd have taken her on. We'd have protected her forever like she was one of our own."

"Yeah, you would and she'd have earned that by then, because ring or not, she was *mine*," Tack ground out. "And bein' mine, a brother moved in on that, I would not be down, Rush. Not ever. Not even close."

Rush's voice dipped when he said, "By then, Dad, you're right, she was yours. She was also ours. Now tell me, who could look after her like we could?"

"No one," Tack gritted.

"Yeah, and she made that play, that was what she wanted, Chaos was who she was and the only thing she could ever again be. If that was what she *needed* to make her happy, who could come after you but a brother?" Rush asked then kept at his old man. "Who would you *want* to come after you to give her what she needed to make her happy but *a brother?*"

Tack shut his mouth so fast Hound could swear he heard his teeth clack together.

And Hound stood against the wall, shaken, because he'd never thought of it that way.

But Rush was right.

Keely was Chaos.

If he'd thought about it, there could be no one else for her but a man whose blood ran wind, fire, ride and free.

"This is fuckin' insane. I can't even fuckin' believe I'm hearin' this shit," Dog growled.

Rush stood, his focus on Dog. "There's love and there's love. My father taught me the right kind of love. It's unrelenting and selfless. There's nothing you won't give up to show it. There's nothing you won't do to protect it." Keeping his eyes on Dog, Rush speared a finger at his father. "Dad taught me that." He speared a finger at Dog. "Black taught *you* that." Without looking Hound's way, Rush speared a finger at Hound. "And Hound's spent two decades showin' us all he's got that."

He moved free of his chair and trained his eyes on Shy sitting to Tack's left.

"You got my proxy. The vote comes up to make Hound stand the gauntlet, my vote is no. But I'm not gonna sit here and be a party to this shit." He finally turned to Hound. "They make you stand, brother, and you fall, I'll be there not to pick you up but to stand in your place." He swept his gaze along the table. "You take your fists to him and bring him low, next up you're taking your fists to me. Now you get done with this bullshit, I'll be at the bar. I need some fuckin' tequila."

Delivering that, he slammed out of the room.

Tack watched his son leave with an intensity that beat even his most intense, and the man could be intense.

Then he drew in an audible breath.

"Shy, you got my proxy too," Brick said, and Hound looked his way. "And it's a no."

"Are you fuckin' serious?" Arlo asked.

"Yeah," Brick clipped. "I don't know where you been for the last two decades but most a' the time I've been here seein' Hound step up for Keely, for those boys, for Black. But I was in that room, Arlo, and so were you, so we both knew just how far Hound went to step up for Black."

"To earn himself brother pussy," Arlo retorted, and that, only that made Hound's neck start itching.

"You know that ain't right," Brick whispered. "You know it."

Arlo moved his head in an awkward way that got Hound's full attention.

"We all know it," High put in. "Whatever we got here, don't go there, brother."

Arlo turned his eyes to the table, looking uncomfortable, and kept his mouth shut.

"We all know Black too," Brick went on.

"And he'd not be down with this shit *at all*," Dog said.

"You sure about that?" Brick asked.

"Fuck yes, I'm sure," Dog answered furiously.

"Well I'm not," Brick returned. "He loved her. I spent years chasin' that kinda love, brother. That gold-plated love that's so fuckin' rare it's almost like it doesn't exist, even when you can see it right in front of you. Love that shines so bright, blinds you but it's so fuckin' beautiful, you can't take your eyes away. Black felt that for Keely. And lookin' back, what I see now is, Hound felt that same thing."

Brick pushed away from the wall and kept at the men at the table.

"What I know about my brother Black is he'd take that blade along his throat again and again and again if somehow doin' it meant he could stop the pain that's been crippling his woman now for years. Black would do anything, give anything, once she suffered that blow, to see her happy again."

"He wouldn't give this," Arlo hissed.

"We all kicked in but it wasn't me and it wasn't you who took those boys trick or treatin', Arlo. It wasn't me and it wasn't you who was the rock of Chaos Keely and those boys could lay their hands on to keep them steady. It also wasn't me and it wasn't you that was the guiding light that led both Black's boys to our Club. And I'll say this, and you can argue it until you're sick but you'd be wrong. All that would mean everything to Black because the love behind it given to his family would mean everything to Black. Now I don't know and you can't know if that would make Black feel Hound earned the place he's now got with that family. What I know is, it's not for me to say it's right or wrong. Black, Hound and Keely'll have to deal with that in another life."

He swung an arm with his finger pointed Hound's way and kept going.

"What I will say is, my brother finally found his old lady and he's got my support. You bring him down, it won't be Rush you raise your fists to next, it'll be," he jerked his thumb to himself, "*me.* And that's the last I'll say. I'm done talkin'. You know my vote. And now I'm gettin' a beer with a chaser of a bottle of vodka."

He didn't wait for anyone to say anything else. Brick walked out with a lot less heat than Rush but he didn't waste time leaving the room.

"Fuck," Dog muttered angrily.

"You love her, son?" Big Petey asked Hound.

Hound looked to Pete. He said nothing. And he said nothing because he was standing there, ready to face whatever they decided, so it was the stupidest question he'd ever heard.

"You love her," Big Petey muttered.

"You went there, you knew it wouldn't stand," Tack said, and Hound looked to him.

He jerked up his chin in assent.

"You knew it'd come down to this," Tack went on.

Hound nodded once.

"You think of Black even once?" Arlo rapped out.

Hound looked to Arlo.

"For eighteen years, almost nothin' else on my mind but him," Hound answered.

"And her," Arlo countered.

"Yeah," Hound said low. "Definitely her."

"He was your brother," Dog gritted.

"He wasn't. He just *is*," Hound returned to Dog then looked to Tack. "I knew I'd be right here. You don't need to call the fuckin' vote. Even a single brother needs me to prove how much what I got with Keely means to me, he can take his shot at takin' my blood. They need me to prove I understand what it means I'm movin' in after Black, he can take that shot to take my blood. If they want to tie my hand behind my back and have a go at me every week for twenty years, I'll stand through it if it means in the end I'll still have her and I'll still have my brothers. But it's not gonna take that. It's gonna take whatever comes from this. So let's just fuckin' get on with it so we can get past this and I can get back to my woman."

"You'll take my fists," Arlo told him something he knew.

"Bring it," Hound invited him.

"Mine too," Dog bit out.

Hound nodded.

No one said anything until Tack called, "Boz?"

Hound turned his head Boz's way and he saw a look on his brother's face he'd never seen in his life.

It was fierce at the same time it was broken.

"I think my brother has taken enough of a beating spending years lovin' her and not havin' her, so I'll not add my fists to it," Boz said, and Hound stared at him, for once not able to hide his reaction and that reaction was staggered.

He had not known Boz had caught on to the feelings he had for Keely.

He had not expected that reaction to what was happening right there in that room.

He had thought Boz's loyalty would be to Black.

Not Hound.

"Right," Tack murmured then louder, "Run it down, men."

"Out," Shy stated immediately.

"That's not a surprise," Arlo muttered irritably.

"No, it isn't. Can't chose who you love, Arlo. You fall in love someday in a way that means you got the skirt you want and you're not chasin' more, brother, you'll get that," Shy replied. "Not me who's gonna make any man pay for somethin' that important that he gets in a way that's outta his control."

"Out," Snapper put in before Arlo could form a reply, but he wasn't done. "And just sayin', I get what this means and that it's important. Especially to the brothers who knew the man that was lost. But we got shit happening. Bounty's pissed at us, probably gearing up for payback and I'm not sure it's in his job description that their vigilante brother is gonna give us a heads up on any of that. Valenzuela's either dead or in the wind and neither are good for us right now. And we got a renegade ex-brother who's got it out for us. We might not have found any surveillance equipment anywhere that's Chaos but there's a woman out there who knows sensitive information about our Club she should not know and she didn't get that knowledge in a vision. This means there's a very real threat out there. So I'm not real certain why we're spendin' so much time on something that's divisive in the Club when we need to be spending time comin' together and getting ourselves and our women safe."

Instinct made Hound look to Arlo while Snapper was speaking and he felt his neck start itching again at the studied way Arlo was staring at the table, the tight in his fame, the hard in his jaw.

"Whatever happens from this meet, Snap, it'll be done tonight and we'll move on," Tack told Snapper, regaining Hound's attention.

Snapper stared at Tack then looked to Hound. When Hound gave him a chin lift confirming what Tack said, Snap looked back to Tack.

"Right, so I'll repeat, I'm out," he declared.

"No fuckin' way I'm in," Speck said. "Because a' what Rush and Brick said, but also because Hound could still beat my ass with one hand tied behind his back even if I'm his third go."

Shy and Big Petey grinned at the table.

No one else found anything funny.

"Roscoe?" Tack called.

"Out," Roscoe answered. "It was a year, two, even five after we lost a brother and another brother moved in, yeah. I get that. Totally. But eighteen years? No fuckin' way."

"Jesus Christ," Arlo clipped.

"It goes that way, I'll let Black kick his ass in the afterlife," Pete put in. "I'm out."

"Joke?" Tack prompted, and Hound looked to his brother who used to fight the underground circuit, bare fists. Hound would go and watch and Joke rarely lost because Joker was a machine.

He was also more than ten years younger than Hound, but that wasn't the reason Joke could beat the absolute crap out of him.

"You need this to feel clean and clear, man?" Joker asked quietly.

The man had never met Black but more than any of the new ones at that table, not including Shy and Rush, Joke was more Chaos than any of them, this before he even joined the Club, so he got it.

"I need you to do what your gut tells you to do," Hound answered.

"Dutch and Jag, been watchin', brother, and you're a third of their world," Joke told him something he knew, but even knowing it, it felt good hearing it.

Hound said nothing.

Joker shook his head. "I'm out."

"High? Hop?" Tack asked, making it clear he wanted this done, but probably more, he didn't want Arlo clapping his trap any more than he already had.

"In," High grunted.

"Out," Hop said.

"Christ, Hop, seriously?" Dog asked.

Hop lifted his eyes from the table to Dog.

"Seriously," he replied.

"I watched Black give you a cigar when Dutch came into this world and another when Jag hit it," Arlo reminded Hop.

"And I watched his woman mourn him for longer than she should. She's ready to find good again, I'm not gonna be any part of makin' it harder for her to grab hold," Hop returned. "I said that for Keely. For my brother Black, I'll say this. He wouldn't put his fists to any brother for any reason, Arlo. Whatever was going down, he'd find his way to understanding."

When Arlo opened his mouth to speak, Hop swiftly went on.

"Yeah, even this. Keely wouldn't stray. Hound would never move in. So if he'd lived, we wouldn't be right here. But he didn't live and I knew him, Arlo, even better than you, and the man I knew would want his woman happy and he'd find a way no matter how deep down he'd have to dig to grab hold of the loyalty he needed to give to his brother."

Hop had been tighter with Black so Arlo kept his mouth shut.

But Hop wasn't finished.

"Last, I'll say I want this for Hound. I do know what it's like to have a good one and that one bein' all I need in a way I know that's all I'll need until the day I die." Hop turned to Hound. "Glad for you that you found that, man. It's about time."

Now that wasn't a surprise. If anyone had the spirit of tolerance that Black had, it was Hop.

And it was Hound's observation, and now experience, when you found that gold-plated love, it did shit to you.

Hound dipped his chin at Hop.

"Tack?" Dog called.

Hound looked at Tack to find Tack watching him.

The room fell silent.

It was Tack who broke it.

"You need this to feel clean and clear," he repeated Joker's words but in a statement.

Hound didn't respond.

Making that a statement, Tack knew it to be true.

"How long will it take her to get over this?" Tack asked.

Tack also knew Keely.

"You put your fists to me, she'll find a way to deal but she'll never look at you with the same eyes," Hound told him the truth. "Me, I get it. That's not from me. Her, you'll lose her in a way you'll never get her back. She'll be Chaos, she'll be that through and through and she'll be that for me, for her sons. But she'll never again be yours."

"Out," High growled.

"Jesus, shit, seriously?" Arlo asked.

"I lost a good woman, by a miracle, got her back," High returned.

"I'm not gonna lose another one in a way I'll never get her back."

"Yeah, and Millie's always been tight with Keely, both of them back, they'll rebuild that, and she hears you took your fists to Hound because of this, you'll find the pussy in your bed goin' cold," Arlo snarled.

High sat back in his chair, unperturbed, muttering, "And there's that."

Big Petey swallowed a chuckle. Hop hid his smile by swiping his thumb and forefinger across his mustache.

But High wasn't done.

"It was me who saw them together and yeah, I was pissed. But what Hound just said, Keely also told me. She loves him. He makes her happy. This won't make her happy in a way any man hurts her man, she won't ever forget it and she said that to me straight." High looked to Hound. "Can't say I still don't wish that, when you found it, it wasn't her. Can say, you found what you need in each other, you're my brother and she's one of the best women I've ever met, so I guess I found my way to wanting it for the both of you. But there's something else she said that's straight-up true. We owe you both this. You already earned it, not up to me to make you put more work into having it."

Hound did another chin dip to High.

High jerked up his chin in return.

Arlo opened his mouth but Tack was done.

"Each man has said their piece. We're doin' this so it can get done," Tack declared. "Shy, go tell Chill to push the furniture back in the common room."

"You didn't say if you're in or out, Tack," Shy noted.

Tack again looked at Hound.

Tack then waited one beat that led into five.

Finally, he said, "He was the best of us."

Hound felt the sudden need to swallow but fought it back.

"And you did the worst . . . for him and for us," Tack continued.

Hound stood against the wall and held his brother's stare.

"I'm torn, brother," Tack said quietly.

"Struggled with this for years because of Black. Struggling with it now, I'm makin' you feel just that," Hound replied.

Tack nodded his head.

"He'd want her happy," Tack whispered.

"That wasn't what got me there," Hound told him. "Makin' her happy did that."

"Out," Tack said abruptly.

Dog blew out a breath.

Arlo made a noise in his throat.

Shy got up from his chair, his mouth twitching. He clapped a hand on Tack's shoulder and strolled from the room.

"You can change your mind, Dog," Pete noted.

"Arlo stands for the brothers," Dog stated immediately and turned his gaze to Hound. "I'll stand for Black."

Hound yet again dipped his chin, this time to Dog.

Chairs were pushed back.

Boz approached at his side.

Hound looked to him.

"It won't happen, but they get a few good ones in, rattle me, I take a knee, you keep Brick and Rush back," Hound ordered.

Boz nodded.

Hound started to move but stopped when Boz called his name.

He returned his gaze to his brother.

"Tack was wrong," Boz said.

"About what?" Hound asked.

"Black wasn't the best of us."

Hound stood silent, now feeling his throat itch.

"You are," Boz finished.

His brother gave him that.

And then he left the room.

<hr />

ARLO, RARING TO GO, WAS the first one up.

Hound had rough rope tied around his waist and also wound around his wrist, securing it to the small of his back.

Even so, for that shit Arlo spewed about Hound taking out Black's killer to earn himself Keely's pussy, Hound ducked the first punch then put all his power in his left fist and dealt Arlo a crushing blow to the cheekbone, quickly spun and caught him with the toe of his boot in Arlo's kidneys.

Arlo spluttered, coughed, staggered to the side, but unfortunately this just served to piss him off even more, so he came back at Hound with everything he had.

Hound knew how to box, trained in a boxing gym, but he wasn't a boxer. He wasn't even a fighter.

He was a brawler and his hand tied behind his back fucked with his momentum and coordination. It wasn't about him not being able to use that fist to throw a punch. It was that he couldn't use it to grab hold, shove, toss, wrestle or use that entire side to stay balanced.

Arlo had opened up his left eyebrow and the right side of his bottom lip before some commotion happened among the men that circled them, catching Hound's attention, but not Arlo's, and when Hound heard Dutch shout, *"Take your hands off me, man!"* he made the mistake of looking toward his boy's voice.

Arlo clocked him, sending him lurching, white invading his vision from the blow mingling with the red that was blood seeping into his eye, and to focus on regaining concentration, he automatically took a knee.

"Piss off, man! Stand back!" Hound heard Dutch yelling. *"Fuckin' stand back!"*

"You are not in this, son," Tack said low as Hound felt a hand land on his shoulder.

He looked up, blinked against the white that was retreating, and the blood that was not, and saw Jag there staring down at him, the muscle running up his cheek flexing.

"I'm not in this? I'm not fuckin' in this?" Dutch asked, sounding enraged.

"This is between the brothers and you are not yet a brother," Arlo stated.

"This is about my father and my mother and my *dad*. And *I am my father and my mother* but most of all, I'm my *dad*."

Christ, that felt better than what Boz had said earlier.

By a lot.

"So I'm as Chaos as you can get, Arlo," Dutch finished.

"Take your brother and go," Hound whispered to Jag.

Jag leaned deep and put his face in Hound's.

"No," he replied.

Then he crouched and Hound felt him at the rope at the side of his waist. He knew Jag had slid in a blade and cut through because it immediately came loose, and Jag stood.

"We got problems with you bein' a prospect, you don't get your ass out and now," Arlo declared.

Jagger pulled Hound to his feet and the rope fell to the floor.

When Jag got him there, he immediately moved to stand beside his brother, blocking Arlo from Hound.

"This was decided by the brothers," Tack explained. "This is how it's done. You need to learn this. It's important. And you don't interfere with it, as a recruit, or as a brother."

"We speak for our father," Jagger stated.

"That's not the way it goes, son," Tack said quietly.

"We speak for our mother," Jagger went on.

"That's definitely not the way it fuckin' goes," Arlo bit off.

"Hound understands this and he wants it," Tack said. "He even needs it, men. So you need to stand down and let him have it."

The boys did not stand down.

"Fair fight," Dutch ground out.

"Dutch—" Hop entered the conversation but he didn't get far.

"Fair fight. He's fightin' for our mother. He's fighting for his place in our family. He's fightin' to stay solid with his brothers. If he's fighting for shit that means that much, shit that means everything, it should be fair fight," Dutch clipped. "You gotta make him raise fists, he feels he needs to take his beating, let him stand free and fight fair."

"I don't give a shit how he fights," Arlo snapped. "What I give a shit about right now is two recruits gettin' up in my face, in brother business, when they're not welcome. You do as you're told, assholes, or I'll see to it you don't earn your goddamned patch."

At that, Hound pushed through Dutch and Jag, taking Arlo by surprise, so he was able to get his fingers wrapped around Arlo's throat.

Arlo pushed back, tried to pull from Hound's grip, but Hound just yanked him so they were nose to nose and he growled, "You're witnessing loyalty, motherfucker, something I'm thinkin' is foreign to you. We'll talk about that later. Now . . ." he shoved him off and lifted his fists, *"fight."*

"Back up," Hound heard Tack order Dutch and Jag.

He felt them all retreat to the circle.

On a roar, Arlo came at him.

And with a roar, Hound met him.

It was brutal and there was a lot behind it on both sides, and none of it had to do with Black.

But all of it had to do with what Hound feared burned deep in Arlo.

Guilt.

And shame.

So when Shy called out, "Time!" they didn't stop.

It took Dutch, Jag, Joke and Hop pulling Hound back, and High, Tack and Boz pulling Arlo back.

"We're not done," Arlo hissed, his focus still locked on Hound, even if now he also had blood in his eyes, covering his teeth and running down his chin.

"No we are not," Hound agreed, spit blood from his own mouth at the floor at Arlo's feet and turned his attention to Dog, shrugging off the men who held him. "You're up, brother."

"Shit," Dutch bit off.

"Just Dog, that's it, then it's done," Boz said under his breath to his boys.

Dog came at him but the fury was not there.

Hound still let Dog have him.

Because Dog was fighting for Black.

Reflex and knowing Dutch and Jag were watching made him duck, lift his arms to protect his face, twist to glance off blows to the body, but he took from Dog what Dog was willing to give, for Black, each fist that landed leading Hound to clean and clear.

And Keely.

"Goddamn it, Hound! Fight!" Jagger thundered.

Right after that came, it was Dog that had his attention turned when another commotion started outside the circle, and Hound heard

Speck mutter, "Jesus, shit, you gotta be kidding me. This keeps up, for a ten-minute fight, we'll be here all night."

"You do not get in this," Tack growled.

"Fuck me," Hop muttered irately.

Shy chuckled.

Dog turned. Hound turned.

Then both shifted back when suddenly a line of women stood between them.

Tyra, Tabby, Lanie, Carissa, Millie, Rosalie and Bev.

Hound looked toward the doors, but all he saw was Elvira scooting her round ass onto a barstool.

Thank fuck, no Keely.

"Reckon tomorrow we should just all come in and paint the Compound pink then go have our balls whacked off," Arlo groused.

Tack came to stand by Dog, his eyes locked on his woman.

"This, especially this, Red, you do not get to be in this," he declared, looking so seriously fucking pissed, Hound moved closer to Tyra's back.

Dog moved that way too, at her front.

"We're here for Keely," Tyra returned.

"Keely does not get to be in this either," Tack fired back.

"Excuse me, but she's clearly coming back to the fold, which means she's a sister even more than she already *was* a sister and as such, her other sisters have to have her back," Tyra retorted.

Tack looked at his daughter and said, "You definitely know better than to pull this shit."

From the back, Hound saw Tabby shrug.

"You can direct all communication to me since we decided that I'm the spokesperson for our group," Tyra put in and got her husband's narrowed eyes.

"I don't know whether I'm gonna laugh or my head's gonna fuckin' explode," High muttered, and Hound looked to him to see him scowling at Millie.

Tack's voice getting louder regained Hound's attention. "How many fucking times do I have to tell you to keep your nose outta brother shit?"

"Since Bev told us Hound and Keely were together and we would need to prepare for this exact thing happening," Tyra flung her arm toward the floor, "it occurred to us this was actually *sister* shit. And Keely was *not* happy this might go down and the last thing the Club needs right now is dissension, so we're here to intervene."

Tack's voice was now dangerously quiet. "Since Bev told you about Hound and Keely?"

Tyra tossed her hair. "Yes."

"How long have you known?" Tack asked.

"Awhile," Tyra answered unhesitatingly.

Now Tack was shouting. "And you didn't tell me that shit?"

Tyra leaned her old man's way and shoveled his shit right back at him. "We sisters have some stuff that's just between us too."

Everyone lost Tack's face seeing as he bent his head so far back to look at the ceiling, all they had was a view of his throat and the underside of his jaw. They also saw his chest expand as he took in a big breath.

Hound felt for the man.

He'd fallen for Keely when she was Black's. Then, it was controllable. She was untouchable.

He'd never fall for Tyra. She was easy to look at, and with her attitude, probably an amazing lay.

But with that attitude, she was also a serious pain in Tack's ass.

Tack totally got off on it (for the most part, barring times like these).

Hound would put up with it for about a minute before he'd get shot of her even before he got all he ever wanted in an old lady.

Finally, Tack looked back at his woman. "Right, get out."

"Kane—" she began.

Tack cut her off. "This is as much Hound's choice as Dog's. He took on Arlo, he's gotta finish with Dog and then it's done. But it's gonna get done with you takin' your ass and your girls' asses and waiting outside."

Tyra sounded confused. "You're not all gonna beat him up?"

"I'm not explaining it further," Tack retorted. "I'm tellin' you, Dog's got about two minutes left of his go and then it's done and you and your girls are *out* until it's *over*."

"But—" she tried.

"*Out*, woman," Tack growled.

There was a long beat of nothing.

Then Tyra said, "Well, since it's only Dog left, we'll go."

Christ, what was going down was going down and Hound was about to start laughing.

He beat that back, looked to Dog, saw Dog was beating his back so they both turned their eyes to their boots.

He lifted his when he felt fingers wrap around his forearm and he saw Bev had hold of him.

"Good luck, honey," she said softly.

Jesus, did Bev just call him "honey?"

"Keely's waiting outside," she finished.

Hound did a very slow blink.

"Say what?" he asked.

"She refused to come in. Said this was your gig and she'd come in after it was over," Bev explained.

His woman had been out of the fold longer than all of these bitches (except Bev, and obviously Tabby) had been in it, and she still was more old lady than the lot of them.

"You think maybe you should have followed her lead?" he asked.

Bev shrugged.

Hound shook his head.

Bev gave him a thumb's up, turned tail, and for once without even a glance at Boz, followed behind Carissa, the door closing them off.

"Give me a shot of that top shelf tequila, boo."

All eyes turned to Elvira, still on her stool and ordering a drink from Rush, who was behind the bar, like she wasn't in a motorcycle club compound but instead just in a club.

"I know you know that you, *especially*, should not have your ass right there," Tack declared to Elvira on a low rumble.

"I do know this, big man," Elvira replied. "We had a powwow and during that powwow I told all your bitches they should be nowhere near here but they wouldn't listen to me. So I'm packin' my Taser in case one of you badasses lost your mind, as, just my opinion, and I'll repeat, not that anyone has listened so far, they were way outta line. Told 'em to let the brothers sort it out among the brothers. It'd go a lot faster, be a lot less painful and not get their asses in a sling on the home front. They were determined to back up Keely. My job is to back them up even if they're doin' stupid-ass shit that in turn might get me uninvited to Chaos hog roasts for the rest of eternity. And that right there is proof of my dedication to the sisterhood, because you boys can roast a mean hog. So here I am," she motioned to her ass on the stool by drawing both hands out down low at her sides, "backin' them up."

"No need for you to be here anymore, Vira," Joker pointed out.

"I like fights," she returned, thought about it and then added, "In fact, I like man on man action on the whole."

Jesus.

"The two minutes left of this fight, you're gonna hafta miss," Tack growled.

Elvira rolled her eyes, but unlike the other women, was wise enough to know when she wasn't wanted. Therefore, she didn't wait very long before she gracefully extended one leg down until her foot in its high heel hit the floor.

She came off the stool and sashayed her way to the door, saying, "I like fights but I'm no nursemaid, so just hope you didn't piss all those bitches off with this caveman shit or you're cleanin' up your own blood."

With that, the door closed behind her.

Tack turned to Hound and Dog in the circle.

Hound looked to Dog.

Dog looked to Hound.

Dog lifted up both shoulders and said, "I just don't have it in me anymore, brother."

Hound nodded.

He got that.

But in the next instant, he rushed Arlo, got him by the throat again and took him, Arlo's feet skidding and sliding, his fingers wrapped around Hound's forearm, toward the bar.

Big Petey, Shy and Snap jumped out of the way as Hound slammed Arlo's back against the bar, lifting him by his throat off his feet, curling him over the bar and bending into him.

"Hound, brother," Pete murmured calmingly.

"You tell Chew I slit that fuck's throat?" Hound rumbled.

The room went static.

"Get off me, man," Arlo wheezed, trying to find purchase with just his toes on the floor and shoving at Hound's forearm.

Hound squeezed and got deeper in his face.

"You tell Chew I slit that fuck's throat?" he repeated.

"Get . . . *off*," he choked.

"Answer him," Tack, now at Hound's side, gritted.

"Get him off me," Arlo gagged.

"*Answer!*" Tack barked.

"Yeah, fuck, yeah . . ." Removing one hand from Hound's forearm, putting it under Hound's chin, and with a mighty shove and twist of his body, he pulled from Hound's hold and scuttled away five feet.

Hound felt all the brothers amass at his back, except Tack, who took one step in front of him, toward Arlo, and there he stopped.

"You told Chew that shit?" Tack asked, the question coming almost as a whisper, furious, shocked and with disbelief.

"He was a brother," Arlo returned.

Dog, at Hound's other side, stepped forward. "At that time, he was not."

"I was tryin' to win him back," Arlo snapped. "He was a brother. Before that shit went down, turnin' him, he was a good brother. Thought, he knew we took care of business, Chaos had what it took to do it right, erase that motherfucker from the planet, avenge Black the way it should be, he'd come back."

"That was not your place, Arlo," Tack pointed out.

"Never thought he wouldn't . . ." Arlo shook his head. "I thought he'd come back. He was Chaos. He was one of us."

"You renounce the Club, you don't get another shot to come back in," Pete said.

"Shit was different back then," Arlo reminded them.

"You renounce the Club, it's done," Tack stated. "It was done. You put your brothers in danger, Arlo."

"It's hearsay," Arlo retorted. "He can't do shit with it."

"You were there, you're not only a fuckin' witness, you're a fuckin' accomplice," High growled.

"I'm not gonna say dick," Arlo hissed.

"You already did," High bit out.

"What else did you tell him?" Tack asked.

"Just that we took care of it," Arlo answered.

"*We* took care of it or *Hound* took care of it?" Tack pushed.

"Both," Arlo spat.

"Christ, brother," Tack murmured. "You pushed for Hound to stand the gauntlet sittin' on knowledge for fuckin' years that meant that's right where you should be to pay penance for doing some stupid . . ." his tone was degenerating, "fucking . . ." he was losing it, "*shit!*"

Then he lost it.

And Arlo was against the side wall with Tack's forearm tight to his throat this time.

The men closed in.

"I was tryin' to pull the Club back together," Arlo rasped.

"You mighta tore us apart," Tack returned. "He's got the goddamned *bones.*"

"Chew won't take it there," Arlo pushed out.

"You better hope the fuck not, man," Tack clipped. "You better hope the fuck not."

He pushed off, took a step back and Hound watched as Tack stared at the floor and took in deep breaths.

Finally, he lifted his head and looked at his brothers.

"The gauntlet is done. The women are outside. Business is concluded for tonight." He turned to Arlo. "We'll deal with your shit later."

Brick came forward, jabbing a finger Arlo's way. "Hand tied behind your back for fuckin' certain, *brother.*"

"We'd lost Black!" Arlo yelled. "We'd lost Chew. Crank had fucked us all. *I was tryin' to keep our Club together!*"

"And now you're learnin' a valuable lesson we all already knew and you shouldn't have needed to learn," Tack said. "Problem with that is you're not the only one who might suffer the consequences."

"There was good in him," Arlo shot at Tack.

"Maybe you're right," Tack shot back. "And now we all gotta hope there's still some of that left and we gotta hope that because of you."

"I fucked up, is that what you wanna hear?" Arlo asked. "It is or it isn't, it doesn't matter. I fucked up. You think I haven't been livin' with that for a long fuckin' time? Shit, I'm *glad* it's out. I fucked up. Now we all deal. As brothers."

"Jesus, that's a fuckin' joke," Dog muttered.

"No it's not," Rush stated. "It's the god's honest truth. We're brothers when it's all good and we're brothers when it's in the shitter, and we're brothers when we fuck up or we're not brothers at all."

All the men looked to Rush.

Rush shook his head, mumbled, "Jesus, now I need more tequila,' then moved back to the bar.

It took some of the men more time than others but eventually they all disbursed.

Except Hound who stood there staring at Arlo.

"I fucked up, brother," Arlo told him quietly. "I laid you out. I thought Chew would hear you delivered justice for Black, he'd know we were on the right path. But it didn't go that way so in the end, I fucked up and laid you out."

"You finally on board with where we're heading?" Hound asked.

"Yeah, man. Yeah. Have been since after Cherry . . ." Arlo jerked up his chin. "Absolutely. Have been for years."

So that night wasn't about Hound moving in on Keely.

It was about Arlo letting out the rage that started building from the shame he felt now that they knew Chew was back.

He'd take that from him.

Because he was his brother.

"Then we're good," he decreed.

"I'll stand the gauntlet, the men put me in the circle," Arlo said.

"You'll want that. It clears the head, cleans the soul."

Arlo nodded and muttered, "Just, on your go, lay off that fuckin' left hook."

He was so into the discussion, he didn't sense her until he saw Arlo's attention shift beyond him and he felt her hand on his back.

He turned.

And there she was.

Keely.

Standing close to him at the Compound, the heart of Chaos, her hair running in shining sheets down either side of her face, her choker around her neck, looking up in his eyes.

Keely, his old lady.

Right there.

Oh yeah.

He would have taken a beating from all of them, both hands behind his back, for that moment *right there*.

She lifted a hand and gently prodded the cut in his eyebrow with her thumb, her gaze on it, then lifted her other hand and did the same with the cut on his lip.

"They opened you up," she whispered.

"Babe," he called.

She looked again into his eyes.

"Kiss me," he ordered.

That was when she stared into his eyes.

He watched her eyes smile.

Then she moved into his arms and rolled up on her toes.

Hound bent his head.

And right there, at the Compound, standing in the heart of Chaos, Keely looking beautiful, being beautiful, now all his, kissed him.

And it was then, for the first time in his life, Shepherd "Hound" Ironside had everything he ever wanted.

The Present and The Future

"THAT, RIGHT THERE, IS SELFLESS and unrelenting," Rush said.

Tack tore his eyes off Keely Black in the arms of Hound Ironside and looked at his son.

"It's everything you've ever fought for, Dad," Rush went on when he got Tack's attention.

"He's right," Tyra murmured, pushing in under his arm at his other side.

Even as he curved the arm she was burrowing under around her, Tack looked down at his woman. "I'm seriously fuckin' pissed at you."

She wrapped both her arms around her man's middle and turned her gaze to Rush. "He'll get over it."

"Yeah," Rush agreed. "Selfless and unrelenting."

"What?" she asked.

Kane "Tack" Allen and Cole "Rush" Allen locked eyes.

Then they spoke the same word at the same time.

"Nothing."

CHAPTER TWENTY-THREE

HALLMARK MOMENT

Hound

HOUND FELT HER WET HEAT close around him as he watched his cock sink into Keely when she bore down on him.

After she'd taken all of him, he lifted his gaze to hers and watched her bend over him, her tits hitting his chest, her hands sliding up his neck, over his ears, into his hair.

She stared in his eyes as they lay connected in his bed in the Compound.

"You gonna ride me or you just gonna stare at me?" he prompted when she didn't move for a long time.

"Shh," she shushed. "I'm memorizing this moment."

He trailed both hands from her hips up her back until he got to her head. He pulled her hair away from her face and held her like she was holding him.

"Baby, I don't do goofy-ass Hallmark moments," he told her. "Especially not when my cock is buried in my woman's pussy. Fuck me or I'll fuck you. You got ten seconds to decide."

"I don't think Hallmark has a moment when a woman takes a man inside on his bed in a motorcycle club hangout," she replied.

"I'm pretty sure it took ten seconds to say that," he warned and watched her smile.

Then he watched her push up.

And with eyes locked to her, he watched her ride him, shifting his thumb to her clit to take her there.

She went there.

Then she took him there.

On his bed in the Compound, his brothers and their women close, carousing, fighting, or fucking.

Hallmark might not make a moment of that.

But it was one of the best in Hound's life.

"OKAY, I SAW THAT COMING from Bev to Boz, but I did not foresee his reaction," Keely declared.

It was after they were done, after they'd cleaned up. They were naked, tangled up in each other and his sheets in his bed. They were front to front but she'd angled herself away and was stroking his chest and abs like she had his tats memorized and could see in her mind the Apache weapons inked into him that she was tracing.

"Yeah," he grunted, not really thinking about what she was saying, instead trying to figure out if he wanted to eat her next or get her to blow him.

"Boz looked destroyed," she noted.

That got his attention because his brother had looked just that. When what went down after the women came back in, after he got his kiss from Keely, and after the booze started flowing, Boz had looked destroyed.

Hound remembered the way he'd seemed during the meet, fierce and broken, and he knew then that wasn't about what was happening with Hound and the brothers.

It was the discussion about Black and Keely and about what Hound now had with Keely.

It was him coming to terms with what he'd had with Bev.

And what he'd lost.

"I almost feel sorry for him," Keely went on and finished on a mutter, "Almost."

Hound dug Tad. He was a good man. Solid. Sharp. He loved Bev.

But he felt for his brother.

He played it out in his head, that time after the kiss when Rush called out to ask him and Keely if they wanted a drink and Keely had ordered a beer like the last time she'd partied in the Compound was the weekend before.

He'd been watching Rush telling Chill to pull her one when he felt Keely's arms get tight around him.

When he looked down at her, he saw her attention was across the room.

He turned his that way and saw Boz up in Bev's space.

Boz was talking low and intent.

Bev was staring in his face looking impatient.

When Boz got finished speaking, she just shook her head, took one step back, another, found Keely and Hound and blew a kiss their way, calling, "I gotta get to Tad's. It's movie night with his kids. I'll call you later."

"Later!" Keely replied. "Love you, babe, and thanks!"

"Anytime, every time," Bev returned.

"Later, Beverly," Tab called out, standing but snuggled into Shy who was sitting on a stool.

"Yeah, later, Bev," Lanie said from her position that was the opposite from Tab's, sitting on a stool with Hop standing close, his arm draped around her shoulders.

"I'll call you, I got that sex toy party sorted," Elvira, on her own stool next to Lanie, said.

"Thanks, Vira," Bev replied. "Later, everybody."

She took off with men and women yelling good-bye while Hound dipped to Keely's ear and muttered, "Sounds like the girl meetings are more interesting than the boy meetings."

Keely turned her head, caught a look at his lip, then his brow, then she looked into his eyes. "Yeah. You want me to help you get cleaned up?"

This meaning getting her to his room, he absolutely wanted that.

"Yeah," he agreed.

He was going to move her to the bar so they could get her beer, one for him, and take them with when she went solid so he went that way with her.

Hound again looked in the direction she was looking.

And that was when they saw it.

Boz staring at the door Bev had walked out, looking destroyed.

"Oh boy," Keely muttered.

"Boz, beer or shot?" Chill called.

Boz didn't move, just stood there, staring at the door.

"Yo! Boz!" Chill yelled. "Beer or shot, man?"

Boz jerked himself out of it, looked to the bar then found Keely.

"That dick's name is *Tad*?" he asked.

"Oh boy," Keely muttered again.

"I mean, that no-dick's name is . . . *Tad*?' Boz asked, this time acidly.

"Um . . . well, uh . . . apparently size is relative considering, well . . ." Keely stumbled along until Hound gave her a squeeze, mostly to stop her from talking, but instead she blurted, "He's actually above average it's just that . . ."

"Shut up, shut up, shut up," Hound whispered in her ear.

She didn't shut up.

"He's got a good seven inches and she's used to more."

The entire room went silent.

Elvira broke it, and when she did her voice was pitched high.

"The woman has seven inches, why she need a sex toy party?"

"Shut up, shut up, shut up," Hound whispered again.

She didn't shut up.

"They're kinda . . . adventurous, um . . . in the sack."

Fuck.

"Well all right," Elvira decreed.

"She's used to . . . *more*?" Lanie asked, sounding strangled and staring with big eyes at Boz.

"Are we really listenin' to bitches havin' a conversation about dicks and sex toy parties in our own damned Compound?" Speck asked.

Boz ignored Elvira, Lanie and Speck and asked Keely, "She's marrying him, isn't she?"

"Yes, Boz," Keely answered.

"She's marrying a man she doesn't love?" Boz pushed.

"I, well . . . no. He . . . Boz, I'm sorry, but he won her over," Keely answered.

"He's a good dude," Jagger put in. "Solid. They were over to dinner and Mom's asshole folks showed, Dad's asshole folks showed, he didn't know dick about what was happening, except they were being assholes, and I thought for a second he'd snap all their necks."

Slowly, Boz looked from Jag back to Keely.

And the destroyed had intensified.

"He had dinner with you and Bev and the boys?" he asked.

Shit.

"Yes," Keely answered.

"I lost her," he said.

Keely nodded. "I'm sorry, Boz, but yeah, you lost her."

Boz stared at Keely then at the door before he walked to and through it.

"Oh boy." This time Keely whispered it.

"Your folks showed?" Tack asked Keely, and she stopped studying the door and looked to Tack.

"Yeah, but the boys kicked them out in a way I don't think they're ever coming back, so it's all good."

"You there when that went down?" Tack asked Hound.

"Yup," Hound answered. "And the boys took care of it."

"Hound opened the door for them after we kicked their asses out," Dutch shared.

"And followed them to their cars," Jag added then included, "So did Tad."

"Then we all shot tequila and ate dessert," Dutch finished.

Hound felt a lot of eyes but only saw Tack looking at him, and he knew right then Tack was seeing yet another part of the good Keely had, having him in her life.

He felt Keely tug at his hand.

He looked down at her. "Your face. Clean up. Let's get our beers and do that."

Hound thought that was a good idea so they did that, ending up where they were.

Naked in his bed.

So he'd been wrong in what he thought.

It hadn't been a good idea. It had been a spectacular one.

"It kinda sucks, I'm back and she's gonna be married to some guy who's not Chaos. But we all bonded over trying to decide what to do about you standing the gauntlet and sex toy parties, so I know she won't lose the girls. She just won't be hanging at the Compound anymore."

"Tad's welcome here," Hound grunted.

Her body went still then it swayed into his and she slid her arm around him as she asked, "Really?"

"Why not?"

"Well . . . Boz."

"He dicked around, let a good thing slip through his fingers, not a brother who doesn't know that. Probably not a good idea Tad shows tomorrow for a brew at the bar, but give it some time, he'll be tight with us, the boys, Bev's always got a place with Chaos and since he'll be with her, he'll have a place too."

She slid her hand back to his chest, up to his neck and into his hair behind his ear.

"I love you," she whispered.

He grunted.

"Are the boys in trouble?" she asked.

"You send them here?" he asked back.

She shook her head on the pillow. "I just told them it was going down. I didn't know they were here until the girl posse got here and I saw their bikes."

He nodded his head on the pillow. "They're not in trouble. They handled it right. Showed loyalty. Didn't take shit too far."

"Good," she said softly.

"The girl posse?" he asked.

She did a bed shrug and answered, "I called Bev, just for moral support.

She told me she was coming over to wait it out with me, but instead she showed with all of them. Apparently, she'd warned them the day after I told her about us. But they didn't get far in deciding what to do if things went south, because she thought they'd have time because she thought I'd warn her it was coming."

"So Bev didn't listen real good when you told her just her, you, me and the boys," Hound noted.

"And Tad," she corrected.

He said nothing.

She grinned at him and returned to her story.

"They hatched the plan to horn in. Elvira, who's a freaking hoot by the way, and I tried to talk them out of it. Tyra and Tab, who, swear to God, if I didn't know Naomi was Tabby's mother, I would have sworn Tyra had birthed that girl, would hear none of it. Lanie was beside herself with fury at the very thought Hop might put hands on you for that reason. Carissa, she's very sweet, but the perfect old lady. She was really calm, supportive of them, but I knew she'd stand behind whatever her man decided to do. It was an interesting decision and says a lot about how secure she is with whatever she's got with her man, that she came in with them. But I figure she knows he'd stand behind whatever she decided to do too."

"They're young but they're tight. I couldn't imagine him with any other woman on the planet," Hound told her. "She does it for him. He's been in love with her since high school."

"That's so sweet," she whispered. "I love that for her."

"He's a good guy," Hound shared.

"Now I love it more," she replied and went on, "Apparently Millie didn't know, until today. Bev knew she and I had history, thought maybe Millie would be the one who would spill with High, so she saved Millie for last."

Hound had nothing to say to that, though he grunted.

Then he declared, "So now it's over."

"Arlo and Dog," she stated.

At that, Hound gathered her closer. "Babe—"

"No," she whispered.

He shut up.

"All those brothers, those two couldn't just let us have it?" she asked.

"Arlo's got issues he needed to work out, Keekee, and it's my place to help him work those out."

"I disagree," she returned. "Especially when that shit leaves you bloody."

"You see him?"

She reached under her. Following his arm he had wrapped around her with her hand, she pulled it between them. She had her fingers wrapped under his wrist with her thumb rubbing lightly across the rope burns at the inside while her eyes watched.

She looked up at him. "You did all that damage with one hand tied behind your back?"

"Some of it. Most of it came after Dutch and Jag made their play, Dutch layin' it out and Jag cutting me loose."

"God," she pressed his hand flat against her chest and melted the rest of her body into his, "I love my boys."

There was a lot to love and their play that day was only part of it.

"Arlo and me worked shit out and you got your own mind, not mine to tell you what to put in it, but know that. Dog, I didn't lay a fist on him and let him do what he had to do since he was standin' in for Black."

Her look shared that did not make her happy.

Her words did the same. "That's not his prerogative."

"It is and we won't agree on that so I'll just say, Keekee, I needed that, he gave it to me and we were good before, we're good now and as for me, I'm *better* now."

"You just let him beat on you, he took that opportunity and did it, and you're *better*?"

"I needed to prove to them what you meant to me. And usin' them, prove it to Black."

"Shep," she pressed his hand deep into her chest, "please get this. It's important. Black is *not here*."

"Not anymore."

Understanding hit her face and her fingers curled tight around his at her chest.

"I'm clean and clear and from this point on, it's Hound and Keely," he declared. "And when I get a ring on your finger, baby, you're addin' Ironside to your name. I know the boys got Black and that lives on. But you're mine now."

The happy was back, shining from her face.

Christ, she was beautiful.

"So when are you gonna put that ring on my finger, Shepherd Ironside?"

"I want time with you. I want a baby with you. And I wanna be in a house with a fire pit by summer. If you can do all that and plan a wedding, we'll go get you a ring tomorrow and you'll be gettin' on all that."

Her head shifted back an inch. "That's not very romantic."

"Whose dick did you just ride?" he asked.

She grinned.

"The man belongs to that dick romantic?" he went on.

"In his way," she told him.

That was when his head shifted back an inch. "When have I ever been romantic?"

"You make me breakfast every day."

"That's bein' a good old man for my old lady."

"Right, then when you yanked my knees out from under me, fell to your own at the end of your bed and buried your face in my pussy," she stated.

"That's romantic?"

"For a biker bitch, totally."

It was his turn to grin, so he did.

He also used his free hand to roam, sharing, "I'm feelin' romantic again right about now."

She rolled her eyes.

He rolled her to her back.

And Hound got romantic not knowing two doors down, Lanie was getting her own version of romantic, one door up, Millie was getting the same, one door up from that, Carissa just finished getting her romantic, and several doors down, Tyra was getting angry romantic in a way the angry part was going to burn out and the biker bitch romantic would be all that was left.

But Tab and Shy were on their way home to their baby.

They'd get theirs later, when Playboy was asleep.

Last, not far away, Snapper was giving Rosalie the gentle version of biker romantic.

And for a spell, all in Chaos (but Boz) were happy.

THEY WOULD NOT HAVE TIME to get used to it.

EPILOGUE

BLESSED

Keely

I WATCHED HOUND DROP TO his knees at the side of our bed.

I also watched him bury his face in my pussy.

After that, with all I felt, all he was giving me, my eyes were closed so I didn't see anything at all.

When Hound made me hit the stratosphere, I was still flying high as I felt his hands come under my arms and drag me deeper into the bed. My orgasm was still burning through me, but it re-ignited as I watched him yank his jeans down just enough to free his rock-solid dick. He pulled my legs apart, covered me and he was then drilling inside.

I shuddered underneath him, took the violent thrusts of his cock, watched the beautiful savagery in his face and did all of that until I couldn't anymore when my Hound sent me flying again.

He was still thrusting when I came down so I held him, stroked him, rocked to meet him and when his head jerked back and I watched and listened to him come, I happily felt an aftershock roll through my body as I absorbed the tremors throbbing through my man.

Hound dropped his head so his face was in my neck and I held on to him with arms and legs, keeping him close, feeling him, smelling him, glorying in his cock buried deep.

But I eventually took one arm from around him so I could lift my left hand, fingers spread, and stare at the back of it.

On the ring finger was a two and a half carat simple solitaire diamond set in white gold.

My old man hadn't lied.

We'd woken up that morning at the Compound. We'd showered together at the Compound. We'd dressed in our clothes from the day before (though Hound had put on a different tee seeing as the one from the day before was bloodstained).

And he'd taken me out for breakfast and then taken me right to the mall.

My first two rides wrapped around him on his bike.

They were perfect.

At the display of engagement rings, he'd asked me to pick.

I'd asked him if he was to pick, which one he'd pick.

He'd immediately pointed to the one that was right then on my finger.

Hound didn't use words to ask me to marry him. He didn't get down on one knee.

He bought me a ring and slipped it on my finger right there in the store.

And we were engaged.

Then he'd taken us home and gave me his version of biker romantic by getting me naked, falling to his knees and going down on me.

In all the agony I'd had in my life, all the disappointment I'd endured with my family, it was right then, laying on my bed, connected to Hound, wearing his ring that I realized it was moments like that, moments like standing at a register in a jewelry store and having my man slide a ring on my finger, moments so simple and extraordinary, there didn't need to be any grand gestures made.

Just as they were, they made all the rest worth it.

"The answer is yes," I whispered.

He lifted his head and looked at me.

"Say again?" he asked.

"Just, you know, to make it that much more official."

He stared into my eyes.

Then he caught my wrist, pulled it in front of him and slid his hand up so he could press the back of mine, particularly where his ring lay, against the vulnerable base of his throat.

"You know, and don't ever doubt, how much I love you," he declared.

I felt the soft smile hit my lips.

I liked it that he said it, especially now, after he gave me the ring, fucked me hard and held that symbol to the life of him.

But he could just grunt and I'd be good.

"I know, cowboy, and trust me, I'll never doubt it," I promised.

He held my hand where it was even when he bent and kissed me.

He did it wet and he did it hard.

And I gave that back.

Harder.

Yes, it was moments like that that made all of it worth it.

When he was done with the kiss and working my neck with his mouth, I put a foot to the bed, shoved up and Hound let me roll him.

I did this because we were who we were, wild like the wind, so we knew to take those moments when we got them.

And tear them up, wringing out of them as much as we could get.

"NOPE, THE OTHER ONE, IT'S got a dining room," Elvira declared.

"Totally this one," Tyra said, clicking back to the one she wanted. "It's got a bigger garage. They essentially have three vehicles and he's a Chaos man. They'll use a bigger garage more than they'll use a dining room."

This was true.

We would.

"But that one doesn't have a very big master," Lanie put in, reaching through the throng of women packed around Tyra's computer in her office at the garage at Ride so she could push Tyra's hand aside and commandeer the mouse.

She clicked. Clicked again.

"There," she went on. "This one. Decent size garage with room to build on. No dining room but huge kitchen so you can get a big table in there. Nice master. And the all-important fire pit."

Elvira shoved through, took control of the mouse and clicked through pictures, bringing up one of the kitchen from the house Lanie liked.

One of several houses Hound and I had appointments to view that afternoon.

"Now stare at that five seconds and try not to get a headache from that wallpaper," Elvira bossed. "I already got a headache and I only looked at it two seconds."

"You can peel off wallpaper, Vira," Tabby pointed out.

"The ghost of that wallpaper might remain for eternity," Rosalie murmured and Lanie started giggling.

"Are you gonna miss the fireplace in your kitchen, Keely?" Millie asked.

I stared at the kitchen on Tyra's computer.

That wallpaper was dire.

But the layout was awesome. I'd have to get rid of my dining room table but that didn't matter since I'd never once filled it. I could fit a bigger table than the one I had in my kitchen now and everyone knew, when you had a party, all the guests ended up in the kitchen anyway.

Further, I had a feeling Hound was an "entertain outdoors" man. I had this feeling because when I'd asked him his requirements for a house that were non-negotiable, he'd said, "Fire pit, built-in grill and no tile anywhere in the house that makes me dizzy."

That was it.

As for me, I needed three bedrooms, meaning a decent master for us, one for our baby girl, and one where the boys could crash if they were hanging, tossing back a few with their mom and dad and didn't want to go home.

The rest, as long as Hound was there, I didn't give a flip.

"I can do without a fireplace," I said, reaching through and taking over the mouse in order to click through more pictures on that house, pulling up the one of the kickass backyard with its fire pit, built-in grill and large covered seating area with raised flowerbeds flanking it, those beds filled with neatly trimmed shrubs. "If I can give my man that."

"I'm not sure 'shrubbery' goes with 'biker,'" Elvira noted.

"Hound's fantastic with yardwork," I declared.

As I straightened away from the computer, I felt all eyes turn to me.

"He is?" Tyra asked incredulously.

"Before the boys got old enough for him to train them to take over, I had the best lawn on the block."

"Well, knock me over with a feather," Elvira said, gaze still on me. "No offense, girl. Just that Hound never struck me as domesticated."

"He unloads the dryer and folds laundry too," I shared.

"Whoa," Tabby whispered.

"And puts away groceries," I added. "All without being asked."

"Yowza," Lanie said.

"And when I'm not working, he prefers to be fucking me, eating with me or drinking beer and watching TV with me, not waiting for me to clean the house, so he vacuums too."

"How did Keely get the housetrained one?" Lanie demanded to know.

I laughed.

"I'm pregnant."

Everyone stood solid, staring at whatever their eyes were on at the moment Carissa made her statement.

Then everyone turned slowly to her hanging back from the posse that was scrunched around the computer.

Except Rosalie. She shifted closer to Carissa.

It was with that I knew that Rosie knew about Carissa's condition. Then again, I'd learned quickly those two were tight, along with Tabby. It wasn't like all the women weren't tight, they were. It was just that the older generation had more history, and the younger generation was building their history.

The way of the world.

"Say what?" Elvira asked.

"I'm four months pregnant and Joker and I are getting married this summer," she announced.

Elvira stepped away from the girl gang to stand at the side of Tyra's desk.

And she did not appear as happy as this thrilling news should have made her.

I didn't know these women very well. I'd only been a member of their club for a week.

What I did know, what anyone would know just looking at her, was that Elvira was fixing to blow.

I had that thought half a second before she blew.

"Are you fuckin' shitting me?" she yelled.

"Uh . . ." I started to intervene, but since I didn't know what to say, I trailed off.

It didn't matter.

Elvira descended into full-on rant.

"Now, your girl Bev is gettin' hitched and you're all a-dither after seein' pictures of him on her phone during the powwow we had where you made the insane decision to march your asses in on serious brother business at the Compound. And they weren't pictures of his dick, which we now know makes that whole sweet package even sweeter. Millie and High are all moved in and playin' house and gonna get hitched. Rosie and Snap are gonna move in in no time, and then for sure gonna get hitched. And Keely and Hound got engaged *the day after* the big brouhaha and we're all clickin' through listings helpin' them find a house. And now *you're* knocked up and gonna get hitched *this summer?*" Elvira demanded that last from Carissa.

Carissa then confusingly said, "I knew you'd be upset. That's why it took me so long to share it with you." She turned to Tyra. "We want our reception at Ride. In the forecourt. Nothing fancy." She smiled. "But a butterfly theme."

"Unh-unh," Elvira huffed, hand up, all her peachy-pink-long-nailed fingers curled in except her pointer. That was wagging back and forth. "No planning. No butterflies. No forecourt."

She leaned in.

We all leaned back.

She blew again.

"You're stealing my thunder!"

"Elvira, you're not getting married until Christmas," Lanie said soothingly.

Ah.

That explained Elvira's rant.

Though I'd already seen the rock on her finger.

Mine, by the way, might be simpler, but it was still more awesome.

"Yeah, and with *four* weddings happening before that you gotta buy presents for and help plan, I'll get the bottom of the barrel with presents and you'll be burned out on planning. Not to mention," she skewered Carissa with her gaze, *"baby shit."*

"Honey, I'm planning your wedding for you, remember?" Millie pointed out. "And it's gonna be amazing."

"And I don't want presents," I put in. "Though, I think Hound would feel a couple of six packs would not be remiss."

"Not to mention, Bev said Tad's off on one," Tabby told them. "She says he's already found the venue and picked the colors and everything. We probably just have to show up for that one."

They didn't have the latest news.

He'd also selected the DJ and decreed the cake would be lemon, "because that taste reminds me of sunshine," he'd told Hound and me while we were throwing some back at Bev's the night before. "And sunshine reminds me of Beverly."

Who could argue that? Especially when it was delivered by a hot guy in a silky, deep voice who had a way with talking about wedding cake that didn't make him sound like a pansy.

Beverly, staring at him all goo-goo eyed and hanging on his arm while he spoke, clearly couldn't argue it.

"And you'd have to bring a present," Elvira hissed at Tabby.

"Well . . . yeah," Tabby said quietly, giving big eyes to the girls around her.

"Do you think, Elvira, my beautiful friend, that the women standing in front of you do not have enough love for you, just for you, that doesn't even include how much we adore Malik, to give you *all* the attention you deserve on your big day?" Tyra asked.

"You better," Elvira snapped.

"I'm beside myself with happiness for you," Tyra whispered, and the feel of the room instantly changed.

Because the feel they were getting from Elvira instantly changed.

Tyra wasn't done.

"After a lot of waiting and confusion and a rocky start with Tack, life has been beautiful and not a small part of that beauty is that during that time, I found you, and since that time, I've had you."

"I've waited for this all my life," Elvira whispered, and the feel of the room changed again.

"I know, honey," Tyra whispered back.

"I thought he'd never come. I thought I'd never find him," Elvira kept whispering.

"I know," Tyra replied.

"And he's perfect," she kept going.

Oh man.

Cool!

I couldn't wait to meet Malik.

"Yeah, he is," Tabby said.

"He loves me, like . . . *crazy* loves me," Elvira carried on.

Oh yeah.

I couldn't wait to meet Malik.

"We know," Lanie said.

"Sometimes I wonder, when I wake up next to him, if I'm dreaming," Elvira shared.

"I understand that," Millie said.

"Me too," Carissa added.

"Me as well," Lanie put in.

"Absolutely," Rosalie declared.

"For sure," Tabby stated.

"Yeah," I whispered.

"Totally," Tyra said.

"Wait until you have his baby," Tabby told Elvira. "I don't know what's bigger than dreaming a dream, getting it, and that getting better.

But whatever that is, a baby is that."

Now I couldn't wait to get knocked up with Hound's kid.

After Tab was done, Elvira looked to Carissa.

"Come here, girl," she ordered.

Carissa went there and Elvira gave her a big hug.

"Butterflies will be perfect," we heard her say in Carissa's ear.

We also watched Carissa's head nod as she held on.

As if on cue, the door to the garage opened and Tack strolled through holding a baby tucked in one of his arms.

His gaze swept through all the women and stopped on Elvira and Carissa, who were breaking away from each other.

"Christ," he muttered and looked to his woman. "Drama?"

"Nope," Tyra answered.

Tack stopped in front of her desk.

"My grandson needs changing," he told his wife.

She tipped her head to the side. "The diaper bag's right there on the couch."

He completely ignored this and turned his attention to Tabby. "Your son needs changing."

"The diaper bag hasn't moved, Dad," Tabby replied.

"I do cuddles," he rumbled. "I don't do diapers."

"You changed both our boys, Kane," Tyra said, again gaining Tack's attention.

"Yeah, and I had a direct hand in makin' those two. This one," he lifted the bundle cradled in his arm, "it was indirect. My job is done. Diapers and shit like that are behind me. With this one," he lifted the bundle again, "I just get the good stuff."

"Oh for God's sake, give me that child," Elvira said impatiently, walked on her high-heeled sandals to Tack and divested him of his grandchild.

"Bring 'im back to me when you're done," he ordered.

Elvira stared at him.

Tack just turned on his motorcycle boot and moseyed his fine ass right back out the door, closing it firmly behind him.

"You know, if that man didn't make such good pancakes, I'd divorce his ass," Tyra grumbled.

"I bet he makes good pancakes," Millie said under breath through a smile.

"Please don't make a euphemism out of Dad's pancakes," Tabby begged. "I love Dad's pancakes and if you make a euphemism out of them, I'll never be able to eat them again."

"Okay, honey," Tyra agreed on a grin. "We'll stop talking about your dad's pancakes."

"Uh, Keely," Carissa called. "When did you say your first appointment was for a viewing?"

I looked at the time on Tyra's computer then cried, "Shit! I gotta go get Hound!" I rushed to Carissa, gave her a tight hug and said, "So happy for you, times two. Butterflies are awesome."

I let her go, dashed around her and grabbed my bag from the couch where Elvira was digging through a diaper bag at the same time juggling Playboy. I snatched up my bag, bent in to steal a quick kiss from the wet lips of Playboy and getting his flirtatious gurgle after I did before I hurried to the door and stopped at it.

"Later, chicks," I called.

"Later, babe," Tyra called back. "Hope you see something you love."

I got more of that kind of farewell, and on a wave, I ran out the door.

As fast as my cowboy boots would take me, I rushed down the steps and across the forecourt toward the Compound, but found myself skidding to a halt while I was dashing between Hound and Jagger's bikes parked beside each other outside the Compound.

The skidding halt was because I'd glanced at Jagger's bike.

And after I skidded to that halt, I stood there and stared at the tank on my son's bike.

Then I stood there and deep breathed as I stared at the tank on Jag's bike.

I'd seen it often, since he rode it all the time, but I hadn't really looked at it, not since he took possession of it.

But right then, I reached out a hand and slid a finger along the top of the tank.

High-gloss clear coat.

Somehow my boy had managed to seal my lipstick on his father's bike.

Jagger's bike.

He rode free taking his mother and father with him everywhere he went.

God, but *God* . . . I loved my son.

I smiled, hustled into the Compound and nearly slammed into Hound the second I entered it.

"Babe," he said, his hands settling on my hips as the door whooshed closed behind me.

"Cowboy," I replied, my hands coming to a rest on his chest. "Carissa is pregnant."

His eyebrows shot up.

That was, his eyebrows under his hair that was yanked back at the top and held in a little pony at the back of his head went up.

Seeing his hotness, I was having second thoughts about spending the afternoon looking at houses.

I was thinking the bed in his room at the Compound was all we needed.

"She let that news loose?" he asked, taking me out of my ponderings of dragging him through the Compound and jumping him.

"Just now," I answered. "You knew?"

He nodded. "Yup. Joker scored himself a box of Cubans and handed them out the day after Carissa told him, which was three months ago." He tipped his head to the side. "Was Vira in hearing distance when she shared?"

Hearing all that, including his question, I felt a wave of happy wash through me because he'd always had these people—these funny, sweet, loving, loyal people—and he knew them well.

And now I had them too.

Carissa pregnant. Elvira finding the man of her dreams. My lipstick sealed on Jagger's bike. Having my Chaos family back. Looking at houses with my man.

That day was another day in what was now a long line of days that

I'd woken up a winner.

"Took a bit but she got over it," I told Hound.

"Thank fuck the men didn't have to witness that," he muttered.

"You knew Carissa was pregnant and you didn't tell me?" I asked.

"Babe, learn now, that shit you gotta get from the girls. I'm not your line on gossip about Chaos bitches."

"Heard and understood, Shep," I muttered through a grin.

He grunted.

I love you too, I thought.

"Wanna go see houses?" I asked.

He gave me a look that made my heart swell, my toes curl and my nipples tingle.

"On the back of my bike, baby," he whispered.

More of the same from all three including a throb at my clit.

Since I'd ridden on the back of his bike to go have breakfast with my man before he bought me my engagement ring, unless I was off to work or the grocery store, my ass didn't get anywhere if it wasn't sitting behind him on the back of his bike.

"You got it, cowboy," I replied.

He grabbed my hand and led me there. He got on first. I threw my leg over and straddled the bike and his ass after he did.

I slid my arms around his stomach, held on tight, smelling leather and Hound, wrapped around my man, being right then in the best place in the world.

He backed out just as I saw Jagger coming out of the Compound.

Hound took a hand from the grip and gave him a flick, Jag gave one back and I blew my son a kiss.

Jag shook his head and threw his leg over his bike.

He looked good on it.

Then again, the amount of pussy that I'd overheard Dutch telling Hound his little brother was nailing, I knew that did not go unnoticed by the biker groupies and probably beyond.

I put this out of my thoughts, happily settled into the knowledge Hound would give me a girl and I wouldn't have to deal with any more of that kind of thing as Hound started us through the forecourt.

We both waved again (well, I waved, Hound did another wrist flick), this time at Big Petey on his Harley trike riding in.

Pete gave us a big smile and a thumbs up as he passed.

I held on tighter to Hound, thinking how good it was to be home.

And we rode out of the forecourt of Ride, off Chaos, the wind in our hair, the Denver sun on our faces, to go look at houses.

⸻

HOUND COULD NOT GET OVER the wallpaper.

I discovered that I was not about to have a house without an awesome master suite.

So it would be the next week when we found what we were looking for.

Hound paid for it in cash and refused to even discuss me putting a penny into it.

I got that need so I kept my mouth shut.

During prime rib for Jag's birthday, we discussed the house my boys had grown up in and I found I was right.

They were attached to me, to Hound, they had the pieces of their father that meant everything to them, so they were good to let go of the house.

The boys lost their trust funds from their grandfather.

So when we sold my place, I divided the proceeds of the home their father gave them and added that to the money they were already going to get from their father and me when it was time to start to get serious about building their lives.

We did a short sale. We were in by the beginning of May.

Hound, Dutch and Jag bitched about having to move furniture again (though the boys kinda got over it when they found out they were inheriting Hound's new furniture, all but the bed, which we put in the guest room).

But with all the brothers and their old ladies helping (plus Tad and Bev), we were in in no time.

⌬

A WEEK LATER, I STOOD with my head on Hound's chest, our arms around each other's waists, holding Dutch's hand with my free one while Jag had his arm thrown around his big brother's shoulders after we got Jean's mezuzah back from the scribe who checked it was still kosher.

We stood this way while Jean's rabbi said a prayer over it as he tacked it up at the entryway to our living room.

When he was done, we shared a glass of wine with the rabbi and his wife (well, I did, Hound and the boys drank beer) and Hound and them shared memories of Jean.

And even though we'd been in the house for a week, since Jean was now there with us, it felt like we were finally home.

⌬

Hound

WHEN HIS PHONE RANG, KEELY made a move against him as Hound lifted his head to look across to her nightstand.

It was twenty-four after three in the morning.

"Fuck," he muttered, twisting to grab his phone from his nightstand.

"Who is it?" Keely asked sleepily.

He did not like seeing Tack's name on his screen at three twenty-four in the morning.

"Just a second, Keekee," he murmured, took the call and put the phone to his ear. "Yeah?"

"All brothers to the Compound. Now."

Fuck.

"Be there in ten," Hound said, and Tack made no reply.

He disconnected.

Hound turned to Keely. "Got Chaos business, babe."

She held on to him even as she looked over her shoulder at the alarm clock.

She turned back to him.

"It's very early," she whispered.

Chew had not contacted them to have a meet, parlay or not. Valenzuela had not reappeared. Turnbull was keeping her shit off Chaos, and according to Knight, dealing with her stable appropriately.

Therefore there was nothing to share with Keely about the shit they were in, because for all intents and purposes, that shit had disappeared.

Even if there was something to share, after they discovered the bones were gone, he wouldn't have told her.

And Keely being who she was, how she was, she wouldn't have expected it.

Not a one of the men thought it was done.

And now Hound knew it wasn't.

"I gotta go," he replied.

"Right," she said, pushed into him and up so she could brush her lips to his.

Then she let him go.

He got dressed, went back to the bed for another touch of lips from his woman then moved out of their room, down the hall, out the door off the kitchen to his bike parked next to Keely's ride. He hit the garage door opener, pulled out, hit the remote he had that he shoved in his back pocket and he rode the five-minute ride to Chaos.

He could have walked it, their new house was that close. That was Keely's deal. He didn't care where they lived, just as long as it was theirs (and had a fire pit).

She wanted him close to his family.

Her family.

So they were.

By the time he hit Ride's forecourt, he saw Tack, Hop, Shy, and Hawk Delgado's Camaro turned in after Hound, following him into the space.

This surprised Hound. When shit escalated months ago with Valenzuela taking Millie, Tack putting all the resources at their disposal—including his relationship with Hawk Delgado, a local badass, and Brock Lucas and

Mitch Lawson, two Denver cops—stopped.

When an old lady had been hauled into their shit, their problem had become the problem of Chaos and Chaos alone.

That problem dwindling down to Hound doing what he did for his Club to solve it.

It had gone unsolved even if it seemed there was resolution.

Now he knew, his headlight and Hawk's shining on the men standing around a picnic table outside the Compound that had a sheet draped over it, shit just got seriously ugly.

His body strung tight, Hound parked, shut his bike down and dismounted, moving toward the men around that table feeling Hawk move in with him and hearing more bikes roar onto Chaos.

He didn't take his eyes off the sheet draped over the table even as he stopped to stand by it.

"We got a delivery," Tack growled.

He sounded pissed, which made Hound relax.

Whatever was under that sheet pissed off Tack, it didn't destroy him.

Finally, Hound looked from Tack to Shy to Hop to see they all looked ticked.

He let out a long breath.

"What we got?" he asked.

Tack looked from Hound to whoever came up beside him and greeted shortly, "Pete. Brick."

More bikes could be heard coming into the forecourt.

"What we got?" Hound repeated, sharper this time.

Hop reached out and flicked up the top of the sheet.

Hound drew in a quick breath.

Camilla Turnbull lay on her back on the table, face white, throat brown with dried blood and red where it was gaping open. There was a thick notecard with writing on it sitting on her forehead.

She'd been done somewhere else, Hound knew that because there was no blood on the sheet, and glancing under the table, there was no blood there either.

She'd been laid out.

On Chaos.

For Chaos.

"Fuck me," Brick whispered.

"Talk to us," Hawk clipped as more men hit the circle around the picnic table and even more bikes could be heard coming in.

"My last calls were Slim and Mitch. They're on their way," Tack told them. "This," he indicated Turnbull with a flick of his hand, "is a gift. We apparently got a new ally."

"And that would be?" Dog, who'd joined them, asked.

"Valenzuela's back," Tack answered.

"And how does him dumping a dead woman on Chaos make him an ally?" Hawk asked.

"I got a text from a burner phone an hour ago," Tack shared. "Said to get down here, Chaos had been left a present. Called Shy and Hop to come with me. We found this, including the sheet. That card didn't move when we pulled back the sheet because it's stapled to her forehead."

"Christ," Roscoe muttered.

"What's it say?" Snapper asked tersely.

"*Cross me*," Tack quoted, not looking at it, which meant he'd memorized it. "*Get crossed. You've got a new friend. Can you slice open an arachnid? We'll see.*"

An arachnid.

Chew was called Chew because he collected tarantulas. Last Hound knew he had at least seven of those fuckers.

Millie had loved playing with them.

And Chew had loved that she did.

"Chew used Turnbull to squeeze Valenzuela out," Hawk surmised. "Either he planted her there to orchestrate the takeover or they've been workin' together all along and Valenzuela crossed a line when he put hands on Chaos property that's untouchable."

"Yeah and they either didn't do a thorough job of it or he's spent his enforced vacation gathering resources," Tack replied.

All the men shifted when they heard a car pull up.

They watched Lucas and Lawson park and get out.

Hound didn't have a good feeling about the looks on their faces as they approached the men around the picnic table, even before both cops took in that table.

"What?" Tack barked.

He had the same feeling.

It was Lawson that gave it to them.

"Got the call on the way here after we called in what you got," Mitch said. "Natalie Harbinger was found dead in the alley behind Scruff's Roadhouse at around one tonight. She was in a body bag, shot through the head, execution style. Done elsewhere. No blood. And in that body bag with her were two human skulls. Both male. Identities unknown but whoever they are, they've been dead awhile. There was also a note that said, *You can fuck yourselves with your parlay*. Last, crawlin' over that mess was two tarantulas."

Hound pulled in breath through his nose.

Natalie had been Tabby's best friend before she went off the rails. Natalie being a cokehead took her off the rails. Her habit was what escalated bad shit between Chaos and Benito Valenzuela. And since Natalie's shit got Chaos's shit twisted, she'd fallen off the grid.

As far as Hound knew they'd lost touch, but Tabby would still be devastated.

What Hound did not get was why Chew would take her out, dump her behind the bar they all used to party in back in the day, and lately they'd started going back, and give the cops Crank's and Black's killer's skulls, which probably would not offer any investigation dick.

Except if it wasn't Chew who did it.

If it was Valenzuela who did it, attempting to frame Chew not only for Natalie, but for Crank and Black's killer.

Which meant Valenzuela had the bones.

"You got anything for us on that?" Lucas asked.

"Valenzuela is back," Tack said as answer.

"You get that note?" Lucas went on.

"Got word an ex-brother might have issues with us. He also might have issues with Valenzuela. We offered him a chat. With parlay. This was weeks ago. We've heard dick," Tack told them.

"The skulls?" Lawson asked.

Tack said nothing.

"We can't be doin' off-radar favors when bodies are piling up, Tack," Lawson bit off.

"There's a new war goin' down," Tack told them.

"And Chaos is caught in the crossfire," Lucas guessed.

The night was opened up by the flashing lights of police cruisers pulling into Ride.

Tack let that be his answer.

WHEN HOUND RETURNED HOME, HE did not find it a surprise walking into their bedroom when he saw Keely wearing one of his tees sitting cross legged in the middle of their bed with the lights on both nightstands blazing.

"You okay?" she asked the second she saw him.

He shrugged off his cut and tossed it to her ridiculous, fur-covered chair.

She hadn't been in their place long enough to get stuck in and make it wild.

She'd get to it and he wouldn't stop her.

If he did, he wouldn't get the fun of giving her shit about it.

"I'm okay," he answered, moving to stand at the end of their bed, crossing his arms on his chest and taking her in, all legs and hair and gorgeous face.

He'd experienced a lot of shit in his life then gone back to his room in the Compound and crashed, or to his crap apartment, and then crashed, never having anything as magnificent as Keely waiting for him to help him drive the shit away.

Now he'd just seen the dead body of a woman he knew, who he didn't like but that didn't mean he wanted to see her dead and laid out on Chaos. And he knew his brother Shy was going home with his father-in-law to land bad news on their girl that would cut Tab deep.

He'd never experienced it so he could never know what it meant to come home to that sitting right there in the bed they shared.

He just lived his life.

Now he shared it.

And staring at the woman he'd always wanted who he was sharing it with, for the first time since his memories started, even after earning her love, he felt blessed.

"You wanna talk about it?" she asked.

Blessed.

"We had an enemy," he told her. "That enemy got a new enemy who doesn't like us much."

She studied him, and then said quietly, "Chew."

"Yup."

"And the enemy of your enemy is your friend," she went on.

"This is not a friend we want."

She nodded.

"Shit got ugly tonight, Keekee," he told her gently, concerned about how she'd react since the last time shit got ugly, she was the biggest loser.

So it shocked the piss out of him when she replied, "We're winners."

"Say what?" he asked.

"We're winners," she said it stronger then.

"Baby," he whispered.

"Do you want a big wedding?" she asked abruptly.

Christ.

Blessed.

"Go to Vegas today, you didn't have to work," he told her.

Keely nodded. "I want the boys and Bev there, you'll want the brothers there. So no Vegas. Not with things getting ugly. We'll ask Big Petey to get ordained or something. Do it in the Compound. I'll wear a short skirt. Then we'll all go out for a big ride, come back, hit the Compound for a party, do it the day before we head off to Baja and make Baja our honeymoon."

"That's two weeks away," he pointed out.

"I need a dress, a bouquet, a cake and a trip to the liquor store. Two weeks is plenty of time."

That was his Keely.

All she needed was him and their boys and maybe a bottle of wine or some beer.

And she was good.

He grinned at her.

"No more birth control, starting today," she declared.

Hound stopped grinning at her.

Blessed.

"We're both committed to riding this fast and wild, cowboy," she said. "I've got my ring. You got your house. We're all in for the win. No stopping us now."

"Yeah," he said, that word gruff.

She rolled up to her knees and her expression grew determined. "No one is going to beat us, Hound. I don't care how ugly they get. It's gotten as ugly as it can be and look at us," she flipped her hands out to her sides. "We came out of it winners."

"I gotta wear somethin' stupid to this wedding?" he asked.

"No," she answered immediately. "Just that black bib shirt and your cut."

"That works," he muttered.

"You're changing diapers," she declared and he scowled.

"Of course I am. Why would you say that shit?"

"Just making sure," she mumbled.

"Keekee?" he called.

"Right here, cowboy."

"Lose the shirt."

She smiled.

Then she took off his tee, her hair flying, and tossed it aside, leaving her sitting naked on her knees in their bed in their house a five-minute ride from Chaos.

Yeah.

They were winners.

Hound had that thought.

Then he joined his old lady in their bed.

HOUND WORE THE BLACK BIB shirt under his cut.

Keely wore a nude lace halter dress with thin straps at the sides of her neck and a crossover skirt that hiked high at the cross, showed a lot of leg and would give her plenty of room to open wide in order to straddle his ass on his bike. She wore this with a pair of high-heeled sandals that made her long legs seem like they went on forever. They also made him make the decision the minute he saw them that she'd eventually lose the dress, but she wouldn't take those shoes off all night.

She looked her usual gorgeous, and then some.

In other words, Hound approved.

On a variety of levels.

Dutch and Jagger walked their mother from their dad's room at the Compound to give her away.

Bev was her maid of honor.

Dutch and Jagger played double duty, since they both stood as Hound's best men.

Big Petey got ordained and sat on his ass on the bar between the bride and groom with a half a glass of beer sitting by his hip while he said enough words that they could commit to each other verbally in front of their family, then say "I do" and finally make out hot and heavy, so into each other, not hearing the cheers and the catcalls, until they heard Jagger shout, "For fuck's sake!"

After that, Chaos rolled out as one, hit Evergreen for a drink, then came back into town and finished the party at the Compound, which was good, because by then the hog was done roasting.

They were both too drunk to ride so they spent their wedding night in Hound's room at the Compound where they fucked tough all night.

That was when Keely gave Hound her wedding present.

And sure as fuck, Hound approved of that too.

KEELY IRONSIDE'S WEDDING PRESENT TO her old man was a tattoo.

When most brides would be getting their hair done, Keely was lying face down in an artist's chair having scripted words inked in around her waist starting at the side and scrolling along the small of her back right where her man draped his arm to hold her close while they were sleeping.

It read,

Shepherd ~ Dutch ~ Jagger

Simple.

Perfect.

Forever.

Harietta

HARIETTA TURNBULL SET THE BINOCULARS down and moved from the window in the apartment over the shop across from Ride. An apartment that had a clear view down the open area of parking spots and driving space into the forecourt of the garage. You could even see some of the building in the back at the side from there.

You could definitely see the front of it.

And what she'd seen right then before turning away was a bunch of bikers and their bitches outside that building throwing back brews, or shots, or swigging direct from bottles, laughing, talking, making out, groping, music blaring so loud, she could hear it all the way where she was.

She left the apartment they'd rented years ago for her to do just what she'd been doing, got in her car that she always parked in the alley out back so they'd never see her (not that they'd known who she was, but they probably knew now), drove a block down so she could pull out where they'd never clock her and then drove home.

He was there.

Him and his fucking tarantulas.

"That one they call Hound married some Indian bitch," she announced coming to a stop across from him where he sat, practically decaying in that armchair. "They're partying at their clubhouse."

"Compound," he corrected her.

"Whatever," she muttered.

"Keely?" he asked.

"What?" she asked back.

"Indian or Native American?"

"Does it matter?" she mumbled.

"Yeah it matters," he returned impatiently. "She Native American?"

"Yeah," Harietta snapped.

"Fuck, he moved in on Black, motherfucker." She watched him grouse. "Made such a big deal his brother got dead, they took out Crank and he was all in, and there he is claimin' his dead brother's property. Knew he was gaggin' after Black's woman. In the end, didn't have the balls to do the right thing and leave her be."

Seeing as he ranted a lot about shit like this, Harietta decided she had a date with a vodka bottle, the only good companion she had in that house.

"What else?" he demanded when she started to the kitchen.

She stopped. "What else what?"

"What else did you see?"

What she saw right then was some stupid-ass fuck who was living in the past who would *not let shit go*.

God, how she wished to have that day back when those bikers showed at Cammy's school to teach kids about safety.

Safety.

What a fucking *joke*.

Angrily, she told him what she saw.

"I saw a bunch of people havin' a great fuckin' time and livin' their lives and gettin' married and goin' on a ride, when two fuckin' weeks ago *my baby girl* was laid out on their goddamned *picnic table*."

He tried to look remorseful but he failed.

Even so, he continued to try that shit verbally.

"Baby, told you how bad I felt about that. I couldn't know Benito would—"

She cut him off. "The man's certifiable and has been since you made a deal with that dick." She leaned back and tossed out an arm expansively, lowering her voice in a parody of his, "Oh, I know where the bones are buried, Benito. And I got an in with Bounty, they're my boys and they're lookin' to expand. You want more manpower, I can bring it to you. You want one over on Chaos, I got the ticket." She leaned back toward him.

"Now *he's* got those goddamned bones and *he's* back in control of his goddamned operation, and *Bounty's* a mess and seriously fuckin' pissed at you and *I'm* puttin' off those two fuckin' cop buddies of Kane Allen's who keep sniffin' around here, looking for *you*."

He slowly stood from his chair, doing it with his hand down so his fucking spider could crawl off then crawl all over everything.

It was creepy.

She hated it. Hated all ten of those damned things.

She'd always hated them.

For eighteen fucking years.

"I'm hurtin' Cammy's gone same as you," he said quietly. "Raised that girl like my own."

She'd had enough.

Cammy was dead.

Dead.

Throat slit and body drained of blood and laid out for a goddamned motorcycle gang.

"And then you sent her off to whore for your vengeance," she spat.

She should have known.

She should have *known*.

When he put the spider down, she should have known.

The last time he put his spider down like that was after she lit into him when she was done listening to him rant about some bitch named Millie that Valenzuela's thugs had taken. He'd gone at her, and after, he'd lost his mind for some bitch he knew *twenty years ago*, and made his play *way* before Cammy was ready for him to do it.

It was bad then, but Harietta didn't learn.

She never learned.

She always pushed it.

He knocked her to the ground with the first strike and it didn't take him long to start getting off on it so he fucked her dry to finish.

When he was done, he looked at her like *she* was a piece of dirt.

"Never learn, dumb bitch," he muttered something she oh-so-knew, pulled out and got up, yanking up his jeans, leaving her on the carpet at his feet.

He retrieved his fucking spider.

Then he sat in his chair, grabbed his phone and made a fucking call.

Harietta dragged herself away, pulled herself up, hit the bathroom to clean him from her, and only then did she keep her date with the vodka, but with that bottle, she added a dishtowel filled with ice to put on her eye.

From the minute she'd met him, she'd never trusted Benito Valenzuela.

Now the asshole had murdered her girl *and* some other girl they didn't even know, framing her man for that bitch's death.

And he was so damned stupid and so hung up on the past, he'd go down.

And drag her down with him.

So maybe, Harietta thought, it was time for a different deal to be struck.

She'd spent years on and off watching Chaos.

Now she was thinking it was high time she paid it a visit.

Harietta wouldn't make an approach to the old guard.

She'd go for the young one.

Kane Allen could take one look at you and read all the words the devil himself wrote on your soul.

But Cole Allen . . .

He was young.

He hadn't learned yet how deep the devil's words could burn. He wouldn't see the black marks obliterating her soul.

He'd be just the ticket.

Keely

THE SHADES WERE DRAWN AS I lay on my side, staring into the darkened room.

Hound entered the bed behind me. He lifted my arm and tucked the hot water bottle low on my abdomen before he put my arm back and covered it with his, holding the heat right where I needed it and holding me against his heat curled at my back.

"Maybe I'm too old," I whispered.

"Baby," he whispered into the back of my hair. "We've only been tryin' a coupla months."

That day, I got my period, and the shitty-ass cramps that had always come with it.

"You want me to make the calls? Tell everyone the cookout is off?" he asked.

It was our first big do since we got the house. Hound had bought enough brats to feed half of Denver. Everyone was coming. Chaos. Bev and Tad. Dutch with his new girl. Jag with one of his harem of girls. And although everyone else was bringing their kids, Keith from work and his wife Megan were getting a sitter for the first time so they could let loose.

"Just downed the four ibuprofen you gave me, the hot water bottle, I'll be good by this afternoon," I muttered.

He pulled me closer and muttered back, again into my hair, "We're winners, Keekee. Yeah?"

I closed my eyes.

He gave me a shake with his arm.

"Yeah?" he pushed.

I opened my eyes. "Yeah, cowboy."

"Makin' you come helps, baby," he reminded me of the times before he'd experienced this with me and we'd found Hound going at my clit until he made me climax definitely helped.

"Not sure there'll ever be a time when I don't want your hand down my pants, Shep."

He kissed the back of my head.

Then he let me hold the hot water bottle and shoved his hand down my pants.

He was right, making me come helped the cramps.

When he'd done that, turning on him and giving him a blowjob took my mind off them.

And after I got done doing that, the cramps were gone.

Hound lay on his back and I lay down his side in the curve of his arm, both of us fully clothed but his jeans were still open and I had my hand in the fly, cupped on his junk because it was my junk and I liked the feel of it, when I looked into his eyes.

"Time to make the potato salad," I announced.

He lifted a hand and rubbed a thumb along my cheek.

"My old lady spoils me," he murmured.

"Until the day I die."

His face changed, giving it all to me, before he slid his hand back into my hair and pulled me down to kiss me.

He ended it with a grunt because he was a good kisser and got me excited and that made me latch on too tight down below.

I lifted my head.

"You break it, you buy it," he said.

I put my mouth to his. "I already bought it, it's all mine and I can do whatever I want with it."

"Fuck, only you could get me hard five minutes after blowing me."

"Mm-hmm," I hummed, feeling his words stir to life in my grip.

"Babe, this is not getting potato salad made and we got thirty people showin' in about three hours."

"Right," I whispered.

"Let go of my boys and let me up. I got potatoes to peel."

Now how did I know my man would help?

"Right," I repeated on a smile, let "his boys" go and let him up, which meant he pulled me up with him.

He righted his jeans and I headed out of our room, but Hound caught me in the doorway.

He put a hand on either side of my face then put his face in mine.

"She'll come," he said gently.

I smiled at him, rolled up on my toes, brushed his lips with mine and rolled back.

"Yeah," I replied.

"Have faith, Keekee," he urged, finishing, "We're blessed."

For most of my adult life, Hound had given me everything I needed.

And for the last months, he'd given me everything I ever wanted.

I was a pawn in life's game, I knew that, so I had no faith in what life had in store for me.

But Hound?

I had all the faith in the world that Hound could do anything.

So put my hands to the sides of his waist, gave it a hard squeeze, and whispered, "Blessed."

SHEPHERD IRONSIDE'S BELATED WEDDING PRESENT to his old lady came nine months later.

They named him Wilder Graham Ironside.

They didn't make a daughter but that was all right.

They had a lot of experience raising a damn fine son.

AND WHEN IT WAS TIME, Keely inked another name permanently into her skin.

But when she did, Hound was there, holding their son in his arms, and he had a few words with his wife.

So finishing the wrap to the other side of her waist, she added one more name.

And in the end, eternally at her back, like it always was, like it always would be, Keely Ironside had,

Shepherd ~ Dutch ~ Jagger ~ Wilder ~ Black.

The End

CONNECT WITH KRISTEN ONLINE:

Official Website: *www.kristeashley.net*

Kristen's Facebook Page: *www.facebook.com/kristenashleybooks*

Follow Kristen on Twitter: @KristenAshley68

Discover Kristen's Pins on Pinterest: *www.pinterest.com/kashley0155*

Follow Kristen on Instagram: KristenAshleyBooks

Need support for your Kit Crack Addiction?

Join the *Kristen Ashley Addict's Support Group on Goodreads*

Printed in Great Britain
by Amazon